C..

Adity Kay has nurtured a secret love for history all through her years of working as an editor in a magazine, a human resources professional and a management consultant. She has lived in various places in India and has been as much of a border-crosser in her career as a writer, writing editorials, essays, stories for children and books for older readers across genres. Her eclectic reading in history – across non-fiction and fiction – and have led to her fascination with the varied possibilities of times past and has also served as an impetus to travel to long-ago worlds, if only through fiction.

EMPEROR
CHANDRAGUPTA

ADITY KAY

First published in 2016 by Hachette India
(Registered name: Hachette Book Publishing India Pvt. Ltd)
An Hachette UK company
www.hachetteindia.com

SRD

Map on p. v illustrated by Bhavi Mehta

ISBN 978-93-5009-568-3

Hachette Book Publishing India Pvt. Ltd
4th/5th Floors, Corporate Centre,
Sector 44, Gurgaon 122003, India

Typeset in Cardo 10/14
by InoSoft Systems Noida

Printed and bound in India by
Manipal Technologies Limited, Manipal

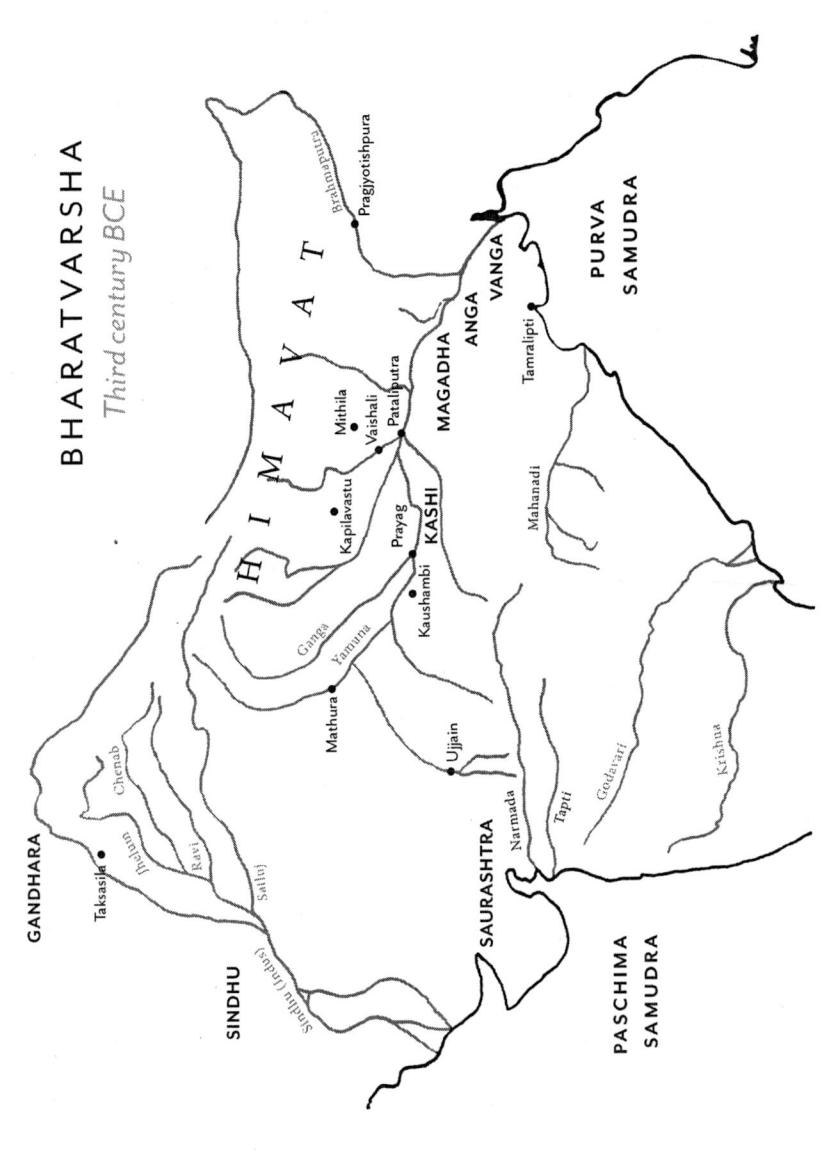

BHARATVARSHA
Third century BCE

GANDHARA

Taksasila

SINDHU

Sindhu (Indus)

Jhelum
Chenab
Ravi
Sailuj

H I M A V A T

Mathura

Yamuna

Ganga

Kapilavastu

Mithila
Vaishali
Pataliputra

Prayag

KASHI

Kaushambi

MAGADHA

ANGA
VANGA

Brahmaputra
Pragjyotishpura

Tamralipti

PURVA
SAMUDRA

Ujjain

Narmada

SAURASHTRA

Tapti

Godavari

Mahanadi

Krishna

PASCHIMA
SAMUDRA

CONTENTS

Part III DHARMA

THE BOY, MORIYA

The arrow sliced through air, turning silver on catching the light. Moriya stood below, crinkling his eyes, watching the arrow rise, following the sharp line of the mountain ridge.

He knew it would get the eagle before that magnificent bird was even aware of the arrow streaking towards him. This eagle, like others of its kind, was alert – its senses catching every nuance, even the slightest movement on the earth far below. But the arrow's rise mirrored the whistling wind, its silver was that of slanting raindrops, or a ray of sun, unexpectedly bright. Even an eagle as splendid as the crested hawk-eagle, with its defiant raised hood and burning golden eyes, stood no chance.

From below, Moriya's eyes locked with the eagle's. He saw the fire bright in its eyes one last time as his arrow pierced its throat. He heard the majestic bird's last squawk before it hurtled to the earth, falling past him, and he caught the smell of life as it left the bird. It was the smell of the earth around, the hard old rocks, the dry grass and the wind that blew in from far away, and as the bird died, it seemed to Moriya, it took a bit of the earth with it.

As Moriya stood on the ridge, he was unable to ignore the plaintive cheeping coming from the nest atop the hill. He had climbed the hills called the Aravallis at the very edge of the desert because he had heard how much of a fight these birds could put up. It was a challenge he had been unable to resist. The other boys, his companions in the tribe of the cattle-herders, had not stopped him. They knew by now that Moriya did things on his own, and they followed him wherever he went. It had always been like that. He was one of the cattle-herders and yet not really one of them.

The crested eagles were lone, wilful and lived solitary lives. He was like them in many ways. The cattle-herders lived close to the plains of the Punjab. They had moved up from the region between the ravines and the desert to the west. Saurashtra and Avanti lay southwest and south, and the river Yamuna ran east, close to the kingdoms of the Matsyas and the Surasenas. Every year they marched this way, up to the pasturelands in the northwest. But now all was uncertain, for there were reports that an invader from a faraway land in the west was very close, just beyond the mountains of the Malayavats and Nishadas. Word was that these foreigners, the Yavanas, led by a golden-haired king called Alexander, could cover immense distances on their quick and strong horses in a matter of days. No king stood a chance against them. People were fleeing towards cities, seeking shelter behind high fort walls, whereas those used to a life on the move, the nomadic herders and other forest tribes, were biding their time, stopping often, reading the signs before moving on.

Every day, the boys, with Moriya in the lead, rode out into the wild scrublands, hoping to meet other tribes or groups on the move for any news about the invader. On one of these mornings, the eagle had appeared, fierce, insistent and far too quick as it snapped repeatedly at a newborn calf before flying away. Moriya had known instantly that he would match himself against it. His eyes had seen how far it travelled, and he gauged he would have to trap it close to where it nested. An animal is always more vulnerable closer to home. In his life on the move, he had learnt that.

Now he climbed, a brutal, rough climb, till he reached the nest, and stopped abruptly. The others below saw him stumbling, the cattle grazed lazily and everything seemed still, but there was that unmistakable tension in the air. It seemed a timeless, short moment between life and death. Only Moriya knew that he had held his breath, felt his fingers quiver as he saw the fledgling the mother had been trying to feed and protect.

He picked it up, looking down as its wide yellow eyes stared, helpless, back at him. This young bird would soon grow up to be as ferocious a fighter as its mother. She could have flown away, he realized now, but had stayed close to her child in the moment of danger. Whose was the greater courage then – his or the eagle-mother's?

The boys chanted his name as he descended in their midst. They were all around his age, with similar dust-encrusted faces, for the journey had left its mark on everyone. Lines ran deep on their feet and their skin bore scratches. All of them, men belonging to roving, wandering tribes, were now being forced to choose between kingdoms. To the east were the Nandas, and to the west the threat of Alexander and his vast army. Anyone determined to fly alone would perhaps meet the same fate as that magnificent eagle.

He saw his companions raise their spears in salutation, he heard their cheers. There was something about Moriya's expression that made them quiet down. No victor could look so forlorn. Then they saw the little eagle he clasped in his hands.

He sat on an old stone seat streaked with mud and dried leaves, crawling with ants, and shadowed by overhanging pipal branches. It was perhaps a place where a sage had once meditated. Now it was a throne where Moriya sat – he was their king. And even if it was all an act, the boys were all willing participants, for when Moriya sat there he told them things they had no idea about, things that took them farther away from anything they had ever known. Moriya, with eyes that could look piercingly fierce one moment and broodingly intense the next, had the answers and always more questions – questions bigger than mere everyday matters.

'Tell me,' he asked the boys, 'do you think, if I had known about this small bird, I should still have killed the eagle?'

'That big eagle was a nuisance. Remember how she would swoop down to snatch our food away? And she troubled the priest to no end,' said one of the boys.

'True, but maybe she could have been driven away.'

'That's what the priest says, too. He says time and again the bird came back.'

'Because of this one.' Moriya nodded at the bird cupped in his palms. The boys fell silent at the seriousness of his voice.

'So what is to be done now with the little one?' Moriya asked, looking down at the young bird resting quietly in his hands, as if it was assured of protection.

'You must kill it,' one of the group piped up. 'After all, he will grow up to be a ferocious fighting bird.'

'And these birds can never be tamed. The priest tried it as well,' said another.

Moriya persisted. 'But it is helpless. Should it be denied care simply because it will turn into a killer? We could kill its parent because it resisted us. But this…?' As he mused over this dilemma he said aloud, 'What would a king's duty be?'

They had no answer but began talking all at once.

'Kings kill those captured in war, or throw them in dungeons,' said one of the boys again, 'because the fear of revenge is constant in their minds.'

'But this is a bird… it is young and helpless. We must take

care of it because it has no one,' said Moriya. 'It is our duty, our dharma.'

'Do you think we can tame the bird and present him to Alexander?'

The question from one of the boys made the others laugh raucously.

'Would he really want an eagle, or demand a lion?' another boy piped up.

They laughed again.

'This eagle stays with me,' Moriya said, in a quiet voice. 'I will use him to send a message to Alexander.'

'A message?'

'Yes, ask him to leave our land or challenge him to a duel to see who is stronger.'

No one laughed this time. Just months ago he had challenged them all to a battle where sticks shaped out of fallen branches served as their weapons. He had taken them on together, and even singly, and finally having beaten them all, offered his hand in help to his fallen victims. His arms had moved faster than anyone else's; he had jumped, whirled, turned around, his stick falling surely and certainly while they had missed the real thing for the shadow many a time. The way he had struck and aimed had never hurt but he had disarmed them surely and effectively. They had been mesmerized by his accuracy and quick movements, and understood with certainty that they had to follow him from then on.

'Yes, a duel.' He had a faraway look on his face now.

Alexander. The name reverberated in his head. *Alexander.* The man who, it seemed, would conquer everything in his path. Who would travel to wherever the world ended, having conquered everything behind him. He made the world seem even bigger than it was – seas, mountains, deserts – all vast and mighty, all waiting to be claimed. Moriya felt his heart race and his eyes blazed. Far away, the wind in the trees made the branches move as if an invisible army lay hidden within them. Alexander. One day he would meet him. One day...

PART 1

THE LOST PRINCE OF MAGADHA

1

A RARE BIRD

The land throbbed as the horse galloped over the arid land towards the forest. Moriya knew of the hard rocks concealed below the dry grass, rocks that were far older than the cold Himavat mountains to the north, beyond the land of the five rivers that was the Punjab. Craggy old trees whizzed by, but in the near distance were low hills, small shrubs and miles of wild grass that cattle were grazing on. As he rode on, the colours on the rocks changed, keeping pace with the sun's movement on the horizon. Moriya rode on, swift and graceful on his horse. The animal was a mere pony, ordinary brown in colour, but Moriya rode it with a majesty and poise that came naturally to him.

He was on the trail left by the peacocks, sighting their soft, silken feathers strewn amidst the rocks. His keen ears had caught their long melancholy calls earlier, more melodious than he had ever heard before. He had wondered whether he had heard right. Was that the cry of the green peafowl – the rarest of rare among birds, far more precious than its cousin, the ordinary blue peacock – its sea-green plumage turning a gorgeous emerald every time it flashed in the sun?

He stopped to watch as the sun rose in slow motion beyond the rocky hillocks that stretched ahead of him, conscious of that one perfect moment before time rushed on. His horse stomped impatiently, flicking its tail nervously. Moriya took a quick look behind him, his eyes straying down the rocks. He could see the ripple of the small stream that flowed close by, a ribbon of water that had appeared when it had rained unexpectedly, and would just as soon vanish. To the west were the dry forests, where he was headed. It was his father who had first told him of the peacocks and Moriya knew he would find them again among the jamun and banyan trees around the abandoned temple at the far end of the hills. Beyond the temple was the desert, a stretch of sand and thorny bushes, uninhabitable for long distances.

Riding up a hillock, he scanned the horizon again, turning his horse around in a perfect circle on a narrow point without missing a step. The wind rose, grainy but soothingly familiar. From this height, Moriya had a view of the world as he knew it. To the southeast lay Magadha, with its capital at Pataliputra, the city by the Ganga. For him, it was always far away, further than his eye could see, though never far from his thoughts. He lived with the certainty that one day he would return to Pataliputra, a city whose rulers had taken away everything he had known and cherished, a city that had taught him the futility of having attachments or lingering memories. A city, he acknowledged, unlike any other place he had ever heard about or seen since. A city he would love to rule from. One day.

He urged his horse on, knowing it was better to chase the peacocks than to give in to thoughts that had no end.

He remembered the first time he had laid eyes on the elusive bird. He had been a few years younger then, reaching only up to his father's shoulder, and was accompanying him on a journey to the forests that skirted Magadha to the north. It was the region where the smaller republics of Malla and Vajji had once existed, long before Magadha became the powerful kingdom it was. The great and greedy Ajatashatru, the emperor who lived in the time of the Buddha nearly two centuries ago, had taken them over, ruthlessly and with cold logic.

His father, chief of the Moriyas, the tribe of the peacock-tamers, had taught him almost everything he knew. That afternoon long ago, Moriya would learn more from his father than he realized. They were in a small row boat, moving in the slow current of the Ganga, banked by forests that were the most dangerous of all forests known, and denser than the forests to the west he now roamed in. Rising dark and thick, green overhanging branches mingling with thick brown weeds that grew taller every year with the rains, the forests of Moriya's younger days ranged from the eastern borders of Magadha all the way to the Himavat mountains. They were peopled by wild elephant herds that could pound through without warning. The speed of the herds always belied their size; they could cross vast stretches of forest in a day. The earth shook and trembled under the massive feet of a hundred and more elephants in spate. Wild buffaloes and deer lived where the forests were less dense, and the elusive tigers had been seen here too.

His father's eyes narrowed as he scanned the forests that came right up to the river bank. The bittersweet smell of sal and tamarind trees reached them, mixed with the feral scent of forest creatures. Moriya noted the way the trees' branches bent towards the water and the stillness of their leaves.

'These forests…they look as if nothing can ever disturb them. Animals can stay hidden forever among these trees; unseen, living their lives just as nature intended,' his father said as they rowed down the river towards Pataliputra. 'But there are some people who will not rest until they tame its creatures, even the magnificent elephants – all for their own ends.'

His father's lips twisted bitterly. He was referring to the Nandas, the current rulers of Magadha, who were intent on destroying the forests and the tribes who lived in it, simply to get their hands on more elephants for their mighty army. As if in acknowledgment of his father's words, there came a loud trumpeting sound from within the forest. Moriya could tell from the way the trees heaved and shifted that a herd was moving through the forest. He rowed faster, gripping the oars tightly and bending forward to exert as much force as he could.

It was then that they heard a long-drawn-out haunting cry pierce through the calls of the elephant herd and the other sounds of the forest. It was a cry that stretched through the expanse of trees and made his father sit up straight and go still in a way Moriya had never seen before. 'That call…it can belong to none other than a green peacock,' his father said in an awed whisper.

Indicating that they must move on, his father guided them shoreward. His father knew where the boat could be anchored securely, just as he knew each path leading from the river through the forest. They proceeded into the vast green, Moriya leading the way, reading the elephant tracks the way his father had showed him. He paused to listen to the sounds of the forest, sniff the air, and break small dried branches to make their way back easier.

Quite unexpectedly, they came upon a clearing in the forest, and that was when both of them caught sight of the bird – the most beautiful bird Moriya had ever seen, perched high on a branch. In the light of the sun shimmering through the canopy of trees, the bird's wings changed colour, shifting from green to blue and then green again, an iridescent dancing patina of green that lit up the trees – its colours always distinct from the leaves that closed around it. The bird stretched out its long slender neck, beat its tail gently on the branch, then called again, a long cry that floated upward, the leaves parting to carry the sound to the skies above.

Let it be. Let it be. Moriya heard his father's soft murmur in his ears.

All they could do was look on, knowing for that one moment the eternal truth – that every creation is unique and wonderful. Every part of creation was worth cherishing and destruction was futile. This was precisely what the Buddha had said.

The moment passed. The bird suddenly turned its head towards them, startled, as if it had sensed their presence, then gracefully hopped off the branch and flew upwards, its wings glittering a luminous green, shaping into a blur as it disappeared into the blue sky.

In its wake Moriya saw a feather float gently to the ground. He picked it up. It seemed to throb still with the peacock's life blood.

'What a beautiful creature...' his father whispered.

'Do you know about it?' he asked his father.

'Yes,' he nodded, 'but you and I are going to keep this a secret. Birds like this one will never be trapped or hunted down. They will roam free, always. Never kill any bird, son, unless it is essential. They make the world beautiful and complete. All creatures – animals and birds and all of us too – are meant to live together in harmony. We are all interconnected. This is what great men and sages have taught us, men whose words will live longer than kings' will. True power lies in understanding that life and death assure the continuity of the universe itself.'

Moriya had, he thought then, understood what his father had meant. Over time, he came to realize there was more to his father's words. Chief of the Moriyas of Pippalivahana, his father believed their tribe was meant to protect birds, to prevent any harm from befalling them. They were the caretakers of the birds and the forest they lived in, he had always said. Moriya took a deep breath, remembering his father's solemn voice. Of course, there were the truths of his father and there were those that Moriya had to learn now that he was older – that killing was necessary, because it proved one's might. Two strong creatures, man or animal, could never rule over the same realm.

Four winters had passed since that journey with his father. Moriya was now far from the forests of the east, where he had spent a little over eleven years of his life. He missed his father, and wondered what he would have had to say now that Moriya had once again sighted the magnificent, elusive green peacock.

This time he corrected himself, fiercely, shaking his mane of dark curls so they lashed against his back. *Don't call him 'Father', not anymore. Call him 'Chief' and think no more of the past… Think no more.* He knew this – that his past was not really his to claim, but there was a time for everything, and the time had come for him to know at least a few things with certainty. He could sense that the boys who were his everyday companions thought he was different from them. And he was, because they had assured pasts, and no doubts and questions about where they belonged and about who their parents were, while he on the other hand was not sure of anything, not even after four winters of being on the run.

Moriya followed the bird with renewed intensity. The brilliant blue-green of the peafowl's feathers was a stark contrast to the grey rocks, brown boulders and the dry keekar bushes of the Aravallis, the biggest and oldest mountains in these parts. It was difficult to lose sight of the bird – it flew low at times, its wings making slender shadows against the rock, and then rose high, its colours a shimmering green as the day lengthened, the sky turning from a gentle morning blue to a raging gold. Squinting against the harsh morning light, Moriya glimpsed the temple again, closer than before. Built by passing herders, it stood amidst a copse of trees, its stone walls blackened with time and the heat of the desert.

He picked up his bow, the taut bowstring whistling in a shrill imitation of the wind as he drew his arrow across. Did he dare aim his arrow at the bird? For a few moments Moriya toyed with the idea. Then he shrugged and let his arm fall away. The arrowhead grazed his horse's mane and the animal shuffled in protest. Moriya bent forward, nuzzling its neck in apology. He saw the bird flying away – almost in relief, he thought – heading further south, where the scrubland and the desert gave way to the forests.

He looked around, unsure if his horse could negotiate its way down the rocks and towards the clump of trees. It was young and skittish and would gallop at full tilt on an open stretch of ground, but one wrong step on these old rocks could send them both hurtling down.

He heard the peacock's call from the forest, which boasted banyan, jamun and amla trees. These were trees of the dry forest, whose brown winter leaves were now turning a golden yellow. Were there two birds hidden among those trees? More? Moriya cupped his hands around his mouth, and soon the air resonated with a melodious, haunting call. Barely had the cry died out when he was rewarded with an answering call from the temple at the edge of the forest. Not one, but two, and then many more. He craned his neck and bent down to pacify his horse, made nervous by the unexpected clamour. The peacocks called again and he saw the branches move as the birds moved about restlessly. Perhaps he should not have disturbed them... Then something else caught his eye.

A tall figure was moving slowly amidst the trees. Moriya became still and watched as the figure limped forward in a fatigued yet determined manner, and a voice from the past flooded his mind – a low, rasping voice that would brook no disagreement, and a pair of glittering, sharp eyes that missed nothing.

The peacocks had brought him here with some intent, Moriya was sure. As he looked on, he calculated that the man would reach the settlement of the cattle-herders, the people Moriya now lived with, by nightfall. Till then he, this traveller from afar, would perhaps rest in the old temple. Moriya dismounted and patted his horse, whispering in his ear as he placed the reins in the creature's mouth. *Go home,* he said, *go back home.* He knew why the other man was here, and Moriya was not going to be taken by surprise – like the last time they had met. In his search for answers, Moriya knew, he would have to be ready to relinquish old attachments.

2

Secret Journeys

That journey with his father held more revelations for Moriya than just his first glimpse of the ethereal green peacock. They had sailed further down the Ganga, the sun sinking in the west, its light a gentle gold on the trees. His father had directed the boat in a distinct southeast direction, and Moriya knew they were headed for Pataliputra, the capital of Magadha, the mighty kingdom ruled by the ruthless Nanda king Mahapadma.

From a distance, the walls of the fortress rose forbiddingly over the lush, thick forest, as though reminding them of Mahapadma's presence. The late afternoon sun added lustre to the hard brown stones, doing little to ease the menacing appearance of the cave-like windows that jutted out from the highest reaches of the fortress. Cruel and unpredictable, Mahapadma Nanda had expanded his kingdom through intrigue and violence, making it far bigger than when the great kings Bimbisara and his son Ajatashatru had been its rulers two centuries ago. Mahapadma was a man of such great power and strength that it was believed he wrestled with elephants every morning. His footsteps made the earth tremble and his voice, when heard from afar, thundered like a lion's roar. It was rumoured, in fact, that he kept lions as pets. He was extremely ambitious – the fort grew bigger and his armies did too – but Mahapadma's quest for more power remained unabated.

When he rose to the throne, the people of Magadha knew they had no enemies to fear. The fort that surrounded the city for miles around was assurance enough of security from invasion. Their fathers and grandfathers had built it, rolling up huge blocks of stone to construct massive walls. With its gigantic columns and forbidding gates, the fort was – along with the surrounding forest, the high mountains to the east and north, and the river Ganga – as sacred to them as the gods they worshipped. It convinced them that, like all their kings, from Bimbisara to Mahapadma Nanda, Magadha was invincible, an empire like none other. But the admiration that the kings had once evoked was now mingled with fear, for to Mahapadma and his sons, the nine Nanda princes, justice and duty came second to supremacy, which they craved at all cost.

This fear had made the people of Magadha incapable of questioning the injustices they witnessed every day and often faced themselves. They knew what had happened to the tribes that had tried to withstand the force of the Nanda armies; how the ancient forests, the free realm of all creatures, were now part of the Nandas' domain; how hunters were forced to work for the Nanda armies and capture wild elephants to be tamed and trained for war. They knew that anyone who opposed the Nandas or questioned them was killed or picked up and locked in dark dungeons. Some never returned; only a lucky few escaped. They saw how their women, even the free women of the tribes, were made slaves for life, passed from one Nanda prince to another, while the brothers' lust never satiated. People spoke in hushed whispers of underground cells and deep tunnels where captured rebels were chained and made to guard the treasures that the royals had gathered over the years – treasures they had amassed by levying excessive taxes on the people they ruled and by demanding more than their fair share of crops from peasants.

Moriya and his father were well aware of these cruelties. That day, their boat secured to the overhanging branches of a particularly leafy tree which kept it hidden from view, and the sight of the peacock still fresh in their minds, father and son started moving through the forest. Once in its depths, Moriya dropped down and pushed his ear to the leaf-carpeted earth. He heard the wind blow, the breathing of a thousand and more creatures in the forest, the sound of a leaf drifting down. He knew that if he listened carefully, he would hear a woman crying. That was the sound of injustice.

His father nudged him. 'We can't linger, Moriya. Not here of all places.'

They moved on, his father leading the way, deeper among the trees, taking a twisted, ever more difficult path. Through the gaps among the trees, the high walls of the fort appeared closer at every turn. Moriya followed his father wordlessly. He knew how his father had held out against everyone else in the tribe and had not acquiesced to the will of the Nandas, but it seemed they were now heading directly into the oppressors' domain. They were both armed only with daggers and, if discovered, any contest would be farcical. What did his father intend to do?

The peacocks and other birds were the special upkeep of the Moriyas, the tribe they were part of, the tribe whose very existence was bound to the birds of the forest. They were the birds' protectors and in a way the keepers of the forest too. But many of their fellow tribesmen were now turning away from that truth. There were some in the tribe who spoke of a compromise with the Nandas. The future of the tribe was at stake if they defied the king, they said. 'They need birds, and they are rich. Peacocks and pheasants and falcons... It could benefit us if we sold some to them,' one of Moriya's uncles said.

'They need birds that will fight each other to death for their amusement, birds to kill for pleasure,' his father had replied calmly. 'Our lives are tied to these birds. We can never betray that bond. They have given us so much. Their feathers are used as delicate quills. Their eggs are ingredients for potions that cure the most resilient diseases. Their beauty and grace gives us happiness. We tame them, teach them to dance to a rhythm so they add to a king's glory. They are of more use to us than we to them, even the greatest and mightiest of kings must understand that. It is us humans that are far more wretched. We forget these bonds that tie us to every creature on earth.'

'Your stubbornness will cost us our lives, our livelihoods, and the very animals you seek to protect,' said another tribesman. 'What you will not do, their soldiers will. Their elephants will trample through these forests, drive the birds away and then us, too. They prey on the weak, derive their power from emasculating others. And you know this.'

Sensing the futility of more talk, Moriya's father kept silent, but his mother took a step forward and slapped the face of the man who had spoken. No one said much afterwards. They had always been fiercely loyal to their chief and in their heart of hearts they knew he had the tribe's best interests in mind. Or so Moriya had assumed.

Now, hiding near the Nandas' fortress, Moriya looked at his father – a tall, lean man, his face withered and wrinkled, not as much with age as from the years he had spent living out in the open, exposed to the elements. He always had the calm and steady gaze of a man who understood his own morality, a man who knew one kind of cloud from another; who could tell everything about a forest from a fallen leaf; who knew, it was said, the languages of animals.

Now Moriya spoke, unable to stop the question that came unbidden to him. 'Aren't you afraid of the Nandas? Their soldiers might find us here any moment.'

'We don't have much to pay them,' his father said, smiling ruefully before sadness descended on his face. 'And no, I am not afraid. Sometimes a challenge is just not worth it.' He stopped and turned around to look at Moriya before he resumed his steady pace, saying, 'Most of the battles we fight are only to satisfy our egos, because we believe ourselves to be more important than the world around us. The biggest battles are those you fight with your soul, when you give up what is dearest to you in the hope of something better in the future, not for yourself but for others.'

Barely had they taken a few more steps when his father stopped abruptly. Moving quickly and soundlessly to the left, he motioned to Moriya to keep low and silent. Slowly, he pushed aside a branch and Moriya crept up behind him to peer over his shoulder. They heard someone's hesitant steps in the undergrowth and then saw the dim light of a taper making its way towards them. Within moments the father and son were face-to-face with the bearer of the taper. As the light dimmed and then rose around them, Moriya saw that the stranger had a slight limp and a hard unwavering gaze that matched his father's steady, calm one. His face was unreadable; a face with harshly etched features and a stern jaw, his head held high. Moriya guessed the man was someone of authority – not a king but one who would find it hard to bow to one as well. Moriya made to take a step forward but his father stopped him, one hand held out almost in warning.

'Is he with you?' Moriya heard his rasping, cold voice from behind the taper's half-light. The man stepped forward. In the flickering light of the flame, Moriya saw his face more clearly now. The lines on his forehead had given him a permanent scowl, he had sharp cheekbones and a stubborn chin, and eyes that saw everything yet gave little away. The shawl over his shoulders seemed of the finest cotton and his dhoti, despite being soiled at the edges, glimmered silver in the torchlight. His hair was knotted in the shikha that gave him away as a Brahmin. Moriya peered into the darkness behind the man. No, there were no soldiers accompanying him. This was unusual. He seemed to be a man of some importance, for he was dressed finely, and yet he had come all this way alone.

His father did not utter a word. It occurred to Moriya that his father had come here with precisely this intent, that he knew the man who stood before them, and that it was all part of something he, Moriya, didn't know yet.

'Step forward, I want to see you,' he heard the voice, sharp and unrelenting. The cold eyes had moved their gaze beyond his father, and Moriya understood.

Moriya's bony shoulder brushed against his father's as he took a step ahead, and he felt momentarily comforted by the touch. When his eyes locked with the stranger's, he did not look away but stood firm as the man's gaze swept over him, scrutinizing him from head to toe. Moriya looked back defiantly and was pleased to see a certain hesitation in the other man's face. So he had surprised him after all. A moment later, the man turned to his father with a deep sigh, a sound of relief. They stood in silence till the man nodded and his lips twisted into a half smile, which on that harsh face appeared little more than a grimace.

'Chief of the Moriyas, you came here at a time of great danger and I thank you.' There was some hesitation before the man inclined his head in his father's direction, a gesture that acknowledged not his father's superiority but his greatness. 'My spies were right. This one is no son of the peacock-tamers.'

Moriya felt his father stiffen beside him. Instinctively, Moriya reached for his dagger but his father laid a hand on his arm and stilled him. He wished he could turn, see the expression on his father's face, but in that moment it seemed to him that his father, standing only a step away, had receded deep into the maze of trees and become a distant figure.

The stranger snuffed out the taper, striking it against the hard trunk nearest him, and said, 'We must bide our time now. I will let you know the next step.' Then he turned and walked away, his unsteady gait making the dried leaves rustle unevenly under his feet.

His father was silent as they made their way back to the river and on to the boat. His mind raging with confusion, Moriya watched the stiff back, the tense outline of a clenched jaw, the whitened knuckles gripping the oar with unusual tension. Eventually, he spoke up. 'Who was he? Why did he want to see me? How do you know this man?'

It took a while for his father to reply. 'I do not know what to tell you. Maybe you will find out and maybe you will understand better than I do. But this you should know – sometimes we blame people too readily for things they were not really responsible for. Your mother...'

He saw his father lower his head. The words had caught in his throat, and he shook his head, unable to go on. They rowed the rest of the way without exchanging another word. The gentle splash of the oars in the water and the calls of the forest creatures were the only sounds punctuating the heavy silence as evening gave way to night.

'Come now. Your mother is waiting, Moriya,' his father said when they reached their settlement.

They reached home to find his mother about to saddle a horse to go looking for them. She stopped when she saw them and rushed forward, her face taut with anxiety.

'Where have you been?' she asked, her voice louder and more high-pitched than Moriya had ever heard. He could see beads of sweat glistening on her brow.

His father only smiled. Gently, he said, 'Why did you have to worry? I have brought our son back for you. He is safe.'

But from that day onwards, his father changed. The stranger they had met, the one with the hoarse voice and sharp eyes, had said little, but Moriya realized his few words and gestures had revealed something his father had not really wanted to acknowledge.

When the Moriya tribe made its decision to leave the forest that had provided their livelihood for generations, everyone from his uncles and the other elders to the impudent young men who had once been Moriya's companions blamed his father. Moriya thought it strange, for his father was gone by then – almost, it seemed to Moriya, as if he had renounced the world in the manner of ancient kings and sages. He had removed himself from their midst in his gentle way and no one, not even Moriya, knew where he had wandered away. But not everyone thought the same of his father's actions.

'He should have foreseen this earlier. He was our chief,' they all said.

'If only he had not challenged the prince... That was what turned the Nandas against us.'

'He should not have dared the ruler.'

'He need not have been so rigid.'

There were no answers to be found, for his father was no longer there. At times anger overwhelmed him, but Moriya kept himself in check. His mother's warning glances were enough for that. If they could speak freely he knew she would tell him that there was a time for everything, and this was no time for rage.

No one knew if the chief was really dead, only that he left one evening and did not return. A few days later, a mysterious turbaned messenger turned up late at night while the last of the tapers still burnt. It was the time when the rains promised to give way to a bitterly cold winter, and the young calves shivered as they were brought into the warmth. The time, as rumours went, when the end of the great Mahapadma was near. The messenger had wasted no time, his words raised in a half shout, half command, harsh and brooking no opposition.

'You must leave. Move fast! I have been sent by the minister Vishnugupta...'

There was confusion and chaos as half-awake elders gathered near the fire that burnt all night long at the centre of the camp and the younger boys came straggling up behind them. But Moriya knew the voice and held his breath. This was no ordinary messenger. Besides, he recognized the limp.

'Do not argue. The existence of your tribe is at peril. Your chief had the temerity to argue before prince Dhana Nanda, the future king. Princes are known to act on a whim and your chief dared to openly oppose one. Do not ask questions, simply leave if you value your safety.'

'Is he dead?' It was the loud and clear voice of his mother, Mura, who seemed undaunted by all the perplexed murmuring. She had to know where his father was and Moriya shivered at her sharp tone.

The messenger hesitated, his voice gentler as he replied, 'We do not know. He was captured by the prince's soldiers. We have no idea if he is dead or...'

In the silence that descended, Moriya felt that even the wind had fallen quiet. No one was known to have emerged alive from the dungeons of the Nandas. Suddenly, and with an unexpected aggression that belied his limp, the man dragged himself to where Moriya stood. His mother rushed forward, positioning herself between the messenger and Moriya, but the man hardly seemed to notice her presence.

'You must hurry,' he hissed in a low, menacing tone. 'Leave… We will meet again…soon.' Then he had turned around and hurried away. Moriya stared after him, his eyes refusing to leave the man's left leg, bent at an awkward angle. The limp, that glance locked into Moriya's – he knew then that the messenger was not who he had said he was. He was the same man that he and his father had met in the forest. His thoughts in a whirl, Moriya turned to his mother only to see her face suffused with fear, a kind of terror in her wide eyes that he would never want to see again in any human being.

The very next day they had headed for the foothills further to the north, close to the mountains from where the Gandaki and Kosi rivers originated. The Ganga began further upstream but they made sure not to follow that river. It was the most likely route the Nanda soldiers would take to track them down. Instead, they travelled up along the course of the smaller Gandaki. If they were chased they knew they had a chance to escape through the mountain passes and head for the kingdom of the Bhotas, far away from the birds that had sustained them but assured at least of survival.

Moriya led the way with the elders. His already tall and strong body was a reassuring figure as they moved on, alert and wary of the ferocious tribes who guarded the passes through the Himavat mountains and who were known to prey on unsuspecting trespassers, dropping rocks from a height and ambushing them. They were rumoured to have strange pets, too – big snake-like lizards and dogs that could smell enemies from a long way off. But once Moriya led his tribe to the terai region, a stretch of undulating hills and deep valleys that lay just before the higher mountains, they met other friendly tribes – people who lived a life always on the move: hunters, animal-herders, traders and even mendicants.

The parting with his mother had followed soon after. He would be safe with the hunters, she said, the ones who knew by sight and smell the lairs and tracks of the wild cats, the tigers and the cheetahs, and who sometimes tamed them for royal pleasure. They could be ruthless slayers too, and having killed these fierce animals, they treated their skins with plant pigments, turning them into fine royal capes to please royal egos. These were useful skills to pick up, and Moriya picked them up fast, learning at the same time to temper his rage and give nothing away of his feelings as he followed the hunters up the terai paths leading northward, and then turned westward, towards the Punjab. This was where the mountains gave way to the five rivers that watered the Punjab and the hunters passed him on to the cattle-herders. Betrayed by his own tribe, he was now bartered to others, his usefulness measured by what other tribes had to offer. The life of the hunters was one lived close to the mountains, but the cattle-herders moved in search of grass, and now that spring was near, they were headed for the Punjab and the northwest. With spring that year, however, had also come the news of the Yavana emperor and his conquering armies from a distant land, a land that lay beyond the Hindu Kush and even farther across the seas.

Moriya realized then that there had been a reason for everything that had happened – his tribe's disintegration, his own life lived on the run, and now the presence of an emperor reported to be almost godlike in his powers, against whom no enemy army had a chance. He looked at the sky and the sun, and felt a strange new power surge in his veins as he remembered his mother's parting words.

'Some day you will go farther than where I am letting you go. It is destined so, for there runs in your veins also a different blood, part that is mine and part that for now has to be kept a secret. For it brings you immense dangers that you must learn to protect yourself from. When you are on your own you must learn most of all to listen to yourself. Give your trust only to the one who deserves it. You are safe in the forests, on the rough earth. It is the men with power you must be wary of.' She paused before she said, her voice dropping to a hoarse whisper, 'You must never let them catch you. Never.'

He knew she meant the Nandas, but there was no time to ask more questions. He knew what they called his mother, those unworthy men who had become chiefs after his father – or rather, the man he would always know as his father – had vanished. They said she was a slave woman, and he, Moriya, the slave woman's son, was not one of them and would never be. But they said it all behind his back. They wouldn't dare say it to his face.

He had looked into his mother's eyes, soft and moist, and she into his, hers blazing with a hidden determination. She had spoken her truth and he had understood, at least in part. One last time, her fingers brushed his shoulder, caressed the mark of the moon, almost crescent like, at the nape of his neck, hidden by his matted locks of hair. For long moments, it seemed, he knelt at her feet. She may have been a slave woman, or whatever else people called her, but she had faith in herself and in her love for the man who was her husband, once the chief of the Moriyas. A love that had made it possible for her to accept her destiny.

Moriya's thoughts returned to the present. Looking down at the temple in the clearing, his gaze never leaving the man heading towards it, he quickly assessed the situation. The man he had once met in the forest had evidently travelled a long distance on his own, for Pataliputra was far away. This probably indicated some trouble at the Magadhan court. His gait was slower than Moriya remembered, and he seemed to be dragging his weaker foot as though it were wounded. Something had happened to make him leave Pataliputra. Something had made him travel all this way. Had he come in search of Moriya again? Why? The truth his mother had not been able to fully reveal lay with this man. And this time, Moriya meant to find out what it was.

3

THE MAN ON THE RUN

In the early morning light, a half-moon still suspended in the sky, the stream was a calm, rippling silver. Weeds had grown through cracks in the cold stone floor of the abandoned temple; a pipal tree had spread its roots generously along the walls, cracking them open in places to entrench itself. The tree's intrusion had caused part of the roof of the main temple chamber to cave in, and now half of the roof slanted in and remained dangerously poised in mid-air, while the other half, overgrown with the spreading branches of the pipal, held on resolute. In another season or so, the branches would stretch farther to overlook the stream that lay just beyond.

A low, throaty growl made the man look up with a start. On the steps below, he saw a thin mangy dog crouching low, his eyes fixed on three cats staring down at it. The glitter in their silver-green eyes was visible in the near darkness. The man, who till then had called himself Vishnugupta, read greed in their eyes. He hadn't heard them yowl in the manner cats did when alarmed and their silence, even with its hint of menace, intrigued him. He wondered warily what the cats were waiting for. Such creatures sensed things that mere humans could not.

The animals seemed oblivious to his presence. Which was as it should be, he thought. For those days were gone when his presence created restlessness among men and animals alike.

The sky was lightening rapidly, the pinkish hues at the horizon stretching into swathes of blue. He decided to have his bath and say his ritual prayers before settling down to the task at hand. Looking around at the still earth, watching the smoke from low burning fires drift moodily over the hill that lay between him and the settlement of the cattle-herders, he knew he had finally found the one he had come looking for.

He went down the steps, feeling soothed as his feet touched cold stone. The long distance he had walked had caused the cracks in his soles to run deep. Thorns and stones had cut into them and he had had no chance to tend to them other than to occasionally apply the juice of crushed basil leaves – a helpful instruction shared by the ascetics called the Ajivikas, with whom he had walked during his early days on the run.

Long years in the palace of that miser have spoiled you, he told himself.

Even as he gingerly took his next step, a new pain shot through his right leg. Looking down, he was alarmed to see a swelling between his toes. He would have to prick it on his own using a thorn – a quick process, only momentarily painful. The Ajivikas had taught him this too.

He knew that the journey had only just begun – for him and for the boy destined to be emperor. The boy, he was sure, was now a young man, and far more certain of his destiny than ever before. Or so he hoped. Together, they would defeat the enemies that followed them as well as those who awaited them at every turn. For he knew the Nandas were on his trail and soon they would follow the boy's too. It was not that difficult, after all, for people such as the cattle-herders travelled on known routes, set and devised from years of nomadic wandering. He had kept close to such routes, on the steps of the wandering saints and lone hunters, and had outwitted the Nanda soldiers thus far. But the two of them, he and the Moriya boy, would evade – and his lips twisted cynically at the thought – even messengers sent by the god of death himself.

He found a spot at the stream where the water was fairly still, flowing gently over the shallow bed. As he leaned over, he caught a glimpse of his shadowy reflection in the grey water. He saw his thin shoulders, and how his face was now framed by long, matted hair that felt hard and dry against his skin. Not too long ago, his hair had been well-oiled and scented, the shikha distinctly knotted, framing his square face. But no more; now his hair fell in hard locks, greying and dull. He had taken an oath to leave his hair this way till the Nandas were defeated and dislodged entirely from Magadha.

The pain between his toes stabbed at him anew and he limped over to the shrubs a little away from the water. Tearing off a thorn, he sharpened it by rolling it on a stone until it became almost needle-sharp. Without giving himself room for further thought, he plunged it into the swelling, now blue-green with accumulated pus. Wincing, he gritted his teeth hard to stop himself from crying out loud. Not that he minded the pain. He had seen cruelty and kindness in equal measure and he knew how useful both were when used in certain circumstances and in small doses. The trick was to always anticipate the circumstance.

He reached for the basil plant that was once worshipped in the temple and now grew neglected and overgrown on the porch. Tearing off some leaves and rubbing them between his hands, he massaged the resulting paste into his wound, its coolness soothing him somewhat. As he felt the pain ebbing away, a sudden movement in the branches behind him made his heart pound. He looked up, just as the cats begin to yowl and, almost simultaneously, a piercing bird call rang out. This was the call of no ordinary bird, but of a peacock that was rare even among its species.

The kings he had left behind were fond of peacock fights. His lips tightened at the thought. If his plans worked out well, their days of debauchery and tyranny would soon be over. He wondered about the boy he had come looking for, the boy who was born to be king. He, Vishnugupta, master strategist and manipulator of the best of men and situations, was but destiny's tool. It was Moriya of the tribe of peacock-tamers who would write Magadha's history anew.

Vishnugupta knew he had put too much faith in his own plans; he had thought of nothing else and had paid the price. For all his machinations against the Nandas, he had never anticipated the envy and jealousy of his opponents who spoke in King Dhana Nanda's ears. Thus Vishnugupta had never expected the humiliation heaped on him in the palace. He should have been more subtle. After all, he had already met the Moriya chief and the boy in the forests long ago; he had also managed to deliver in time the warning to them, so that they could escape the prince's wrath with haste. If he had waited, the situation might have been different. But it was not to be. Events moved faster than he had anticipated. With Mahapadma's sudden death, Dhana Nanda, always power-hungry and far more arrogant than his father, was now king, and things would never be the same for Vishnugupta.

He knew he had been too careless and had paid the price for his overweening confidence. He should have kept his temper in check, reminded himself in the heat of the moment that it was imperative he stay within close quarters of the royal court and strive, despite his unwillingness, to hold the king's trust till the time was right. Instead, he had exposed himself to ridicule, to accusations of being too stubborn and too ambitious, and so to save himself from certain death by execution, he had been forced to tender an ingratiating apology to that vain and most undeserving of kings, Dhana Nanda. And then he had walked away into self-imposed exile. But he knew Dhana Nanda's men were never too far away, and that even in Pataliputra, the stories of the boy who had been reared by the tribe of the peacock-tamers were now more than just a rumour. Dhana Nanda and his soldiers would do everything they could to silence those rumours and put an end to the threat forever.

Vishnugupta remembered that morning well, the morning of the debate between him and the visiting scholar from the Chera kingdom in the south. He had been looking forward to pitting his knowledge and learning against his opponent's, assured and certain that in the end the triumph would be his. As a student at Taxila university, famed for its learned Brahmins, there had been no one who could debate with him and win. There was still no one.

Like every other morning, his wife had filled his pitcher with water and waited by the gate. Just as he was about to step out on to the porch, there came from the distance the sounds of a horse's whinny and an elephant's trumpet, in ominous chorus. As he sprinkled the water from the pitcher his wife held out over his forehead, he heard her say, 'Don't go out so soon, my lord.'

He looked at her and noted the alarm in her eyes. For a moment he considered assuaging her fears, but realized immediately that he could not afford a delay. He had to get himself ready for the debate; the king and a hall full of spectators were awaiting his arrival. He shook his head and smiled at her, gently touching her cheek. 'It's all right. You shouldn't believe in these things.'

Vishnugupta had prepared for the debate in advance, and knew nothing could go wrong – except that it did, in ways he, even with all his foresight, had not accounted for. Apart from the omens in the morning, the day seemed as usual. The sun glinted on the fort walls, turning it golden brown in places. As he walked down the road to the royal courtroom, through the high archways of the fort, he saw everything had been decorated for the event – marigold garlands on the walls, painted floral patterns festooning the floor and the fragrance of sandal and jasmine everywhere. At the forecourt, elephants stood in perfect order and at a gesture from their mahouts, they raised their trunks in Vishnugupta's honour as he passed. The drummers stood high on the ramparts, the silk in their turbans glowing orange in the sunlight. Soldiers stood at every column that lined the archway to the courtroom, the tips of their iron spears glinting with a new coat of polish and menace. Vishnugupta stared ahead, adjusted his fine silk shawl over himself and acknowledged the soldiers as they bowed to him, and the rice and rose petals that were sprinkled on him by the palace attendants.

The courtroom was an oblong chamber, lavishly decorated. At one end was the high dais with the king's throne, still unoccupied, for Dhana Nanda was a late riser, and a step below, arranged in neat rows all down the chamber, were the low seats, with bolsters and cushions, for the king's advisers, ministers and officials. The colours progressively dulled as one moved down the order, for the lower officials had to be content with dull brown cushions and the roughest of mats. Scarlet curtains draped every open window, attendants stood ready next to pitchers of water and some were at work already, waving their palm-leaf fans. The chamber looked cool and inviting as Vishnugupta stepped in. There was a rustle of clothing as the officials rose to greet him. They bowed low and as he acknowledged the gesture, he felt pride sweep through him. He took in everything with one quick glance: the obeisance of the lower officials, and the hesitation and dark glances the high ministers exchanged before they bowed low in welcome, inclining their heads only at an angle and not as obsequiously as the lower officials. The protocol of greeting was well-entrenched but he missed the hesitation that marked some of these gestures, and did not heed the dark malice in Rakshasa's eyes as he stepped forward from his place right near the king's throne to greet Vishnugupta.

He waited, and it was Vishnugupta who moved towards him and bowed first. Rakshasa was the prime minister and deserved the honour of being greeted first. If Rakshasa had noticed the hesitation or even the contempt that Vishnugupta made little effort to hide, he did not show it. He raised his hand to pat Vishnugupta on the shoulder. Rakshasa was the shorter man, and his silken robes swirled and fell off his rounded, oiled shoulders as he did so, the thick gold necklace on his chest heaving with his every move, but Vishnugupta's mind was already on the debate. Rakshasa's quick eyes took in everything about Vishnugupta; his lips moved under his thin moustache, and only then did he smile.

Turning aside, Rakshasa pointed to the carpet that had been arranged in the centre of the courtroom, lined with cushions and pitchers of water for the two learned men who would now debate in full view of the court. As Vishnugupta looked on, his rival from the Chera kingdom bowed low and almost mockingly. He returned the gesture before he turned to face Rakshasa again, composing his face suitably to show his respect to someone senior to him in the palace hierarchy. He was surprised by how difficult the effort was.

'Greetings, O Vishnugupta,' said Rakshasa. 'In you now vests the prestige of Magadha and the court. We hope you will acquit yourself with honour and worth.'

There had been signs everywhere and he had missed them. Never before had Rakshasa spoken to him this way. His debating skills, his victory in any contest of learning had always been a foregone certainty, yet Rakshasa's voice had carried a taunt he couldn't quite place.

Instead, he allowed himself a thin smile as he replied, 'Your trust in me is gratifying, Maha Mantri, and I will do my best to live up to it.'

'Hear, hear,' said Rakshasa. 'This time the great Vishnugupta agrees to bring glory to the emperor and not himself.'

Their glances locked and he heard the low subdued laughter that broke out, before it was all drowned by the fanfare of trumpets, the blowing of conch shells and the ululations of the women attendants as the emperor Dhana Nanda walked in. Vishnugupta realized Rakshasa was trying to bait him, but he dismissed it as inconsequential. He missed Rakshasa's dark glance as they bowed together before the emperor.

Dhana Nanda did not deserve to be king. Of all of Mahapadma's sons, he was the most worthless. Vishnugupta had come to believe that royal birth was just one criterion for kingship; learning and courage mattered as much or even more. Destiny still had the last laugh though; after Mahapadma's death, Dhana Nanda had seized the throne. He had already outlived several of his brothers and overpowered the rest. But not for long; Vishnugupta would ensure that. Magadha deserved more righteous rulers than the vain Nandas. Vishnugupta clenched his teeth, reined in his thoughts and waited for Rakshasa to make the announcement. But the emperor looked drowsy, while Rakshasa busied himself in comforting him with obsequious platitudes, and it was only many moments later that Vishnugupta bowed again and took his place on the cushions facing his rival.

The topic of the debate was the duties of a good king. Was a king good if he defended the state, or was he good if he taught his subjects the way of dharma? Was the good king a saint or a warrior?

'War is an essential duty,' said the learned man from the Chera kingdom. 'The king is first and foremost a soldier, leading his men to victory and securing his kingdom from all threats.'

Vishnugupta disagreed. A king's duty encompassed much more. He was more than a mere soldier; he was the state, or the most powerful and potent symbol of it. He had to be both a soldier who led armies and a saint who upheld dharma, as and when occasion demanded.

'It depends on the context,' he had said. A king had to be a step ahead. He had to have foresight and then take action. Politics, he said in the argument that clinched the debate once and for all, meant understanding and anticipating what could happen. A king did not have to be a god or one of the devas to do this but simply be blessed to have trusted advisers who would not desist from giving even unwelcome advice, if it was so needed.

The visiting scholar was left speechless, the listening audience burst out in applause, the emperor too smiled sleepily and Vishnugupta's victory appeared complete. He blessed the other scholar and advised him to continue learning but not to believe too much in what the old texts said. 'After all, in politics, learning only helps you trust your own counsel,' he advised before proceeding with satisfaction and pleasure to take his own place among the king's council of ministers.

It was already noon and the assembly would disperse in no time. Perhaps that was why Vishnugupta had dropped his guard. He smiled absently as the ministers and officials recounted amongst themselves the debate and its proceedings but it was Rakshasa, rubbing his hands on his thighs, whose voice, silken and cutting, rose above the low murmur and commanded attention.

'Ah, Vishnugupta, you said all the right things but left much unsaid,' he said in his quiet voice, deliberating over the words he uttered. 'You would equate the king with God and yet not so.'

Dhana Nanda sat looking on with a bored expression. Vishnugupta knew the king had had a sleepless night. Spies had reported that the nomadic hunters who had asked for permission to camp in the forests of Magadha had been ordered to supply the palace with some of their women.

Vishnugupta replied calmly, 'For a king's subjects, he is God, but he needs the help of well-functioning state machinery – absolute loyalty and devotion from those who serve him. Loyalty that would make them secure, enable them to voice truths necessary for the state's welfare and not just the king's. Freedom from fear is far more necessary than the freedom to flatter.'

'Are you saying that the king's advisers don't serve him well enough? That we are parasites, just toadying up to him?'

The answer that came to his lips died away just as quickly: Yes, I do think you are. That you are hypocrites and don't know the scriptures well. You know only how to flatter him. Instead, he had replied, confident of the knowledge he possessed, 'The state is like a body and the king is at the centre. Every part of it has to function well and only then can the state be a healthy state.'

But his words were drowned out by a loud burst of familiar laughter. The king, resting on his cushions, was now doubled over, his entire body shaking with mirth. Vishnugupta knew the king occasionally indulged in such reactions to ease himself of boredom. He had in truth followed nothing but as always, his ministers followed Dhana Nanda's cue. Vishnugupta's opponent looked sympathetic, but also relieved. The debate was over, and he had no argument to offer. Besides, it was not his place to do so.

Vishnugupta waited for the laughter to subside. Instead, the laughter spread among the lower ministers, the visiting dignitaries, and the court's attendants too. It was this that first alarmed him. All of the dignitaries aligning with Rakshasa was definitely a sign of conspiracy.

'O Vishnugupta, this time you have truly surpassed yourself.' Light filtered in from between the pillars, lighting up Dhana

Nanda's robes and his sparkling jewellery. For a moment, it diminished the sad, sick pallor of his face. He was a shadow of his father, the late Mahapadma.

'The king is the state.' This time it was Dhana Nanda who spoke, enunciating every word as silence fell. 'There is no distinction between the two. That is why the people pay him taxes, because without him they will have no land. There will be no one to protect them, no one to perform sacrifices for them to appease the gods.'

Vishnugupta shook his head, aghast at the king's interpretation of his duties.

The king's eyebrows rose as he slowly sat up, pushing away a cushion. It rolled away, and even the attendants were too stunned to do anything for a moment.

'You disagree, Vishnugupta. Does it not occur to you that you may have got the scriptures wrong? Or that you have not changed your thinking with the times?'

Dhana Nanda's voice rang out in the silence. It rose in strength as the king put the debauchery of the night behind or perhaps it had just been a ruse all this time. The king's eyes bore into Vishnugupta and he lifted a lazy hand to finger his moustache.

'Maybe you need to learn the scriptures anew, Vishnugupta. I do think you are not fit to be my adviser.'

Vishnugupta felt himself go very still. Now Rakshasa laughed gently, as he placed a cushion somewhat extravagantly against the king's elbow. Every action was measured. Everything had been prepared, Vishnugupta realized.

'Vishnugupta has been at the court since your father's time, oh king,' said Rakshasa.

'Do not tell me of things in my father's time. He was deceived by men like him…' he rose now and spat in Vishnugupta's direction, '…men with false learning. But I am no fool; I saw through him when I was a prince and now, as king, I cannot help but laugh at him. Yes laugh at him and all his silly learning.'

He laughed then – a strange high-pitched sound like a cackle that was soon picked up by everyone around. It was nervous laughter that went on for a long time, and faded slowly as the king raised his hand. He patted himself on the stomach as if restraining the laughter that still threatened to break out.

Silence filled the hall once more. Vishnugupta's lips were clenched, he did not look away from Dhana Nanda. He had always prided himself on his learning and his habitual caution had slipped for that moment. He spoke. 'You misunderstood me, oh king. A king becomes a ruler by the will he exerts over his subjects. They give him the power to be king.'

Murmurs of surprise filled the hall, and the emperor raised a hand in command.

'Oh, vanity! Vishnugupta, do you think that you can say whatever you want because my father gave you a prominent position in court as a minister?' the king asked, leaning forward, his eyes sharp and tone exacting, his boredom all but gone.

'The arrogance of the man,' commented the prime minister. 'Vishnugupta, you will have to admit you have been wrong. Ask for the king's forgiveness and you will not be disappointed.'

Vishnugupta saw the cunning speculation in Rakshasa's eyes and sensed there was more danger than had been apparent before. It was there in the way Rakshasa's eyes looked slyly away, and in the way he sidled a little closer to the king, as if his petty powers could be boosted by that proximity.

No one had ever been able to look Vishnugupta in the eye; he had never allowed it. The superior intelligence and cunning that shone through in them, the particular expression of authority he had cultivated over many years, left anyone who dared confront him decimated. Yet, that morning, at that moment, Vishnugupta had faltered. He could feel now the hostile glances boring into him from around the hall; he could sense the malice, the pleasure at his discomfiture. He understood that Rakshasa was behind this. Vishnugupta lowered his gaze.

He knew he had to leave at once. If he lingered, the punishment for disagreeing with the king in an open court could be lethal. He stared at the floor, then leaned forward with folded hands. Blood rushed to his face, and he could hear his heart pounding in his ears. Never before had he felt humiliation so acutely.

'My lord, I made my arguments too hastily. I forgot myself.' He stumbled over the words, looking at the intricate, painted designs on the floor. He knew if he leaned closer he would smell the fragrance of the crushed basil used to wash the floor every morning. He forced himself to think of everyday sounds and smells. His hair came loose from the knot he had so securely tied and fell forward in loose strands, hiding his face. He gritted his teeth. *I will not dress my hair till I see the end of you and your dynasty, you rogue.*

When he spoke again, he heard his own words as though from far away.

'I would request you to allow me some time away from the court.'

'Hear, hear! The great Vishnugupta is admitting his mistake!' Rakshasa chimed in.

Vishnugupta straightened up, suddenly aware of his every gesture. His hands shook and he clasped them together tightly. 'I wish your rule every prosperity and greatness, O son of Nanda, king of Jambudwipa.' He could barely believe he was mouthing the same inanities the other advisers poured into the king's ears night and day.

What if the king recognized the hollowness of his words? He expected the king to clap his hands or drop his scimitar – which was a sign ordering someone's imprisonment or worse. Vishnugupta was suddenly glad of the king's revelries the night before. The effort to silence Vishnugupta and to impress his sycophantic court had left Dhana Nanda somewhat drained. Now he lolled among the cushions, urging his attendants to fan him harder, as a smug smile played on his lips. He revelled in short-lived triumphs like these, which gave a boost to the ego and showed off his power. He smiled as his eyes closed and Vishnugupta's quiet words rose over the audience.

Vishnugupta took care not to betray the relief he felt at the king's now dulled demeanour. He walked a few steps towards the king, willing his knees not to tremble, and when he was only a foot or so away from Dhana Nanda, he prostrated himself. He could see the king's feet, the fat stubby digits and the rings on his toes. He felt the hard floor graze his knees and his elbows as he lay on the floor, his head on the cusp of his palms.

'I am truly sorry if I have given cause for offence, my king. I can only pray for your mercy. Please spare my life. I promise not to show my face here ever again.' The jangling of the attendants' bangles as they waved the pankhas and the occasional crunch of the walnuts being crushed by the king were the only sounds in the great hall. He continued, 'Only great kings know how to forgive.'

It would be the last time he would say these words to anyone, he swore, until he met one worthy of such advice. As he lay in supplication on the floor, the face of the boy he had met in the forest appeared in his mind. In a blinding moment of clarity, he knew what he had to do.

He stood up, slowly. The danger was not over. It would not be over till he had left the borders of the Nanda empire behind him, till he had reached the north, and the land of the five rivers. Somewhere beyond there was a Yavana invader who was drawing closer and closer with every passing season but Vishnugupta had to find the boy, and quickly. His search had to commence immediately; it would begin once he had left the palace walls. He bowed once again, took a few tentative steps backward, and said, 'My king, I beg your permission to leave. Not until I have obtained knowledge that will please you, that will answer your questions to your utmost satisfaction, will I show my face again.'

The king's eyes flew open. He looked on dazed, before he gestured to Rakshasa. The minister took his time and smiled thinly, his eyes gleaming, as he re-arranged his silk robe over his shoulder. 'That might take you an entire lifetime.'

'I am ready for every hardship,' Vishnugupta said, his voice low, studying the patterns on the pillars as the sunlight played on the fluted columns.

The minister nodded, looked towards the king and then clapped twice. It was a sharp, cutting sound that startled everyone but the king. Pigeons flew out of their roosts on the high corners and everyone craned their necks to look up. So it was just Vishnugupta and the king who saw the guards come to his side at the sound of the claps. Vishnugupta bowed one last time and took quick steps backward. Then he was out into the ante-room, out through a corridor, walking briskly, ignoring the shooting pain in his. leg that caused him to limp. He expected to be called back at any moment and stand accused of insulting the king.

'I can see myself to the gates,' he said through clenched teeth to the two guards accompanying him.

Once out of the palace grounds, he did not even look in the direction of his home. Trying not to think of his wife, he lowered his head, watching his feet tread the ground, the way his robe moved around his knees and his ankles, and walked towards the city's gates. He would change his name and from now be known by the same name as his father – Chanakya.

The memory of those events had so preoccupied him that he did not notice he had turned back towards the temple. As he climbed the steps once again, the sharp crackle of a breaking twig made him look up. It was as if his thoughts had conjured up the boy he had come to meet.

4

AN OFFER

They stared at each other, the youth's fearless eyes never leaving Chanakya's as he advanced towards the older man. Chanakya sensed hostility, but what he saw pleased him. This boy was no slave, even if his mother had been one. His hair was longer, brown and matted from long years of travel; his eyes, grey and deep set, revealed a wisdom far beyond his fifteen years, and he walked with the steadiness of a soldier and the stateliness of someone born to rule.

'You are the man I met at Pataliputra,' Moriya said, stopping at the first of the steps. 'The man who took my father away, who scattered my tribe by pretending to be our friend…'

'I am no fair-weather friend, but a practical man,' Chanakya replied, drawing back his tired shoulders, 'and our destinies are entwined with each other's.'

Moriya did not seem startled by the unexpected revelation. His eyes darkened a fraction and he tossed his head back as he asked, 'Why are you here?'

Chanakya folded his arms at his chest and said, 'I came to find you.' Then, choosing his words carefully, he continued, 'It seems I do follow you around, don't I? Your father's enemies are yours too, but their intent now is far more sinister and nefarious than before. Now that I have left the court, they will know that the rumours are true. They know you exist, the lost prince, and they know the threat you can be to them. The Nandas are tyrant rulers. They will not be content in driving you away but will want your death at all costs. You have to prepare yourself to beat them, outwit them, crush them once and for all. The question is – how deep does your need for revenge burn? And is it just revenge that you want? Will you claim what destiny ordains for you?'

Chanakya found himself breathless as he ended. It had been days since he had spoken to anyone. The younger man shrugged his shoulders impatiently and with a certain contempt. It was as if he knew what Chanakya had to offer, but there were other things on his mind as well.

'I want to know about my father.'

'Your father was – is – a brave man,' Chanakya searched for words. 'But what matters now is how brave *you* are.'

They watched each other, the careless confidence in Moriya's eyes matching the studied caution in Chanakya's.

It was the older man who blinked first and broke the silence. 'Your father, the chief... I only know that he was made a prisoner of the Nandas. It was a time of transition, when Mahapadma was dying. Your mother, as you may know by now, had been a slave in their chambers before she escaped.' He waited before he uttered the next few words, words that left his lips reluctantly because he knew what their impact would be. 'These men humiliated your mother even as they offered her every luxury.'

Moriya's eyes flashed shock and anger, Chanakya noted. He saw that the boy did not trust him. The person standing before him was no more the boy he had met just a few seasons ago in the forests near Pataliputra. Here was a young man certain of where he wanted to go. The task would be easier if they both held on to their vision. He smiled, acknowledging Moriya's distrust, knowing they were now equals like never before.

He continued, 'You may feel you have to avenge your father, your mother, and all those oppressed by these tyrannical kings, but you must reach out for more, for what destiny clearly has in store for you. If you are a worthy son of your mother and the man who was such a fine leader to his people, you will consider matters beyond revenge. Will you use your passion to good effect, to defeat the unjust and cruel Nandas? Will you choose to lead, to establish a much-needed reign of justice in Magadha?'

Moriya listened in silence, watching the other man closely. He noted again the dirt on the man's feet, which even a dip in the river had not cleansed, the recently treated wound, the cracks that showed signs of having bled. There were patches of dried blood high on Chanakya's waist, and scratches and bruises on his thin, skeletal torso and arms. If this man had indeed travelled far to meet him, he had also braved dangers along the way.

'I have seen your qualities of patience and observation. You have also watched me for a while,' Chanakya said. 'But then, you are not really a hunter, are you? Or even a roaming herder.'

'I am far better than a hunter or a herder. I gather all these skills in what I am,' the boy retorted.

Chanakya laughed, a note of freedom and lightness ringing in the sound. It echoed off the temple walls.

'What do you think the future holds for you?' he asked, his gaze intense.

Moriya looked thoughtful. It seemed to Chanakya that he was full of answers which he wouldn't give away easily.

'Come,' Chanakya said, 'let me show you something.' He climbed the steps of the temple and limped over to a slightly damp patch of land. Looking around, he picked up a twig and sat down on his haunches. Moriya watched as he drew lines, shapes and patterns on the ground, not looking up even once. A while later Moriya felt those intense dark eyes focus on him.

'This is where we are. Here, in the west, by the desert and close to the land of the five rivers, which is two days away. The grasslands and the passes leading to Persia lie ahead, to the northwest. And here, to the east, is where the land of the Nandas begins. The empire of Magadha. Because we are beyond the borders of that empire, we may think we are safe, our past well behind us. But that should not be your story. Your past has no bearing on the future that is yours to make.'

Moriya listened, the words seeping into his being.

'Imagine then, this land that our sacred Vedas call Jambudwipa. It stretches from the Himavat to the unknown seas far away. With its fertile lands, its life-giving rivers, its hardened plateaus, its people, its animals – this land is yours to rule over. *You* can rule it with a just hand. It is not just the mark you wear high on your back, but your destiny that ordains who you are, even if you may not believe it yet.'

He paused to allow his words to have the desired effect, then said, 'I know your story... You have it in you to do great things. If you want to be king, an emperor, then I can help you. I hope you will accept.'

Moriya had been listening with great concentration, and now a chuckle escaped his lips. 'No one would turn down an offer like that... But, tell me. You are...were...a member of the court of the kings you profess to hate now. How do I trust you?'

'Call me Chanakya, and accept me as your teacher and adviser. I have risked a great deal to find you. We have a common enemy who will not hesitate to kill either of us. They know the truth of your lineage and that I know their secrets; that I can best help you defeat them. I can see you have already learnt a lot since we last met, but I can teach you the ways of power and of the men who possess it. I trust in your potential. I am now asking for your trust in my words and what I offer. Will you accept this? Trust me as your adviser and one day you will be king. A king Magadha has never seen the likes of before; a king even more luminous than those stalwarts Bimbisara and Ajatashatru.'

He paused, before he said, 'The Shishunagas – does anyone remember them? And these sons of Mahapadma Nanda – what mark will they leave? Their names shall one day be mere dust, while yours will be etched forever into this land's history, because your kingship will be splendid, noble, magnificent, and as the sun glows, your reign will too. That mark you have on your back...' He smiled thinly as he saw the look on Moriya's face. 'Yes, I know about it, as do your enemies. That birth mark shaped like the moon – it sets you apart from everyone you have known, and from the people of your tribe... I have thought about this for a very long time. I do believe that you will be the very best student I will ever have the honour of teaching.'

Moriya smiled. He realized that the latter's voice was no longer as harsh as it had been during their first encounter. It was tempered with humility and there was something else Moriya noted – a desperate wish for his acceptance. Chanakya responded with a wide, open smile, as if he had read Moriya's thoughts. 'You must not be afraid to ask questions or disagree with me. And that is as it should be. It will be an honour to prove myself to you.'

He went on, relaxing his guard now, knowing he had Moriya's full attention.

'I have seen more of life than you have. A king has many loyalties, to the land he owns and to the people of his kingdom. He is alone, even when surrounded by courtiers. Perhaps this makes him afraid, and so the power of a king is diminished. But, with the right advice a king can fulfil his loyalties and ensure there is never a threat to his power. You want to be a king, Moriya, and you will be one. And I promise, I will serve you and make you a king like no other.'

As though remembering something of import while he allowed his thoughts to coalesce, Moriya responded slowly, 'I have felt this too, these days and years, as I wandered with the tribes of our land. And yes, I wish to be a king – not merely the best among equals but the best of them all. I would have done it on my own, but with you as my adviser, I will surely find success.' He did not miss the appreciative gleam in the older man's eyes before he turned away.

In the distance, Moriya saw dust clouds rising. He let himself imagine that they belonged to the Yavana emperor Alexander and his armies, furbished with horses that could run faster than the wind. He had already heard much of Alexander, the tall golden-haired emperor who could race faster than any horse; the emperor who wanted to conquer the entire world, even the seas that stood in his way. *Alexandros*, the tribes moving away from the northwest called him. One day, and it seemed no longer a dream, he too would be king – one better than any king who had ever ruled. He had it in him, no matter what Chanakya or anyone reading his destiny had to say.

5

THE JOURNEY BEGINS

Moriya and Chanakya started out on the long trek that would take them from the desert to beyond the Malayavat mountains. They would travel as men of the land, changing their story and their disguises as required by the circumstances. If they encountered herdsmen on the way, they would offer their services as men who had knowledge of cattle and who could even cure the ailments that afflicted these creatures. When they fell in with monks leaving the east for the monasteries higher up north in the mountains, Moriya and Chanakya travelled as a young monk and his aged teacher. Lone villages and hamlets on the way willingly offered shelter to men of learning, while Moriya's skills as a hunter and trapper saw them through at other times.

They moved forward cautiously and warily, taking the rough roads to the northwest, as life around them changed evenly and surely, evident in the food they were offered, the modes of barter that were accepted and the dialects that were spoken – and Moriya, from his days as a roving hunter and herdsman, had always had a keen ear for language. Magadhi to the east, Prakrit closer to the west and Aramaic farther north. Words and meanings never changed abruptly and he was alert to every shift in nuance and change in inflection. Chanakya was familiar with these parts of the kingdom. Moriya learnt that his teacher had many talents - not only had he mastered many texts, he spoke multiple languages as well.

This first journey would lead them close to where the Persia of the Achaemenid or Farsi empire had once begun. There was no longer any empire, for King Darius's forces had been defeated by Alexander and his army - the very man they were headed to meet.

Some day in the future, though it would all take a while and danger was never too far away, they would be face-to-face with the man who Chanakya said was the greatest king of them all - Alexander. Even the name fell from Chanakya's lips with a splendour of its own. 'He is the greatest conqueror ever, the embodiment of all that an emperor should be. He is very different from the Nandas, with real power and strength. That is why we must meet him. You must see for yourself what an emperor must be like.'

But there were other reasons too. Their destination was the borderlands - regions that had no permanent ruler, and where loyalties changed easily. They would be safe here because there were few chances that anyone would pass on information about them to Nanda's men. In these hostile, inhospitable regions, everyone was a stranger to one another; even assistance - for no one turned away someone in need in such desolate places - came tinged with suspicion.

It was during their last days at the edge of the desert - for on clear days the mountains were now visible - that Moriya went looking for blackbucks. Chanakya, tired after yet another long day, chose to retire early. Following their tracks and the smells the wind brought him, Moriya detected in no time the gleaming, fast-moving creatures of the desert, their sword-like horns glinting in the low evening light, as if set afire by the setting sun. A large herd was moving away from the dry scrubland in an erratic manner. Something had evidently disturbed them and he had to find out what it was. If it was an army of men, he needed to know who they were. They had to be alert to the presence of anyone, even nomadic herdsmen.

He rode on, knowing he and Chanakya had to remain unseen. Moriya understood why Chanakya always picked the most difficult routes and the hardest paths, for he knew even the most benign of situations could prove dangerous. Chanakya was schooled in the world of manipulation and power, and continuously stressed the advantages of always being a step ahead. Moriya, used to a life in the open and the wild, knew that the instinct for survival existed in all creatures, but some creatures had more advantages than others. For Chanakya and Moriya it meant always being alert and staying as inconspicuous as possible. Yet the danger was even greater now that they were together, two sworn enemies of the Nandas.

Moriya followed the dust plumes that had troubled the herd and betrayed the presence of other travellers. Alexander was someone he would love to match skills with, and yet he made him think too. Did an emperor primarily have to be a great conqueror? Was Alexander different from the Nandas because he had conquered a larger area of land? But then, he had not stayed in any place for long, which begged the question – was conquest enough to establish an emperor's rule?

At last Moriya saw the merchants, who he surmised had reached the settlement at the edge of the desert in the twilight hour. The hooves of their Arabian camels, Moriya noted, did not look worn out, which meant the men had not journeyed far. No salt had caked around the soles of the men's feet or marked their faces, as would have happened if they had travelled through the Rann, as native tribes often did. These were men from distant places. Among them were guides – evidently local men, shorter and leaner than the others, who were leading them through the desert. The merchants were tall, their skin bronzed and dusty. They were desert men all right, but not men of this desert. They had rugged features, hook noses like the eagles that flew overhead and it seemed to Moriya that the songs they sang evoked their far away homelands.

It was Moriya who asked to join them. As the evening grew darker, there was safety in such companionship. He and his master, who was resting at present, Moriya indicated, intended to journey towards the Malayavat as well. At night, Chanakya and Moriya conversed with the merchants. They were frequent travellers to this region, their leader – who spoke in Prakrit and also a rusty Gandhari, spoken further north – explained. But he had more news for them, something that made Chanakya stiffen while Moriya tried hard to hide his excitement. The news was that King Puru, monarch of the regions beyond the Jhelum, had been defeated. Alexander, it seemed, had no able rival.

'The wind brought us here, but more than that, it was the news. We must rush with our business before it is too late,' said the leader. He was the oldest man Moriya had ever seen – with wrinkles that spoke of the many journeys he had undertaken over the years and eyes that gleamed like gemstones in the night sky. It made his face seem wide awake and indeed, as his companions fell asleep around them, resting their heads against their frisky camels, the old chief stayed up to talk with them. He held his staff upright in one hand and spoke in a low, gravelly voice.

'We are on our way to the old city of Kalibangan, and the smaller kingdoms of the northwest. Our business was always good there and we hope it will continue,' he shook his head, a trifle sadly. 'Did you ever hear of the good king Puru?'

Moriya shook his head, giving nothing away. Stories were of

many kinds and one learnt much from the way a man told his stories. Besides, he liked hearing stories of kings. Puru, he now learnt, had been defeated by Alexander, betrayed by some of his own men who refused to fight. But he had been a true king, one who had led and ruled.

'Puru the magnificent,' said the old merchant. 'He knew what being a king meant. For a long time no one even knew what he looked like, he was so shrouded in mystery. He would go out at night to check on his subjects. Some people said he looked like a giant; he could walk over houses, jump over rivers and canals. Others said he knew magic so he could slide through walls, become invisible, rise in the air and float away.' Even after his defeat, no one criticized Puru; no one ever would.

Moriya had heard many stories of King Puru, as he was called in the lands farther east. He had recently witnessed the wandering bards performing in the land of Avanti, which they had just left. He had watched them in the village square, transfixed by the light of the lanterns. They were heavily disguised, with masks covering their faces, and they wore long robes. They did not want to be recognized, or punished, for in their stories they told the harsh truth, minced no words, and everyone – king and subject, rich and poor – was equal. They made fun of all and spared no one, but even they had nothing bad to say about King Puru.

'Puru was a great king, and also blessed,' the old merchant continued, and he could have been echoing the bards. 'He ruled the most fertile of all lands; lands that were watered by the tributaries of the Sindhu. Alexander's Greek and Macedonian soldiers now call it the Indus – as if a different name will make it a new river altogether!' the merchant laughed. 'Puru's kingdom stood on the trade routes that led to the middle kingdom and stretched eastwards, to Magadha. It was blessed with fine weather and rich soil but its soldiers had forgotten how to fight. Soldiers will fight when there's something to gain. Alexander and his men knew that.'

As news of Alexander's advance spread, fear came raging in its wake. Alexander's soldiers included the elite Macedonians – tall, rangy and golden-haired. Then there were the agile men of the land of the Nile, the ferocious soldiers of Persia, the small, sharp-eyed men of Central Asia, and the swift-footed men of the mountains of the northwest, who knew the secret passes and how the snow moved in the mountains. Each group wanted to prove itself superior to the others.

'It's his ability to dominate every type of soldier that makes Alexander successful,' Moriya said in a reflective tone. 'He is able to command the loyalty of such disparate groups while Puru could not persuade his own people to unite. When it really mattered, they all fought their separate wars.'

The old man mulled over his reply. 'True, but Puru never really lost. When he was defeated in battle, his honour was still intact, because of the noble king that he was. He demanded that he should be treated like a king, even if he had been defeated. He honoured what he represented but it was Alexander who embraced him. Who then showed the greater honour?'

The question of honour intrigued Moriya. Could a defeated king demand honour?

'He is a king who had grace even in the face of defeat,' the merchant continued, 'so the gods watch over Puru. He is no tragic figure.'

Then seeing Moriya's keen eyes on him, he shrugged and began speaking again. 'Let me tell you of the kings of Egypt. The pharaohs – that's what they are called...'

So many stories... Moriya listened quietly, late into the night. He was so fascinated that he had forgotten sleep.

'Do you know about the afterlife?' he heard the old man ask.

Yes, he did. He knew of the pain brought on by the endless cycle of birth and rebirth. That was what the Buddha had said, the sage his father had revered. Mahavira, the Tirthankara, had said almost the same thing – that violence towards other creatures was sinful, and all creatures were deserving of the same compassion. Did kings also go through this eternal cycle with little hope of salvation? If attachment caused suffering, was conquest and attaching oneself to power a way of bringing suffering on to oneself? Or was it a matter of duty?

'The kings of Egypt wanted to go to heaven,' said the merchant chief. 'They wanted, above all, a wonderful afterlife. Even if they killed people, fought wars and treated people cruelly.'

Moriya knew that Chanakya slept lightly and there was every chance the latter had overheard the old merchant's words. He had also learned this vital strategy – to never let down one's guard, even during sleep. It was this half-asleep, half-awake Chanakya who spoke next, his voice rising out of the darkness, 'It is their duty to fight wars to make their kingdoms secure and sustainable, even if people get killed. Wars when fought wisely bring peace. Doing one's duty in the right way can help one seek heaven.'

'Does Alexander consider it his duty to conquer the world? And can a king get too attached to duty or power?' Moriya asked.

The other men at the campsite, some of them awake now, laughed.

'He is no ordinary king,' said one of them. 'He does not even bother to be a god. He is now the master of the known world. And greater than God.'

'Isn't that blasphemy?' asked Moriya.

The old man laughed, locking eyes with Chanakya, who was now wide awake. 'He is already a myth bigger than himself. Isn't it best to find out what the reality is?'

'A myth can burn itself out just like a rumour,' was Moriya's quiet response in the darkness.

There was silence. Moriya knew he mustn't give away their plans. He sensed his teacher distrusted these men and did not want the conversation to continue.

The stories faded away after a while, and the fire smouldered. The sounds of animals nearby permeated the silence. Owls screeched, nocturnal insects chirped and jackals howled to each other as they claimed the night.

Chanakya and Moriya rode out at dawn as the merchants slept. The sand dunes moved in the wind, shifting positions and drawing new patterns, and yet everything appeared to be still. It was the time before dawn that Chanakya read the position of the stars and the clouds, and his weather predictions set the tone for their journey every day. It was best to give the merchants the slip, Chanakya said, and travel on their own, or move among different groups. Besides, merchants and the goods they carried drew attention from soldiers and commoners alike.

'The onyx bracelets the merchants wore tell us they are from the land of the two rivers,' Chanakya's voice interrupted Moriya's thoughts. 'The region of Mesopotamia. They have been travelling to this land for thousands of years and more, from the time when there were great cities all along the Indus, even along the plains and deep in the desert. Some of these cities are lost forever so even conquerors and the changing weather cannot destroy them anymore.'

Kalibangan, the word uttered by the old merchant chief, remained in Moriya's mind. He would remember the merchants too, as he and Chanakya travelled farther upland, joining a caravan of camel-herders a day later. The settlements they now passed were more scattered.

'Merchants play a useful role for kings once you learn how they function,' said Chanakya. 'They are itinerant beings, who travel in and out of kingdoms and regions. They can be dangerous and yet can become useful allies. The king's men and spies should ask them what goes on in other kingdoms and what they saw on the way. They can be valuable informants for your kingdom. And as king, you must regulate them. Bind them to your rule with duties, with a fixed place to stay, ensuring they report to you, while your spies dog them at every step, unseen. In this way, your power will grow beyond your kingdom. All merchants are happy with regulations, with law and order, with getting a fair price for their goods. In the long run, it works well in your favour.'

Moriya let his camel run on ahead, throwing up a huge cloud of dust. He rode a long way off, thinking of the merchants. He envied their free lives, but were they really free? He longed to see new cities, new worlds, as they did, but how trustworthy were these worlds? Being a king meant taking on everyone else's uncertainties. His relationship with his subjects would be one of regulation, devoid of the personal. As Chanakya said, he would always be alone, when really, no man was truly alone. Even the merchants who came from so far away, sailing overseas and walking vast distances over the desert, had to move in groups for their security. Men belonged in groups because they feared being alone and helpless, they feared the uncertain.

He shook his head and looked around. His camel had covered a great distance and was now truly lost. A sandstorm had begun with no warning. The softly stirring sand became a shrieking gust that rose from every direction, biting into Moriya's skin, clawing at his eyes, as if with evil intent. The sound of the screaming desert raged in his ears and he knew it would last for a long time. Moriya sank low, crouching beside his camel, soothed by its warmth and calm breathing. Still he felt the dust everywhere, even on his lips and lashes. Exhausted, he fell back against the camel. He must have slept, for it was a long time later that the group of camel-herders found him.

'You didn't really want to remain lost, did you?' Chanakya's voice was calm, although his expression betrayed the worry he had felt.

Moriya said gently, 'I have never been lost anywhere, whether in the forests or now in the desert. I was merely familiarizing myself with it.'

Chanakya only smiled tightly in response. This was a young man sure of his destiny, but one could never trust that all would be well, and it was up to him to ensure that they were always cautious.

Travelling across the unyielding, unending desert, Moriya settled into its rhythms. At night, as they sat before a fire, taking turns to sleep, Chanakya told him more about what kingship meant.

'A king should have foresight,' said Chanakya, 'he cannot entrust his kingdom to the workings of destiny or even nature's ways, unlike these nomads and herders. He should be prepared for any eventuality and ensure he has people in the right places – priests to read the signs, farmers with enough grain to fill granaries… He should be ready to do anything to stop people's suffering.'

'What about the king's own uncertainties, his own sufferings?'

.Chanakya smiled. Moriya always asked the most difficult questions. 'This much I do know – it is the need to alleviate the sufferings of his subjects, those he has power over, that keeps his own suffering diminished. A king is important for others – he, of all creatures, lives for others.'

Moriya looked up at the sky, a universe more vast than anything he knew. He felt it all seep into him, infusing him with strength and calmness. He understood that being one with the universe brought peace to the self. 'If a man is ordained to rule and he knows his duties, what makes a king a tyrant hated by his people?' he asked.

'Of all people, a king's position has to be secured on his own. So kingship can never be ordained or divine, one has to prove oneself worthy of it. A king becomes a tyrant when he seeks to destroy, to overpower man's will.'

Chanakya was quiet after that. Moriya knew some answers could be elusive, while others would emerge with time.

6

EARLY LESSONS

Moriya raised his arm and pulled his bowstring as far as it could stretch. He had caught the sun glinting on the long slender horns of the blackbucks far away in the desert. He aimed, then his arrow melded with the light as it streaked across soundlessly.

The cry that followed was shrill and long-drawn. He saw the lone vulture joined by another as they began to circle over the dead blackbuck. He rode his camel forward, sending shafts of sand in his wake. Unnoticed, the sand moved again, erasing their trail.

The younger herders were with him. It hadn't escaped his attention that the boys hovered around him wherever he went be it hunting blackbucks or chasing falcons.

But Moriya's gaze rested absently on them. He was used to such devotion by now. Sometimes he found it an impediment. He knew who he really wanted to see – the dark-eyed girl with her heavy, swinging plaits – the chief's daughter, who always joined them on their daily expeditions. She was nowhere to be seen now even though he gazed across the dunes in search of her. He felt the same excitement at the thought of chasing her as he did when he sighted the blackbucks. It was a challenge he could not resist.

Chanakya, of course, had noticed the hostility in the chief's eyes because of his daughter's interest in the young Moriya. They had some more days to go before the desert was crossed, and travelling in a group with men who did so regularly was the safest option they had. But Moriya knew there were other reasons for Chanakya's wariness. By now, as news travelled and the merchants and other smaller groups they had met moved to the interior, Nanda soldiers and assassins would be hot on their trail. Chanakya hid his nervousness while Moriya tried to allay it as best as he could. He had never felt a threat to his life and the need to save himself appeared to him as a challenge. He would not let the thought of a tyrant king like Dhana Nanda subdue him.

Finally, the girl appeared, a mocking look in her eyes as she caught his stare. Moriya smiled, almost in triumph. With a careless flick of his wrist, he waved the young herders away. 'This one,' he said, indicating the distance where his arrow had travelled, 'I will track on my own.' They left, but the girl remained, her gaze defiant as she stayed her camel, which had wanted to follow its companions. Moriya didn't wait, he gave his camel a free run in the direction of the blackbuck he had killed, knowing she would follow him. Although the sand ate up the sound of the hoofs, he heard the tinkling of her anklets in rhythm with his own harsh breathing.

They must have ridden for a long while, for a glance back confirmed that their temporary hamlet was no longer in view. The blackbuck lay on its side, a vulture or two had descended and were now gazing beadily at him as he dismounted. The girl watched him as he cut off, with his carved dagger, the blackbuck's prized horns. It was a symbol of a true warrior, for blackbucks were swift-moving animals and difficult to catch. He waited for some praise, but she said nothing. Only her darkened eyes gave him a hint. On their way back, she rode alongside him and every time she pushed her braids behind her ears, he caught her mocking smile.

Was there something she knew that he didn't? Then, suddenly sensing danger, he turned his head. Riding out from the desert were six stern-faced men brandishing spears, their turbans glinting silver and gold. They were men of the desert – the protectors of the blackbucks.

They stopped in front of Moriya and, pointing their sharp spears at him, one of them said, 'The blackbucks are sacred. You have sinned by hunting them.'

Moriya turned to the young woman with him. 'You must go and let no one see you.' She had gone very still, but obeyed. He watched her dig her heels into her camel's sides and prod it into a run, her braids billowing behind her head like a black cloud. He drew in his breath and waited. He was one against six. It would be an unequal fight but he was prepared for it. He looked at each one of the men in turn, his gaze meeting theirs fiercely and proudly. Only the true hunter knew how hard it was to chase a blackbuck and claim its prized horns as a trophy.

The men waited. They offered no contest, nor any more accusations – they knew the time-honoured rituals of the desert. They did not have to wait for long; the chief of the camel-herders turned up in no time accompanied by his daughter and his men. Chanakya was with them too.

'Ten camels in exchange for a blackbuck,' he heard his host say.

'That is hardly enough atonement. A blackbuck is rarer and more sacred.' The men and the chief continued to discuss terms for a while.

Chanakya didn't say a word till the very end. He knew when to prolong matters and when to step back. 'If a warrior does not hunt down an animal, for prey or pleasure, who else will? His dharma demands it. And he,' his eyes flicking over to indicate Moriya, 'is a warrior, who one day may be the ruler of all these lands. The stars that tell the future can never be wrong. It is just a matter of time.'

Chanakya paused; he knew he had the full attention of his audience. 'You, O chiefs, have the duty to maintain the harmony of the desert, hospitality towards its guests and the need for preservation of all its creatures. You must be just.'

Moriya watched them, knowing Chanakya wasn't going to let the moment slip. He turned to the chiefs, and gesturing towards Chanakya, said, 'If I chose this means to prove myself, it is because I desire to command your respect. I beg forgiveness for this act of mine, and give you my word that when I am king, I will uphold all that you hold sacred too. It shall be my promise just as you must forever swear to uphold the harmony of the desert.'

Something about his confidence, his unwavering look, assured them. There was a chorus of agreement all around, and he swept past on his camel, his eyes mocking the girl, knowing he had impressed her with his self-assurance.

As they rode away, Chanakya turned to him. His voice was low and somewhat distant as he said, 'We mustn't give away our reasons for being here unless it's necessary, as it was just now. And you...you mustn't give yourself up to unnecessary attachments. The desert is not a place for that.'

Moriya pursed his lips, hiding a smile. He should have known that his wily adviser would guess his intentions. Chanakya shrugged and confessed, 'I saw you riding off with her. She was less discreet. Women in the throes of attraction seldom are, and they bring on grave dangers to themselves and others. You must learn to deal with desire of this sort without giving in to it.'

Chanakya hadn't finished and Moriya knew he was deliberately taking his time. 'Attachments that present themselves at the incorrect time can stunt one's progress. A tree that grows too close to the soil never looks up to the sun.'

Moriya nodded, but his thoughts had already turned to the chief's daughter, her smile that constantly challenged him – as if daring him to trespass on her father's hospitality. As for attachments, those he cared for, he carried forever in his heart. He had been on the run and away from the people he had grown up with for years now. There would never be chains tying him to anything or anyone. It dawned on him, as he turned to look at the girl now riding away with her father, that he was already irrevocably attached to his destiny, and his desire for her was part of it. She held his gaze with her kohl-rimmed eyes, her smile caught in the beads embedded in her veil, and their eyes exchanged a forbidden promise.

The desert vegetation was now less sparse where they were. Past the low hills of sand, over the craggy rocks, down the abandoned wells that contained water which had turned salty, there was a shady copse of trees with small thorn-like leaves. Skeletons of animals, given up by the desert, lay scattered across the land. The days were long in the desert, the nights bitterly cold. Looking up at the cloudless skies, Moriya had that feeling of timelessness again, that he might see his peacocks here. It was the sensation that always filled him when he was restless and he rode out on his own.

She came to him, as he knew she would, as he waited under a tree, letting his camel graze nearby. His heart began to beat erratically as he recognized the force of his own desire. He touched her cheek, feeling the lines of her face. For a few moments, for the first time ever, he would know what it felt like to be with a woman. It made him feel vulnerable yet exhilarated.

She tossed off her veil and ran deeper into the grove. The sun was harsh and golden on the sand as he followed her, his hand briefly straying to where his dagger was sheathed close to his waist. The sand ran and danced over his feet like a soft flowing river before he caught up with her.

'Is this what future kings do?' Her question surprised him. He recognized her teasing but paid it no regard.

She giggled, but his gaze silenced her as he reached for her. He was taking off her blouse now. It had already slipped down one shoulder, the ribbons trailing across her skin, the mirrors glittering. He saw a million pieces of himself in these mirrors, the glass glistening with the fire in his eyes. Every other sound was soft in the shadows, the tinkle of her bangles, the shifting sand under their feet, the leaves bending in the sun.

'I will be your slave,' he whispered suddenly thinking that the man in her many mirrors mouthing those words was a stranger to him. Did desire and lust change a man so? And was a woman always aware of it?

He remembered Chanakya's words. 'Don't form unnecessary attachments, not when they will come in the line of your duty.'

But he didn't intend to forget his duty; there was too much distance he had already covered. For these few moments, while he gave himself up to the girl's desire, he also felt secure knowing his dagger lay very close. He looked down at the shadows that fell across her face, and with his rough fingers, he traced her face.

'Your father would never agree to our being together,' he whispered. 'He is sure to drive my teacher and I out of the camp, into the desert. We could end up being devoured by the lions.' He knew these were untruths the moment he uttered them but it did not seem to matter as they lay close, not an inch apart but for the harsh grains of sand that grated on his skin and hers.

'We've never come across the lions, there aren't any really,' she said.

He bent low towards her, feeling a stirring deep inside him.

'Would you run if a lion came?' she asked. 'Would you? The

brave warrior who chased a blackbuck for its fine horns?' He understood she was teasing him again, and could only look at her as her voice fuelled his raging desire.

She ran her hands down him, till he felt the heat blaze within him. Then she was pulling him down, the jingling of her bangles loud in his ears, her breathing soft on his cheeks. She let her nails scratch his chest, tossing aside his flimsy cloak and the diadem he wore with the peacock feather.

'I am strong, you know that. So if a lion does come, I will face it,' he murmured against her skin, pinning her down.

She gently bit his ear, his neck. He uttered words that he forgot the moment he said them, as he held her close. Words spoken in moments of love are fragile. He had a vision of riding long distances alongside her with their camel herd in tow. He laughed as he trembled with the force of his own desire.

The frenzied jangling of her bangles, changing their rhythm with every touch of his fingers, filled his ears and his every sense. He heard the tearing of cloth, felt the rough desert grass on his skin. He felt alive.

The gentle firmness of her limbs gave way to a delicious softness. His hands cupped her breasts, letting them spill out of his hands before he held them again, wanting his hands full of her. She moved under him. 'This isn't the place, not here.' From the prickly grass under them, they moved to an old, empty hut, where camel-herders would often seek rest. She was deeper in the shadows, and for a moment the thought crossed his mind that she would slip away too soon, tossing that mocking laughter behind.

Instead, she pulled him by the hand and on to a bundle of hay. A gust of wind came in through the open window, a tree branch swished – he was suddenly glad of these other sounds.

She lay under him, her hands on his back, soft and insistent. She touched his face, ran her fingers down his neck and lingered on the sign of the moon he carried on the nape of his neck.

He felt heat envelop him. She was holding him, rising under him, and then her hands were on his hardness, gripping. He felt her softness give way to a warmth and moistness that enclosed him. He felt the rush of heat in him, just as he felt when he was out riding alone, far away from everyone. Moments later, he felt his breath dying away, mingling with hers, and he was filled with a sudden peace in the darkness, the reassuring presence of stars everywhere. He knew he had been with her a long time.

The long, mournful call of the peacock roused him. Bird of the forest, he remembered, the bird of the dry scrubland that had been his home all this while. It was a bird totally of this land, a creature unlike him. In its call he heard the reminder that he must never forget his destiny. He frowned, aware of his hesitation. He wanted these moments of pleasure to linger for as long as possible.

She helped him with his garments, while he caressed her face one last time. He would have to let her go; he might perhaps forget her, but she would always be dear to him. He wanted to touch her again, but she was already far away. A woman of the desert, she understood some truths far more easily than he did.

He heard the branches swish against the mud walls, like a warning. He pursed his lips, using every ounce of his will to leave this immediate past behind forever.

'They are waiting.'

These would be the last words he would ever hear her say.

Barely had he reached the settlement when he saw Chanakya, leading two horses. 'I got them from some merchants,' Chanakya's tone was urgent, and he was looking up, studying the stars and the clouds.

'We have to leave at once. There may be people close on our trail. Two lone men, neither soldiers nor herders – we draw attention everywhere if we stay too long. Forget the woman,' Chanakya said quietly, unwilling to be harsh, as they rode away.

As always, Moriya rode ahead, but at every pause, he waited to hear the sound of her bangles and anklets, even her laughter, behind him. *You will forget her. Don't let yourself think of her.*

'Does destiny decide everything?' Moriya asked, though the answer was clear to him and he didn't need to hear it from Chanakya.

The answer came slow and unhurried, his breath falling hard as the horses, young and agile, set a fast pace. 'Yes, we have already lost time, and now we have to move eastward to avert suspicion; take a circuitous route to reach our goal. The merchants from the far west, the incident with the blackbucks – such news will travel and will only draw unnecessary attention to us.'

Chanakya fell silent, waiting as if he was weighing his words, but Moriya knew Chanakya wanted his full attention. And then he threw down his trump card, his eyes gleaming.

'And that goal is not too far now. Alexander. He has stopped his march – perhaps he will not come further even if he wants to. I am told he is being deserted. His soldiers have fought for many years now and no longer believe in his war.'

Moriya did not let his expression change. 'What is a king's worth if he is being deserted? Is he truly a king then?' he asked casually.

'That is what we have to find out. A king who couldn't win absolute loyalty despite having conquered so many foreign lands. A king who is an outsider.'

Moriya shook his head. Suddenly, what he had experienced with the woman seemed ordinary. He gazed at the skies and the desert he had come to love. He shut his eyes, closing his mind forever to the woman who belonged to it, who would always belong to it.

'There is another reason, more important, why we need to get to Alexander and fast,' said his teacher, leaning forward to emphasize his every word. 'His deserted soldiers, men without a master, can be made to serve a new master. We can shape a new army of our own. We must hurry else we will lose the opportune moment.'

There was no mistaking the urgency in Chanakya's voice. Moriya knew he had to leave some more of his past behind in the desert. But the thought of moving ahead, the prospect of coming face to face with Alexander soon, gave him an unexpected thrill.

The roads to the northeast were well-traversed routes, frequented by nomadic tribes, where it was possible to travel undetected in big groups. But they rode at night too, hoping to reach Viratnagara in a few days. Sometimes, as dusk fell, Chanakya would fall asleep over his horse. Then it was Moriya who led him, holding the other horse's reins, still riding fast.

Some mornings later, they joined horse-traders who were travelling to the cities. The traders were from Arabia, their horses majestic and stately, meant to grace only royal stables. From the desert, they crossed once more the ravines they had left behind only a season or so ago. The ravines and the plateau stretched all along the centre of the land they called Jambudwipa, bordered by mountains to the north and the sea in other directions. This was where the Narmada had its origins; and was ringed to the east by the forests of Chitrakuta, with its deer herds and dense sal groves. On the hard stony ground, the horses set a fast pace, the sound of their hooves ricocheting across the low hills, mingling with the stones and pebbles that scattered below.

They camped by the Narmada one night, by other rivulets on other nights. The high ravines provided protection from unexpected attack, and also gave Moriya ample scope to slip away undetected by the men sleeping around him. He knew how to feign sleep and then rise when all around him had given in to slumber. He knew how to walk silently over the cold hard surface of the plateau, how to make his horse trot noiselessly across the stones and not send a single one falling from a steep height. He discovered for himself all the intricate passages that led into and out of the ravines and valleys. He would plunge into the cold river, delighting in pitting his strength against it. He would reach the highest boulder after a rigorous climb up the steepest cliff and lie bathed in the moonlight. It was in these moments, when he could defy everyone – the spies on his trail and even Chanakya – that he felt truly alone. He liked his solitude, and the more he missed it in his journey with Chanakya, the more zealously he looked forward to such moments. If Chanakya noted his absence, he did not say a word.

Deep in the ravines, where the dry forests rose like a series of steps to the skies above, Moriya once encountered a sage deep in meditation. Riding up to him, he was caught in his trance. He liked the serenity and calm that pervaded the sage's face, and it seemed as though the animals of the forest enjoyed his presence as well. Snakes slithered by the man even as Moriya watched; birds danced on his shoulders, pecked at his ears.

Moriya also saw the traces of kindling left around the sage. He commanded the loyalty of the villagers who looked after him. If loyalty could be achieved by peaceful means, why did a king need to use force? Was force, or the fear that made its use necessary, really needed?

He could have stayed there for hours, watching the sage meditate. But all of a sudden, he heard the sharp tapping sound of another horse's hooves behind him. He turned sharply, suddenly realizing that he had been followed.

Moriya bent forward, pushing his horse through the trees. With no other warning apart from a hissing sound, a spear cut through the branches. It struck a tree with brute force, and the air filled with the harsh cries of frightened birds. The skies darkened and Moriya looked back to see the stunned face of the man who had wanted to kill him. It was someone Moriya had never seen before and yet he knew him, for as their eyes met, for the briefest of moments, he saw hatred contort and twist the other man's features before he fled.

Moriya followed him, his hand on his horse's mane, calming it. The horse calmed down, its jerkiness easing into a quick canter. Moriya could hear the thudding of the man's horse not too far ahead. The trees were thick around him, but he could make out where the assassin was headed. To follow him further into the forest depths, Moriya would have to abandon his horse. It would give away his presence. He dismounted and patted it, placed the reins in its mouth and whispered urgently, 'Go. Now!'

Staring ahead and with the trees crowding around him from all sides, Moriya spotted a cave, hidden by branches and cleverly disguised by rocks. In a trice, he had mounted the boulders and the steep sharp-edged rocks. He slid into the cave, glad for the refuge it offered. It was a mere hole in the cliff and he flattened himself against the walls, feeling the welcome dampness of moss on his hands. In no time, he heard the nearby thudding of horses, and he knew there was not one but several men on his trail. Almost a small army, all out to get him.

From across thick rock walls, he heard men shout.

'Find him, that mongrel half-caste, that slave woman's son.'

'King Dhana Nanda will never forgive you if he escapes.'

'We cannot return to Magadha if we do not find him.'

'And find him we must. As well as Vishnugupta. The two of them have long given us the slip.'

'There's his horse, look!'

'A fine specimen indeed,' said a second voice.

He hoped it was a different horse that had wandered away, and his ears strained to catch every sound.

'This horse has certainly run away. Look, there's the torn end of the rope.'

'Traders from the Arab lands bring these horses to sell them to the hill kingdoms. They are the finest Arabian horses you will have ever seen.'

'Let's take it and hand it over to the king. It will rid him of his obsession with elephants.'

Amidst raucous laughter, they debated over the horse. The creature protested, shuffling and neighing. Moriya felt a twinge of sympathy.

'We will find that young pretender once he enters the city. He has to find shelter there for he cannot survive this inhospitable land for long. But let's go at once. This forest will not give him up now.'

It was almost dawn when he felt it was safe enough to emerge from the cave. He made his way cautiously, calming his raging heart. Now he knew for sure. Chanakya had been right. The truth about his real identity, the threat he posed to Dhana Nanda, was neither a secret nor a mere rumour. These were men determined to hunt him down. He would have to do his best to thwart them.

In the forest, he saw the tracks the men had left behind, their footprints embedded on damp earth. Then he saw the upturned stones, the trampled leaves, the broken branches and the white lime stains on the trunks. He realized someone had drawn a path for him to get away – it could only have been the sage.

He followed the path cautiously a short while later came upon the sage hanging upside down from a tree. As soon as he saw Moriya, almost as if he had been expecting it, he intoned the solemn warning, 'There are spies set on your trail. Now and always.' In moments he had righted himself and now, seated on a long tree branch, he delivered his next warning, 'Some sages in this forest are spies too. Someone will soon track you down. You must travel on your own.'

Moriya nodded, heading in the direction the sage pointed to. When he reached the camp, Chanakya was waiting for him with a worried look on his face. Moriya heard the older man out, then said to him urgently, 'We must leave soon. You can tell me more when we are on our way, but not here.' As they left Moriya told him of the sage's warning.

'They are as much on my trail as yours but I am just a petty catch for them; you pose the biggest threat to the Nandas. The nearest town is to the east, and we must go there. True, cities may be unsafe but they have crowds we can hide in,' Chanakya said.

7

TREACHEROUS CITY

Viratnagara was a city people had inhabited for centuries – traders from lands down south and from farther away; soldiers from the north; travelling sages from the east; and descendants of a royal family from the south.

'No one knows us here. This is a city we can hide in,' said Chanakya. 'We must plan our journey to Taxila and beyond until we reach Alexander. We can gather information here and prepare ourselves. We must also work, on raising an army of our own, comprised of men on the move who can give us their loyalty.'

They found shelter in one of the hermitages on the city's outskirts. It had an inn and an animal dispensary inside its precincts. Its monks served everyone willingly and for long hours. It was sanctuary to many a wanderer. On their first day there, a young monk noticed Moriya and said, 'You look a fine young man. I saw you with the horses and how ably you handled them. You should join our order.'

Moriya was taken by surprise but he bowed humbly and walked away. Compliments were a sign that he had been noticed: he had to take care to remain inconspicuous.

Soon after their arrival, a notice appeared on the monastery wall, asking for soldiers to guard the treasure in the monasteries.

Most of these monasteries housed holy relics, like the Buddha's sandals, gold statues carved in his likeness and the imprint of his hand on a wall.

Moriya thought of a soldier's life given over to devotion of this kind. The monks were warriors too, devoted to the Buddha – he who had walked this earth and preached the way of peace more than two hundred years ago. Monks who travelled to different corners, crossed hills and deserts and braved every inhospitable condition to spread his message of peace were no less than soldiers of the Buddha. The distinction was that they were men of peace who used force only when it became imperative to do so.

In one of the monasteries that Viratnagara was known for, Moriya came across men of robes who were also expert swordsmen. He watched them from his spot, hidden in the branches of a neem tree, fascinated by the way they flew up high, twirling gracefully, and the clashing of their narrow swords. Some of them used sharply pointed spears, their ends made of finely carved ivory. The men were like flitting moths as they practised their moves in the growing darkness of evening. Their bodies lit up in a golden glow, and as their spears clashed, he could hear their harsh breathing.

Then, without warning, a spear pierced the night sky like silver lightning and embedded itself in the branches right below where he was hidden. The tree cracked but before anyone could look up, Moriya had leaned forward and pulled the spear out. Straddling the twin branches of the tree, which were bent low under his weight, Moriya threw the spear right back, knowing he would not miss his aim. The spear zipped back the way it had come, between the torches, blazing like a flying stream of fire. No one but a warrior blessed by the divine forces could have done this, and Moriya knew he had given himself away. Even if no one knew or recognized him yet, people would soon be on the lookout for him.

The other monks stared at him, more amazed than suspicious. Then the first three came forward, swords drawn, and Moriya recognized the unmistakable challenge. He jumped down from the tree, snatching the sword of the one nearest and leapt into the fray. The sound of swords clashing rose to a musical crescendo, the bells around the men's ankles and wrists tinkled, and then increasingly grew more clamorous. Those watching could see nothing after a while but ribbons of silver striking each other, and while other ribbons fluttered and wavered, there was one that flashed clean and neat, like a thing of beauty. Moriya had no shield but he moved around his three challengers with a fluidity that could have put rivers to shame. They never knew when he faced them or when he had turned and moved away. His feet barely touched the ground, and his arms holding the sword high were like strong firm branches that held on even in the roughest winds. No one knew when it was over, until the quiet fell moments after the swords of the defeated challengers lay on the earth, and Moriya stood tall, his sword raised skyward, the gesture of all triumphant warriors.

The next moment, he had flung it away and raced down the roads to the hermitage. He knew he had revealed himself but he could not help rejoicing in the thrill of victory.

'There were some men here who came representing the king of Magadha and insisted we were hiding fugitives.' The chief of the horse-traders took Moriya and Chanakya aside to tell them this. A few days ago, he had graciously accepted their request to join his men when he had seen Moriya's skills with the animals. It was a part of the plan that Chanakya had made for them to travel out of the city and beyond. But now the chief clearly looked distressed, his eyes flickered to a point behind them as if he were worried about being seen. His words were measured and halting.

'The Nandas are powerful rulers, and the Matsya king of Viratnagara will never displease them. We are assured of Viratnagara's generosity because we have been supplying horses to the king for years. He believed us when we told him that the two of you were Brahmins whom we were escorting from Bharuch to Ujjain and onward to Mathura. But we cannot carry on this way.'

The chief of the horse-traders seemed regretful as they made plans to leave. Moriya gazed at the line of departing carts, the wagons carrying young foals, and his short-term companions on their fine ponies. In his short life, he had already said farewell to far too many people.

'We are not to leave immediately, for that would arouse suspicion,' was all Chanakya said through pursed lips, his eyes, like Moriya's, scanning the crowds. 'And look at you, it isn't your warrior skills that will give you away, but these scratches all over your arms for all the world to see.' Chanakya meticulously set about creating a disguise for them. 'We must not be recognized at any cost. You heard what the trader said. The news about us is out.'

His hands were coated with wet mud and he worked harshly on Moriya's face. 'Do we look like poor monks now?' he asked, his lips twisted in a semblance of a smile. 'And starving too?'

'This should work,' Moriya said as they looked at each other. In the space of a few seasons, Moriya had grown as tall as Chanakya. Looking down at his shadow, he saw how his hair now fell below his shoulder, his arms rangy and lean.

'You look more like a warrior than a monk,' said Chanakya, understanding his thoughts, 'but that is what destiny has decided for you.'

They walked on till they reached the old Jain temples west of the city. The hermitage of the sage who presided over the other priests and pandits was not far away. Soon they met the sage Bhadrabahu himself, who had wise, all-seeing eyes and a gentle manner about him. As he bowed before him, Moriya knew instantly that Bhadrabahu had guessed the truth about them, but the sage made them feel welcome. After offering them nuts and fruit and asking an acolyte to wash their feet as was the custom of the hermitage, he said, 'It's the day of the seasonal debate. I am glad you are here. Men of learning will want to challenge each other. Would you like to participate?'

The bland expression on the old monk's face caught them by surprise. Viratnagara appeared to be seething with hidden dangers. Could Chanakya resist the idea of a debate or was it a trap? Moriya felt Chanakya's stillness, and understood it was a suggestion he could not turn down, for the great monk was their host. Chanakya nodded his agreement.

Bhadrabahu looked at them with amusement. 'Things may not be what they seem. Scholars can even be spies, soldiers, or assassins.' The message was delivered so softly that the words came to Moriya only after the sage had stopped speaking. He was warning them that there were spies in the crowd – assassins, too – lurking among all those gathered to listen as scholars debated and argued.

The monk led them out into the courtyard where several people had already gathered. In a crowd, even assassins would have a hard time finding their mark and getting away. Silence fell, only broken by the sound made by the rustling of robes and the scraping of mats, as everyone rose at Bhadrabahu's arrival. He raised his hands in welcome, and then addressed the gathering.

'An important topic will be debated here tonight. Scholars have been trying to study the planetary positions, trying to see if there are patterns, if they have an impact on disasters on earth. If we can read planetary positions, can we can stop disasters? Or do we think that it is the old wisdom that holds good?'

It was Chanakya who answered. 'They might only give an indication of our lives here on earth. It has been observed that the stars can take years and centuries to move.' He went on, 'When the comet passed, it meant the death of Bimbisara – that he would die under suspicious circumstances. But another comet appeared later and Magadha celebrated with great fervour because it was at the time of the accession of Mahapadma Nanda.'

There was hearty laughter. Someone said, 'No one really knew what a tyrant he would turn out to be.'

Voices began to rise.

'The king who outlived his own sons.'

'The best wrestler there ever was.'

'With the strength to beat an elephant.'

'And they say the dynasty's days are now numbered.'

A shudder passed through the crowd. Moriya heard the stray voices rise and fall all around him. Somehow the rules of kingship had changed with Mahapadma's passing. Dhana Nanda had none of his father's strength, and all of his miserliness. In these turbulent times, he had also surrounded himself with all kinds of charlatans, driving away those who had merit, whose wisdom could have saved the kingdom from ruin.

Chanakya was quiet; it was clear he did not want to be drawn into a political debate. But the great monk spoke up again, and this time he spoke to the two of them.

'Do you see the position of the stars? Today the moon is in an unusual spot.'

There was a low urgency in his voice that compelled Chanakya to look up. It was early evening and the moon was half-full and appeared to be a strange purple. It was accentuated by the strange sight of birds suddenly lifting themselves from trees and flying around in wild, inchoate circles.

He looked at Moriya and said abruptly, 'We must leave.'

'Yes, in a few moments. We are all out in the open. We will be safe,' the sage acquiesced.

'Be prepared to run,' said Chanakya, speaking in a hushed tone.

As if in response, the earth began to rumble. There was an ominous roar that began reluctantly, then an angry rumbling broke out from the deepest bowels of the earth. The trees shook, veering wildly from side to side, swaying in abandon. The wind moaned as if frightened, followed by the cries of a thousand and more alarmed birds. The sounds of more than a hundred men and women, panting and screaming hoarsely in a bid to make their escape, mingled to make the explosive noise of one elemental, final destruction. A pillar crumbled and toppled over, a thatched roof plunged, almost inexplicably. A tree's branches shook heavily and then it toppled over two people who had taken shelter under it.

'The river – Chamanavat – head for it!' Moriya wasn't sure if it was the monk's or Chanakya's voice in his ears.

In the turmoil, Moriya led Chanakya by the hand, willing his legs to move. He stepped on earth only to find the ground sink under him, so he leapt, taking the other man with him. He could feel Chanakya's hand tighten in his own.

Run, Moriya.

They ran, and there was no looking back. They were on an open stretch of ground and the roar of the earth and the terrified heaving of the trees persisted as they fled. Somewhere Chanakya lost his balance and Moriya stopped, his hands reaching out to support him. His upper garment slipped and he felt the cold wind on his skin like the lash of a whip but it was all momentary. They must have run swiftly for, after a while, the screams faded. He heard the pounding of feet, but it seemed like a distant noise. As he ran, he felt himself plunge into deep cracks that had opened up in the ground. The sound of the earth in the throes of pain died away, then rose again. The birds were like swirling grey clouds in the sky, their calls harsh in his ears. Not too far away, he could see the boats and the erratic way they bobbed in the waters.

He willed himself on, holding Chanakya's hand, refusing to let the older man falter, knowing he had to keep the river in sight at all times. He ran on even as the earth trembled under his feet. The sound of their harsh breathing was all that they could hear, and only after what seemed like a long time, did it strike Moriya that the earth had now stilled. It was the river's waters that swirled close, lapping at their feet.

When the quiet descended once more, Moriya heard the creaking of a boat drawing up nearby and signalled to the boatman that they wished to board. He found that he was unsteady on his feet, unable to trust the earth for a few moments.

Chanakya fell over into the boat, exhausted. Moriya stared at his limp body before the older man turned to give him a half-smile of assurance. What had happened appeared strangely ordained – the earthquake had struck at an opportune moment, letting them escape.

Moriya picked up one of the long oars, ready to lend a hand to the lone boatman. It was already late evening, with the early moon rising behind him in the western sky, no longer the strange purple shade it was before. Chanakya closed his eyes.

'Sail towards the west, the west,' he said in a weak voice. 'To the east there will always be more enemies.' The low hills and dense copses of trees they passed cast black shadows on the waters in the low moonlight. They could hear the jackals and hyenas that had gathered on the shore. 'Where there are scavengers around, you can be sure that more terrible animals are waiting.'

'Lions?' Moriya couldn't suppress the note of excitement. It carried over to the older man who cautioned, 'Don't try and go looking for them, Moriya.'

'You are always trying to teach me to be careful,' he said ruefully. Both knew that despite Chanakya's warnings, Moriya would still take risks, brave dangers and win. It was that serene mocking confidence he read on Moriya's face that made Chanakya smile. He could say nothing more.

Sometimes in that altering light, Moriya thought he saw the hills move again. He heard a rumble and wondered if the earth was shaking again or if it was a trick played by his senses. The moon moved ever so slowly behind the mountains, paler now and closer than he had ever seen it.

'Chandra – that is your name from now on, after the moon,' said Chanakya. 'You will have the moon as your companion always. You carry him on your shoulder anyway, the mark that is your secret, that holds the key to your destiny. You are no longer Moriya of the tribe of peacock-tamers. Row on towards where your destiny calls you. We have to reach Alexander soon, for the Nandas know where we are now and they will never give up.'

The last sound that remained as Chanakya's voice faded was that of the oars splashing in the Chamanavat, a young feckless river that held great danger and yet could be tamed. After a short silence, Chandra heard thunderous roars and felt himself tremble with excitement. He had heard of the lions first from the entertainers who had come to Magadha. No one had ever seen those lions, concealed in their cages covered with cloth, for the great Mahapadma would not allow it. A special enclosure had been built for them and the rumours only grew that the lions, who were special to the goddess the Nandas worshipped, would fight Mahapadma, and the scratches he sustained would be washed with their blood.

'Those animals were never meant to be caged,' Chandra remembered his father saying. When a few men from the tribe had tried to bribe the guards of the fort at Pataliputra to let them look at the fabled lions, he had not been a part of the mad scheme. As fate would have it, the men were caught and handed over to the king.

Chandra knew the story, one that shamed him and filled him with sadness. The memory of it was still fresh in his mind – the entire sequence of what he had been told, the succession of events and the probability of what happened. A messenger from the new Nanda king – for Dhana Nanda had ascended the throne on his father's sudden death – had appeared before the chief of the peacock-tamers as they camped in the forests by the river Gandak. His father had been summoned before the king to answer his questions or else pay a heavy price. The chief, surrounded by his tribesmen, held himself straight and tall as he listened to the messenger. It was a lesson he had taught Chandra too. Never bend to anyone, especially to someone unjust, he liked to say.

The messenger's voice rang out booming and loud, as if he relished being the bearer of bad news. The king Dhana Nanda had placed the most difficult compromise before the chief of the peacock-tamers. 'The meat of the wild peafowl is the most delicious food on earth! You can have your men back only if you supply me with peacock meat.'

That was when his father had decided to surrender. Chandra had been away hunting at the time and had returned to find his father gone. The chief knew he had to accede to a tyrant's demand or have his men, his own tribespeople, executed. He knew too well the consequences of those actions. The Nandas' greed would never be assuaged, and their tribe would be forever enslaved to them.

When he returned to the court of the Nandas, he refused the request and found himself made prisoner, as was inevitable. Orders were given to destroy the tribe that had so foolishly rejected an emperor's demand. But they were warned just in time by a mysterious turbaned messenger who got to them before the Nanda armies did…

The stories we remember are those that shape us, or we shape our stories to make the remembering bearable. The river was now quiet as Chanakya slept. Chandra leaned forward and touched the boatman on the shoulder. 'It's time you slept too. I will row for the night.'

The grateful boatman only managed a tired smile as he handed over the oar. Chandra lifted the heavy oar effortlessly. He felt the moon's gentle light on him. He looked up for a moment and, balancing the oar against his shoulder, he cupped the moon in his upturned palms. Chandra, he heard his name again in Chanakya's raspy voice. Chandra. He remembered his frantic race away from the earthquake, his other narrow escapes from death or capture and knew Chanakya was right. He had been born anew. There was no going back on destiny now.

'There are those who have deserted Alexander…' said Chanakya, looking up at the stars as the boat moved at an even pace. They were on the river Satadru now, just the two of them for the boatman had been persuaded to leave once they had passed his relative's village of Chandpur. The river would take them towards the land of the five rivers. Chandra had already rowed for a long while and his arms ached, but at least they were beyond danger for the time being.

'Soldiers from every part of the land, of every hue, with mastery over different weapons – we need to speak to them, get them to join us.'

Chanakya rummaged in the small sack he always carried over his shoulder. After rustling through some palm leaves, he pulled one out. Penned in elegant calligraphy was the incendiary prose that only Chanakya could speak and write in.

'There is a secret message inscribed in the main note. I have had to write this in secret, in the late hours of the night. Those who read carefully will know who it is from.'

The moment Chandra looked at it, he knew instantly what it was about.

Chanakya wrote about two penniless travellers, a Brahmin and his young student. They possessed nothing, except knowledge of the land they were travelling in. But the prose changed complexion as he read on and the older words vanished to give way to new ones, written in ink that gleamed in the low moonlight.

It exhorted the people of the land to think twice before bowing meekly before a foreigner. 'A foreigner whose ways are totally different,' he heard Chanakya's voice in his mind. 'There have been people from alien shores who are welcome in our land. Traders, even soldiers, have come and made their lives here. But Alexander is a king who has come from afar, across the seven seas, and wants to conquer and humiliate us. He would shame us into subjugation and return as a world conqueror. We are a people from a land that will make the foreigner welcome but we should never agree to be conquered...'

'Wherever we go, we drop these scrolls,' Chanakya instructed. 'The scrolls will inspire those who are willing to fight to join our cause against the Nandas. It is not just in the cities where we will find our soldiers, but also among the wandering tribes, the herders, the nomads who live in the forest, the robbers and the bandits.'

He closed his eyes and the sounds of the dry forests closed in around them. A cold dry wind blew in from the west over the low bushes. An old monastery, now falling to ruins, stood forlornly by the bank. It was nearing winter, Chandra realized. Several seasons had passed since their first meeting.

'A monastery that once had more life in it,' said Chandra, rowing closer. They could stop here for the night, he thought, mooring the boat at the bank.

They stepped into the deserted building. The windows gaped vacantly, the door had long broken down and the low roof had crumbled. They brushed past the drooping hay as they entered, and the green-blue eyes of slumbering monkeys they had awoken peered at them. It was the stillness that warned Chandra, and only he caught the sweet sharp sound of a dagger slicing through air, cutting between Chanakya and him menacingly, then whirling around, seeming to return the way it had come. The voice that burst through next appeared startlingly loud in contrast. 'Don't look around for us, for we are the Atavikas, the men of these forests. And we can see you wherever we may be.'

Chandra replied, his eyes searching the darkness for any giveaway move, 'And we are two travellers moving through your forests. We come with no hostile intent.' He spread his hands wide and glanced at Chanakya, asking him to do the same.

The men emerged, silent and purposeful, from behind the trees and the broken walls of the monastery. In a trice, they whipped out coils of twine and bound Chanakya and Chandra so tight that it was impossible to break free.

Then a man – turbaned and masked like the rest of them, though seemingly older, for his grey beard slipped through the thin mask over his face – came forward.

He said, 'If you came with no ill intent whatsoever, what are you doing in these forests?' His voice mingled with the sounds of the forest. 'Usually we hang trespassers upside down from a tree.'

Chandra knew he was one against many, and it would be foolish to battle these bandits. A battle had to be fought first in the mind, where deception and a false front were equally powerful weapons. He saw how Chanakya too kept his expression carefully wooden. Even the older man knew his own voice, its harshness and the blaze in his eyes, could offend many.

'We are indeed travellers...'

'Travellers?' the man laughed, shook his head. 'Try telling me another story. Travellers know which roads to avoid. They would hardly take the river or the path through the forest at night.'

They were surrounded now. Chandra saw their faces in the reflected light. They were all small-built, lean and with sharply defined features.

'One of my men was on your trail. We watched you as you came down the river. But we have our principles too. We do not attack an unarmed man.'

Smiling in a slightly sinister fashion, another man said, 'We prefer hearing their stories first.'

'I also like listening to stories,' Chandra said impulsively and unthinkingly. He could feel Chanakya twitch in surprise.

The chief roared with laughter. 'Oh, you do, do you? We have stories that could make you wish you had never ventured outside your safe comfortable homes...but you...' he looked at them, running his eyes over them quickly. 'You are no spoiled, pampered men of the city. Who are you running from?'

It was Chanakya who spoke up this time. 'We are running for the same reasons that make everyone seek refuge in the forests.'

'If words were a method everyone employed to save their lives, you would soon die,' said the leader, the man who had spoken first. 'But you are both here for a reason. Which makes us very curious indeed. Even sages would not wander around in these forests, so very close to the ravines. Your robes are wet and muddied, you have the smell of more distant rivers on you. I can tell your story right from these clues.'

Chandra saw the chief smirk and knew his life rested in the man's hands. Yet, after living and wandering among such people, he knew that they lived by a certain code of honour. They would not kill a man who was disadvantaged. Chandra looked back, a smile of open mockery on his face. He knew they would not kill without reason. It was a battle of wits from then on.

'Untie them,' said the chief of the Atavikas. 'We can tell them our stories, entertain them for the night before they tell us their secrets.'

They left the old monastery behind and trudged through a narrow forest path, which had grass growing high in places. More men joined the procession, holding up fiery torches. They passed by a graveyard where criminals and unwanted people had been tossed and left to die. Chandra heard the hissing of snakes, something furry brushed past him, and every so often he saw glowing eyes staring at him through the trees. As he stumbled on a branch, he caught a whiff of harsh animal breath.

They finally came to a settlement after a journey that lasted half the night. Chandra had carried Chanakya on his shoulders when the older man had started shivering. Chandra felt his shoulders sag, his legs trembled, but he wouldn't give in to fatigue or admit to any weakness.

8

ALL CREATURES OF THE FOREST

For days Chanakya's body raged with a fever that refused to abate. Chandra kept watch, tending to him even as he carried out menial duties for the Atavikas. A mutual trust, at first grudging and watchful, developed over those days but it was one forged out of necessity. Every few days, some groups would return and the chief and others would huddle and whisper among themselves. Then they would leave again. Chandra and the still recovering Chanakya were left in the camp with a few others – some wounded bandits and the old ones who were too impaired to do anything. Chandra chafed at the wait but knew it was necessary. The camp of the Atavikas was deep in the forests and their whereabouts were secret and unknown. The Atavikas were men with hidden lives and their loyalty would be secured with some difficulty. But during the days they spent with Chanakya and Chandra, they came to realize the two meant no harm to them, and that they too were fugitives from the Nanda dynasty.

One of the old bandits was in agonizing pain. He had been mauled by a lion. It was Chandra who bathed his wounds regularly as they waited for the others to return. He foraged for herbs, laid traps for small animals and waited eagerly for the sight of a lion. The wounded bandit would smile at his efforts.

'It is only a particularly hungry lion who ventures near humans,' he would say.

Nothing seemed to heal his wounds, while Chanakya recovered very quickly. Chandra awaited the bandits' return and prepared for their move up north. 'I am certain Alexander will make his plans for the future now. The rains are over and there is a period of a few lunar cycles before the winter comes. His men will either want to leave or advance. We will lose the right moment if we do not leave soon.'

Chanakya was always bent over palm leaf scrolls, writing his message of revolt and hope. Two nights passed and the men did not return. 'It will be some time before they do,' said the sick man. 'They can get carried away when they have made a victorious raid. So they will go to the nearest town or city to revel and make a kill. Always separate, never in groups. They'll spend days there to satiate their hunger for women and indulge themselves in every forbidden pleasure that we deny ourselves in the forest.'

The sick man looked at Chandra, his yellowing eyes enfeebled by age, his brow furrowed. He looked painfully ill and spoke in a faint voice that made it seem like he was already conversing with spirits, those who inhabited in the in-between worlds.

'But we are partly animals, aren't we? You know, when the lion attacked me, and I was fighting him off, I understood his need. He was driven by what he was, he could be nothing else. He was only following his instincts. And what was I doing, fighting the laws of nature?'

'And yet you did, and the lion let you go.' Chandra could listen to this story any number of times.

'He wasn't very hungry,' the man laughed. 'He waited, with his paw on my face.'

Chandra forced himself to look at the injury on the man's face again. The flesh there had fallen away, the mark of a sharp claw now stretched from his forehead to his lower cheek.

'I think he felt alone,' replied the old bandit. 'Usually lions hunt together in packs and this one was by himself. It struck me that he was left to fend for himself. Just as I am now.'

For the third night in a row, there was no sign of the bandits. The old man shivered, the blanket failing to soothe his rising fever. The hyenas sounded nearer, their hysterical laughter reminiscent of men gone wild. Almost simultaneously, they heard the menacing, low growl of a lion which sounded ominously close. Excited at the prospect of spotting the lion, Chandra could barely sleep.

As dawn broke the next morning, Chandra followed the river as it narrowed up the old stone valley where the lion hunted. The lion was alone and old, a creature left to himself. The old bandit's words rang in his ears. 'There used to be more lions here in my youth, but they moved away once this area became more inhabited. Even they choose to stay away from humans. We are the worst of all creation. Animals kill because they need to, but we do so because of the evil in us...'

It was afternoon when Chandra reached the riverside. He had walked all day. The river looked sparkling blue and the rocks he stepped on were black and barren. He stopped in his tracks, transfixed by the sight of a pugmark – a huge, square-shaped paw, with one broken claw. The lion had staked his claim to this territory.

He suddenly felt defenceless and tightened his grip on his sword. He had his bow and arrow as well as his spear. But he knew he was powerless if a lion, four times as strong as an elephant, leapt onto his back in a surprise attack. He climbed a rock and looked around. The settlement was hidden by the shade of spreading trees, and over the low rounded hills, he could see a trade caravan passing by. The music of the drummers reached him in short bursts as his gaze returned to the hill. He caught his breath sharply and froze. For there, a little above him, standing on a rock, was the lion.

The animal was watching him and Chandra held its gaze, slowly moving his hand towards his spear. If he unleashed it quickly enough, he could get the lion. As they stared at each other he couldn't help but notice that it was a lovely day, and the sun was catching the animal's wrinkled brown skin, turning it into burnished gold. The lion shook its mane, the fluttering sound making Chandra hold his breath. He took a step back, gauging his movements. The creature lifted his head and opened its mouth, giving Chandra a glimpse of its reddened gums and yellowing teeth. Chandra raised his spear, standing rigidly, as the lion gazed down at him. He waited for it to spring. But, to his surprise, the lion raised its front paw instead. Chandra saw the smear of red, a patch spread in an irregular circle.

The lion was wounded. That explained why it was alone and why it had not been able to kill the old bandit. The lion opened its mouth again and the smell of age and decay assailed Chandra. He winced, but to let down his guard even for a moment might be fatal. He stood there as the light flashed in the lion's tawny eyes.

Never abandon someone wounded, even if he is an enemy, his father's voice rang in his ears.

Without flinching or taking his eyes off the animal, Chandra advanced, spear in hand. Taking one step and then another, he approached carefully, catching his breath as he neared the lion. It now stood above him, unblinking, slowly flicking its tail. It smelled of old flesh, of the frightening and mysterious smell of the earth and the forest, and of its own power. Chandra did not look away. Was he doing something foolhardy? A practical man would make a rational choice and save his own life. But it was cowardly to leave the lion to its death.

Determined, he stretched out and clasped the lion's paw. It weighed heavily on his hand, but he refused to tremble. In that one moment that stretched forever, Chandra quelled his fear and felt a deep calmness surge within.

He saw the piece of bone stuck deep in the gaping wound. A smaller creature's bone, perhaps one discarded by a hyena. The bone had cut deep. Pus had festered in the wound. The lion raised its head as Chandra bent before it. The creak of his knee on the rock and the scraping sound of his bow touching the earth were the only sounds to break that silence.

The moment he could have made a different choice had passed. He held the paw in his hands and looked at the creature. He saw himself reflected in those old eyes, and there was no fierceness in the lion's gaze. The moment was bigger than either of them, man and beast. The lion whimpered, evoking a tenderness in Chandra as he held the animal's paw, the offending bone thin and sharp as a small dagger. Chandra prised it out carefully. The animal's whimper rose to a low painful moan, then a howl that filled the forest, reminding Chandra oddly enough of the sound peacocks made when they were hunted. If all animals felt the same pain and expressed it in almost the same ways, what was the difference between them?

He clamped the wound with his hands and felt the lion's warm blood flow over his hand. Looking into the creature's eyes, he felt a deep kinship with it. He knew then that he need not have been afraid. The lion would not harm him. He smiled as he felt the animal's pain diminish.

I have to go now.

He was not sure if it was his own voice he heard. He patted the injured paw, ran his hands over the sleek, hot forehead and the glorious mane. He would always remember this moment.

He took a few steps back, facing the lion who stood watching him, unmoving. More boldly then, knowing the descent was steep, Chandra turned away, leaping over the boulders. When he looked back, the lion was gone. He stared, hoping the creature would emerge out of that emptiness. But he saw nothing. The lion's presence hung everywhere even if it had vanished in the forests and, as he waited, he thought he heard the soft rustle of the bushes, a whimper as the rough gravel touched its recovering paw, and its harsh breathing that made the leaves sway. And then, even the presence was gone and Chandra knew he was once again alone.

He started to walk back towards the settlement. Had he been away too long? The sun was still high and it was a day hotter than any he had known before. He stopped under an old babul tree, drenched in its shadow, letting its leaves caress his face. On an impulse he picked up a sharp thorn and carved his name on the trunk, watching the letters take shape slowly and certainly on the wood. He felt himself shiver and the hair on his arms rose. Would anyone believe what he had just done? Or what the lion had let him do? Was it its pain or had the creature understood his desire to see a lion and generously let him come near? The lion could have killed him with a swipe of its other paw. And yet it hadn't.

As Chandra walked on, he understood one thing: this was an experience he would not share with anyone, not even Chanakya. It was beyond his own understanding, and telling someone who would offer his own views about it would dilute it, make it into something he knew it was not.

He stopped at an old well, fetched water with a rusty bucket and drank heartily. The greyness reflected in the water told him the day had lengthened. It was nearing evening. His eyes burned, a raging fire that the water did little to calm. He ran his fingers through his hair; they tangled in his locks, and he was reminded of his long journey over the last few seasons. His hair had turned brown in his travels through the plains, the ravines and the deserts. As he bent to pour water over himself, he saw in his reflection that he was taller now. He stopped still as this knowledge sank in. He was no longer a boy of the forest but a man with a destiny.

There was a heavy silence that reigned in the bandits' camp when he returned. His footsteps stilled as he understood why. No welcome fires burned – and he knew in his heart that the old bandit warrior was dead. When he walked further, he saw Chanakya leaning over the body of the dead man, anointing it with balm and herbs he had gathered. He spoke without turning back, 'Took you quite a while.'

Chandra came near and the older man looked up. Chandra gazed into those angry red-rimmed eyes, disconcerted as he remembered how the old lion had gazed at him the same way. He asked Chanakya, jerking his own head towards where the old bandit warrior lay. 'When did this happen?'

'He was in great pain and perhaps death came at the best time,' Chanakya's eyes never left his face, and his voice was low. It was growing dark fast and the owls had begun calling, too near, too loud.

'That is a good sign. We must cremate him, give him an honourable death,' said Chanakya. 'A warrior like him deserves one. Like a kshatriya, not a mere forest bandit. In the manner of his death, he earned honour. He cannot be left to be eaten up by carrion birds and vile hyenas.'

They gathered wood and Chanakya performed the rites, chanting the sacred hymns that consecrated the dead. The black smoke rose high as Chandra lit the fire. The wood burst into flames, logs falling over each other, crackling as the fire leapt high. In a matter of moments, the fire destroyed the flesh and bones of the warrior. Chandra thought sadly how easily a human life could fade away.

'The soul is eternal, isn't it?' he asked Chanakya.

'Yes.'

'And there is rebirth?'

Chanakya shrugged. 'There is indeed, as the great monks and followers of the Buddha and Mahavira say. It is also what you do in this life that matters. Never forget that.'

In the fading light, his back turned towards Chandra, Chanakya looked smaller and painfully thin, yet he held himself upright. He was a man with a mission, and more importantly, a vision that he believed in. Chandra, his hand still on the flaming torch, knew it was time to leave the bandit warriors behind.

He placed the torch in the blazing pyre and stepped back, closing his eyes.

'Never waste time on unnecessary emotions,' advised Chanakya. 'Besides, what was he to you?'

'I knew him,' Chandra said after a long time.

'Briefly.'

'Sometimes that is all that matters.'

He looked back now and Chanakya held his gaze. 'All this, even death, is impermanent. That is what every religion says. We did our duty, and now we must move on. First thing tomorrow morning.'

Did he imagine Chanakya say it or was he hearing his father, the chief's voice in his ears again?

9

BUILDING AN ARMY

Etched across the vast expanse of the cloudless sky were the seven great sages, the seven stars that assured travellers with their constant presence. The seven sages, known for their wisdom, endured through time and the ages. Chandra thought once again of the vision Chanakya and he were chasing, a dream only they held.

Tonight they would not hear the lion roaring. As he slipped into sleep, Chandra thought of how majestically the lion had shaken its mane, the way its tawny eyes had left his face and looked to the sky. It was a moment that revealed the lonely splendour of a creature he had been privileged to see. A loneliness that truly befitted a king – one who ruled alone and fearlessly. He would be a king like that lion, an emperor, alone yet mighty in his magnificence.

He awoke to low voices, interspersed with the crackling of twigs and the neighing of horses. He looked through the leafy curtain of their shelter. Chanakya was reading from his scroll, surrounded on all sides by fierce-looking men. The Atavikas had returned.

Chanakya read aloud: 'You have had a narrow escape this time. But you cannot live a life on the run forever. It is temporary, a raid here, a booty earned there. You have your pleasures but then you must run and hide each time. A life meant for taking risks is in your blood. But if you are part of an army, where you offer your services when they are needed, and when a truly righteous king assures you his protection, then you no longer need be afraid for your families.'

It was the beginning of an impassioned speech about the Nandas that Chandra had already heard many times. The Nandas were unjust and greedy rulers and Mahapadma had been one of the worst. Driven to test his strength as he grew older, his power had proved too great for his sons, who had collapsed and died before him. It was Dhana Nanda, the youngest and puniest of them all, who had survived. Despite his unimposing stature, Dhana Nanda's greed and love for gold knew no bounds. It was known that he had sent soldiers to look for giant gold-digging ants that he believed could find gold in the hills and ravines. His miserliness was legendary and he married only for dowry and gold.

'The Nandas still have the mightiest army,' said the chief of the Atavikas as Chanakya looked up from his scroll. And that indeed was the truth everyone knew. The people of Magadha could not rebel against their rulers, for the Nandas had power and force on their side. Their mighty elephants roused terror and fear in equal measure.

'Even here, in this forsaken part of the forest, we find those elephant-hunters trapping elephants to serve the Magadhan army. Frightened villagers are taken away to train these elephants. Then every year there are contests, when elephants battle men.'

'That is because the bonds between man and animal are made of fear. They are not naturally bloodthirsty creatures,' Chandra broke in.

Chanakya acknowledged him with a glance but there was also a warning in his eyes: *Be careful what you say.*

But Chandra continued, 'The Nandas have to be defeated. There is no doubt about it. Here is what I propose.' He held his breath. This was a moment when he would either be committing treason or winning the Atavikas over. He looked around quickly, observing every face carefully, but all of his audience stood still, watchful and alert.

He took a deep breath and began, 'You could become part of an army that will advance towards Magadha. And when the new king – the prince who vanished – will return to claim his kingdom, you will serve him as loyal soldiers. He will be a king worthy of your loyalty. In return, you can continue your old ways, but as protectors, as keepers of these forests. Forests that will be the king's resources, used only to serve the interest of the kingdom.'

A silence had fallen over the men and he knew they were thinking over what he had said. Their eyes moved from him to Chanakya and then back again. They knew what he meant, and from their silent acknowledgment it seemed they already had an inkling of who he was. He continued, 'You will accept the king and in turn, he will accept you. Live and let live. A relationship of the fingers to the hand, every part essential, every part for itself and yet for each other.'

Chandra knew then he had to persuade them with all the power he had. His eyes moved over every face as he spoke, 'All of you will have a new life, but one without fear. You will no longer have to hide. You need never be afraid.'

Never be afraid. The last words were picked up by the listeners and repeated. Their hushed tones rose like a sibilant cloud.

'The word will reach you, soon.' It was Chanakya who spoke now. 'It will be a new beginning, you will see,' he said, holding Chandra's arm high as the light of the tapers shone on him. 'There will be a new king, far greater than the Nandas. A king who will be your protector. In return, he will only demand your loyalty.'

Chandra held their gaze, and then he let his eyes move over every face, steady and unhurried. Already he stood tall and graceful over them. If he could look a lion in the eye, he knew he had nothing to fear from a crowd. Besides, he knew this crowd had its fears too, its uncertainties.

The moon glimmered and somewhere an owl hooted. A mournful call, as ancient as the world itself, which lifted any uncertainties the Atavikas were feeling – it was an auspicious sign.

'There is no time left. We must begin at once,' said Chanakya. His voice was no longer harsh, though his eyes glittered with triumph. Only Chandra knew he had been afraid. It was a gamble they had pulled off.

They bade farewell to the men and rode off into the night on two of the finest horses of the camp – a gift from the chief. The chief had told them of another tribe, pirates along the rivers of the Punjab and the regions farther north. 'They will take you across the many rivers of the Doab. You will not draw undue attention, as they do not harm monks and solitary travellers. When you meet them, show them this ring.'

It was a ring with a crescent moon embedded in it.

'It has been with our tribe for generations – given to us by a king whom we rescued when he got lost in the forest while hunting. A king born of the lunar dynasty.'

They rode for several days, away from the dry forests that slowly gave way to grassier patches. They were nearing some foothills and already in the far distance they could see the blue of the mountains merging with the sky. One morning, they came across an outpost, a small patched-up tent amidst the low trees. An old monk sat resting on a rock, flanked by his disciples. On conversing with them Chandra found out that their intent was to cross the high mountains of the Himavat into Bhot, the Land of the Dragons. It turned out they had left Magadha only the previous monsoon.

The monk said, 'We had a hard time in Magadha. Everyone is suspicious there. Dhana Nanda never emerges to meet his people anymore. His fort is stronger than before, and it is lit up in a ghostly green light. The light is not from tapers, people say, but reflections from the gold he has gathered. He demands gold from everyone – from traders who come from afar, from kingdoms his father had conquered, even from those who stray into his kingdom. And his officials demand their bit too.'

Then one of his disciples spoke up, his voice shaking with nervousness, 'And because we had no money to pay them, no gold for our permits, they took us for spies.'

If the monks were curious about the new arrivals they did not show it. Instead, following a lull in the conversation, one of the acolytes said, 'Every day, a boatman comes with our supplies from the village on the other side. You are welcome to share our meal with us.'

'Forgive us but we do not have time to share a meal with you now,' Chanakya refused politely. He shot a quick glance at Chandra. They had to reach Alexander. That was Chanakya's vital strategy, for he believed his suspicions about Alexander's soldiers were correct. If things went according to plan, they could make use of Alexander's soldiers – who were now deserting him in droves – press eastward gradually and in time, decimate the Nandas. But, it was important to reach Alexander first, to see things for themselves.

'We have the advantage of time,' he told Chandra as if to explain his haste. 'We cannot afford to let this opportunity go. Sell the horses. It is a boat that will take us away from here soonest. And in secret.'

Hidden behind the rocks that overlooked the river, they watched the boatman and his assistant deposit small bundles of grain and baskets of fruit for the monks. The boatman was an old man, but his assistant was much younger, although he looked weak too – it was the way he waded through the water that told Chandra he was a cripple.

Now. As Chanakya gave the signal, Chandra swooped down from the rocks, reaching for the boat in quick strokes as the boatman and his helper looked back in surprise. They had been too slow, giving Chandra little challenge. He could hear the surprised yells of the boatman, and the slap of water as the crippled young assistant dived into the water, making a desperate attempt to pull the boat back. The boy, who had a stump for a left leg, floundered in the water. Realizing that the struggle was unequal, Chandra knew he had to turn back and save him, ignoring Chanakya's surprised stare.

The boy shivered in gratitude as Chandra pulled him over the boat, then passed him a rough cloth to dry himself.

'He would have drowned,' he said later to Chanakya, once he had reached the bank and apologized to the boatman. 'He was doing his duty, which made him a man of virtue. How could I wrong him? Even if, the end, as righteous and honourable as it may be, justifies any means one adopts…but not when the dice is so loaded against someone. How could I act against dharma?'

Chanakya's harsh laughter rang in Chandra's ears. 'As a king, you must make a choice between what is virtue and what is foolish. Did the boatman's helper need to be saved? We have gone no further towards our goal and the threat to our lives can still close in. What do you think you have done?'

'It is still early. We will find a far sturdier boat, I am sure, without having to steal it from someone.'

Chanakya said sardonically, 'At this rate you will become a monk. Whatever happened to the boy who was chosen as a leader by his mates? Whom destiny ordained to be king?'

That afternoon as they thought over what to do next, the rain came down heavily. Falling down like a thick curtain, it was unwavering. Suddenly they were disturbed by the sound of rustling as leafy branches struck wood and water. The boatman's helper with his shy smile and intense eyes beckoned to them.

'It's a raft,' said Chandra in some amazement. 'Will it stay afloat in these fast-moving waters?'

'It will. It will,' the helper assured him. 'It has been built to negotiate small channels and canals. Follow those when you are going upland. And in the colder reaches, where the current is far swifter, palanquin-bearers will help you. They have always ferried monks and lone sages up to the mountains.'

His voice dropped. 'That ring on your finger,' he said, pointing to the bandit chief's ring, 'means there may be enemies after you. Men from the Nanda state will attack you if they find you. We who lead itinerant lives recognize that ring and now we know that you are friend, not foe. We have encountered the Atavikas before. Once they came as far as Benares, drawn by a monk to hear a sage's teachings, and someone reported them to the king. We helped them escape in the middle of the night. Now we want to help you too so I have brought you this raft.'

Thanking the boy, Chanakya and Chandra boarded the raft and left immediately. The river proved unpredictable and unruly as they rowed northwards. The water flowed so swiftly that it took all of Chandra's skills to keep the raft on course. He pressed hard against the current, but was out of breath in no time. But pitting his strength against the river quelled the raging torment in his mind.

He wondered how long they would have to lead a life on the run. He knew they could not afford to let their guard down. He heard Chanakya's voice behind him, quietly detailing all that was left to be done. 'It is men on the move who will give us our best chance at forming an army. Alexander's men, their hands already bloodied by many wars, offer us our other best option. In the big cities, men have fixed lives, and will do little to change their situation – they will even suffer a tyrant. We must look for those who can help us, men with their own stories of injustice and suffering. Men such as the Atavikas, tribes, herdsmen and even robbers. Men who are in a position to believe that a new order can come into being.'

They were sailing upstream on the Asikni, having turned northward from the settlement of the Atavikas. The Asikni was one of the Sapt Sindhu, the seven sacred rivers. The wind was sharp and cold on their faces and the tangy smell of leaves drifted down from the high forest trees. They passed plains on either side, flatlands rich with new crop. Sometimes towns appeared on the riverbank, some with temple spires that rose high and some with flat-roofed monasteries. They saw the washing laid out neatly on the banks and boats bouncing in the tide. After more than a day's rowing, Chanakya told him they had reached Sakala, a well-planned merchant town endowed with great wealth, that had seen new monasteries built over the last few years. The people of the town lived in red brick houses all along the riverbank.

They stood before one, in the manner of all poor Brahmins, and asked for shelter. A servant appeared first and bidding them to wait, returned a few moments later with the lady of the house. She addressed them through her veil. Her voice was well-modulated and soft; she spoke with the authority of one used to being obeyed. Chandra looked down at her hands, soft and heavily ringed. 'I will ask the servants to attend to you. Some of them may be dawdling because it's the day of the great festival.'

They were shown to one of the inner rooms, which was equipped with every comfort. Young women, veiled like their mistress, washed their guests' feet with scented rosewater. They were offered sweets and wine. As they reclined on their couches, Chandra fell asleep, exhausted by their long journey. When he came to he realized he had slept for a long while, having been jolted awake by a young woman of the house. Her veil had fallen off, her skin glowing as the sun shone in gently through the windows, where the curtains danced beguilingly.

'Young master,' she said, 'there is a messenger at the door. It's about the festival…' she gestured towards the corridor. Chandra looked over to Chanakya, who was wrapped in a blanket, asleep. In these hill towns of the north, the air could suddenly turn chilly and Chanakya always liked to be prepared.

'Not him, only you.'

Chandra was wary, yet curious. He followed the woman down the corridor, her anklets jingling as she walked. They emerged in the open and, standing by a peepul tree, he saw a man who looked familiar. It took Chandra a while to place him. It was the warrior he had only had a quick glimpse of at Viratnagara. The one whose spear he had extricated from the tree branches, who was also one of the three swordsmen he had outmatched thoroughly.

The man stared at him with mocking eyes, and spoke in a taunting voice, 'There's a limit to how far you can run, isn't there?'

So they had been tracked. Chandra wondered if they had ever been safe.

The man laughed at his shocked expression. 'Have no fear. When my friends described two men, coming from a long way off, travelling secretly, I suspected it might be you. And only I know of your superior fighting skills, unmatched by anyone. So, do you think you can match your skills once again? Only against me?'

Chandra stared at the man in silence. The man laughed and spoke again. 'My name is Bharata. The mistress of this house is my sister, and she told me you had come here. When my father died, I went away to study sword-fighting, hoping to become one of the sastropajivi-srenis, the free warriors. No king owns our services but we offer ours to the best of them.'

The competition, he explained to Chandra as he led him away, was held every year. He pointed to two drummers a few steps ahead on the road. One stopped to unfurl a scroll and read out an announcement, calling all sword-fighters to match their skills against the best. It was not a war, but a true contest of brave warriors.

Chandra could barely contain his excitement. The itch to match his skills against the best was simply irresistible. It was a challenge he could not pass up especially now that his new friend had invited him to participate.

They soon came upon an open ground. An excited crowd was milling around, waiting for the competition to begin. On a bench nearby sat important-looking officials. Unlike the warriors, who were bare-chested and had only a diadem around their foreheads, the officials wore jewelled turbans and soft cotton robes and were being fanned by attendants. There were many tents around the main one that stood right at the centre of the expansive grounds.

'I've come on my own. My masters in Viratnagara wouldn't give me permission to compete. Some of my companions wanted to join Alexander's army but I wanted to come here first,' Bharata said.

Chandra lowered his voice, 'There is in any case little honour left in fighting for Alexander.'

Amused, Bharata glanced very deliberately at his finger and said, 'I can see why you have that ring.'

Chandra had forgotten all about it. He shifted the ring but it wouldn't move from his finger. Noting his discomfiture, Bharata patted him on the shoulder and laughed. 'Think instead of the contest and the men you will fight against. Men who, if they see your worth, will give their lives for you.'

Bharata said the last bit quietly but the import of his words was not lost on Chandra. The contest was a chance to prove himself before like warriors, and to convince them to join the army that Chanakya and he were looking to form. His pulse raced with excitement and he laughed, almost defiant of any challenge. 'I can't wait to begin,' he said, his eyes shining while the sun lit his matted brown hair.

Warriors from many places, far and near, had entered the competition. Men from the Dragon Kingdom; fine-featured, rough-haired men who had run away from Alexander's armies; soldiers from Darius's Persian army who hated Alexander; others from lands south of the Narmada.

Chandra chose his sword; it was made by the finest metal-workers of the region. He raised it to his lips and against the blue sky and felt a power flow into him from the sun overhead. He knew then that this sword would be with him for all time to come.

The competition began and Chandra strode into the arena. He was so fleet-footed that his opponents couldn't keep up with him. His movements had a fluidity that seemed magical – he could fling his sword and rush to catch it, just before it fell, and deal a mighty blow the very next moment. One by one, he defeated every swordsman who confronted him.

In the final contest he faced Alexis, the warrior famed as the hero who had jumped up and killed the elephant on which King Puru had been seated. The sight of that falling creature, who only a few moments before had towered majestically over everyone, had spread panic on the battlefield. Other soldiers had then surrounded King Puru. He had been captured soon after and his armies had capitulated to Alexander. Alexis, for his part, had not rested till he had subjugated the elephant, emerging finally from under its belly, holding a bloodied tusk high in his hand.

In this contest, with several hundred onlookers, Alexis proved no match for Chandra. Time and again Alexis jumped high in the air and neatly twirled around to attack but Chandra was unfazed. At one point his blond locks caught on Chandra's sword and his neat topknot came undone. In anger and humiliation, he flung his sword away. It flew in a small arc, slicing up the air. As he knelt at Chandra's feet in the manner of the vanquished, he handed over his sword as well. He said in a whisper no one else caught, 'If you ever need help from soldiers like me, you will find me here, in this town.'

10

AN EVIL PRINCE

Malayketu was an angry man. He gnashed his teeth as he thought of how he had been betrayed of his legacy by his own father, the once great king Puru. Ever since his father's defeat at the hands of that usurper, Alexander of Macedon, Prince Malayketu had been living a life of exile in his own land. Now his ambition was to get back the throne of Gandhara, and get rid of his father. There was something menacing about Malayketu – a man who would stop at nothing to achieve his evil ends. He trusted no one and never slept in the same room twice. He was as paranoid as he was conniving. It was when he was charming that he was most dangerous. He distrusted women the most because he thought they were a wicked, manipulative species; that they could deceive even when engulfing men in their charms.

'My lord, come back to bed,' a voice from the shadows interrupted his dark thoughts. It was exactly this sort of woman he was most wary of. Dinner had been delicious, leavened flat bread, goat korma and fragrant rice with saffron and raisins – the innkeeper had gone out of his way to make a fine meal for his honoured guest. But the woman had spoken too much, asked too many questions. 'Do you like my dress? See the henna on my hands, isn't it beautiful?' And as the evening wore on, the wine made him wild with lust for her. He had taken her roughly, tearing her blouse and squeezing her breasts tightly till she whimpered, her moans of pain inflaming his blood even more. Then he had collapsed on her, unmindful of her whimpering, rolling over after he was satiated and then pushing her away to a corner of the bed. Her moans had drifted to him in odd bursts, yet she called him back to bed, but he had other matters to think of now.

Malayketu's thoughts returned to the news his spies had brought him. They had said Dhana Nanda was planning to march north and then westwards with his army and his battalion of elephants towards Alexander's armies. Spies had told the Magadha ruler of Alexander's gold but although Malayketu knew the greedy Dhana Nanda would stop at nothing to enhance his coffers, he did not really have the courage to face Alexander's armies. There was another story too, one that Malayketu was intrigued by – of a warrior prince who was on the run and who now posed a threat to the Nandas. But his angry thoughts returned, as they always did, to his father, King Puru of Gandhara. Malayketu had abandoned him even before the battle with Alexander, for his father hadn't formally anointed him crown prince yet, and Malayketu had been sick of waiting.

There was no need for that now, Malayketu thought with contempt. Puru didn't deserve to be king; in fact, how could he still be called king when he had been defeated by that foreign upstart? His kingdom, Gandhara, long admired by rival domains, had been taken over by Alexander. But the land was now rife with the absurd story of how Puru, surrounded by his enemy's soldiers, their swords pointed at his throat, had still stood straight in defeat and commanded Alexander to treat him like a king! What a farce, Malayketu snorted. He deserved to be eliminated in the same way as Ajatashatru had eliminated his father Bimbisara. Had anyone said anything then? Where was the talk of parricide at that time? It was a matter of shame that people still fawned over a worthless man like Puru and actually looked at a defeat as an act of honour!

Yes, Malayketu sat up as the realization struck him – his biggest enemies were indeed Alexander and his father – and he had thought of a way to get what he wanted. Those rumours of a warrior prince on the run in the kingdom had to be true. Malayketu had also heard that the prince was now heading towards Taxila. The marketplace that evening had been full of such news and then more – about a brave warrior who had vanquished every opponent he faced in the festival contest. This was a warrior who could be of good use. Malayketu ran his fingers down his thin beard and then laughed out loud. There was a possibility that the warrior was the prince in disguise. Malayketu would find that out very soon.

Excitement surged through him at this thought. He reached out and pulled the woman back towards him.

Chandra smiled, glad that he had found a worthy companion in Bharata. He was someone Chandra thought he could trust. He felt satiated and still raw from the many duels he had had. The gleam in Bharata's eyes had been unmistakable when Chandra's eyes met his, as a defeated Alexis knelt at his feet. Now as evening fell and they walked away from the festival crowds, Chandra felt the two of them were bound together as only two brave people who revelled in the challenge of a duel or a contest, could be. It was Bharata who explained the nature of soldiers – while they loved their freedom, it was necessary for the brave, temperamental sastropajivi-srenis to always serve a master. 'They cannot hold their temper, these warriors. It urges them on, they say it makes them forget fear. That is why our loyalty is only for those who can rise above ordinary temptations and inspire us.'

He stopped and then very deliberately winked at Chandra. 'But for that we need to journey across the Punjab, all the way to Taxila. That is where you are headed too, are you not?'

Chandra nodded, hiding his surprise at how much Bharata had guessed. It was indeed time they headed towards Taxila, where news of Alexander and his moves would be more certain and accurate. And now that he had gained fame at the contest, he was sure to have drawn the attention of Nanda spies. He knew Chanakya was wary about returning to Taxila for fear of being recognized. It was, after all, the city he had lived in as a much younger man and he had even taught at the university there. But Chanakya was also excited. Returning to Taxila, they both knew, was inevitable and necessary. It was the chief city of the kingdom of Gandhara and it drew the best stock of warriors, traders, scholars and philosophers. Any campaign for Magadha had to begin from Taxila. It was a place that granted recognition and acceptance.

It was a night filled with long conversations and much easy laughter. Chandra had little idea how the hours passed. They were now walking through a lonely part of town, where most people had retired for the night. Stray sounds of revelry – laughter and the rhythm of drums beating – reverberated in the distance. Animals brushed past them time and again, lonely abandoned creatures who emerged only when it was dark. Closer to where they walked, dogs yelped and ran away. Cats watched them, green-eyed and wary.

Chandra knew then that they were being followed. It was evident in the way the sounds stilled behind them. The way a door shut quietly, although it could have been the wind. Someone was, perhaps, watching them from a window.

Chandra raised his hand, cutting Bharata short, all his senses screaming at him to be alert.

'We are being watched,' whispered Chandra. For a moment,

he had seen a long shadow on the ground, as the moon moved ever so slowly in the sky. All around them, the earth suddenly seemed to come alive with dancing shadows, moving leaves and the slap of feet on wet mud.

The town has a life of its own, he couldn't help thinking. They flattened themselves against a tree, trying not to breathe, seeking to hide in the darkness the tree offered. Chandra smelled the bittersweet fragrance of leaves around him, the trunk of the tree that pulsed with its own life rhythms and sometimes, the whiff of different animal scents. From above he heard the hissing of a snake.

The darkness lengthened, the shadows spread, dissolved and reshaped themselves. A bird swept past suddenly, obviously disturbed from sleep and then they saw a man slink out of a doorway. 'Come, that is the person to follow,' whispered Chandra.

But the chase was more difficult than they had anticipated. The man appeared to almost fly through air. He ran across streets, slithered up houses, jumped across courtyards and terraces, and vanished into trees before appearing again. He could be a ghoul, Chandra shuddered, his hands tightening on his dagger. But no ghoul could leave behind shadows.

'He is one of the choragavas,' whispered Bharata. 'Highly organized groups of brigands who sell themselves for a prize. They can be worthy allies.'

They followed the man into a quieter part of the town. Here the buildings were bigger with larger courtyards, and the porches were festooned with garlands.

There were guards now at every corner, but their quarry still managed to give them the slip, flitting from pillar to pillar, shaping himself to fit every column, his body sinuous and graceful. In a trice, he had leapt on to a gate, crawled along the wall, and then hoisted himself onto a window ledge. He waited before breaking out into a whistle. The curtains parted and the man vanished inside.

Chandra was about to follow when he felt the pinprick of a spear in his back.

Don't look back, he heard a whisper. He knew for sure that even if he did, he would not see him. For the man's voice was muffled, revealing that he was masked.

'We will go in through the gate, and you will keep your hands away from your dagger,' said the muffled voice.

He held himself straight. A brave man had nothing to fear. 'I am a warrior,' he said. 'I give you my word I will not try to run or give you the slip.'

There was a moment's silence, then a short, sharp bark of laughter. 'You have the cheek, the audacity to make such a promise when you are virtually my prisoner.'

But the spear no longer hurt. The man stepped into the light and, grabbing a taper from one of the guards, held it up.

'So it is you. You are the one who got the better of Alexis in the contest.' His captor spat on the floor in disgust. 'Those Greeks.' He called to a guard who was no older than a boy. 'Bal, is the prince asleep, do you know?'

'Yes, he is. No one's dancing for him now. They were all called away to the inn,' said the boy, smiling up at Chandra. 'I saw you fight,' he said, looking at him with awe.

'Enough of that,' said another man, who emerged from the darkness. He was the one they had followed. Chandra saw that he was small and slightly built. He shifted his weight from one foot to the other, as if he did not know how to stand still.

'Who is your master?' Chandra looked around and tried hard not to show his shock, for Bharata was not with him. Had he managed to give them the slip or – he could not delve on this treacherous thought – had it all been a trap of Bharata's making?

'It's the prince of Gandhara, the man who would be king, except for his cowardly father.'

'You mean Puru?' Chandra couldn't stop the sharpness of his tone. 'But Puru is a brave man.'

'Brave man?' the man spat again. 'He should have preferred death to dishonour.'

'But how was he to kill himself?' asked Chandra, who had heard the story so many times that he knew where the truth lay. It was recited everywhere, the story of Puru's stubborn bravery and his insistence on being treated with honour.

'He should have refused to be made a prisoner.'

Chandra shook his head; his long hair flew and settled around his shoulders. He brushed it away from his eyes.

'How? When Alexander's soldiers tied Puru's hands and dragged him away, he still held himself straight. If he showed a moment's fear, he would have been killed. And then his soldiers would have fled in disarray, and his kingdom would have been ransacked.'

'Well, how do you know? Were you there?'

Chandra shook his head. 'He demanded honourable treatment. He said he was still a king. He was born one,' he repeated the lines that would soon become the stuff of legend. 'And that was how, unchained and escorted by soldiers, he was led before Alexander.'

'His son thinks he doesn't deserve to be king,' said the other man.

Before he could speak further, a window on the floor above was flung open against the wall and a screaming woman was hurled through it. Chandra rushed towards her, lunging down on the courtyard stones, hoping to catch her before she hit the hard earth. But her veil flew and caught his face, his arms reached for her and failed. She now lay on the ground, breathing heavily. Part of her veil still covered her face, the other end flailed against his stretched arm.

'My lord, what have you done?' someone shouted.

'That is no dancing girl, but a spy. And it is your fault, Bhrigu, for getting her here. Take her away, this instant.'

Chandra glanced down at her. Her breath came fast and in ever fainter gasps. She smiled, a fading smile, like a mirage. It was a smile of life hoping to triumph over death but failing. And then her breath stopped. The man looking down from the window smirked as if the incident had meant nothing at all.

'People who cross me had better be careful,' he said threateningly.

'That does not mean you can throw a woman out of a window,' Chandra retorted. The man next to him stiffened and the man leaning over from the upper floor glowered. This was a bully, a man who savoured hitting the weak, and Chandra should have held his tongue. Perhaps that was what Chanakya would have advised.

'A man who wields his tongue as a weapon.' The man laughed.

This was a dangerous man, Chandra realized, someone who was laughing moments after he had pushed a woman to her death.

Malayketu now rushed down the stairs and came up to Chandra. As he neared, Chandra realized Malayketu was much shorter than he had first thought and his breath reeked of drink. Malayketu wiped the spittle from his moustache and then growled at Chandra, 'Tell me if there is a reason I should spare your life.'

Chandra did not flinch. He shrugged, saying, 'If there was no reason, your man would have killed me straightaway.'

His captor grinned. He leaned forward to whisper in his master's ear, the prince's lips taking on a mocking twist as he heard him out.

'So you are indeed a brave warrior, the vanquisher of Alexis. But do you think you can escape with my men surrounding you?'

'There must be a reason why you still haven't had me killed. Though,' Chandra said, his eyes never leaving the other man's face, 'it would be cowardly. I am unarmed, one against all those who guard you.'

Malayketu threw back his head and laughed. 'You have a way with words. And so did my father.' He stopped and his eyes glittered with malice. 'True warriors, I think, don't waste time on words.'

His long thin face wore a nasty look. 'So what shall it be? Do you think you are up to a challenge?'

'Yes,' Chandra said under his breath, 'not that you give me much choice.'

'Your life or your word that you will see this through,' Malayketu said, his eyes glittering. 'Here's what I propose... Bhrigu, fill him in.'

The man Chandra had followed emerged silently from the shadows. He told him about Alexander, the man Malayketu had set his sights on, whom Malayketu wanted killed as an act of revenge, which he could not, or would not, carry out himself. Chandra heard him out, holding his breath. Bhrigu proposed a plan for Chandra to meet Alexander alone, for him to bring the latter to his knees. A close meeting with the emperor, alone in his tent, with no one around. He would know then what really made an emperor, what drove a conqueror on, thought Chandra. Perhaps he would challenge Alexander to a duel too, for then he could kill the man honourably. Malayketu's plan was diabolical but if it meant a way to reach Alexander on his own, Chandra was all ears.

'He is camping somewhere near Gandhara,' said Bhrigu. 'King Puru gives him every help. An enemy on our soil.'

'And we want him dead. As for my father, I will take care of him on my own.'

Chandra shuddered at the venom and the hatred in the other man's voice, soft and snake-like, as slippery as the silken garment that repeatedly slipped off his shoulders. Chandra willed himself to hear the rest of the plan, as Malayketu, impatient with the leisurely way in which Bhrigu told his tale, took over the narration himself.

'Alexander is heavily guarded. Prove your worth and do it. And no,' he smiled slowly and cunningly, 'don't try and give me the slip. For there are people like Bhrigu here on your trail. This time you will not know they are there.'

As Chandra looked at him, Malayketu said, 'Even now, there were others. You were surrounded. You could never have escaped.'

Despite all this, Chandra thought, Bharata had still managed to disappear.

Malayketu seemed an impulsive, excitable young man. And suddenly the picture was clearer to Chandra. He was a man who could be a small-time king, but never an emperor. An emperor never waged a futile war, or expended his energies in small battles. An emperor, as one of Chanakya's dictums went, chose to make allies of smaller enemies.

'I am told Alexander's men are frightened of elephants,' said Malayketu, mockingly. 'Are you?'

He had never been afraid of elephants, Chandra said defiantly. He had grown up in forests where they roamed wild. Malayketu smiled his lazy smile and told him about a mad elephant that needed taming.

Chandra was led out through the gate and into an open courtyard. The mahout rose and pointed out the enclosure where the elephant now dozed. 'He has been sedated,' said the mahout, 'otherwise none of us would ever get a decent night's sleep. The other creatures would go mad too.'

The mahout handed Chandra a wide knobbed club. The man's eyes were wide with fear as he walked Chandra to the gate leading to the enclosure. He delivered his warning as if he could not help it – 'He has been deliberately driven mad. He can...'

But Chandra held his hand up, silencing the man. He held the club with both hands, then moved it from one hand to another, checking its weight and strength for himself. Scanning his surroundings for the best strategy by which he could confront the elephant, he climbed up a nearby tree and attempted to leap across the low wall of the compound and onto the elephant's back. Twice he fell, missing the target. After each attempt as he landed neatly on the ground, loud screams of laughter, the most hysterical from Malayketu, mocked him. Chandra bit his lip, furious. He could barely control his intense dislike of the man. He wished he could leap right onto him and strangle him as he sat, a false king among his sycophants. Instead, he shrugged and looked straight at the elephant. Chandra could see the whites of the elephant's eyes, the way its head swayed, the way its tail twitched uncontrollably as it rose.

The men laughed raucously, taking their cue from Malayketu.

On his third attempt, he jumped neatly into the enclosure, close to where the elephant stood. A cry of surprise passed through the onlookers. The elephant trumpeted shrilly, swinging its trunk around Chandra and picking him up effortlessly. Those watching looked on in alarm, and Chandra saw himself looking down at the creature's huge, all-seeing eyes, red-rimmed at the edges.

'Listen to me,' he said as the elephant tightened its grip around

Chandra. He breathed in so his chest became taut. The elephant's trunk felt hard and scaly on his well-oiled, mud-bathed skin. The smell of damp earth, grass and rage was strong on it. Animals and men smelled the same; perhaps at this moment of contest, they felt the same way too.

'Listen,' he had to pitch his voice to get the elephant's attention. 'Listen,' and for a moment, he felt the trunk loosen. He drew in his breath cautiously and deliberately, pressed his hands on the creature's huge lined forehead, catching the elephant by surprise. Chandra wasted no more time. He slipped out from the elephant's grasp and lunged forward, jumping onto the ropes on the creature's back. The old leathery skin felt hot and scaly under his hands. Chandra leaned closer and bit the elephant's ear, always its most-sensitive part.

Listen.

He gestured to the mahout to cut the creature's ropes, the ones that tied him to the posts, and to throw the gate open.

Several of those watching rushed away with howls of alarm. It angered Chandra, for the noise would frighten the elephant even more. The dust rose, gravel hit him, but the elephant ran at a thundering speed. Chandra saw the green-brown colours of the earth flashing past. Branches brushed his face, some scratched and grazed him harshly. But – stretched out flat on the elephant's back – not for a moment did Chandra let go of its ears.

The elephant must have run a long distance, stopping every now and then as if it remembered the unwelcome presence of someone on its back. After a while, his efforts at resisting Chandra stopped. The trees were taller and denser now. They must have run into the forests outside Sakala which stretched right up to the Punjab and a little beyond. Chandra felt the sharp nip of air, the smell of the river, and knew the elephant had led him deep into the forest.

As he lay on the back of the shuddering beast, now totally exhausted, he heard thunderous stomping nearby and recognized the sound for what it was. An army of elephants had surrounded him.

'He did give you a long ride, didn't he?' someone called out.

The words were spoken close enough to make Chandra nearly lose his grip on the ropes; his arms were already stiff with exhaustion.

'In the end you got him.' It was Bharata. He sat on a low branch, just above a mild-looking elephant, and both stared at him placidly.

'Where were you?' Chandra's breath came out in exhausted gasps.

'I gave those men the slip and returned with help.' He smiled, seeing the suspicion on Chandra's face. 'You need rest.'

'I must tell you that I made a promise I don't intend to keep.'

Bharata seemed to know about this already. 'We will see to that, we will.'

Chandra looked away so Bharata could not see his expression, hating himself for his doubts about his new friend. Had Bharata deliberately deserted him and was this all a conspiracy on his part? After all, they were sastropajivi-srenis, their bravery sold to the highest bidder. Perhaps someone had bought his services already. Chandra sat up on his own elephant, touching its ear gently. The animal was tired, but his heavy breathing eased at Chandra's touch.

Bharata said, 'He is breathing too hard. That long run through miles of forests and villages has left him spent and I doubt even you know how far you have come.'

Chandra leaned down and placed his ear on the animal's hard leathery back. The elephant was breathing laboriously, in slow painful gasps. He could feel the animal's heart thud loudly against his own hand, the sound of the earth in distress.

'He was driven mad,' said Chandra through clenched teeth, his hand gentle on the elephant.

Understanding that this was a man driven to anger very rarely, Bharata nodded. 'Yes, Malayketu is known for his random cruelty, his abrupt changes of mind. He has been consistent, however, in pursuing one aim – his desire to kill his own father. I think he really wanted to test you.'

Chandra's skin prickled on hearing Bharata, it surprised him that the latter knew so much. He knew he had to be wary of him; a warrior had to impress with skills other than mere bravery, he thought. They moved slowly, Chandra's eyes on Bharata, whose elephant led the way, parting the trees for them to walk behind. The other elephants walked sombrely around them. The forest was alive with a certain tension, of quiet elephants and a dying one – one whose legs wouldn't hold him up much longer. His laboured breath seemed to send shudders through the entire forest. The sounds of birds died in their path.

'Someone will be surprised to see you.'

'Someone who I am sure is equally furious,' Chandra replied, for he knew Chanakya must have looked all over for him. Suddenly he missed him, longed to see his teacher's harsh, gritty face and hoped he had not made him worry too much.

Chanakya had indeed been worried. He had come to the festival soon after he had awakened in the mansion. Though he had heard of the brave warrior who had easily defeated all his opponents in the competition, Chanakya's face had given nothing away. He wouldn't speculate about the truth and would rather wait for it to be confirmed. In his harsh, imperious way, he had demanded a look at the roster, where every competitor's name had been entered. But just as he had expected, Chandra's name wasn't on it. The young man had evidently used an alias and that would make it more difficult to trace him. As Chanakya went around the festival, looking for clues, he heard about every duel, the victor's graceful moves and nothing else. It was as if Chandra had come to epitomize courage and bravery itself.

But he still wasn't sure; unless reason confirmed things, Chanakya wouldn't give in to mere beliefs or rumours. Holding his breath, and closing his mind to the worst, Chanakya had then forced himself to look at the faces of dead warriors whom the doms were taking away for their last rites. He did not shudder as the wild dogs yapped close by him, and even in the twilight, the vultures swooped low. The fires burning the dead rose high – the flames fanned his cheeks but Chanakya did not flinch.

Bharata described it all to Chandra. 'Into the late hours of the night, I am told, he looked at every face. And I knew then who he was looking for.' Bharata's face turned suddenly serious. 'He had the saddest and sternest expression on his face. The face of a man who has seen many a tragedy. I had to then tell him the truth about you. His relief was great.'

The elephant sank to its knees as the end of the forest appeared. At the same time they had their first clear glimpse of a settlement, which they had come upon unexpectedly.

'They are mostly soldiers on the run. Deserters from Alexander's army,' Bharata whispered. 'Don't try and get into a scrape. You have been in too many of them...'

Chandra smiled because he sounded like Chanakya.

They watched the elephant die, its eyes now blinded, the whites gleaming like an old tired moon. Its breath emerged in pained, shuddering jerks, like a lost wind in the forest. An elephant driven mad, Chandra thought, a lost life, an unfair death. The animal deserved better.

Chanakya wasn't as angry as Chandra had thought he would be. He had a hard smile as they stood face-to-face, Chandra looking down at him, wearing a rueful smile. 'You took a risk but they told me you fought like a lion. And I knew no one could have fought like that except you.'

There was an unmistakable note of pride in Chanakya's voice, but he was stern the very next moment. 'You will give yourself away if you take such risks. It won't be difficult for the Nandas to track you down.'

Chandra asked, 'So even if I am a fine warrior, I should hide my skills?'

'No, you should learn to use them wisely and discreetly. Choose your battles – and your friends – carefully.'

Then Chandra told him about Malayketu's offer, his voice unable to hide his contempt of the Gandhara prince. Chanakya heard him out and then surprised Chandra with a conspiratorial grin. 'You need not keep your word with Malayketu. You can, however, appear to do so.'

The smile didn't just indicate the pleasure Chanakya evinced at outwitting Malayketu, but his relief on seeing Chandra safe. Chandra nodded; he already had no intention of falling in line with Malayketu's demands. It was in a sense reneging on a promise, but a warrior – even if he were made a prisoner and his oath secured under threat – needed someone worthy to serve, to obey. The thought of Malayketu, the undeserving son of a misunderstood father, the memory of the woman he had flung out of the window and the elephant he had driven mad, made Chandra's lips tighten in anger. Chanakya saw his expression, and was assured that this time Chandra was following his own counsel, in spite of the risks that would be involved in thwarting Malayketu.

They had Bharata with them now, and Chanakya offered his grudging trust to the other man. It was Bharata, after all, who had brought him news about Chandra and who had brought him back after the episode with the mad elephant. Bharata could help them reach other mercenaries and warriors who were looking for a new master to serve. He was a warrior himself and, more importantly, he was resourceful. He had already left to fetch them elephants for their journey northward.

Chanakya also knew that their lives were in even greater danger now. There were men waiting and watching, who could kill them at any moment, especially Chandra, if he deviated from the mad prince's plan. And a warrior like Bharata would be an ideal companion – someone who would bravely defend and fight for Chandra.

Besides, Chanakya needed all the time he had to write his scrolls and spread the message of the new king. He had to ensure that these reached the right places, that they moved from city to village and even reached the wandering tribes and the nomads. There was now little time to be lost. Chandra, he knew from the younger man's determined gaze and assured voice, would reach Alexander soon. His own role, Chanakya understood, was to offer the future king of Magadha the best advice.

'We cannot be beholden to anyone,' said Chanakya, his voice rising as he felt himself sharing Chandra's confidence, 'even if we owe them our lives. Everything is subservient to the main cause. Till the enemy sits on our frontier, there is always a threat. And we have our own goal in mind. There is no other cause or bond we must recognize.'

They left the city in the night; there were no soldiers out on patrol, no one to man the roads. It was strangely peaceful despite the ever-present threat of lawlessness and the soft rustling of their elephants treading the path.

Close to dawn, they stopped to rest at a temple and let their elephants bathe in the river. It was the river Vitasta, a tributary of the Sindhu. Gandhara was not too far and, as Bharata pointed, Alexander's camp was only a few days away.

Wading into the cold river, Chandra splashed water over his face and played with the elephants for a long time. In that early morning light, he saw himself in the waters, and noted the long, matted locks of hair that now reached below his shoulders.

Using his dagger, he cut his hair then, brutally hacking off the locks – quickly, sharply and unflinchingly. He watched the strands of his hair float away in the river, long loping curls that had been part of his journey. The forests, valleys, mountains and rivers, all swept away in a flash.

There was traffic on the river even at that early hour. Orange-robed monks passed by in a boat, raising their brass vessels as they passed. In another boat, there were bears, tied with thick ropes and their tamers, brooding and tired. A mangy bear, its frame skeletal and with a long drooping neck, lost its balance and fell into the water. It was speared to death in no time. An old infirm bear could never be a performing bear. Chandra saw the bear's blood mingle with the water before that too vanished.

Chanakya joined the two younger men in the water and they waded along the riverbank slowly, appearing like ordinary travellers. Their untidy locks of hair, gaunt appearance and dishevelled robes would not have aroused suspicions except for the men still on their trail. Chandra looked across at the temples on the banks, the low flat roofs of mansions and the long brown line of huts, and he wondered briefly what made people live such settled lives.

For that moment, he felt the fatigue seep into him, like the soldiers he had recently seen, spent after their battles. Then he felt his mentor's eyes on him. 'Never let your guard down. Play with distractions but never let them own you. A king never does that, not even when he has guards around him.'

There would never be a time when Chanakya would not teach him something, and looking away, Chandra also thought – would he accept him as a teacher all his life? His teacher believed in a life of action and Chandra did too, but action always invited immense contemplation. An emperor was especially duty-bound to be aware of the consequences of his every action.

Chandra smiled ruefully. He thought of the self he had already lost – the boy who loved riding out on his own, who lived in the deep forests and the open scrubland. He would never find that self again.

PART II

THE WARRIOR-KING OF MAGADHA

11

MOVING NORTH

Rumours travelled in the wind as Chanakya, Chandra and Bharata moved northwest towards the mountains that lay beyond Taxila and Pushkaravati, rumours that could only have had their origins in Gandhara and Kamboja, the frontier states that had waged the first futile battles against Alexander. These rumours carried with them the scent of fear, the excitement of a contest and the uncertainty of a future that defied prediction.

The whispers said Alexander, insatiable as ever, was making plans for an invasion. He was not willing to hold off any more. Almost everyone they met coming from that side said this, and yet no one could be certain about whether it was true.

· 'You should hear him speak,' said Bharata. 'I have heard his voice carries the strength of thunder and the lightness of the breeze. He speaks just one line and everyone falls silent, even the birds in the sky. Really, I have never heard anyone speak like that.'

'The Buddha did, two centuries ago, when Magadha was the only empire in these parts,' said Chandra quietly. 'He was quiet and simple, yet his presence was totally imposing. That's what I heard.'

'Well, Alexander wants to move eastwards,' said Bharata, and then his eyes twinkled in their usual way, 'but perhaps he hasn't heard of us and our intentions.'

'No one is really sure of what Alexander wants. What I have heard is that his soldiers are tired of the heat and the long journey,' Chanakya interposed clearly and deliberately.

'They are indeed tired and want to go home. So the time for an invasion is now. There will never be a better opportunity,' said Bharata. Chandra noticed how his two companions sparred frequently with each other. The older man was disapproving of what he thought was Bharata's impetuousness and garrulousness. The latter, for his part, chafed at Chanakya's constant attempts to correct him. For Chandra, it was a novelty to have a friend who was near his age and athletic prowess and who shared his hopes and dreams for the future. He wondered whether the calm, implacable Chanakya was capable of jealousy.

The next morning they rode their elephants into the Sindhu, close to the bank, where the waters never ran deep. Ahead, a procession of boats formed a straight line. On the main boat leading them all, the flag of Alexander fluttered proudly – a golden sun blazing on red cloth. Chandra held his breath; there was a palpable power in that flag, as if its owner was already stamping his authority on areas he hadn't yet conquered.

He saw the soldiers – tall, their faces harsh in that gentle morning light as they lashed at the boatmen to speed up. He saw the scowls on their faces and the wariness in the eyes of the boatmen as Chandra and the others came close. Their own elephants were slow and graceful, wading in the quick-moving, cold waters of the Sindhu. The ripples widened and knocked against the boats as they approached. The boatmen flinched and the soldiers cursed.

'Keep your elephants away!' One of the soldiers raised his spear. He spoke a Greek dialect and repeated it in Aramaic, running a disdainful glance over them. In his days as a herdsman in the grasslands to the north, Chandra had picked up some Aramaic. Chanakya was already familiar with it, from his student days in Taxila but for now, neither man was giving anything away.

Chandra raised his bow in turn, and the soldier smiled.

'A spear aimed at your elephant would fell you. Just one spear.' The soldier smiled mockingly, but lowered his spear at the look in Chandra's eyes. In anger and frustration, he kicked a boatman hard as he hunched over the oars.

'Who asked you to stop?' he shouted.

Bharata leaned forward, seeking to restrain Chandra. 'We are on our way to meet Alexander as well,' he said in Aramaic.

'Who is he?' asked the soldier, looking pointedly at Chandra. Though he stumbled over his words, the sneer in his voice was unmistakable.

'Chandragupta,' said Chanakya, speaking up at last, his tone very deliberate. Then he added in Aramaic, 'He is a prince of Magadha.'

The words had a ring of finality. Chandra felt no shock or surprise on hearing them. Somewhere along this journey he had left his past behind and emerged a new man.

The river rippled by, playful as always, but the menace in the air became a thick, invisible wall between the men and the soldiers. The boats stopped, rocking with a reassuring rhythm against the water, and the elephants stood still, water sliding off their backs with the motion of the river.

Chandra spoke up now, continuing where Chanakya had left off. 'And we are heading to meet Alexander. We have travelled a long way from the east.' He glanced quickly at Chanakya and Bharata, a frisson of apprehension running through him as he continued, aware of the patent untruth of his next words. 'We wish to offer our support to Alexander. We will fight in the battles of his choosing.'

Chandra knew the soldiers drew their confidence and aggression simply from their position as Alexander's soldiers. He had decided that even if he used lies to get his way, he had to meet Alexander. Chanakya believed that Alexander would not venture further east; he had left it too late, but Alexander's armies, in the secret plan of Chanakya's making, could be used for their purposes.

The soldier sneered, but he lowered his spear, nodding to the others to do the same. 'Not many princes and kings want to do that. They are all too ready to surrender. And then demand fancy terms for themselves.'

The soldier was obviously referring to King Puru and Chandra could well understand Malayaketu's hatred of his father. But it angered him to hear Puru being referred to so disparagingly.

'Not very many can understand how practical surrender can be,' he said out loud. The soldier blinked and looked at him again. It took a moment for the sneer to reappear on his face. 'Ah, words of wisdom. The emperor will indeed be happy to meet you.'

Chandra recognized the sarcasm in the soldier's words but he was not pressing for a confrontation. He saw his elephant's eyes droop in exhaustion, for it had waded through the waters a long way. He bent to caress it on the forehead and soothe it. A boat would be a faster way of travelling towards Alexander.

The boats commandeered by the soldiers for Alexander's mission had turned around now and they were clearly headed northwards, where the river was narrower and far more treacherous and its pristine blue waters hid the jagged rocks beneath. At the river's northern reaches was the border that had once divided the kingdom of Kamboja and the Farsi empire. Alexander had set up his camp there, a day's journey from where they were. The boats, made of light forest wood and steered expertly, were setting a fast pace. The elephants waded alongside, their usual placid contentment intact, and soon the boats had swept past and disappeared from sight.

'They won't go too far,' mused Chandra. In all likelihood the soldiers were making for a fairly large village where they could billet for the night. It was best to befriend them, offer their services at a more opportune time in the morning and hopefully join the fleet of boats all the way to Alexander's camp.

He was right in his surmise. Only a few hours later, as the sun dipped and the evening air turned chilly, they saw the first smoke plumes drifting upward not too far away; an indication of village hearths. No sooner had they crossed a bend in the river, that the long line of boats moored on shore came into view and with it, all signs of a village abuzz with activity. Some of the soldiers were taking a dip in the waters, shivering in the cold, and others were warming themselves by the fires that had been lit. Buckets clanked as they pulled up from wells, the slapping sounds of bread being prepared by the women echoed near the hearths, and the mattresses made scratching noises as they were pulled out on porches.

As their elephants climbed slowly out of the water, a hushed silence fell. Some of the soldiers rose from their place by the fires. One of them, a tall man who walked with a distinct swagger, and who, as Chandra noticed from the flickering fires, still wore his imperial diadem – a plain band of yellow cloth, its ends dropping to his shoulders – approached the three. His eyes drifted lazily over them and the elephants, who now shook themselves heavily, showering those around with water and forcing the man to wince and take a step back.

'Aren't you the men going up to meet the emperor?' he asked, his eyes locked with Chandra's. But it was he who looked away first, letting his glance, now full of contempt, run down Chandra's wet, soiled clothes and his matted hair. But Chandra stood tall, his grey eyes giving nothing away.

'Yes, we have a special mission. To tell the emperor of conditions in the east and of the battles that must be fought.'

'Indeed. Then you must join us,' said the man, as he came up even closer and confirmed Chandra's suspicions that the man was someone important, the commander who was leading this particular fleet up to where the emperor camped. He lowered his voice, but there was a steely note in it, almost a warning, 'Make sure you present a feasible plan. The emperor needs to convince his men.' He paused and then, with the sneer back on his face, he said, 'yes, a whole lot of his men.'

Their eyes locked one last time, and the commander lifted his hand in an expansive gesture of welcome. But the import of his words was not lost on Chandra.

That night, after they set up camp – on a small boat with a wooden roof for all the other huts had been occupied, Chandra walked out alone, far away from the spot where the elephants slept. The sounds of the forest picked up and dulled again, almost mimicking the river's rhythms.

Alexander was one of the greatest conquerors the world has seen, but even he could not command the complete loyalty of his soldiers. As they had eaten their simple meal of flatbread and mutton, he had been privy to several conversations. He had overheard some soldiers say that for many days Alexander had been pleading with his soldiers to stay but they were deserting him in droves. They were tired of the fighting, tired of being far away from their homes. Each day would see some tents empty, the sound of horses being ridden away, indicating that more desertions had taken place. Alexander had forced those who remained to pledge their loyalty to him in blood. Each soldier cut his flesh to draw blood, which was collected in a bowl and then passed around in a rite that silenced all doubts about Alexander's predicament.

Had Alexander indeed thought that conquering all these kingdoms, achieving magnificent victories over kings, would be enough? Why did the craving never end? Did not Dhana Nanda's craving for gold have the same tragic intensity? Even his father, Mahapadma, had been desperate to live forever, but in the end, he had died a lonely death, calling out in turn to all the sons he had outlived.

As the moon dipped in the northwest and the darkness of the night diminished to a thin grey, Chandra walked back. He saw a taper's light in the direction he was heading. His breath quickened. The taper stood, affixed to the crossbows of a boat, *their* boat as Chandra soon realized, that lay moored some distance away, beyond the other boats commandeered by Alexander's soldiers. The sound of water lapping against the wood punctuated the other sounds of the night – of snoring soldiers, the sighs and curses of the drowsy few keeping guard and the movements and stirrings of animals.

As the boat creaked, swayed gently in the night breeze, he saw Chanakya bent at his task. He was writing, the sound of his quill scratching on the leaf mingling with the whispering of the wind and the rocking of the boat. Chanakya did not hear Chandra come up to him, for he was hard at work, penning his scrolls as he always did when he was alone, and absolutely assured of his privacy. As the night stretched, even the soldiers had dropped their guard. The stillness that gripped Chanakya was the only indication that he was startled when he picked up the sound of Chandra's steps on the wood. The leaf blotted as he blew on it and all that he had written disappeared. He took his time looking up and Chandra recognized that look of smug contentment on his face that appeared whenever he outsmarted someone.

'This is invisible ink, made with special herbs. It vanishes if you blow heavily on it.'

Chanakya looked around cautiously, but they were not overheard. 'It's not just you that destiny has marked out. It's my life's mission as well. I have seen kingdoms, small and big ones.

I have seen kings but there are no great emperors. Even...' His voice dropped, 'No, not even Alexander. He is a conqueror who is no emperor. But we must still meet him.'

Chandra bent to splash water on his face. He looked at his reflection, blurred in the taper's light. Yet his eyes stared back at him, darker than ever, always questioning, knowing that somehow the answers never kept pace with the questions themselves. He found his voice after a long time, watching the ripples settle down through his cupped fingers. 'Alexander does not belong here, he never will. If he moves on, he will not stop at Magadha. Magadha will never be the centre of his universe. And maybe Alexander doesn't really want to settle down and be king. For there is more to being a king than mere conquest. What does being a king mean? You might want more and more power, so where does it all end?'

'That is a good question. Power is of little use if, as king or emperor, you see yourself as separate from your realm and your people,' said Chanakya. 'Power is not for yourself, but for your kingdom. Power is not merely for your own glory but to rule justly and efficiently, to preserve your kingdom from enemies, to safeguard your people.' They gazed into the darkness for a while and then decided to rest.

In the morning, Chandra busied himself with fetching the kindling and lighting the fire. He roasted dry flatbread over it, then ate it with the bananas their village host had offered them. Chanakya performed his ablutions diligently, his eyes closed to the world. This time they travelled on the boat, keeping close to the shore, as their elephants swam alongside. They followed Alexander's fleet of boats which were being led by the commander.

There was already a trail of boats behind them as well, all readying for the journey upriver. By nightfall, they would reach Alexander's camp. The boats had all been commandeered from the villages by the river, and now the boatmen were forced to serve Alexander's armies. In the clear light of day, the boatmen seemed none too happy about the long journey they were about to undertake. They bent over their oars, not looking each other in the eye, too afraid to protest.

The commander was pleased with what his men had achieved. 'A bridge of boats, that is our plan. Something that has never been done. before,' he boasted. 'These boats will make the rivers of the east easily fordable. For the rivers are in spate this time of the year, and their unpredictability is what makes the soldiers afraid.'

He spat, his contempt swallowed up by the water before he went on. 'All these soldiers are from the dry deserts and treeless plains. They have never seen rivers or elephants. Just yellow sand and those sleepy camels that can't run for all their size.'

A bridge of boats. The idea struck Chandra as marvellous. There was really no obstacle that couldn't be breached, and the rules of war were always flexible. He thought of the high palace walls around Magadha, high as the eye could stretch. He had never seen such towering walls since. The Nanda kings had made their palace impregnable but perhaps there was a way to enter it.

Chandra remembered Chanakya's words about humans being the weakest links in the strongest of defences – and that everyone had a price. He sighed and stared at the moving sky. The clouds scudded by and he felt his own heart soar. He missed the old days when he could ride out on his horse for long distances, chasing the day, and waiting for the sun to come up again the next day. The forests never seemed to end. Then there were the strange tribes who offered him their hospitality. He looked at the scars he had as mementoes, the rings and promises that he had exchanged with others. One mark of friendship on his wrist had been placed by tribals living among the bears in the mountains. He remembered the men who escorted monks over the mountains

– he had their word that if he ever needed help in these parts, they would appear.

Impatient with his thoughts, Chandra dove into the water. He intended to swim to the elephants. At times when he was assailed by too many questions that had no answers, he liked matching his strength against a stronger force. But he had not anticipated the current, that the river, though narrow, would have such power in its waters. Just within a few feet were sharp pointed rocks that looked more menacing as he neared.

The current knocked against his chest, pushing him back. Before he could react, a wall of water overwhelmed him, bearing down on him. He struggled but could feel his body giving up, feeling weaker, when he felt something forceful tug at him. A hand pulling at him. His head on someone's shoulder. And that someone was pulling him up and away with strong strokes. He felt his rescuer pushing the water away and the wall gave slowly to fresh air. He was lulled by the twin sounds of water rushing by and a man's arms cutting through it.

It was one of the boatmen who had jumped in upon sensing the danger. He pushed Chandra back on to the boat and hoisted himself up. Bharata and Chanakya looked on, the anxiety on their faces slowly giving way to relief. The other boatmen too were smiling. Only the soldiers looked on with displeasure and anger at the delay. Then one of the soldiers, without warning, lifted his spear and dashed it straight at the boatman who had saved Chandra.

It struck the boatman deep in the shoulder and blood gushed out, spraying Chandra in the face. He stared, speechless with shock, at the soldier, who was gesturing angrily at the boat that was being borne away by the currents.

'How dare you strike him!' shouted Chandra.

'How dare he let a boat go?' snarled the soldier in response. 'One boat less can make all the difference. Alexander's bridge cannot have a boat missing.'

'But he is a brave man, and you, a rotten coward,' Chandra turned and with one swift, graceful turn, grabbed Chanakya's upper robe, for his own had been swept away by the river. The spear had pierced deep and its pointed end was still in the boatman's shoulder. Chandra bent forward and pulled the tip out with his teeth, his lips tasting of iron, salt and the man's blood. Clenching his teeth hard, he proceeded to tie up the man's gaping wound with the cloth from Chanakya's robe. The man lay helpless on the boat, his stricken eyes looking at the gentle blue of the sky. The soldier only shrugged as he turned aside.

Chanakya shook his head and his harsh features went soft for a moment in the sadness he felt. 'Let it go. It is unjust and unfair, but this defeat is one you have to accept. The wound on his shoulder is deep but you have done all you can to help.'

Chandra lifted his head to ask him in turn, 'Do you remember the crippled boatman's assistant?' Chanakya nodded, a bleak look in his eyes. 'In the same way, I cannot abandon him,' Chandra continued. 'We will leave him at a nearby village, where he will find help.' Chandra squeezed blood out from the cloth as the man who had so spontaneously and generously come to his rescue, looked on with gratitude. They chanced upon a village much later in the afternoon as the boatman lay exhausted on the boat's prow, his head against the cloth, reddened by his wound. His eyes looked deep into Chandra's as together, he and Bharata, took him ashore and left him in the care of a fisherman's family, whose two young sons looked on, goggle-eyed with amazement at the long flotilla of boats on the river.

The soldiers muttered to each other. They flogged the boatmen mercilessly, cursing and goading them to go faster. The boatmen hardly looked up, wincing and groaning as they pulled at their oars, while the lashes came down on them over and over again. The blood from their wounds sometimes struck Chandra in the face as he bent at his oars too, looking up defiantly as the soldiers neared. The soldiers marched up and down, shouting at them to row faster, but they stopped as they came near him. For some reason, where he was concerned, there was now a wariness in their eyes.

They came upon the camp only as the last greyness eased from the night. In the near distance were the Malayavat mountains, rising grey and white in the soft darkness, beyond which were the satrapies – the provinces of Gedrosia, in the region of the Makran and Arachosia to its west – once part of the old Farsi empire and now in Alexander's possession.

Stray fires were flickering in the camp, the sound of kindling crackling as the flames rose and leapt high. Dogs standing guard barked as the boats were tied and one could hear the soft pattering sound of animal feet, the quick urgent breathing, that meant the jackals were near. Periodically, the guards called out. Horses neighed and sometimes laughter erupted, the sound carrying far. Chanakya emerged from beneath the boat's awning, his shawl draped over him, for it was colder up north. He cursed under his breath.

The sprawling camp was adjacent to a village. There were men sleeping on the porches of the dwellings and as dawn descended, they could see the rounded houses and their low thatched roofs. An encampment of soldiers drawn from all over had come together to create the biggest army ever.

The soldiers from the camp sauntered up, gazing at the boats in the river. The black line of boats presented a fascinating sight. There were smaller boats ahead of theirs and larger ones in a long line behind, stretching so far that they melded into the darkness. In that grey dawn, the boats stood like orderly soldiers themselves, in a clearly arranged formation, swaying ever so slightly. Their own elephants moved closer to the banks, their heavy breathing fanning out over the rippling waters. Behind them were other elephants, picked up by the soldiers. The boatmen's arms stretched far on their oars in a sign of their utter exhaustion. Yet the river was full and alive with the presence of these boats. One journey had ended but as the boats bobbed, sank low and creaked, everything, even the morning, seemed to have just begun.

One of the soldiers on the shore asked, 'Where is the emperor?'

He was speaking in a Greek dialect. Bharata roughly translated what the soldier had said for Chandra and Chanakya. If they were surprised by the fact that Bharata appeared to know the language, they did not show it. For the moment though, Chanakya and Chandra exchanged a quick glance with each other, and watched the scenario unfold around them.

'We thought he was with you,' said one of the soldiers on the boat. There was consternation among the men on the shore, and more soldiers came out. They were talking to each other, and there was considerable confusion as to where Alexander was. The soldiers who had been on the boats looked flustered and disappointed for they had wanted to impress their emperor. Instead, there was now even more agitation.

'We cannot possibly have him with us. He gave the orders for us to get the boats.'

A crowd of soldiers had gathered, and everyone had soon forgotten about Chandra, Chanakya and Bharata.

'Where is Alexander?'

Though the soldiers were speaking in different languages, they were all calling Alexander by his name. Sikandar – Chandra picked up that name too, as it came floating in the wind towards him;

soldiers speaking in old Persian spoke of Alexander by this name. His army had men from all over. But he had melded them into one army, his own. He knew how to march as one with his soldiers as well as lead them. He could assume any role, either of a ruler or that of a comrade-in-arms. That was how he had managed to conquer so many lands.

'We do not know,' the soldiers on the boats said, perplexed.

Barely had this exchange died away when a shout came from a distance. 'His horse isn't there! Isn't that the first thing you should have checked, you dolts? He's gone hunting.'

The atmosphere lightened. There was laughter as they rushed to the riverbank, where the tired and still frightened boatmen sat in their boats. The boats rocked slowly as if being lulled to sleep after their long sail up the rivers that watered the upper Punjab and beyond. The sun rose higher, lighting up the boats in its golden glow.

The soldiers were talking among themselves. Some of them cast curious glances their way. Chanakya struck an unusual figure with his pronounced limp, his craggy face and the shikha dangling like a thick knotted snake below his shoulders. Chandra stood by his elephant, patting its trunk, murmuring as he looked into the creature's huge brooding eyes. But he was alert to the conversation around him. 'The boats...will these be enough to cross over?'

'We will need many more elephants too.'

They stared at the clumsy elephants that lumbered up the bank and snuggled close to each other, their trunks swishing lazily at flies. Some of the soldiers came closer for a better look.

'They do look difficult to ride.'

'Someone just told us you rode on its back here? Part of the way?' asked one of them a bit incredulously, turning to Chandra. Chandra nodded. He stood to one side with Chanakya, absorbing the new voices, soaking in the scene around him.

Then he replied, assuming a deliberate nonchalance, 'Most of the way. For all their size, elephants swim fast. Perhaps they just need a skilled hand to guide them.'

'They look like cows, just bigger,' said one of them and the rest of the soldiers broke into loud raucous laughter. They laughed so hard that they did not notice the horses till they rode right into their midst.

12

THE CONQUEROR

The sun shone bright on the tall, golden-haired, broad-shouldered man who had come riding up. Chandra knew this was Alexander. It could be none other. The men fell silent. Those in front sank to their knees and the soldiers behind bent at the waist before they hastily made way for him.

Alexander took the deference for granted. As he neared them, Chandra could see the dishevelled locks of hair and the puffiness on Alexander's face. He realized that Alexander was also a much troubled man. Raising his hand in lazy acknowledgment, Alexander looked at the man next to him, who was seated on an equally magnificent white horse, and pointed out imperiously. 'So we have the boats – can we now cross the river?'

'We will need more boats than these, sire. These rivers can be unexpectedly dangerous.'

Chanakya stepped forward, decisive and impatient, quickly nodding to Chandra and Bharata. 'Sire…please give us some time to talk to you. We have come all the way from Magadha to meet you.' He spoke haltingly, his speech a mix of Greek and Aramaic. Bharata, whose Greek was more fluent, repeated it all, looking up at Alexander.

The emperor was taken by surprise at the sudden request and he turned in the direction of the speaker. His gaze fell on Chandra, who stared back. It became a contest of who would outstare the other; finally, it was the emperor who grinned. 'Some upstart there. Don't you know that you're not supposed to look the emperor in the eye?'

Alexander's remark made the soldiers converge around the three of them. 'It's all right,' said Alexander, laughing, gesturing with his hands. 'He is one against all of you – he can't do me harm.'

'Your Imperial Highness,' said the man on the horse, 'he does not know how to behave.'

Chanakya passed Chandra a brief, warning look. Though Chandra could not understand the language he could gauge the tone of the men.

But a smile filled Alexander's face. It was taunting, yet it brightened his face. Now he replied in Aramaic, his words distinctly meant for Chandra. Chandra was surprised that Alexander could speak the language but then realized that the latter's long campaign in Persia meant he had some acquaintance with languages spoken in these parts – old Persian and Aramaic. Chandra himself knew Aramaic from his days of wandering with the herders and the tribes.

'You do not expect barbarians to know any better. Their king is not really worth much. Maybe all those big stories we have heard about the Nandas are not true.'

It was the moment Chandra was waiting for. Exchanging a quick look with his companions, he spoke up, his voice clear and loud in that throng of waiting soldiers. He refused to lower his gaze as he spoke, 'That is what we have come to speak to you about. There are brave warriors from the east to the northwest who will fight to ensure the defeat of the Nanda king. Maybe you have not met enough brave soldiers yet...'

A soldier whispered quickly to Chandra. 'You should come back later. He must not talk of another war in the open. Many of his soldiers don't want more war. There could be a mutiny.'

Alexander was running his fingers through his hair. It caught the light of the sun and glinted gold. Then he turned with a mocking smile to Chandra again.

'That is interesting. Do you consider yourself to be one of these brave warriors? Would you prove your might and challenge me to a duel?'

His question silenced the crowd while Chandra looked him back in the eye. He remembered his childhood dream. *Yes, I'll ask him to leave our land, or invite him to a duel to see who is stronger… A duel it will be, and I will win.*

It was Alexander who nodded and finally looked away, a shrug of his shoulders indicating his indifference. He was shaking his head, running his hand over his horse, and then he sighed, as if to himself. 'Not now… If only Hephaestion were here…' There was an unmistakable note of longing in his voice, of a sadness that would remain forever.

Chandra knew he was referring to his friend and specially chosen bodyguard – Hephaestion, who had died a season ago in Baghdad. Alexander had trusted Hephaestion with his life and it would take him a long time to recover from his death. Chandra was so caught up in his reverie that he missed the moment Alexander began speaking to him again. 'Everyone will tell you he was the finest swordsman there ever was. He could strike you dead with just one blow.'

Then, as if he was bored with it all, he turned to the men nearest him and gave the terse command, 'If they are new here, and warriors,' he flashed a smile Chandra's way, mocking and also amused at the younger man's effrontery, before he continued, 'they need to feel welcome.'

As the three of them made their way through, following Alexander, they felt a few hostile glances from the soldiers. Then Chandra caught the whisper that came to them in the wind – 'Don't you dare try to influence him into moving east. We have moved far enough with him. The end of the world doesn't really ever come. The world goes on and on.'

Over the next few days they discovered that the encampment was like a small town. As morning dawned, children from the nearby villages would turn up with their cows and pails of milk. After the morning meal, the soldiers bathed, polished their weapons and armour and then set about matching their skills against each other. Chandra, warned by Chanakya not to reveal himself too soon – there was a time for everything, as Chanakya always said – would spend most of his time with the horses. The fabled Arabians in Alexander's army were a joy to ride and Chandra did so every morning, riding out far, sometimes towards the desolate Makran ranges west of their camp. Beyond the ranges stretched the desert and many rivers lay further east. He would often explore the area and try to catch a glimpse of the desert beyond the ranges. Standing tall with his horse among the craggy boulders, Chandra knew Alexander would have to take a decision soon. A decision made harder by the fact that many of his soldiers were now sullenly making their resentment clear. They had had enough of conquests.

By early afternoon Chandra would return to camp after his work with the horses. Sometimes he would also practice his javelin throwing skills with the tribesmen of the area who had thrown in their lot with Alexander. Around this time, the big tent at the corner of the encampment would turn into a huge kitchen. Chanakya would also appear then and he would exchange a conspiratorial grin with Chandra. Chanakya had offered to translate Alexander's message to the rest of the kingdoms, the story of his life and his many conquests into the languages of the east – Prakrit and Magadhi, in the hope that this would compel other rulers in the east to bend before Alexander.

But both Chandra and Chanakya knew this was all a pretext; this work gave Chanakya a chance to work on his own scrolls, passing on his own message among Alexander's soldiers about the brave prince of Magadha who would soon challenge its tyrant ruler. It was all done discreetly – the message was passed on to a few soldiers and then after some days, to other groups. They knew that for now they had to play an elaborate game of waiting and watching.

As for Bharata, he had become elusive these days. He was with soldiers of his kind, showing off and perfecting his own sparring skills. When Chandra came across him, Bharata would nod and fill him in with information he had gathered – of the many soldiers who comprised Alexander's army, whom among them were the disaffected, the rumours they were privy to, and Alexander's own health.

'He is getting angrier by the day,' whispered Bharata, as they stood before the trays of flatbread and vats of steaming curry one afternoon. 'He wants to go on. This area offers little wealth. But it's hard to go on beyond this point and he's finding it difficult to persuade his soldiers otherwise.'

Yet supplied by the adjoining villages and the herds who lived around, Alexander's soldiers always had the best of food – cattle was also sacrificed every day and birds were hunted down in the dozens. Walking in their midst, carefully nonchalant but very curious, Chandra could see these things for himself – that the soldiers were indeed all exhausted with the warring and some desperately needed rest.

An emperor's army lived by its own set of rules, framed as the men marched along, especially when the men came from varied regions and each had their own customs. 'It is a state on the move,' said Chanakya. Chandra knew that Chanakya was as fascinated as he was. 'And rules have to be made. If the king or his advisers fail...'

He was careful to keep his voice low. Any word, for they could easily be overheard, could be misconstrued as being against Alexander. Their presence had been accepted by the soldiers grudgingly, and any small error on their part could cost them their lives. So Chanakya went on, casting a careful look around, 'If kings and their armies fail, they have largely themselves to blame. An army that marches needs rules to live by, just as much as those who fight wars.'

During such afternoons, the area near the kitchen would be bursting with soldiers. There was a clear hierarchy in how the meal arrangements were made. The Macedonian and Greek soldiers were served first. Laughing raucously and swarming as a vast, unruly crowd, they dipped ladles into the steaming vats; some leaned over, their sweat and saliva flowing freely, as if they had been starving for days. The Persians and other men from the hills watched in barely concealed contempt but when it was their turn before the vats, they reached out just as greedily. Their weapons lay by their sides, amulets and armbands clashed and rang out every time they bent towards their plates.

'With soldiers, there is always the risk of disaffection,' said Chanakya. 'It is very difficult to keep soldiers happy – some of them are not warriors by birth. They could be farmers and hunters, so at best they are only half-hearted soldiers. That is why a state needs its own army – professional and committed. A king must provide for a regular, properly maintained army in which the soldiers are given a salary. The source of the money is the taxes imposed on farming, on forests, on trade. From the state, and for the state.'

It was a conversation that even Bharata had been privy to, and as Chanakya paused to take a breath, Bharata leaned forward to interpose. Chanakya bristled for he especially did not take kindly to interruptions.

'It would be nice to always be a soldier, and not forage for a living as a mercenary,' Bharata said, his voice fading as he dreamt of better days.

There was that same flash of wariness in Chanakya's eyes that Chandra had noted before, like the time they realized that Bharata spoke Koine Greek, the language spoken by Alexander and his elite group of soldiers. It was different from the irritation Chanakya had expressed whenever Bharata spoke out of turn or too impetuously. Now Chanakya looked away, gathering himself before he went on, 'The mercenary is soulless, he is not above committing treachery – against emperor, state…' and this time there was a distinct pause before Chanakya went on, '…and friend. In the end, the state is what matters, and it is represented by the emperor. He protects the state, defends and kills for it because it is his duty. It is not a question of his survival, but the survival of the state.'

Chandra looked down at his meal, knowing Chanakya was passing on a subtle hint about Bharata. He was useful in getting them information about Alexander's army but his loquaciousness could get them into trouble.

There were some days when Alexander did not emerge from his tent; he was ensconced with his advisers and commanders, thinking up strategy and ways to convince his army about the campaigns that still lay ahead. Some days, he went out hunting as he had done the first day when Chandra and his two companions had joined the camp.

In spite of Chanakya's advice, Chandra found himself growing impatient. He was exasperated at the fact that he was unable to approach Alexander directly. He longed to burst into Alexander's tent and blurt out truths he knew for certain – that the army was now disenchanted with his conquests and they needed a new leader, one who knew the land. But for now, as Chanakya readied his scrolls and the message moved on among the different groups of soldiers, Chandra explored the encampment.

There was one late afternoon when he stopped to observe the beginnings of an impromptu contest among some of the soldiers. A group had challenged another to throw a spear the farthest and so prove their prowess. Remembering Chanakya's warning that he mustn't show off his skills and attract attention, though he longed to, Chandra watched the proceedings before walking on with a practiced indifference, making his way through the assembled soldiers and their living quarters. Some of them could be his soldiers one day; Chanakya's scrolls would do their work, of that Chandra was certain. If the soldiers looked up with suspicion and hostility as he passed them, it was soon allayed for Chandra was alone and most likely unarmed. No one knew of the dagger he always carried close to his waistband.

It was a long time later, as the sun was setting, and before the night fires were lit, that he realized he had reached the very end of the camp. Standing at the edge of the forest, Chandra looked back at the camp enveloped in a smoky haze; it was as if it did not exist. A flimsy dream that could easily be blown away by harsh winds.

He heard his own breath, and realized his legs would not hold him much longer. He lay there, on a dry patch of grass, with the low rocks nearby, and the hills not too far away. In the distance, he could hear the laughter, the shouts that seemed farther and farther away as he lay very still. He was sinking into a languor. The grass now felt surprisingly soft as the sounds drifted away. He told himself he would get up soon and make his way back to the camp but was unable to make the effort. His eyes were closing and the last thing he remembered was seeing the clouds drifting past and how one of them seemed to resemble an elephant.

Later, when questioned by the awestruck and mystified soldiers, Chandra would say that he did not remember. For he had barely closed his eyes when he imagined that the lion he had saved had come looking for him. It no longer limped with pain. And like the boatmen who had been his companions, the camel-herders he had left behind and the forest bandits who had given them their trust, the lion too, was now part of his army in his fight against the Nandas. He flinched, for the lion's breath was hot and felt like a heavy cloud on his face. It was like the heat from the campfires leaping up for a final surge before dying out. The animal's breath stayed hot on his face, and he felt the touch of a raspy tongue on his cheek.

That was when he opened his eyes and saw the lion above him. He was sure it was the one he had saved. Whiskers tickled his nose roughly and abrasively ran against his cheek as he felt himself enveloped in animal warmth. He looked into tawny golden eyes. He heard a low humming noise to his side and turned his head – to see that there were at least five more lions, and young cubs too. He wasn't sure if the strangled sound he heard was his own or the lion's. He felt himself burn, his breath turning to steam, the dew now rising on his skin as if it were sweat before he realized it was something else altogether.

The lion's scaly tongue was hot on his neck, its whiskers trailing on Chandra's skin. Its tongue felt raspy, the touch abrasive yet lingering, and Chandra felt the fear leave him. The heavy paw brushed against his chest but, as if the lion knew that it could hurt Chandra, it lifted it aside. The beast lowered its head, its breath heavy and hard, and Chandra had the sensation of an immense rock hovering over him, dangerous, yet casting a protective shade. Its rough mane moved against Chandra's face one last time, leaving him with a scent of the forests that stretched all around and beyond the encampment.

All animals smelled almost the same, he realized. They smelled of the earth and of death and life. Morning was breaking, taking its time, blue spreading where the blackness of night had stretched before. He had spent the whole night here. The lions left slowly, congregating in a group as if they realized morning had come. In place of the hot breath Chandra had felt earlier, the cool air of the morning was now cold on his face.

He rose to his feet slowly and then heard the shuffle of feet behind him. A group of soldiers had been watching him and the lions from a distance. Now that he was alone they had come forward and the air was alive with tension.

They were soldiers from Alexander's Greek army. Men from the dry islands, close to the mainland, bodies hardened by the sea, the uncaring and changing climates of the lands they had traversed upon and the long battles they had fought – against conquerors from the north; against the enemy kings from the Persian kingdoms; against the pirates who roamed the seas. The power that came from destroying, killing, pillaging at will, had gone to their heads. But now they looked at him, their faces showing stunned surprise. They made no effort to hide their admiration. But he also noted the hostility on a few faces. A couple of soldiers, hidden in the small crowd, who were of shorter build and had thicker beards, had their eyes trained on him in a manner Chandra had learned to recognize. He gave nothing away, grinning indifferently as he walked away, his senses alert to every danger.

When he reached the camp, he did not tell Chanakya about the lions but it didn't matter; Chanakya was preoccupied.

'We should be even more careful now,' Chanakya said abruptly.

'Isn't that what we have been all this while?' Chandra asked in amazement.

Chanakya looked around in his usual cautious way, before he said, 'The scrolls are now bound to draw attention. They will convince the soldiers who are wavering and want to leave. But the others will be warned,' his lips twisted cynically before he went on, 'perhaps helped by our very talkative friend, and they will alert Alexander. So we must act fast. It has been some days after all. Apart from the soldiers who will pledge to fight for us against the Nandas, we can gather our vast army now. The cattle-herders, the animal-tamers, the sword-fighters, the farmers.'

He paused and then Chandra spoke, his voice so hushed that Chanakya had to lean forward to listen. 'I saw some unfamiliar faces, but clearly from the east, from Magadha. They were trying to blend in, but I sense danger. We can still play our cards well and get out soon. The boats are still moored on the banks.'

Chanakya nodded quickly. His face betrayed nothing as he gazed towards Alexander's tent, its yellow flag gleaming in the sun. 'He may have lost a bit of his heart, and some of his hunger. But they are all still his soldiers. Hungry, untamed soldiers. We can use all of them. We must have our scrolls reach them all in the time we have left.'

Slowly, they walked around the camp, dropping newly written scrolls, discreetly among the tents they had learned were inhabited by unhappy soldiers. On their return, they chanced upon two men hurling maces at each other in mock battle. Chandra stopped to watch, his interest returning automatically.

'I didn't know these soldiers could use the mace or that they prefer it to their spears and swords. They don't know how to use their weapons properly.'

'Let them be,' scoffed Chanakya with some contempt. 'Some of his soldiers do seem to be untrained. That's hardly the way armies should be organized.'

'They can be of use to us,' Chandra said thoughtfully. They were close enough to the two men now to see that the maces they wielded were light in weight and had spikes on their surface. 'That can be painful.'

Chanakya nodded. 'It can drive elephants mad. These are the men from the mountains, they are light on their feet. They know about small battles, and would prove to be useful soldiers for quick assaults. But they will not suffer the arduousness and sacrifice that long wars need; they will give up during a long siege. Also, they are men of fickle loyalty.'

The same thought was racing through their minds. Pataliputra – the capital of Magadha – with its walls of stone, would be difficult to take. The hills on its three sides made the city almost impregnable.

'We will have to try another strategy to get into Pataliputra. The usual way of storming the fort won't work,' mused Chandra, his eyes on the contest.

They paused as someone else came up to take the place of one of the men wielding the mace. The newcomer looked very different. He had pale golden, cropped hair, kept in check with a head band, and looked near to Chandra's age. The slender newcomer, however, proved totally ineffectual with the mace, and grinned unrepentantly as Chandra and Chanakya came nearer.

'Oh, I will never get to be a soldier – weapons forget what they are meant for in my hands...'

He spoke Greek, a language no longer unfamiliar to Chandra owing to his days in the camp. The newcomer had an open, friendly manner, and even his whining had a tinge of the comic. Chandra smiled involuntarily at the other man's humour.

'It is such a waste of time fighting. I would rather travel and see interesting things,' the newcomer continued. He would have gone on had not someone shouted, 'It's time for the hunt. Get ready, all of you.'

The man shrugged. 'See, there is always some action or the other. Say, aren't you the one who played with the lions in the morning?'

Chandra smiled wryly, not just at the man's infectious friendliness but at the fanciful way the man constantly changed topics. The man went on, now more enthusiastic than ever, 'I was always curious about lions; they aren't really the scary creatures they are meant to be. For example, the people of the Nile worshipped them. Can you worship creatures you are afraid of?'

Chanakya replied in clipped tones, 'You worship them because you hope they will use the same frightening power to protect you.'

His voice was drowned in the thunder of hooves as a group of men riding horses came rushing out of the camp. One of the horsemen swiped the friendly newcomer on the head as he rode past, sending the young man sprawling to the ground.

'Megasthenes, no one can ever make a soldier out of you.'

The young man grinned, his eyes crinkling up and creases appearing all over his face. He shook the earth out of his eyes and hair. 'Who wants to be a soldier anyway?' He called out to the disappearing cloud of dust the horsemen had left behind but they did not hear him. 'There are always too many of them and too little to do.'

Chandra took a last look at the blond Greek, who was still tossing the mace into the air and completely missing it on its return. Then he yelled out to Chandra – 'Megasthenes. That's what I'm called.'

'I am Chandra.'

'That's a short name for a brave man who battled lions.'

Chandra stared at Megasthenes. He found himself liking this young warrior – who was not really one – despite Chanakya's misgivings. 'Then you can call me Chandragupta,' he said first to himself and then again, loudly.

They were walking back to their tent when a soldier stopped by them. 'The emperor wants to see you.'

They did not look at each other, but Chandra knew that Chanakya shared his thoughts. Had the news about the scrolls reached Alexander and was he now suspicious of them? Chandra noticed the lines on Chanakya's face, his deeply worried look as they were escorted to Alexander's tent, led by soldiers who held their spears and swords menacingly high. Then Chandra realized that Bharata was missing, and had been for some time now – he knew then that something was very wrong.

13

THE TRAITOR WHO WASN'T

Alexander's tent was bigger than the others, and well-guarded. Men drawn from all of Alexander's conquered territories made up the special legions under the emperor's command. There were those of short stature who were lean and had inscrutable slanting, almond eyes; others who were taller and golden-haired; and some of Persian origin who looked on with open hostility.

The guards formed a column as they neared the tent.

'They are here,' announced a tall, broad-shouldered man who had a mean smile on his face.

The tent wings parted for Chanakya and Chandra to enter. It took them some time to get used to the darkness inside the tent. Candles burned in beautiful stone urns, soft carpets covered the ground and the air was redolent with a pleasing fragrance. Alexander had collected perfumes from Persia and Egypt, whose rulers were known for their fine aesthetic sense. Chandra saw the tic beating in Chanakya's cheek, a sign of his worry, but his own resolve to face the situation only grew stronger every moment. He wondered again where Bharata could be.

Alexander rose from the tub behind them. He walked half-naked to the divan, his body lit up by the candles. Droplets of water that fell on the floor turned to gold and silver by candlelight.

He waved at them, and it was Chandra who stepped forward.

The emperor grinned, then he spoke in Aramaic again, assuming that Chanakya and Chandra still could not understand any Greek. 'So you, brave warrior, are the one they sent to assassinate me?'

Chanakya spoke up quietly and firmly, 'There has been a misunderstanding. We came to advise you about the situation in the east.'

'I was not talking to you,' said the emperor in a lazy voice, but there was no mistaking the menace in it.

Chanakya stiffened and Alexander burst out laughing. It was the laugh of a man who was in control, a man who could twist fate to his own command – who feared nothing.

'I think there should be an agreement between the two of you about who will make the confession.'

Chandra did not look at Chanakya but spoke up boldly. Suddenly he had a vision of the lion staring down at him, its breath hot on his face, and it filled him with courage.

'No, sire. We came to tell you that should you wish to do so, the time to advance is now. The ruler in the east is weak, his strength built up on rumours.'

Before he could finish, there was a burst of activity outside. The curtains were shoved aside roughly and sunlight flooded the tent. Alexander rose to his feet in anger. He was immediately surrounded by his soldiers.

'Sire, a thousand apologies. But it's a conspiracy. They are from the east and can weave a spell with their words.'

Chandra.

From the midst of the soldiers, Chandra heard a familiar, but weak voice. He felt waves of relief and a raw fear. He almost ran to Bharata but Chanakya's hand reached out to hold Chandra by the wrist.

'Ask this man, sire. He comes from the camp of the prince of

Gandhara. The man whose father you defeated – and released honourably. He was found skulking around your tent at night. Said he was looking for someone.'

Then another voice rose, 'A sword was found on him and a scroll, that had poison on it. It turned Polonius's hands blue when he opened it.'

'Sire,' said Bharata, panting heavily. 'I am a warrior and can explain my actions. Please let me speak.'

But Bharata was flung to the ground and the Greek soldiers stepped forcefully on him. The sound of leather on skin made a terrifying noise within the closed confines of the tent.

'So if he is a traitor, a conspirator – who are they?' Alexander asked, glancing towards where the two of them stood. 'Are they with you? I understand some inflammatory messages have been passed among my soldiers.'

Alexander's eyes glittered as he looked at the three of them in turn. Bharata did not reply. Chanakya held on to Chandra's hand, pressing it tightly.

'Are they with you? Answer the emperor, traitor!'

The soldiers prodded Bharata's chin with their feet, but now his eyes gave nothing away, his face bathed in sweat and blood.

'Are they with you?' barked a soldier again and kicked him hard on the head.

'Sire, you did not treat King Porus like that!' burst out Chandra, his hand on his dagger. He was called Puru in these parts, but soldiers from the west, Alexander's men, called him Porus.

Alexander looked at Chandra with surprise. 'Ah! But the King Porus was no traitor.' He lifted his hand to forestall the soldiers who had made to rush towards Chandra.

'You may have had an encounter with the lions, but you forget who you stand before now. If I had my way, I could have you beheaded. You could meet the same fate as this traitor. He was, after all, found with a traitor's message on him.' He gestured at Bharata, his armband slipping down to catch the light from the tapers.

'Take him away!'

'Sire…'

Chandra turned to look at his friend one last time, at his wounded, terribly ravaged face, the tears mingling with sweat and blood. As Bharata was pulled away, he gathered his strength and spoke up, his voice cracked and ravaged with pain.

'You…you invaded our land, and your soldiers ravaged it. I had to take revenge. These men…these two, they don't even understand how you have begun to destroy our land!'

He was breathless by the time he finished. For one moment, his gaze met Chandra's but it was clear Bharata saw nothing for his eyes no longer focused on anything in particular. But he would never expose his friend, and the realization stabbed at Chandra's heart.

'Sire,' Chandra looked towards Alexander, making no effort to hide his anger, 'this man is a warrior. He would not behave like a common traitor.'

'You speak well for your friend, who has only incriminated himself,' Alexander rose to look at him now. They were the same height, and Chandra saw his own eyes, dark with anger, reflected in the hazy green of the emperor's before the latter turned away. 'I like a brave man,' said the conqueror. 'So, believe me, even if my men here bayed for your blood, I would let you be. The world needs more men like you.'

Alexander looked out absently, his attention drawn to the laughter he heard outside.

Chanakya picked that moment to deliver a hurried warning to Chandra. 'Enough, you really can't do more. Do nothing to spoil your cause.'

But Alexander spoke up, 'Tell me more about the lions – I want to hear it from you.'

He leaned back on the couch, waving to an attendant to fan him. It was as though he was totally indifferent to the fact that he had just sealed a man's fate. Chandra wondered how much a king could bother himself with the consequences of his actions. Or were his actions guided solely by what his people wanted?

'A few lions found me alone in the morning,' Chandra answered vaguely. He remembered the smell of the lions and felt his courage surge once more. Courage, he knew, would never fail him if he thought of the lions.

'Yes, you did,' said Alexander, his voice quiet as he made his admiration obvious, 'That is how a conquest should be. That you win over a creature, anything, even land, not by force…but something else…'

His face took on a preoccupied look as he searched for the right word and then they were interrupted. A small band of soldiers rushed into the tent at that moment. They bowed low, falling in a neat line at Alexander's feet. 'It is all prepared, sire.'

'The stake has been set up for the traitor,' said another. 'We are waiting for your orders. It will teach traitors amidst us a lesson.'

Chandra drew in his breath, and Chanakya nudged him quietly. Bharata had not really come with the mission to kill, or had he? Chandra realized he did not really know his friend. Had Bharata deceived him all along? Or had he played a lone hand to keep him, Chandra, safe?

At that moment, Chandra realized another truth – he was impressed by Alexander but not overawed. A king was bound to the loyalty he commanded from his men, and this in turn constrained his decisions. Alexander's men wanted Bharata to die and it was a show of their power that Alexander had acquiesced to. How free then was a king, even with all his power? Chandra asked himself this question as they followed Alexander out of the tent.

The sight that met their eyes was enough to make him feel sick. A scaffold had been erected hurriedly. A thick rope dangled from the top, shaped into a noose. A crowd had gathered to watch the proceedings. Bharata had been stripped and was being urged to crawl towards the scaffold. Bent on all fours like an animal, he was kicked and whipped by the soldiers in total abandon, some of them shouting, 'Come, let us see how far you can go. Let us see.' He was bleeding profusely. The guttural sounds he made each time he was kicked were painful and elemental. The crowd roared when they saw Bharata being dragged forward.

Chandra turned his eyes away. He wished his friend would be put to death soon so his misery could end.

'Quiet!' loud voices rang out, failing to silence the crowd once and for all. And yet with every pause in the din, they could hear Bharata's low moans.

'Listen! The emperor shall speak now.'

Alexander stood near the scaffold, smiling and waving. The gestures of an emperor had taken over the man and it seemed an effortless transition from the decisive general he was known to be, the soldier who respected every warrior and even the curious man who had asked Chandra about the lions. It was as if Alexander could change face any time he wanted, as the situation demanded. One of Alexander's advisers whispered in the emperor's ear. His voice carried clearly in the silence – 'He is a traitor, sire. And we must teach all traitors a lesson.'

'A traitor. Yes, indeed.' Alexander nodded, a grim expression came over his face. His eyes assumed a stony, imperious look. Then he raised his hand, and his words carried far, his gaze ran over his advisers and the crowd, but it seemed to Chandra that he did not really see anyone. 'A traitor is a coward. A man who can stab you in the back. He corrupts bravery by his very presence.'

'No. No!' said Chandra but the cheering of the crowd drowned out his lone protest. He thought of the spear that had whizzed past him that evening in the hermitage in Viratnagara. Only he had seen its force, and no one else would ever remember it. He steeled himself as he watched his half-dead friend being dragged to his feet. Bharata was made to raise his arm and shout, 'Long live Alexander!'

But his strength was ebbing out fast. 'Long live...but not...' was all Bharata could manage, defiant to the last, before he was kicked in the mouth, viciously and repeatedly. His head dropped limply onto his chest. The silence of the long dreadful moments later was broken by a voice that rang out above the crowd.

'The man is already dead, he cannot...'

Chandra had no idea it was his own voice. It was only when the enraged crowd turned to him that he realized he had spoken. He said angrily, 'You are like hyenas now, dancing over the dead.'

He saw the mad hatred in every eye now; faces that had lost all compassion. He felt singed by their hot breath. But even in their murderous rage, the men were civilized enough to realize whose orders they obeyed. It was Alexander who raised his hand to still the men.

'Listen!'

Almost miraculously, a hush fell over that crowd of angry, seething men. Chandra saw the value of a king's power then – by his sheer presence he could hold a crowd at bay and bend it to his will.

'Listen, you are courageous men. Brave warriors. Never forget that.'

Alexander's voice rose effortlessly over the crowd of soldiers. Chandra felt the rage among the men subside. The hot angry waves no longer swelled and heaved around him. He met Alexander's gaze over the crowd. The soldiers between them were on their knees before the emperor, submitting to his authority. Alexander stood on a mound of raised earth, his body covered by the thinnest of robes, which was fluttering in the light breeze. The afternoon sunlight bathed everyone in a welcome warmth, shining upon the dusty tents and the flag high over the emperor's tent. The sky's only occupant was a lone kite.

Once Alexander saw that the men were under control, the grim look came over his face again. Then he said with some finality.

'Kill him. But don't get distracted. You are soldiers, so choose your battles well.'

He stepped down from the knoll, the crowds making way for him as he returned to his tent.

'It's hot,' Chandra heard him muttering as he passed by him. Alexander held himself ramrod straight and yet, just before he stepped into his tent, his body relaxed. Perhaps the peaceful darkness inside was a relief, allowing Alexander to let down his guard. For in that single moment before the excitement surged through the crowd again, Chandra's eyes met his through the thin gauze curtain. Alexander looked angry, and then helpless, knowing the bloodlust that surged through his men's veins could hardly be controlled – even by him, the world's greatest conqueror. The next moment he turned away from Chandra, and hurled away a wine glass that was being offered to him. The hollow metallic sound it made as it struck the wooden pole inside the tent was drowned by his men's shouts.

The loud protests were unending, echoing their disappointment as they converged on Bharata. 'The man is already dead!'

Chandra held up his hand and shouted, 'Stop!'

A few soldiers who made up the outer circle around Bharata stepped back in surprise. Their hesitation was noticeable.

'Stop. He is already dead. You will get no pleasure now. Your victory is complete.'

He raised his hand and looked everyone squarely in the eye. It forced them to lower their gaze. In disparate groups, they began to slink away with heads bowed. From the shrieking above, Chandra knew the vultures had already gathered.

'We must give him an honourable farewell,' said Chandra. Chanakya nodded in agreement.

The soldiers moved away, muttering curses at being deprived of their fun. In a matter of miraculous moments, there was no one left at the scaffold. The sounds of the camp returned. It was as if the violence of a short while ago had never happened. Someone broke into song somewhere, then came the sound of weapons being sharpened and water being poured. Forgetting was easier than feeling shame.

Chandra pulled down the poles and undid the knots of twine binding Bharata's hands and feet. His body – broken, bare and bloodied – was difficult to lift. And then he saw Bharata blink, taking long moments to shape his mouth to form words. Chandra, his heart quavering painfully, leaned closer, unobtrusively, wary of drawing attention from passersby. There was something Bharata wanted to say to him.

'Your time...is now. He will soon be deserted. Take his men.'

Bharata's words died away and his heart beat one last time. Chandra ran a hand over his forehead, stilled his eyes, and saw a calm expression on his friend's face. He had not died a traitor but a warrior...and a friend.

He covered the body with his own upper robe and then, as he made to lift Bharata over his shoulder, he was, to his surprise, joined by a few others. A couple of soldiers and then one or two more had drifted out quietly from their tents, and now extended their help to Chandra.

'He was our friend too,' one of them said, his words muffled for his upper robe covered the lower half of his face and the evening had spread a shadow over his features. 'We are men of the Makran, O prince, and have your message. But you must get away fast, while the revelry is still on.'

The encampment was some distance behind but they could hear the raucous laughter of soldiers who were now celebrating – with a drunken feast – their capture of a traitor. The men with Chandra did their work quietly. They stacked some wood into a pile, and withdrew a short distance as Chandra placed his friend on it and lit the fire.

'Did he deserve such a death?' Chandra asked Chanakya as the bier caught fire, the flames rising greedily.

Staring thoughtfully at the burning body, Chanakya took a long while to reply.

'You can never choose when you will die, but you can choose the manner of your death. And he died a warrior. He did not fail himself.'

They stood there until the flames had died away, leaving but a handful of ashes. Chandra felt the dryness on his own skin, as if his friend's soul had seeped into him. The vultures stood still, not too far away, looking on with beady, hooded eyes.

Chandra realized that it was Bharata's death – an unnecessary one – that had affected him more than the meeting with Alexander. A king could have stopped the torture. Alexander should not have appeased the evil in his soldiers' minds. Death offered no solution when it came to evil intent. A king with his sense of justice should have known that. Chandragupta would be a far better emperor than Alexander, who was a world conqueror but no king.

14

ESCAPE

'It is a matter of strategy,' Chanakya said, a few hours later. The darkness of night stretched into purple and dawn could break any time now. It was the time soldiers and sentries relaxed their guard. It was also the time they had chosen to leave Alexander's camp.

'Why do people prefer living in kingdoms more than republics?' Chandra thought to himself as he kept guard. He provided his own answer – because more than equality, men prefer order and will be loyal to a ruler who imposes it. Why do we worship God? Or believe someone else has the answer to our salvation? It's because we want to believe, to give our faith and loyalty to deserving people. Everyone hopes for a settled, more certain life – if not God, a king will ensure it in His stead.

He stretched out on the boat. The soldier, Gawdar, who had fervently promised his help after Bharata's funeral, had been waiting for them, having snapped the boat's moorings and rowed with the boatman a short distance upriver so as not to arouse suspicion. The boats were counted every morning and would not be missed for now. Chanakya and Chandra had waded and then swum towards it, wincing as the cold water struck their bodies, struggling hard to ensure the precious scrolls which were wrapped up in rough cloth, stayed dry. Gawdar had left, assuring them that he and his fellow soldiers, around twenty in number, would soon leave camp and join them in Taxila, for that was the nearest city where Chandra and Chanakya intended to go next.

Right now it was crucial that they put as much distance as possible between them and Alexander's camp, which was teeming with suspicious soldiers who, once their heads had cleared of drink, would be on the lookout for them.

Chandra stared up at the starlit sky, his hair lifting in the breeze, often brushing his face. He must have drifted off; it had been a long night. A soft scratching against the wood followed by the sound of something falling woke him. In the manner he had learnt from his days in the forest, he let the outside world seep quietly into his senses so that he would not be taken by surprise. Beside him, Chanakya slept, sitting up, head resting on his raised knees. From the corner of his eye Chandra saw the shadow of the boatman, whose head had dropped onto his chest. He heard a low moan of pain, noticed the spear that had neatly pierced the boatman's back and felt the boat's quiet movements.

He was on his feet in a flash, just as the soldier's head bobbed above the boat's prow. Their departure from the encampment had not gone unnoticed. He did not hesitate, reaching out to pull the spear that had struck the boatman. When the man leapt on board, Chandra spun around and swung the spear into him. It was over in a matter of seconds. The attacker fell over the boat, the cold spray of water splashing against Chandra's face and clothes. He stood still, feet planted apart, waiting for the boat's violent shaking to subside.

Chanakya had woken up during the struggle, startled. Their eyes followed the dead assassin now being swiftly borne away by the currents. The corpse, caught against sharp rocks, was tossed and lifted, making for an eerie sight in the dark murky waters. Chandra saw his teacher step towards the murdered boatman.

Chanakya chanted his last mantras for the dead and dying. Then they tipped the boatman's body into the river and he too was gone, carried away in moments.

Chandra realized he was getting more inured to death.

'Destiny has a say in what happens. And there is a pattern to all this,' explained Chanakya tersely, looking up at the stars. He was trying to gauge their position to find the quickest route to their destination.

They had decided to sail upstream from the encampment, knowing that in a matter of a few hours, before the sun appeared, they would have to leave it far behind. They changed their plan and aimed at reaching Pushkaravati first. Taxila was not too far away either, but for now, it reeked of danger. Pushkaravati, on the other hand, was closer to the mountains, and it was a city with magical narrow passes that led through to the mountains on the other side. Chandra felt a shiver of excitement, for there the mountains were majestic, with crevasses that cut so deep they reached the very heart of the earth. In the hidden caves were sages and monks who had perhaps been meditating there for centuries, aloof from the world, away from every material attachment.

'We can disappear more easily in Pushkaravati,' Chanakya was saying. 'Taxila is more settled and orderly. If anyone is following us, and they are sure to, Taxila is not the right place. It is full of people. Besides, they will never think we have gone up to Pushkaravati.'

He waited, watching the smile play on Chandra's lips. 'Yes, and that is where we wait. But not for long. The soldiers deserting Alexander will be sure to make their way to Taxila soon. Soldiers left hungry and unpaid for too long. Soldiers who know of our message and will be waiting. And that is the time when we make our move.'

'Do you need help?' A high-pitched voice called out to them as they travelled down the track to Pushkaravati. The call came again, in Old Persian and then in Aramaic. Chandra stared as a young man made himself visible in the drooping branches of the deodar trees not too far away. Flocks of goats and sheep were milling around below the tree.

'My village is beyond that hill,' the youth pointed. They walked towards him and in no time, the goats and sheep were all around them, their jostling creating a welcome warmth.

'What are you doing here in the trees?' Chandra asked.

'I keep looking out for soldiers,' said the young man. 'We faced a terrible drought some seasons ago so many of our men left to join Alexander. They are now returning; there are others with them too. We heard that the plans for an invasion to the east have been put off. It will never happen. But the soldiers think differently…'

'Oh!' Chandra said. 'Why do they think so?'

The watcher in the trees lowered his voice, 'The word is that Alexander has lost heart. We are travelling herdsmen and know these stories. My friends had a glimpse of him – he is spent from his efforts in trying to convince his men to advance. And some of his own men have already decided to leave…'

Chandra let the young man's words rush over him. He sensed Chanakya's quick intake of breath, his stiffened stance telling him he was excited too.

'See, those scrolls have had an effect,' Chanakya whispered to him.

The young man gave them water to drink from his skin carrier. Chanakya drank first and then Chandra bent forward, his hair sweeping away from his back as he cupped his hands for the water. His upper garment slipped off his shoulder at that moment, exposing the moon birthmark for an instant.

'The lost prince of Magadha,' breathed the young man. He looked unblinkingly at Chandra. 'They are all looking for him now. The one who left behind the secret messages. The one who will march east, carry out exploits that Alexander did not dare to try. The prince who was exiled and who will march now to claim what is rightly his, to oust the tyrant Nanda.'

So in the secret, haphazard, magical way messages spread, this bit of news was now everywhere. Chandra heard the younger man's words and saw Chanakya's lips twist in triumph. The time for war truly seemed near.

There were shouts coming from the village, calling for the young man. He raised a horn to his lips and blew in reassurance. 'They think,' he said wryly, 'that I am a wastrel and a daydreamer. But I just dream of a better life, that of a soldier's.' He looked at them with fire in his eyes. 'There are others in my tribe who want to do that too. But our fathers and grandfathers, who have always lived a nomadic life, won't hear of it. While we long for settled lives in a king's army.'

He looked from one to the other, a gleam appearing again in his brown flecked eyes before he lowered them respectfully. 'Prince of Magadha, I assure you of my loyalty always.'

From the distance, the shout came again, rising up and down with the dust that swirled. 'These are my friends, we are the Paktyans of this region,' the youth said. 'You can trust them. And our small tribe in this land, where tribes pass each other every new season, can spread your word in secret. We have our own tattoo and drum signals, and we own the very air around us.'

Chanakya cleared his throat. It was evident he approved. As they walked towards the group now advancing towards them, Chandra heard him say almost to himself, 'And thus from small rebellions are big ones created.'

The Paktyan elders of the council, however, were more wary. It was Chandra who had to convince them. He stood tall in the open assembly, held under the chinar trees, holding his spear by his side. His voice rang clear and strong – he knew the moment he had been preparing for was near.

'We live in chaos and in times of great danger,' he said, with Chanakya looking on. 'We have to think of the future beyond our own communities. Alexander taught us that a big empire offers us so much more. More security, ease of movement and a better life in the end. When he leaves, there will be anarchy, chaos and an utter void. People used to a settled way of life will find disruption of their peace. There will be more violence and evil than before. Even those who want to continue,' he said slowly, looking around the crowd of assembled elders, 'with their old ways of life may find it too late.'

'What do you want us to do then, Prince of Magadha?' said the oldest – a half-blind man with grey eyes – in a tone of pleading mixed with sarcasm. They were proud men who had braved harsh conditions throughout their lives; who had seen the terrible cruelties man could inflict on his fellow beings.

'You can continue your old ways. But give us your men as soldiers – your own who have returned from Alexander's army. And in a time of peace, you will have the king's protection to live alongside your flocks and herds.'

Everyone in the council, even the veiled women standing at the back, looked at the old chief, Chandra's words dimming the hostility in their eyes. The nods were slow to come but Chandra saw them everywhere and tried to hide his triumph.

'All right,' said the man who had first spoken, 'we pledge our loyalty to you. But remember, it is a risk we are taking.'

'A risk,' interposed Chanakya, 'that is worth taking. This is a choice we make in the interest of the future generations. We want to restore Magadha to its most glorious state, restore it to its rightful claimant and remove that debauched weakling who rules there now. There can be no going back.'

15

TAXILA

That night, the sound of drumbeats reverberated across the high mountains. The tribe that had so willingly offered them shelter and loyalty was now sending messages to their fellow tribesmen – to prepare for an important event. In the morning, a messenger would ride across with directives from the elders.

Many years ago, Chandra thought, he too had been part of a tribe, a tribe whose unity had been broken – in part by his parents' loyalty to each other, a loyalty so deep that it had antagonized the others. But now Chandra's words had brought closer the tribe who had pledged their loyalty to him – he had seen it in the nods of agreement among the people who had gathered at the assembly. The decision made by the elders was unanimous and in the tribe's best interests.

'When the time comes, we shall be ready,' said the chief. He looked old and weary in contrast to the excited and eager young people at the gathering.

'You have unleashed a keenness in them, even while there is danger,' said the old chief. 'But there is a time when the future is so near that you have to step in…with anticipation. I think the time for that is now.'

The Paktyans gave them two of their best horses to carry them to Taxila. 'They are of the finest Arabian breed,' said the young men proudly. 'These horses are in great demand in Taxila and in the east. They were given to us by merchants in return for escorting them to safety to the plains farther east. They are faster than elephants, and easier to train.'

'Our men and those from other tribes will follow you,' said the old Paktyan chief as he came up to them before they were to leave. 'But Taxila is King Puru's city. A large group of armed men will cause alarm. King Puru, and he is quite troubled these days, has never meant us harm. His son gives him no peace, and his own people are angry with him. He surrendered. And now Alexander's army demands too much. You, prince of Magadha, have every answer and we place our trust in you.'

In the chief's words, and in the expressions of all those gathered around, Chandra knew there was no mistaking his role now. He was riding to Taxila as a challenger, a power in his own right, and claimant to the throne of Magadha. Chandragupta – that was the name they would call him. The name in which the message of unity had gone out. He could now look onward to his future.

Chanakya's expression lightened as they neared Taxila. It was the city he had grown up in; he had taught at its famed university before ambition had taken him east towards Magadha, the land of his father.

They came across caravans and other travellers on the way to Taxila. The road was no longer a dusty rough track, but wide and lined by trees and wells. There were outposts where horses, camels and weary travellers could rest. At places they stopped at to rest, they heard the same story – a once thriving city was now almost on its knees thanks to the war and Alexander's conquest.

'Some of the caravans are stopped by his soldiers,' a merchant said, 'who pay us nothing.'

'Indeed,' said another, 'we are looted one way or another. King Puru doesn't want to send soldiers to protect us, for he wants to show he is a man of peace. The farmers demand a high price thinking they have a good market but how can we buy at their prices when our profits are dwindling? Indeed, peace does come at a heavy price.'

'Surely you are not seeking your fortune in that godforsaken city now?' the first merchant asked.

It was the moment Chandra had been looking for.

'No, I come to claim my own fortune and to restore the city's glory.'

The men stared in surprise, for there was an intensity in Chandra's gaze and in Chanakya's watchful silence.

'The glory of our land begins with Taxila. And to restore its former glory, we need a ruler who remembers what it once was and values each one of its people, and what they need in these times.' Chanakya held out a scroll. 'You are merchants and traders. Kings need you as much as they need soldiers. In your prosperity lies the kingdom's too. When you travel to other lands, you carry with you the message of your own land. This is the message the prince of Magadha has for you. And the message that you in turn must pass on.'

The two merchants stood and bowed in unison.

'We heard the drumming across the mountains, and one of our horsemen told us about you. We dismissed it as a rumour,' said one of them, laughing nervously as he took off his turban to reveal a sweaty bald pate. 'But now we know you are indeed the prince of Magadha whose stories we have been hearing. You have our support. And there are many like us, O prince, who travel up to Mathura and even Kusinagara but not to Pataliputra any more. The tyrant there demands too much from us.'

They met more merchant caravans as they rode on. Groups travelling in bullock carts, usually four or five in number and accompanied in some cases by armed horsemen. The merchants they had met before had told them how in earlier times they used to be far more in number. Trade had suffered and with it, the city.

When they neared the outskirts of Taxila, they saw its hamlets ringed by verdant green fields and the strong mud walls reddened by the slow rising sun. A few more miles in, they passed bigger brick houses, seemingly prosperous looking villages ringed by acacia and date palm trees. Passing children stopped and counted the carts, clapping in joy as they rode by. The dust blew in the streets and rose to a small storm as Chanakya and Chandra were about to enter the city.

'The university of Taxila is the biggest of them all,' Chanakya said, unable to keep the pride out of his voice. The old harshness on his face was now considerably diminished; there was actually a twinkle in his eye. He looked much recovered from their arduous journey, and a flush – partly a result of their long ride and partly due to the excitement of coming home – now coloured his cheeks. If he loved Taxila so much, why had he left? Chandra wondered. He decided to ask as much.

'It is the story of my father as well,' Chanakya said wryly. 'He could not stay in Magadha because he could see things so very clearly. There is a time to leave, as my father understood, and a time to return. If nomads see life as a movement of seasons, men of the cities see it as a progression of life – from a student to a householder to an ascetic. Here in Taxila, I had students of statecraft and the laws. I felt they would become mere advisers, while the kings they served would be incompetent to act on their advice. Birth and a long illustrious lineage can often stunt one's intellect. All that they had learnt needed to be used wisely and well, in the creation and service of a true, powerful state. I saw these things clearly, but no one else did. And after a while I wanted more.'

He got off his horse as if this reminiscing made him restless. They had reached the gates of Taxila.

'That is what I saw in you. I knew your story,' his eyes glittered. 'I saw it in you too. You've long moved beyond your family, and even your community. You are finally ready to embrace your destiny.'

Taxila was a crowded city; it absorbed them completely. They mingled with the crowds, deliberately drifting away from the merchant caravans that had accompanied them into the city. The Nandas had still not given up. Malayketu would know them as his enemies too. A city like Taxila, made up of disparate people, could be unpredictable – challengers could be read as upstarts, or even a threat.

The sounds of many conversations rose and fell and the cries of traders and sentries calling for order filled the air. Chanakya and Chandra were enveloped by the sounds of a thriving city pulsating with life, a city that also held presentiments of chaos. It was evident in the tension barely reined in and lurking everywhere. The road leading in through the city's main gate was crowded with oxen-drawn carts and men on horses, all wanting to get in, and impatient that it was all taking so long. The guards at the gates were having a hard time, unable to make themselves heard over the crowd that sought entry.

Rumours floated in the waiting crowd, thick and fast, growing more fantastic with every telling.

'It's true. The great emperor Sikander has decided to go.'

'A huge ship came over the land and carried Alexander away.'

'No, it flew up into the sky,' said another. The speaker was from the tribe of the wandering bards and he clashed his cymbals as his words died away.

There was nervous laughter at this and the storyteller was mocked. 'You will fly up yourself with all your jingling bells and fanciful tales.'

'But there will still be war,' said a pompous looking man who looked like an important trader, 'between the challenger who forced Alexander away and the Nandas. There can after all be only one emperor in these domains.'

'It is indeed a story to make us let our guard down,' said the watchful soldier at the gate, looking grimly all around.

'And who cares for Puru anyway?' said another man. 'He will offer his loyalty with a grand bow and a short speech.'

Everyone laughed and a guard took a swipe at the speaker, who dodged just in time.

'It's about time there was some certainty. People loot in Alexander's name, believing there is no authority,' said a horseman at the gate, and he pointed to a low spire of smoke rising from within the city. 'Many of Puru's soldiers left to join Alexander and so this goes on.'

'There are hardly any guards left between here and the frontier,' another voice piped in. 'King Puru will now need to travel to Persia to welcome Alexander back.' The sneer was evident in the man's voice. What use was a man's honour, thought Chandra, if he could arouse such contempt in his subjects?

But there were more signs of disturbance as they rode on as unobtrusively as possible, through the city. There was a strain in the air as if people expected danger. Chandra and Chanakya passed by a looted shop; a sack of grain, ripped open and its contents spilling out, lay abandoned on the road. A pair of chickens, drawn to this unexpected feast, flew with raucous cries up to the roof as they rode by.

They had passed a few soldiers on the way, who were now riding around the city's streets in small groups. They had their hands full in an effort to keep order. From a liquor den, two men emerged, their hands on each other's throats, calling each other Alexander and Puru. It took the best efforts of some nearby soldiers to prise them apart. Even soldiers, it seemed, had forgotten how to assert themselves.

Chandra and Chanakya rode towards the university. Taxila's university was the centre of all learning and now they had to win the sanction – even if this was, in some measure, forced – from its scholars and other men of learning.

The university was located at the southern end of the city. It was housed in a low structure made of mud bricks, standing in the middle of a huge ground that sprawled around it. Benches stood next to peepul and deodar trees. A few students stood talking, but the buzz of conversation died away as they saw the newcomers enter. The grim looks on some faces gave way to curiosity but no one came up to them or shouted across asking their business.

Then, in the silence, a stray voice rang out, perhaps from an open window on a higher floor. 'Taxila has no need for teachers any more. You should offer yourself to the army.'

The comment evoked some nervous laughter before it was all swallowed up by a watchful silence.

The tension was palpable the moment they stepped into the old corridors. From outside the walls they could hear, in odd bursts, stray shouts and the sound of horses riding past. Time and again Chanakya would stop and touch the stone walls around him, as if he secretly rejoiced in the fact that he was back. Chandra had rarely seen his teacher show such emotion. He wished he could see

Chanakya's face but his mentor's gaze was fixed, at a door at the far end of a corridor – the room where the head of the university sat. Chanakya had previously referred to him in contemptuous tones.

'Chitravirya is his name but that is not important. Someone who took the position because the old master retired, unwilling to serve under a foreign conqueror. His name will never be remembered in history.'

No one cared to stop them as they walked in. Some tapers along the walls had died out and no one had come by to light them again. Other doors opened into empty chambers. It looked like a university that had forgotten its dharma. Perhaps that was what made Chanakya's steps angrier as they walked further and it seemed to Chandra that his limp foot left deeper and deeper lines on the clay floor.

The master, Chitravirya, was poring over some palm leaves as they entered. They saw his bull-like shoulders, the knot of hair on his head, and his stubby fingers closed over the quill as he wrote, slowly and haltingly. He sighed in irritation when he heard them enter and looked up. His eyes widened as he saw Chanakya, and then narrowed into slits, sharp as twin daggers.

'You? How dare you come back here?' he said. But he could not say more for Chanakya stood over him, glowering.

Chitravirya tried to rise but failed. He was too cowed by that fiery, insistent glare. He searched for something to say.

'You remember how enraged you were when none of us listened to you about the Yavana invader? You wanted us to branch out, move to other kingdoms and cities, to exhort and urge kings and commoners to fight together against the enemy king. I agree we did not understand then. We are teachers and scholars first, I said, not orators in the least. And at least our lives and those of our students were safe. Everything we have worked hard for – the great scholars, artists and teachers who have made Taxila a great city and Gandhara one of the most cultured kingdoms in the known world – we could not give it up. Scholars are not meant to fight; our battles are waged with words.'

'Bah!' Chanakya spat out. 'You were and still are cowards. What good is knowledge if it does not help us understand the present? If it does not help kings and commoners believe in a better future? The king Puru had poor advisors in men such as you. He would have been better prepared for battle had he had the fortune to have even a single good adviser. But he was betrayed first by his scholars, and then his soldiers. '

Chitravirya flinched but made no response. Then a cunning look came over his face.

'But you had no chance in Magadha? Why are you back here again?'

'Just to tell you that things will change now, for the better. Magadha shall have a new king soon. All the lands we walk on, all the lands our students come from – everything will be under his sway. Mark my words. Nothing lasts for long, especially a period of chaos. Nothing can stop your black tongue from spreading perfidies; you, who have never spoken up for truth or courage. And yet before you now stands the rightful king of Magadha.' He stepped aside to reveal Chandra, the light of the tapers glowing on him.

A shout came in from outside, and then the sound of something breaking – a potter's shed nearby had been attacked. In a time of chaos, Chandra realized, the poor were the most vulnerable. He heard more horsemen ride down a nearby street. Chitravirya's eyes widened. 'So it is true. All the messages, the rumours.'

'Yes, they have the force of truth. A truth that is greater because it was secret. A truth you will sanction yourself if you value your life. Because, as you have seen, I can come back from the dead, and you can never escape.'

'You would not dare! You cannot make me misuse my position.' For a moment, a look of utter hatred flashed across the man's face.

'I would. I dared to march into this room and no one could stop me. I was recognized but now I have protection.'

He gestured to Chandra who moved decisively out of the shadows. Chitravirya gasped and fell back on the cushions. Chanakya bent to lift the taper and it was then that Chandra saw his changed self again in the mirror. His hair fell around his shoulders in matted, heavy locks. He was taller and his face had a narrow, almost gaunt look. But it was his eyes that for a moment made him think he was looking at someone else. They had a haunting light, burning with an intensity that came from within.

He stood over the master, dagger in hand, as Chanakya once again wrote in his scroll, using the finest quills he could see on the master's low table: *Fellow citizens of Taxila, people of Gandhara, prepare for a new dawn. An emperor came and he could not hold us. Now the time for a new emperor is here. And he needs your loyalty.*

He wrote fast while Chandra looked over the manuscripts placed in the master's room. They were compilations of the Buddha and the Jain masters. He longed to read them and pulled out one to browse through. It contained the teachings of the Jain saints that had been compiled at the first council. The palm leaves crackled as he turned them over and drew Chanakya's attention to him.

'If need be, you will have to speak to the people. Matters are progressing too fast.'

Chitravirya, lying on the cushions, moaned in his fear and helplessness. He said, 'Look at the way your prince eyes the books. He has none of your boorishness. This one seems more a scholar than a warrior.'

'A king needs to be both. How would he set up an empire if he spent his days fighting? He needs his head and his hands.'

Chitravirya said sardonically, 'What use would his advisers be then?'

'They can give advice but the king has to take the ultimate decision. The responsibility lies with him. On him alone rests everything, and he alone has to face his maker.'

When he was done, Chanakya simply held out his hand demanding the master's seals, whose face contorted with hatred. Chitravirya would have spat, had he not glanced up to see Chandra pointing his dagger at him. 'Read it, and place your seal on it,' said Chanakya coldly. 'Else we'll do it ourselves. In this time of chaos, it is up to us, the learned people of this hallowed university, to show the path to peace once again. The rightful king will soon take his place and we will support him all we can.'

Chitravirya spat this time, and a spiteful look crossed his face, as the ink ran fast across the scroll. But Chanakya pulled it away just in time.

'We can do it without your permission,' said Chanakya, the calmness never leaving his voice. The earlier harshness had utterly vanished, now that he was guided even more surely by his convictions. Chandra raised the taper, let the wax run on the seals, and felt the skin of his hand burn. The seal transcribed itself on the scrolls and then became an indelible, permanent stain. It was a fact now, imprinted on a scroll and marked with a seal of the university.

'This is an important step,' Chanakya said, turning his back on the master. 'Once the university makes its position clear, we'll have won considerable ground. This scroll will make things work.'

'No it won't!' Chitravirya shouted. Before Chandra could react he had grabbed the bottle of ink and swallowed it. It dribbled past his lips, down his chin and there was a last look of hatred on his face before he fell forward on to the floor, giving himself up to the horror and pain of death.

Chandra lifted him up roughly by the shoulders, trying to make him spit out the poison. But the man was now muttering under his breath, his eyes had a vacant look, and drool was leaking from his mouth. This was no way to die, Chandra thought, horrified. Had he expected to die? Or did he think, arrogant in his learning, cloistered in his magnificent chamber, unchallenged by all his peers, that he was above death?

The room was quiet except for the dying man's last gasps, the slow drip of the oil falling, and the sound of a mouse scurrying around by the walls. Chandra caught a glimpse of its tiny blue eyes as he, lifting the taper again, cast a quick glance around the room.

'There is a time for everything, and it was time for him to die,' Chanakya said, indifference lacing his words. 'No one will miss him.'

Chanakya picked up a gong that lay on a wooden shelf nearby and struck it. The sound was loud in the silence and echoed down the corridors. The first steps that could be heard in response were hesitant. He struck the gong again. It clanged its way down the corridor, almost like a demand. Footsteps sounded closer and louder, a tread that became more measured as they neared. Perhaps whoever had heard the sound of the gong had been waiting in the darkness for a while.

The next moment, a startled voice broke out as the gong vibrated once again. 'You are back!'

'Yes, I always said I would be,' Chanakya said quietly. 'Now do you believe my way was indeed superior?'

There were more steps rushing towards them, figures emerging from the shadows, their white robes melding together in a swirl. As Chandra and Chanakya watched the other scholars approach, they saw how their agitation gave way to confusion.

'The master, Chitravirya, is dead,' said Chanakya, crossing his arms, looking steadily around. Only Chandra saw the tic beating in his cheek. 'He took poison.'

The scholars stayed quiet.

'He did not have answers to my questions. There is chaos and uncertainty all around us. Remember the exchange I had with him? We were so afraid that Alexander's men would destroy our university and now the alternative is much worse. Do you want the rampaging hordes of Dhana Nanda's elephant army to run roughshod over you? Or the small tribal armies up north to launch small skirmishes against your city? Are you willing to witness the fratricide that will be unleashed now that Alexander is no longer Puru's protector?'

There was silence. Chanakya had been right. They were men of wisdom but they were small men too, fearful that their carefully carved domain would be lost. It was the university that made them what they were.

'We all need a strong state, a strong king. Everyone – soldiers, farmers, scholars, traders...everyone – even monks in their faraway monasteries, no matter what they say, need a strong king to lead and protect them. Justice must prevail.'

The scholars had gathered in a small half-circle, facing Chanakya.

'Most of you do not remember the debate I had here. It's now part of this university's legend,' Chanakya paused, crossing his arms, allowing himself this little conceit before going on, 'I said that the state must matter if we are to have peace. It isn't just belonging to our own castes or groups, but belonging to a state too. One far bigger and stronger than these small groups, which will unify us all under one rule. We need a state represented by a king, a warrior and a ruler. Only a true king of the soil, a true prince of Magadha.'

He gestured and Chandra stepped out to face them. The taper was by him on the wall, strategically placed so that it lit up his figure.

He stood there for a moment, his shadow rising on the walls behind. Chanakya gestured to him before he went on, 'This is the son secretly born. The son who Dhana Nanda tried to kill. He was saved because destiny so willed it. Just as destiny willed so many other events.'

As the audience drew in its collective breath at the momentous revelation, even the walls shuddered before everything fell silent once more. It wasn't merely an empty silence, but a silence that engulfed them as what Chanakya had said sank in. He pressed on. 'When disturbance breaks out in a time of no clear authority, it only spreads. We understand there have been riots in Magadha after the king Dhana Nanda's soldiers killed someone by mistake. A murder committed all because a harmless play was enacted – a play they thought was about the king. But it was a prayer to the rain god, asking him why he was hoarding all the rain, like a miser. The murder was an act of cowardice. If a king is so insecure, how long can he stay on the throne? How long before his people turn against him? And if it has happened in Magadha, you can be sure the end of the Nandas is near. They are false rulers who have ruled under false pretexts.'

The assembly of scholars stood in silence. They were men of learning but this time their knowledge gave them no answers. But in their whispers, some of the truth emerged. Things were happening in Taxila at that very moment; a chaos that was engulfing the university – a guard's hurried order, conches being blown to ward away alarm, and then the horses neighing frantically, as soldiers tried to maintain order. 'The rumours are spreading', said one of the scholars, the desperation now clear on his face. 'It seems there are messages that the prince of Magadha is here to wage war. That is causing fear.'

Chandra looked on grim-faced. This wasn't the effect he wanted the messages to have. Now they had to move out, from beyond the university to the city. The false rumours had to be put to rest once and for all. Then he remembered the king. Yes, King Puru, for all his ineffectualness, had his honour and this had to be upheld. King Puru was not his enemy, Chandra knew.

Chandra undid the drapes at the window and looked out beyond the high walls of the university. Spirals of fire rose upward from the city's north where some merchants had their warehouses. The smoke was visible like a grey cloud, and spread like a hydra-headed monster in the sky.

Now the stray shouting was clearer; they heard voices rising in panic as people fled the streets. The scholars looked nervous and muttered conversations broke out. There were also rumours that hungry soldiers who had once served Alexander had returned in droves and were now looting the city. Afraid for their lives, people from surrounding villages were also moving towards Taxila, seeking comfort in a city that no longer recognized itself – a city that was enveloped in a smoky grey haze, a city that had erupted in turmoil.

It was Chanakya's voice that carried an assurance. 'If you think the way of truth is dharma, if you are men who believe in truth and justice and the power of your words, now is the time. Go out into the city square and tell the people this. There is a new king, the true king, and he will fight all false ones. Only then can peace prevail and you, men of learning, have the duty to make it happen.'

There was a knock on wood, three taps and a tap again. Chandra whirled around, dagger in hand. The swiftness of his movement made everyone draw in their breath.

'It is a message from my master,' said a voice at the door. His voice sounded young and tremulous. The other scholars stood aside, lowering their gaze as Chandra made his way to the door, his hold on his dagger somewhat relaxed. But he had learnt never to let down his guard. A young monk stood outside. He was breathless. He trembled as he gazed up at Chandra, for he barely reached his shoulder, and a pulse beat furiously on his forehead.

'You are just as they described,' he said in awe. 'In the streets outside.'

He swallowed, bowed somewhat awkwardly, and then began again, as Chandra gestured to him to enter the room. 'My master said to tell you this. The respected Bhadrabahu will lead us, monks of his order, through the streets, spreading the message of peace and to inform all that the time for tyranny to end is near. There is tumult here and in Pataliputra. Rumours spread fast and become the news of the day,' he gulped before finishing the rest of his statement, something he had evidently memorized, in a rush. 'Our brethren travelling north brought us worrying news; that Dhana Nanda's demands have laid waste to once prosperous cities like Ujjain and Shravasti.'

Chandra raised his hand in a gesture at once commanding and reassuring.

The transformation that took place in the room was amazing to behold. Chandra said, in a kind tone so as not to intimidate the young monk, 'I am a warrior, and my dharma is to offer you my promise of protection. I thank you for your master's assurance. We will lead you – no blood will be shed in this city of learning.'

Followed by the scholars and Chanakya, Chandra mounted his horse and rode out into the street, which was eerily quiet, though in the distance they could hear shouts and the sound of swords clashing. The stables and the elephant sheds that abutted the university walls were filled with the loud noises of hooves stomping on stone floors and elephants trumpeting in evident distress. The fires all over the city cast an orange glow on the night sky.

The echo of hoof-beats behind them was reassuring. But soon that echo appeared to elicit a like response, almost in a pattern – it was clear there were other horsemen out on the streets too. Chandra drew his sword out and rode out in front, leading the crowd of students and teachers who had followed him out of the university. Their faces were set in resolute masks for there was no turning back now.

The monks were waiting for them outside the university. They walked behind the riders, just as they had promised, in an orderly procession, holding up orange tapers so that there would be no mistaking who they were. Chandra thought about how their group must look. Monks, teachers and students of one of the greatest universities of the world were out in the streets and Chandra was leading them. He held the scroll in one hand, sword in another. No one could question his destiny any longer. But the king, who ruled over this city and the kingdom of Gandhara, had to give his consent as well. It was a question of honour. A king who upheld peace deserved his dignity. Moreover, Chandra and Chanakya meant to make Puru an ally, and by extension be granted the services of his army.

The scroll and Puru's support would help them in the journey that lay ahead. Outside the city and even in some of its precincts, men and soldiers who had pledged allegiance to Chandra, waited. It was time for the final campaign for Magadha to begin. He lifted his sword, it caught the light of the tapers and it seemed the sun had risen a second time that day.

They rode past deserted streets and locked shops. Every door was shut – frightened householders had bolted themselves inside. Every window quivered in rhythm with the trotting horses; every bolted door braced against the dust raised by their hooves. The monks held their tapers high, the horses rode on in perfect rhythm and thus, a silent message of assurance was passed on.

As they turned a corner, they came face to face with other horsemen – soldiers with yellow and purple streaks on their cloaks. They stopped and faced each other.

'We are King Puru's men. We are here to make sure that peace prevails at all cost.'

'I am the prince of Magadha,' declared Chandra, 'and I respect your king. I mean no challenge to him. Peace will be maintained.'

The soldiers kept silent and then made way for their leader. Riding past them on a magnificent horse appeared a regal figure wearing silver armour. He said proudly, 'I am King Puru, ruler of the realm of Gandhara.'

The monks behind raised their tapers in respect and stood still, as did the others. The solemnity of that moment was palpable.

'My lord,' said Chandra and inclined his head briefly. It was a gesture between equals. The older king smiled.

'My spies have told me many stories. That Alexander is having second thoughts. He is rethinking his conquering rampage. I was not sure Alexander would leave his territories so soon,' he stopped and looked long at Chandra. Then, casting a quick glance around, he let his horse take a few paces forward. Lowering his voice, the king went on, 'There are other stories about a challenger prince from the east. Is that you?'

'Alexander's soldiers are afraid, driven to fear by the power of a rumour. Rumours based on lies have no standing. But I am the true heir to the Magadhan throne,' said Chandra.

'You believe that you stand for the truth based on a rumour?

That you are the true heir, who the Nanda ruler wanted to see killed since the day he was born?'

Chandra held his head up proudly. 'He could not kill me. Now it is his turn to face me and I will not fail.' Chandra felt proud knowing he had never sounded more assured. He held the other king's gaze. He saw the sternness dim in Puru's eyes, to be replaced by a steely, amused glint.

'I like your confidence. But you should know a king's days are numbered, too.'

'What matters is how well a king honours his dharma. And that he makes his state matter more than anything else.'

Puru smiled faintly again. 'You need better armour than the one you have on now, prince.' But his smile held no mockery as he took in Chandra's robe of rough tent cloth and the belt made of animal skin. He went on, 'We will meet again, I hope. There will be no more unrest here in Taxila and Gandhara. My men are still restless, eager to regain their honour, having lost it not too long ago.'

A moment later, his lips had tightened into a grim line. 'By fighting for you, they have a chance to do that. They are yours. May the Magadhan king rule for long and be glorious in every way.'

The import of that statement was not lost. The king was offering his men, and more significantly, his support to Chandragupta. Chandra was no longer an upstart but a prince claiming his right to the throne of Magadha. The news would reach Pataliputra, and Dhana Nanda would now have cause for alarm.

'Our land has not seen a great war for a long time. Perhaps it shall not happen again but it might come to that.' said Chandra, accepting King Puru's decision.

Their horses were neck to neck and the king's glance slid briefly down Chandra's horse. He spoke in a low tone, his voice harsh. Chandra could see he had difficulty breathing.

'I am old and I know my kingdom will not survive me...'

Chandra made to interrupt him but the older man raised his hand. 'We cannot even choose our own time, but we try to play with destiny. And who knows if it really matters? If it is all pre-determined, why did I submit to Alexander? Because for a moment, I thought a king's duty was also towards peace. To try and prevent war at all costs. My soldiers were afraid; it's the same fear that drove Alexander's men away. But ordinary men have a chance to atone. We, as emperors bear our sins alone, and remain answerable to the maker himself.'

'What about a king's duty?' Chandra said, knowing that he had to say it. 'Perhaps it was yours to take away their fear.'

The old king flinched, but he held his head up. 'Maybe I failed – everyone, even my own son, says I did. And I shall pay for it.'

He reached forward and touched his horse's mane – a sign that he was ready to move. They had lingered long enough. 'I allow you to go through my kingdom. Taxila is still my city, and Gandhara the land I rule over,' he said proudly. 'My ideas may not be accepted or even be popular, but I see you have nobility in you. No one can stop you.'

Chandra raised his hand and the soldiers moved to one side. His group passed through quickly, their horses moving in unison. The monks followed, their wooden flats striking the hard earth a moment after the hooves sounded. As they marched through the street, flocks of people began to join them. Chandra's eyes widened as he saw the number of soldiers and men from the town who were now following him. They raised their bows and swords, then bowed deferentially as his eyes ran down the ranks of men. The soldiers included Alexander's men and some who had once professed loyalty to King Puru. They had flocked to this city to find refuge – and to find a new master. They stood in orderly lines, showing an innate discipline that reflected their commitment to their beliefs. They were soldiers who believed in a just fight. Chandra felt an exhilaration sweeping into his heart; the time for doubt had ceased. He was their leader and he had to prove himself every moment from now.

'We have come all the way from the east, Prince of Magadha,' said a soldier. 'We will fight for you against that tyrant.'

'It is a fight for dharma then. A fight to the finish!' Chandra said, throwing his hair back. He raised his sword high, its tip glinting gold in the light of the tapers.

'A fight that will not end soon. But a fight that will end tyranny once and for all. A fight that will mean your continued loyalty to Magadha.'

'We are prepared for it,' said another soldier. 'Our hearts have burned ever since the Nanda ruler's soldiers ran his elephants over our village.'

'And when he ignored us during times of famine.'

'Or when our crops were destroyed by his soldiers.'

One by one the voices spoke up. Chandra silenced them by raising his arm high.

'The anger you hold is effective, but anger dissipates like most emotions, even love. You long for shelter, for a peaceful life for those you have left behind. As king I promise you peace and justice – in return for your loyalty.'

'We promise!' They spoke as one. And so an army was born.

They rode out till the sun was high and from afar they could see the silver rope that was the river Satadru. The land stretched before them, filled with dangerous possibilities yet promising hope. There was a distinct sense of exhilaration among them. The soldiers had covered the distance faster than anticipated.

'Here we must disperse into different groups,' Chandra said, 'and make our own way across.'

He saw doubt appear on the men's faces and knew he had to assuage it. He rode amongst them, watching them as they held their weapons by their side in a sign of acceptance and submission.

'We are not marching for war, not right away,' he chose his words carefully, scanning every face. 'There is still time for that. There is a long way to march to Pataliputra. The Nanda ruler's hold is weak here and our messages have worked. The cities are what we take, one by one. The villages stay unharmed; we must never expect too much from them. I say all this for we must not let our passion dissipate too quickly.'

He had seen it happen among Alexander's men. Many of the soldiers who were now in his camp – and every day there were more of them joining in – were those who had deserted Alexander. It had been a long wait, and all to satiate an emperor's ego. But many of them had seen the message about the new king and been touched by it in some measure. Chandra felt his skin singed by the fire in their eyes.

'We will now march in separate groups and meet in the wide plains outside the big cities, where the mighty rivers begin, the Ganga and the Yamuna.'

As he rode among them, the words came to him unbidden – 'There will be many battles we will fight. But as true soldiers, we do not kill or loot unnecessarily. The villages will look after us, for they will believe in our message, our promise. Our creed is never to harm the weak and the unarmed, but to come to their defence. You are the king's hands, and loyal as his hands are.' It was the soldier's creed that he believed in. His father, the man of the forests, would have called it the creed of life itself.

Some of them had questions but in the end he realized Chanakya had been right. Everyone wanted to belong. They hungered for it, wanting the warmth and security of belonging to a group that believed in the same things.

'We follow the river's course down to the plains. The Yamuna and then the Ganga itself. We ride on till we reach the cities on the plains. Remember my words.'

They raised their swords and spears in agreement. He heard the rousing clash of shaft hitting blade, not once, but twice and then again. The sound was unexpectedly joyous and, looking through the arch formed by his soldiers, he saw Chanakya smiling amidst the upheld swords.

16

THE BATTLE FOR MATHURA

The army was on the move. There were some who insisted on riding ahead and others who rode out into surrounding villages. At night they camped in forests lining the foothills, the fires rising high to ward away wild elephants. As they marched along Valhika and Madra, down the passes of Mainaka Giri, they were met by men bearing news and soldiers willing to join their cause.

The true test would come in the cities. They were still a ragged army on the move. They kept to the river valleys and the foothills, helped by herders and nomads. Orders were carefully passed on and obeyed. No one was to be harassed and troubled on the journey, Chandra made that clear.

Every second night, Chandra spoke to his people, observing faces he was familiar with and those who were new. People came from nearby areas, drawn by the message that had been passed on. Some were curious, some watchful, some attentive and hopeful. 'Their faces, always watch their faces,' Chanakya had said. 'That is when you know people are ready for change. You must make every move carefully, taking your cues by what you see.'

Between Magadha and the kingdom of Kuru stretched the smaller kingdoms of Kosala and Panchala and the smaller principalities of the Mallas and the Vajjis, all of whom were once beholden to the Nandas. In a time of flux, loyalties shifted, and nothing was sacrosanct any more. In the battles that peppered their long journey eastward, Chandra led from the front. Armies clashed only when negotiations failed as with the Sauviras, a kingdom east of the Indus, and part of the Punjab region. The Sauvira commander was felled by the javelin Chandra threw from a long way off.

Many a time, when his soldiers formed a protective circle around him, Chandra swung through them, leaping past them with his horse, to clash with enemy soldiers, sometimes taking on several at a time. The sight of his sword rising high, flashing in the sun, strengthened his men's resolve. Time and again he heard them call out his name. The name that had created his legend, the name that had travelled with stories about him. *Moriya. Moriya*

It was a wonder that Chandra slept at all during that long journey eastwards. One early morning, as he took his horse out for a ride, he told Chanakya, 'The first thing I will do on becoming king is sleep peacefully for a few hours.' When he saw Chanakya's fixed stare, he asked, 'Why are you looking at me like that?'

'A king never sleeps. Or no one knows if he does, or where.'

Chanakya never joked. His every response held a deeper truth. Chandra accepted these truths; he was being swept away by the momentum of events.

That night, a soldier who had professed loyalty to his cause came running to find him. He was a soldier from the eastern hills, as was evident from his shorn hair and narrow eyes, who had been stopped moments before he could enter Chandra's tent. He had a mad look in his eyes and held a dismembered head in his hands, the blood dripping down to form a small puddle near where he stood. But the soldier was unmindful to all this as he shouted, 'I need to see the king. This man was trying to kill him!' He held the head up, presenting a grotesque sight in the dim light of the tapers. But he was cut short when another soldier arrived on the scene and slashed him with a sword. The soldier made a defiant explanation to Chandra – 'What he said was not true. He had sold himself to the claimant, the prince who would be king at the cost of his father's life. The prince impatient to be king of Gandhara.'

Malayaketu.

The name was whispered quietly, the vile demon who still cast a shadow over him.

'He has set a reward on your head, O master,' said the second soldier. 'This soldier was trying to trick you into believing in his loyalty and then kill you with deception.'

'No one raises a sword against another unless I say so,' Chandra told him. 'You are my soldiers and will fight only my battles.'

'My lord,' said the dying man. 'I speak the truth. I am a man from the east, someone whose homeland is close to yours.'

Chandra did not know whom to believe and yet he had to act decisively. This man was dying, his last words lost in his heavy breathing.

All at once, he made up his mind and said firmly, 'Give me my sword.'

In the next moment, in exactly one stroke each, he drove his sword into both the soldiers and killed them. A hush fell over his men.

He announced calmly, 'A man who could sell himself even momentarily is no use as a soldier. A soldier who acts without orders is no true soldier either. There is a soldier's code that we must follow to ensure justice.' His sword dripped with blood, and he held it away from his body as he walked back to his tent. 'As soldiers, I need your loyalty, nothing else.'

In the morning, he raised his bloodied sword and let the sun wash over it. It was an act of cleansing.

'A new day, new battles. Is there any virtue in conquering a kingdom?' Chandra asked.

'It is your dharma now,' said Chanakya. 'You have little need of me now,' he went on. 'Your heart and head will now tell you what to do as a king.'

'And you, what will your role be?'

'I am your adviser. I will serve your state,' Chanakya replied. Perhaps he imagined the hesitation, before Chanakya went on, 'Until you want it to be so.'

He bowed before Chanakya, his head at a slight incline. 'Will Magadha be the strongest state ever? And will you help me make it?'

It was a king's question but Chanakya also heard the young man who had been fired with ambition, one who had chased a dream many years ago in a forest.

'You will make it so.' He smiled wryly. 'It will be my privilege to be a part of it. You have seen how things change, and so quickly too. The trick is to never let down your guard, or show your uncertainty and weakness. You acted well last night. You cannot take half-measures, not anymore. A king is different from commoners.'

As the sun rose, they rode their horses into the water. Chandra cupped the cold water in his hands. His face became one with it and he felt rejuvenated once again.

'After a while, I must part ways with you. I cannot stay too long with you now,' said Chanakya. 'We have different roles now that we are on our way to Magadha.'

Chanakya raised his hands high, chanted verses honouring the sun and sprinkled petals over the man he was now committed to obeying. They rode forth, closer to Magadha than they had been a day earlier. They would march to Mathura and from there find a way to Pataliputra. The taking of this city was vital. Right by the Yamuna, it was a premier outpost for the Magadhan empire. Only a little beyond and around Mathura lay cities like Ujjain to the south, others like Ahichhatra to the north, with Kaushambi and Vaishali further east.

It was here in Mathura that the empire's might was most evident – an empire weakened but still powerful in its name; its soldiers might chafe at the tyranny of Dhana Nanda but they knew no other king to whom they could swear loyalty. Possessing Mathura would send an important message to the people as well as the Nandas. It would constitute a decisive moment in the contest for power. And planning for it was vital, Chandra knew. The battle would involve force, cunning and secrecy. Henceforth, every battle and every victory would be crucial. It was now clear that he was not just an upstart, but a rival, a challenger to the Magadhan might.

Looking back, he saw his army behind him. A long unbroken line, yet orderly, that stretched a long way off. There was no doubt that Dhana Nanda knew of its approach. The cities under his control, beginning with Mathura, would put up a fierce fight. It surprised Chandra that he had not been challenged yet. His spies informed him that cities such as Mathura were alive with tension, now that the rumours about his campaign had come true. Soldiers were arming themselves anew – and every day, proclamations were read out in Mathura's main square reiterating the might of the Nandas.

'But all the long speeches by the king's stooges have little weight against the stories that are whispered. Everywhere they talk of a new era of peace and justice,' said one of his spies.

It was at night that new men drifted in as well, shadowy creatures who crept in from the dark fields around where the army camped. Chandra saw the haunted look in their eyes, and also the hope that he would give them something worthwhile to fight for. These were soldiers who had been unpaid for long, or peasants whose land had gone to waste with no help from the king, who were now determined to regain their lost lives. Laying their swords or bows before him, they bowed low as they promised him their service.

The night before they reached Mathura, his soldiers picked up two men.

'These men wanted to speak only to you and would not tell us anything,' one of his soldiers said. The soldiers were careful now. They did not kill so readily.

The two men shook their heads and bowed before him. Their nervousness was evident in the glimmer of tears in their eyes and their trembling hands. One of the captured men, dressed in what had once been fine robes, now muddied and torn in places, held his turban in his hand. He revealed haltingly that he had come as a representative of the traders.

His voice trembled as he told his story. 'Everyone is demanding money from us. The soldiers who are supposed to protect us demand money to do so, since the Nanda king has promised them his gold only after the war. We've been robbed till nothing of value remains. The roads down south and east have become unsafe as bandits prey on those of us who are fleeing. We have had to pay off so many people that we are left with no money or possessions and no peaceful way to go home.'

The man broke down and wept. 'I am not a soldier and Mathura was always a city that welcomed traders,' he said. His next gesture made everyone gasp, while Chandra moved back instinctively a step or two – the man had flung himself at his feet and was now moaning piteously. 'We are forced to live out in the open, and rogue soldiers, even those loyal to you, are demanding their share in everything, even the water we drink.'

Chandra looked at the men around him – men who had promised to fight for him and could turn into altogether different creatures when they saw someone helpless and weak. His eyes moved down the circle of men, saw some gazes drop, some who looked back defiantly but who could not hold his stare. He did not know what they saw. Did they see the fierce dark brilliance in his eyes? The nerve beating in his jaw? The lips held firmly, not cruelly but with a determination that seemed to will destiny itself?

'If you must join me,' he said to his soldiers, his voice low and firm, 'there is only one writ that runs here. It is our rule that traders and monks, those who travel peacefully from kingdom to kingdom, shall forever be unharmed. And it is a king's dharma to uphold this and his soldiers must follow suit. When merchant groups depart from areas under our control, you must ensure they are safe. The time to uphold dharma is now, not just after the battle with Dhana Nanda and his men.'

It was a battle for their minds he fought now, the fight to convince his men to follow his principles.

They stood outside the city of Mathura, preparing to breach its gates. A grey dawn had broken but no one on either side had slept. For Chandra's army it was part of a deliberate act. Some of his soldiers had kept at their drums and trumpets, setting up a thunderous clamour that had made the birds circle over the city, spreading out in ever widening arcs across the sky. It was evident that the spirits of those inside had frayed. The tapers on the ramparts had wilted and not all were relit. The enemy soldiers were afraid to reappear for a few had been struck down by expertly aimed spears, some of them Chandra's, and he never missed. As one soldier was felled, and then another, the drumming rose to even more frenzied levels, always followed by the cry of *Moriya! Moriya!*

Within the city, stray skirmishes and short battles had broken out. A few of Chandra's soldiers had stealthily entered the city, from the western side, crossing the Yamuna in small fishing boats. Others had joined the traders' caravans only a few hours ago. For any strategy to work, it had to have secret as well as open elements acting in consonance.

As the darkness lightened, Chandra knew this was the best time to strike. It was when subconsciously, everyone, but especially, the enemy, let their guard down, as they accustomed their eyes to the growing brightness, and acknowledged to each other, in unspoken ways, their growing fatigue. Chandra knew there could be no letting up, no relaxing of their own guard. With his men, he had been up all night and now he rode among them, encouraging them, readying them for this final battle for the city.

Some more time passed. Neither side had let loose the first arrow and yet a watchful, nerve-wracking tension filled the sky. His soldiers – buoyed again by the presence of their young leader by their side, who had ridden by them at frequent intervals through the night, encouraging and reassuring them in turn – arranged themselves in order, as the drums continued their beat. Battering rams were readied at the city's gates, and then the final shout rang out in a moment's stillness as the drums and trumpets stopped for the first time in several hours, demanding the city's surrender.

The gates did not open, the ram slammed against the hard wood once and then again. The huge iron bolts rang out with a metallic clang, and Chandra looked up to see a defiant spear rise high in the sky, but it went clumsily awry. His men, as one, raised their own weapons.

He lifted his bow as the battering ram did its work and his arrow caught a Nanda commander right in the throat as he made to ride out with his army. The man fell from his horse and Chandra urged his troops, shouting the command to advance and attack.

He heard the stamping of a thousand and more feet behind him, the smell of dust as horses picked up pace and the stinging swish of arrows. A familiar thrill surged through him. He pulled his bowstring, and the silver light flashed in his eye time and again as he fired his arrows one after the other, barely pausing to catch his breath. He urged his horse forward, making sure he was always seen by his men and was never at the same spot for too long.

He saw the arrows fly past him, some finding their mark and others embedding themselves on the city's walls and its buildings, stamping the conqueror's authority with a finality. The sky darkened; the din and clang of arrows striking each other and of spears zipping through the air mingled with the soldiers' battle cries. The sounds were never-ending, rising, then falling, only to rise again to an ever increasing clamour. Chandra noted the gate still looming open behind him, and his men advancing around him and spreading out, stepping over fallen soldiers and things – sacks and items bundled up in cloth – abandoned on the way by citizens who had chosen the loud, seemingly endless night to flee the city.

Chandra raced through the city, sometimes in the midst of his men, at other times leading them, watching the morning spread over Mathura. 'No one harasses the innocent here,' he said as he rode through the city's main street, and cheers rang out loud around him.

The enemy soldiers, clearly unprepared and uninspired, were no match for Chandra's army. As they went deeper into the city, the battles were shorter and fought between smaller groups of soldiers. Chandra led his men forward, indicating with quick gestures that they must break up into smaller groups to fight on. Inside the city, their enemy had the advantage, for they knew of hiding places – roads and side-streets from which they could strategically attack or defend.

But the entry of Chandra's army into the city signalled the enemy's ineffectiveness. Some enemy soldiers stood with swords turned down in a gesture of surrender, others stood over their dropped quivers. There were some enemy soldiers who had not given up, who waited in ambush at the first corner. Chandra's men, having tasted victory, were unrelenting. There could be no mercy for those who had chosen resistance. Felled bodies littered every street they passed. It was only a matter of time now. The sounds of victory soon grew louder than the groans and cries of defeat and pain.

After hours of battle, Chandra and his men reached the river that stretched beyond the city's walls on its other side. He saw the boats sailing out, carrying away the still fleeing citizens. He knew then that it was finally over. His men had run through the city and made it theirs. Mathura was his. The sun was now high in the sky, and when he wiped his sweat away with his hand, he saw the blood on his fingers.

Later, his men would say how inspired they had been by him in the battlefield – Chandra sitting high on his horse, letting arrow after arrow fly, never missing the mark. His shield caught the light of the flares and it shone on his face; and the soldiers beheld him, aflush with the glow of possible victory and rightful conquest. Now that victory was complete, they rode to where he stood, horsemen and infantry still in their perfect lines. They raised their bows and swords and the cry that rang out resounded across the city – 'Victory to our king, Chandragupta of the Mauryas!'

He raced along the river now, ahead of his men; the heady sense of being a conqueror was exhilarating. The sound of hooves was hard and rigorous on the earth, as if inscribing itself forever on time.

17

SHRAVASTI AND KANYAKUBJA

The sounds of life on the plains, where rivers flowed wider and more serene, were entirely different from the sounds of the northern mountains. Green fields stretched wide and canals flowed, busier than the narrower streams of the north. Pataliputra seemed closer now that they had claimed victory over a big trading city. But now they were deep in the domain of the Nandas, and while every further advance had to be planned with extra caution; they had to act fast, for any loss in momentum could be fatal. Moreover, the danger they faced grew with every territory they conquered. Either the Nanda army would soon give decisive battle, or those on their side would rebel and capitulate, for even allies could prove fluid in these uncertain times. No one could be trusted.

They moved relentlessly ahead, planning every move. Between the conquest of cities, Chandra and his soldiers would return to the foothills in separate units. This was to deceive the enemy, to keep them guessing their next move; this was also a way for Chandra's army to recoup, for a battle depended on quick-thinking and staying several steps ahead of the enemy.

They journeyed past where the kingdom of the Kurus had once stood, between the cities of Ayodhya and Hastinapura. His soldiers would announce as they rode past, the words that now appeared engraved on the land he conquered – *All this land is now under Chandragupta, of the Mauryas. He rules over this land and promises his subjects a just, fair rule.*

This was the land between hill and plains where he had once felt at home. He was its ruler now and was prepared to fight to claim it as his. But so far, nothing untoward had happened. Victory had seemed easy, and it was more evident to him now that evil and tyranny exercised at best only a superficial, hollow power.

When they reached Shravasti, close to the Gomti river, a general of the Nandas was captured along with his army. The general had been headed to secure the eastern forts of Kanyakubja and Shravasti on behalf of the Nandas but had reached too late. Chandra knew by now that it was breaking dawn that provided the best time for a surprise attack. Shravasti's soldiers, waiting for reinforcements from Pataliputra, had been caught by surprise. The general's army had been ambushed just as bugles sounding Chandra's victory rang out across the fort and over the river.

'I don't want him killed,' said Chandra after his soldiers reported the general's capture. The man had struggled to free himself and even after he had surrendered, he had tried a devious way of escaping, using a dagger he had kept hidden in his clothes.

'He is a true soldier and a true soldier from the enemy's side can serve our cause well,' said Chandra. Men of the Nandas could be his best followers if he, Chandra, played his cards well. His way of dealing with an enemy general would send an important message to the Nandas. If one of their generals had been caught so easily, Chandra thought with some contempt, it didn't say much for Dhana Nanda's army.

There were others who insisted the general be put to death. Put him up on the gallows and display his corpse for all to see, they demanded.

'We cannot be like the kings we wish to depose,' he said, thinking quickly of how to deal with the general. This man knew the Nandas' strategy well and could be used to good effect, especially as the eastern forts on the way to Pataliputra needed to be conquered quickly.

'O king, This is one of the Nanda generals and his execution will send a strong message.'

The general had been dragged in, and was now bound with ropes that had not too long ago tethered cattle. His robe was soiled, his hair hung about his face, and his lips, stained with betel, were twisted in savage contempt.

'In my court, I speak first,' said Chandra. He was in the assembly hall of the famous Shravasti palace, the hall that would have honoured any king with its finely sculpted columns and arches. He felt restless and uncomfortable on his grand throne despite the soft cushions, for there were more battles to be fought, and sitting on a throne seemed premature.

'The end of the Nandas is near, and you must see that. Do you hear the silence everywhere? There is no protest as we enter the cities and pass through villages. Did the Nandas really rule over this area?'

Fear crept upon the man's face as he sensed the contempt in Chandra's voice. Chandra turned his head away. He couldn't stand the inevitable emergence of cowardice that lay inside even the bravest of men. If it wasn't cowardice, was it some other weakness to which they succumbed? Even Alexander had given it all up eventually. Were soldiers, whose dharma it was to fight, ultimately cowards? Was the dharma, their life's work, a false one, an illusion?

A soldier spoke up, 'To the west of the Yamuna, nothing belongs to the Nandas anymore. King Puru is our king's ally. And the days of the tyrants are numbered. You can see that around you. The question is – do you wish to throw in your lot with our new ruler?'

They waited for the general's answer and Chandra hoped the captured man would say no. That would be a soldier's answer.

'My duty as a soldier is to fight. I follow my master's commands.'

They loosened the ropes and pushed him forward, kicking him as they did so. Chandra had to raise his hand to stop that shameful degradation.

'My lord, spare my life,' pleaded the general piteously.

Chandra gripped his sword, a weapon that was both his friend and enemy. A stench filled the air; the man had defecated in his fear, and the smell of impending death mingled with the condemned man's excreta. The soldiers surrounding him laughed, and Chandra thought of Bharata's death.

'My lord, spare me.'

Chandra shook his head. 'You don't deserve a life anymore,' he said, as his eyes held the defeated general's. 'You will not be able to bear your own humiliation if I let you live. Die a soldier's death. Kneel before me.'

This man who had once been a general dropped to his knees in front of Chandra who was now king. Both of them were in roles that destiny had writ. Chandra raised his sword and slashed off the man's head in one blow. The blood splattered his robes and those of the men standing nearby. The head fell to the earth, a dull thud eaten up by the long silence that followed.

'Tell them, tell everyone. Have his head placed on a pole for everyone to see, and the message will be carried long and far,' he said, his voice calm and steady. He handed his sword over to the soldier who would wipe it clean and sharpen it again on a whetstone. 'This is what happens to those who oppose us,' he said, knowing he would never have to repeat those words, his ruthlessness stamped now with his every word and gesture. 'Either they join us or they pay with their lives.'

He looked around in the silence that followed; his army was bigger than it had ever been, and he would do all he could to keep it together.

One night, someone left a mutilated peacock near his camp. Its throat had been slit and most of its feathers ripped out. It was the dogs' barking that alerted some soldiers nearby, who brought it to Chandra. For a few moments his hand rested on the bird, wishing he could assuage it in some way, even in death. He knew the warning for what it was. In its mutilation was an evident insult to him, and to his past, but he would never consider it as one. The peacock was ceremonially burnt to ashes and he turned his gaze even more resolutely eastwards. Pataliputra would soon be his and such senseless cruelties would be a thing of the past, he vowed. He would always remember the peacock, its neck torn off, blood turning its feathers black.

But on the way, there were battles to be fought, blood to be shed, lives to be lost – it was all an inevitable part of war. As his men prepared to lay siege to the ancient city of Kanyakubja, they learnt of the large numbers of enemy soldiers already assembled there. Some of Chandra's advance troops had been easy targets, as the soldiers of the Nandas had shot arrows from their vantage points on the town's ramparts. Many of the men who had sworn loyalty to him had died in their first attempt to take Kanyakubja. Some had betrayed him, unprepared for the siege and the other long hard battles that lay ahead. Yet there were battles he had already won by strategic negotiation such as when he convinced the ruler of Malla that he would not interfere in his small republic; that Magadha would instead protect Malla from external aggressors.

Chandra also did not shy away from coercion. When the king of the Matsyas who ruled east of the Yamuna, beyond Mathura, was taken captive by Chandra's army, he was released only when half his treasury was given over to Chandra, along with the support of his immense army. Chandra basked in these victories, knowing that every battle was different. His army's strength lay in its very unpredictability, in its ability to improvise, to spread itself into different formations – an arc, a complete circle, or even an ambiguous snake-like form – so as to confound and confuse the enemy.

As the full force of his army rode up to Kanyakubja, it was clear that the Nandas would not give up easily, especially as Pataliputra was so close now. The gates stayed shut and were heavily guarded – even the ones to the south, his spies told him. This was evidence that it was well supplied and there was no shortage of food for its inhabitants. This time, Chandra realized, the battle would be even longer and harder won.

He gave commands for his army to spread out on the city's northern and western sides along the river Ganga. Beyond the city lay Nanda territory. Kanyakubja was in the heart of the plains. His army camped in the surrounding villages, in small units that stamped Chandra's presence on the land more effectively. This also made it difficult for the enemy to estimate its numbers. They were far enough from the enemy to prevent an effective attack, and close enough to keep relentless watch on it.

During the day, flaming arrows were aimed at the fort. Horsemen rode by the fort many times, their spears held high, mouthing the war cry in Chandra's name and making the enemy fear an immediate attack. Elephants were readied for battle. Shravasti's entire stable had been added to Chandra's army and they were many in number, stretching from the city's northwestern gate to the low hills that led to the river, their grey hides at times making for a perfect camouflage, especially during the twilight hours. Their trumpeting accompanied the sounds of the drums and made the enemy restless. Chandra would order for these sounds to cease at night, but there was always the continuous calls of the night creatures and the cries of sleepless birds that ensured there was never complete silence.

Two cycles of the moon had gone by when Chandra received the news he had been waiting for. Some of his soldiers, helped by farmers from the neighbouring villages, had managed to dig a long tunnel that led inside the fort. The tunnel had begun near the banks of the Ganga and had entered the city after traversing a distance of around two yojanas.

He gave the command to withdraw. In the clear afternoon, a soldier's voice announced that the king Chandragupta, having waited for long, was now retreating. He heard the cheers ring out from inside the fort and his lips twisted in anticipation. His horsemen would encircle the city in an arc and the elephant units would retreat into the nearby forests.

As cries of joy rang out inside the fort, Chandra rode among his men again, advising them to be patient. It was only a matter of time now, and they had to be completely prepared.

In the evening, as the sounds of revelry inside the city rose to a crescendo, he led a few of his men through the tunnel that ended in a warehouse in the western part of the city. In the meantime, above ground, his men fanned out, making for the city's gates, which were still guarded by alert soldiers of the Magadhan army. Their killing was quiet, swift and certain in the form of a quick, brutal slash across the throat.

As Chandra and his men climbed out of the tunnel to attack the city from within, the gates were opened; their clanking drowned out the cries of horror and realization from inside. The sounds of a thousand and more horses riding in accompanied by the thundering sounds made by the elephants and the war cries of the soldiers filled the city as they stormed it by surprise. His army made for the stables, the treasury and the soldiers' encampments, sealing their presence there. Then, in smaller units, they rode into the residential precincts where some of the enemy soldiers had taken refuge. One of Chandra's commanders, Pratyusha, led his men down every lane, resolute in his commands as his men stopped at every house. Whenever an enemy soldier was found cowering, he was put to death instantly. At dawn, a new victory proclamation rang out, and Chandra'a messengers raced in every direction, carrying the news.

Over the next few days, as Chandra made plans for the rest of the journey, he formed new allies. Kings from the Vatsa region to the east, Vidisha to the southwest and the Asmakas to the south pledged their allegiance to him. The Nandas were slowly being encircled by kingdoms that now bore loyalty to Chandra.

18

KASHI AND PRAYAG

The rains arrived as they rode eastwards – there were days when the downpour was so heavy that they couldn't see their way ahead. The river roared around them, no longer gentle but a menace that they had to respect and keep away from.

For many a day they were stuck in remote villages between the cities of Kashi and Prayag, but they could not take the risk of going too close to the riverbank.

Kashi was a sacred city, its monasteries and small shrines celebrated the presence of the Buddha and Mahavira who had preached here barely two centuries ago. Priests and monks who ventured out to the river to offer their ablutions were not to be harmed, Chandra insisted, nor were the common folk and the farmers. From the looks of agreement on his men's faces, he knew his insistence had wide approval. The people – his future subjects – mattered, and they would never take kindly to the ravaging of a city long held sacred. And Chandra knew how people themselves could aid in conquest. Merchants on their way to Kashi and even artisans and a few acolytes from the monastery were stopped by his men for information about the way the city was laid out. The laymen knew the city and its different parts, and with their help Chandra and his commanders sketched out a map of Kashi.

With this handy information, Chandra and Chanakya were better equipped to plan their strategy to take over Kashi. They observed how the city operated, the hours followed by the guards and the kind of vigil they maintained. His soldiers drifted into the city disguised as merchants and even as monks. They were careful to remain inconspicuous, hiding away individually or in small groups in cowsheds, stables and warehouses, waiting for nightfall to launch small, surprise attacks at key locations.

Finally, just as the guards changed shifts at the gates and the last calls were sounded by the city's watchmen, his men emerged from their hiding places. They made for the army camps which, thanks to the information they had gathered from the map, were easy to locate. A few deaths were all it took for a surprised platoon and its commander to capitulate. By cleverly manipulating the upper levels of the army, Chandra's men were able to take the city without shedding much blood.

The next morning, Chandra entered the city flanked by his commanders and issued a proclamation from the city's centre. The chief monk of the Buddhist monastery stood by and blessed Chandra as he bowed before him.

'The Nandas no longer rule over this most sacred of cities,' Commander Pratyusha read out. 'Chandragupta of the Mauryas is your ruler and a new era of peace and justice has begun.'

The other monks stepped forward and showered flowers on him, and the city rang out with sacred chants and ululations. He rode through the city in the midst of his men, and saw its citizens smiling at him from their homes. This wasn't just an ordinary army, he realized, but one that was truly welcome. He felt heartened by the thought. The most difficult battle – the capture of Pataliputra – awaited them but he felt a renewed sense of confidence now that he had met with such success.

He wrested Prayag by taking a risk that his adviser, Chanakya, would never have approved of. His army spread out in the 'asamhata' formation – horsemen, elephant units and his infantry broke into detached units. Every few days, these units changed place with one another and the enemy was left confused, unable to estimate their exact numbers. It disturbed their preparation for war but it served well as a strategy to delude and deceive the enemy.

One night, Chandra and a few loyal men scaled the southern city walls. He had deliberately chosen a part of the city that his spies had confirmed was most vulnerable and unguarded. Again, a period of watching and waiting had helped. It wasn't just a matter of taking the enemy soldiers by surprise, but also one of causing as little bloodshed and mayhem as possible. Working stealthily and quickly, they overpowered the soldiers manning the city's gates and crucial posts like the central warehouse and treasury. Closer to Pataliputra now, he could not afford to be seen as bloodthirsty and violent. In the plains, every city was linked inextricably to the other, and the destruction of one would have an impact on the economic and social constructs of all the others.

But there were still deaths, and they were always more than he anticipated. Deaths of his own men and those of the enemy as well as the city's people, many of these innocent lives caught in the crossfire of battle – women out washing clothes by the river, monks asking for alms, and small-time traders and merchants whose lives were dependent on constant movement. At the end of a day's battle, the dreariest of all chores awaited him – counting the men he had lost, picking up bodies abandoned and unclaimed, and ensuring an honourable cremation for all warriors. Then, much later, as the shrieking of the carrion birds died away in the sky, while his soldiers took turns keeping guard, Chandra would stay up, reconfiguring strategy, planning anew, determined more than ever to win.

He tried hard not to show his impatience as he worked out a way forward. Already there had been two monsoon seasons since Mathura had capitulated. His army was now three times its original size but then he had lost many men too. It was crucial to minimize the loss of his men during battle. The Nandas, his spies informed him, had more men and more elephants. To his two thousand elephants, the Nandas had five thousand and perhaps more. His twenty thousand horsemen and foot-soldiers were no match for the Nandas. Their armies, his spies insisted, numbered in lakhs.

Yet his army was more flexible and had on its side the element of surprise. They were the men on the move, the men to be wary of. The Nanda army, forced to be stationary in its defence of Pataliputra, was clearly vulnerable in this regard. But there were other worries for Chandra too. Beyond Prayag, the movement of the trading caravans had diminished. Merchants knew best how to read the signs of war and made haste to leave for more peaceful locations. This made the people vulnerable as their markets saw lesser influx and higher prices. No matter how unpopular their rule, the Nandas were the established rulers of the region. It would be his army, Chandra understood, that would soon come to be hated if this state of affairs continued. He feared this just as much as he feared running out of supplies. Unsated, unsatisfied soldiers were the hardest to please and assure. His spies kept him informed not only of life in the cities and kingdoms around but also about the state of his own army – whether they were happy or unhappy with the long campaign and battles ahead. They were a disparate group of men drawn from all over but bound by their allegiance to him. He did as much as he could to retain their loyalty. He went on hunts with them, practised his fighting skills with the most skilful among them and also shared every meal with his men, always insisting on eating with the last lot to be served.

One morning, Chandra rode out earlier than before. The previous night he had been up late for Chanakya had rejoined him after having established relations with the Vanga kingdom that lay southwest of Magadha. The kingdom had once been an ally of Magadha. Their distinct support, as indicated by the arrival of an elite guard force with Chanakya, was an encouraging sign. Chandra was elated, but not for long. He wanted to end his long wait, to march ahead and finish his battles once and for all.

'It's the road from here that is the hardest, O king,' said Chanakya and it no longer surprised Chandra to be addressed this way. 'The pinnacle of your long journey lies there,' Chanakya continued, pointing to the east, 'and our wait and planning have been well worth it. What our soldiers have done, our messengers and diplomats have done too. They have carried your message, your promise of a just rule to every small kingdom, especially to kingdoms that were always ambivalent and undecided about their support to the Nandas.'

Chanakya pulled out a scroll from the cloth bag on his shoulder. 'This, O king, has the list of kingdoms to the west and southwest who have pledged their support to you in secret. The Asmakas to the west and the Gangaridais to the east have promised to send their soldiers only once the Nanda tyrant has been driven out.'

He leaned forward and touched Chandra on the shoulder – the earnest and affectionate gesture of a teacher towards a favourite pupil. 'But it is how you decide on the capture of Pataliputra that matters. This,' he whipped out another scroll, 'as you can see, is a well-protected city and also one of the greatest ever known. You cannot destroy it, for it has the seeds of your past and the glories of your future. To conquer it, you will need to be deceptive, strong, persuasive and always generous – especially to your enemies. Remember that you will be closely watched and judged for generations to come.'

Chanakya's words remained with him as the night eased and dawn broke. That was when he harnessed his horse and rode out, dismissing the offers of some soldiers to accompany him.

They withdrew with some hesitation, and Chandra spurred his horse onward, away from the makeshift stables and out into the open country. There were always too many soldiers with him and he was not used to that. He breathed in the solitude and realized how much he had missed it. The wind was damp and cool on his face as he rode out towards the village of the peacock-tamers. It was something he had intended to do for days since one of his soldiers had brought him the news that they had been sighted – his lost tribe which had vanished, or it was assumed, been wiped off the earth, unable to withstand the demands made by the Nandas. He was riding into forests once as familiar to him as his father's tread, forests as dense and cluttered with secrets as before. But he was no longer Moriya, the boy.

The fact that he would be recognized was the last thing on his mind. The settlements of the peacock-tamers were not where he had first thought they would be. On the way he saw that some of the forest land had been cleared. In some places, trees had been set aflame to keep away elephants but the people had since moved away.

He continued his journey, stopping when he saw crippled people on the way. Everywhere the story was the same. 'We had to move away from our homes because of the Nandas. The Nanda soldiers put some of us to work cutting down the forests. They needed more and more wood for Pataliputra and their weapons, and fences to enclose their elephants. Some of us, no longer young, could not move far. There is nowhere we can run to for safety.'

There was nowhere he could run to either. It was Chanakya who found him as he rode up, awkward on his horse, with a troop of men from the mountains.

'You cannot go off on your own, O king,' he said, his dark eyes hiding his disapproval. 'It could create confusion among your men especially now that we are closer to Pataliputra than ever before. It was lucky a passing water-carrier saw your horse and he brought us the message.'

Chandra rode up to him, smiling for he had had no idea he had ridden so far. 'I was seeing my kingdom for myself. One day I hope it will be so vast that I will lose myself trying to cover every distance of it.'

'Your hair,' his old teacher replied almost mockingly in a half-whisper, 'it gives you away.' Chandra bent over a pool and saw his hair, matted and twisted into locks that fell wild despite his efforts to keep it all leashed in tightly with a rough strip of leather.

'I was looking for the peacock-tamers.'

'Men of a tribe lost or scattered,' Chanakya snapped. 'Stop going back to the past.'

'The past has its lessons and they may not be the people I once knew,' Chandra said quietly, 'but the peacock-tamers will know how to tame the enemy soldiers too. I have a plan.'

Chanakya looked at him, understanding dawning slowly on his face. 'They can't be far. Follow the river and the tracks going uphill.'

The plan was devious, and he didn't delve too much on it. 'Poison everything that enters the city,' was his only terse command. 'Poison carries its own rumours. When people suffer, the blame will fall on those who rule, and when the rulers can offer no cure or help, it will show that they have no power. Our plan won't fail. We have to use every means to take Pataliputra without destroying it.'

He knew well that the destruction of the cities would prove to be the undoing of his rule too. Kingdoms, big, strong and secure ones, depended on cities. Pataliputra was the most splendid of all cities, its glory, the envy of all conquerors. It was the countryside that had to be conquered; the cities had to be tamed into submission. He made sure his orders were understood as he waited for the chief of the peacock-tamers to be brought before him.

'We know the stories. And we believe you are, or were, one of us once,' said the chief. The tribe had dispersed into smaller groups, divided as they were by strife and fear. Some had capitulated to the Nandas's demands, others had sought refuge in the mountains, and no one knew where they were now. Chandra did not acknowledge the chief or his statement in any way. Instead, stony-faced, he had one of his men outline his plan to the chief. A heavy silence fell; the chief bore a resigned look but Chandra knew he would capitulate. They were not made like the chief he had once known, the man who knew all of life's secrets from the forests he loved. He knew what his father would have said – 'We do not hurt the forest's creatures by force-feeding them poison.'

Those days were over. Impatient with his thoughts, and at the slowness of things, Chandra stepped forward.

'You have given up your birds for dead long ago. You have no might to match the Nandas,' Chandra snapped. 'You are trapped by the silent war that has already broken out. Defeated and angry soldiers will avenge themselves on weak beings. Our demands are for a cause. One that will matter to you, to your own people. You won't have to leave your homes to escape all the time once we rule.'

'It is against our dharma.' The man's recalcitrance surprised him momentarily.

'Is it not your dharma to care for the old and the helpless amongst you? Those you leave behind in your life on the run?'

The man was silent. Chandra lowered his voice to a more persuasive tone. 'When change comes, it also demands a change in your dharma. You have to know what you do is right, else someone else will always decide for you.'

Chandra had the man's attention. 'Our plan is to target Pataliputra, to end the tyrant's rule and restore Magadha to its old glory. We have to ensure that their soldiers succumb easily, or are so weakened that they yield readily.'

There was an unshakeable resolve in his voice. The Nanda army was huge; at best this measure would affect only a few, if at all it worked, but this was just one strategy among others. The conquest of Pataliputra was what he had been dreaming of for years, even subconsciously as a young boy, and now he would put all the skills at his command to make it happen.

'The time to strike is now and by using every means possible,' said Chanakya, almost as if had read his thoughts. 'We have to make sure that the Nanda soldiers are incapacitated one way or another.' That old, cynical look came into his eyes as he continued, 'All means, devious or foul, are right when considered in the light of the final goal. All creatures have a mission.'

To Chandra these were bleak words of comfort, knowing he had made the decision no matter how much it tore him up inside. The poison would simmer inside the birds as they were cooked, and the unwary soldiers of the Magadhan army who ate them would meet a terrible death. Some of its people, too, would be its unsuspecting victims, innocent but for the fact that they were citizens of Magadha.

'The fear and other rumours will work their own poison, you will see.'

19

THE BATTLE FOR PATALIPUTRA

Chandra found the wait hard to bear. It had been days and he had consulted every map he had of Pataliputra – the old ones that Chanakya had reconstructed for their battle and the new ones drawn up with the help of spies. It told him of the grand houses the king and his nobles had had built, and the storehouses and warehouses that numbered more than before. The treasury and granaries were located at the city's centre or close to where the elite guards were stationed so the city's wealth would be the most difficult to secure.

His spies told him that the roads leading up to the city were now even more strongly guarded. Elephants stood for miles around, and soldiers stood at the ramparts ever ready with vats of boiling water.

He was heartened by the arrival of soldiers from the north. Men from the mountains were better trained and more skilful, especially with swords. But he had also been warned about their fickleness and how they changed sides easily. Magadha's spies would spare no effort in buying his men's loyalty either. He found it constructive to observe and interact with his men to make sure they stayed loyal to him, often sizing them up as if it were just their first battle.

To ensure their loyalty, he also made promises to them that he would fulfil once he was king. The soldiers from the mountains would have the finest weapons from the Nandas' fabled armoury once the battle was over. To the hardy soldiers from the northwest, he promised they could serve in his empire's northern and western provinces, close to the regions they were familiar with, if they so chose.

For the smaller, disparate groups, he made sure they were answerable to higher authorities – every soldier would belong to a unit which would serve under a commander and every commander swore their allegiance in blood to him, their emperor.

Before the first battle was to begin, all his men retook their oaths. A huge fire was lit on the banks of the Ganga and every soldier came up to it, extended their swords to the fire and then raised it to the sky, chanting his name and their loyalty to Chandragupta of the Mauryas.

The first battle took place right where the border of Magadha began. Chandra recognized the forests he had once travelled as a young boy, and it was from here the soldiers of the Nandas launched a surprise attack. It took all of Chandra's wits to ensure his soldiers did not scatter in disarray. 'Follow me,' he shouted, his sword raised high. Then, spurring his horse on, he rode into the river, intending to break into the forest from behind, taking the attackers by surprise.

His men let out their war cries and blew on their trumpets often, and the birds scattered in alarm. As the sky darkened, Chandra charged through the sal and deodar forests, followed by his able horsemen. The ambush took the Nanda army by surprise. In the skirmish that broke out inside the forest, Chandra, his eyes long attuned to seeing well in the dark, felled many a soldier. He heard the sound of their crashing bodies on the undergrowth, the creaking of branches as these broke too, and the sound of swords clashing with each other as the men fought bravely.

It was a hard fought battle and many lives were lost. But one side was clearly the winner. Chandra knew this victory was significant. This decisive battle would affect morale on both sides. His soldiers were now eager to press on, and many of the Nanda soldiers were now switching loyalties to him. They knew, as did many others, that the days of the Nandas were numbered. His army grew with every battle that was fought and Chandra knew it was imperative to keep his men and forces together. Every evening, they took their common oath and the next day's battle plans were shared with them.

Over the next few days, his army advanced closer to Pataliputra. Their movement was purposeful, designed to sow the seeds of terror in the enemy. Under the cover of darkness, the elephants crossed the river, as did small groups of soldiers in boats that had been commandeered. Other soldiers, armed only with small daggers and cleverly disguised, had already entered the city, sneaking in along with the trade caravans, eluding the eagle-eyed guards. The horsemen, led by Chandra, set up a furious pace, galloping to the sound of beating drums and the blowing of conches. His men later said they had never ridden as fast as they did on their journey to Pataliputra. They covered a distance of a hundred yojanas over a few days, and they reached the gates just as the sound of the first temple bells rang out in Pataliputra on a new morning.

'It's the last time these bells ring for the Nandas,' said Chandra grimly but his heart was pounding fast. In a few hours, the battle for the city would begin. The Nandas had lost half their kingdom but they still had Pataliputra and the land that stretched beyond.

The walls of Pataliputra rose like a thin brown mountain not too far away now. But Chandra's armies did not advance further. On the vast open stretch of land that lay between them and the city, the Nanda army had already set up camp and was waiting for them.

'Your numbers are smaller but you can deceive them,' insisted Chanakya. The army then spread out such that the units at the back were barely visible from the fort while the units at the front were scattered so as not to look too large in number. This deception would compel the enemy to launch a reckless attack, confident of their own numbers in comparison. But the hidden units of Chandra's army made up of horsemen and soldiers on elephants, were waiting for precisely such a moment. Once the Nanda soldiers rushed in, using the conventional front attack, his hidden units would spread out, and some would even take a route by the river to attack the city's other gates.

Things unfolded just as Chandra had anticipated. He knew well enough that the enemy – in believing that their strength lay in launching the initial offensive – would commit the first mistake. The attack occured near afternoon. The bugle sounded and all at once the earth shook as several thousand elephants rushed forward, swaying wildly, their soldiers letting fly arrows and hurling their maces. Chandra had some horsemen stationed at the front; between them and the unseen horsemen behind were his foot-soldiers, flanked by soldiers on elephants on either side. Such a formation enabled his soldiers to advance quickly, breaking through the enemy's elephant ranks and spearing the elephants. This was enough to drive several of them wild. Their wild trumpeting turned to cries of pain, which was picked up by the other elephants. The Nanda commanders had committed all their forces to that initial onslaught and this soon crumbled when it was met with equal and forceful resistance.

Dhana Nanda was absent when the battle began. As Chandra led his horsemen in, riding in and out expertly through the enemy elephants, his horse rising high over the awestruck foot-soldiers of the Nanda army, he heard the stray shouts and mocking comments that soldiers uttered to each other in times of war.

'I see your king is invisible,' said commander Pratyusha.

His opponent, an enemy commander, lashed out ineffectually with his sword, panting in some desperation, 'He has us, doesn't he?'

But his sword went flying in the air as Pratyusha lunged at him with a surprising agility, and this time the laughter ranged louder among Chandra's soldiers, 'May your king disappear just as your sword did.'

In surprise and fear, a Nanda commander leading another unit ordered a halt. Some more of the Nanda army's prized elephants had bolted, turned tail, and were now running amok, trampelling their own soldiers. It was in these moments of chaos that the hidden units of Chandra's own army emerged. The horsemen covered the unguarded, open stretch of ground in no time. Some enemy soldiers tried to fight but by now they were hopelessly outnumbered and confused.

At the centre, Chandra's horsemen had made more headway through the elephant ranks. His foot-soldiers, already trained in several battles, were getting the better of the Nanda infantry. His elephants moved in from the flanks and caused more fatalities on the enemy side. In battle, it was always important to strike the enemy's animals first, compelling the creatures to either shake off their rider or run wild.

This was the most important battle of his life; it was a fight to the death, it was a fight for ultimate glory. This thought played on his mind as he made sure his men saw him at all times, leading from the front, a figure of inspiration and courage. He rode his horse among the elephants, among his foot-soldiers and horsemen, standing high on his rough stirrups, to engage with the Nanda commanders. As the Nanda soldiers saw their commanders fall one after the other, they lost heart. Some dropped their swords or bows and admitted defeat. Some cowered behind their shields asking for mercy. Many ran towards the river chased by his soldiers. In this, the final battle for Pataliputra, there could be no mercy.

It was late afternoon when Chandra and his men reached the gates of the city. Only a moat stood between him and his destination. A spear flew past him, grazing his horse, and Chandra immediately lifted his bowstring from his shoulders and let fly his arrows. He counted the men as they fell. His men followed suit, shooting their arrows at the Nanda soldiers guarding the gates, determined to take the city.

'Not now,' he said. 'We must look to our army and plan a final surge. It is best we gather our forces and take the city in stages.'

He walked among his soldiers then, counting his losses, mourning the men who had given their lives for him. Looking back, he saw the city was not as well lit this evening, there were fewer welcome fires burning now that the war had begun and lives had been lost. As night descended, the glow of several hundred funeral pyres shone both outside and inside the fort. The wailing of mourners and the menacing flutter of great birds circling above created an atmosphere of doom. Once in a while, the gates would open and traders' carts would rush out, taking the main road that led southwards. As the night stretched, Chandra saw the birds circling over and over again, and heard their harsh calls. The poison had indeed done its work, Chandra realized grimly. The city had been defeated, both from within and in battle.

In the dead of the night, the eastern gates of the city were opened. It was a sign of surrender, an admittance of defeat. The sound of iron bolts being moved and the slow creaking of wood in the wind as the gates drew open reached Chandra and his men clearly. Tension filled the air as his soldiers waited, alert, for any impending attack. A small group emerged from the gates. Only one torch was lit up to show the way, which was then quickly snuffed out. Chandra felt no impatience, only a quiet certainty.

'You can be sure their cowardly king has already left,' said Chanakya, a contemptuous chuckle followed his words. 'I wonder how much treasure he managed to carry away.'

'Those who can are indeed leaving,' said Chandra, with some satisfaction. 'It is now only a matter of time.'

Chandra led the way in, accompanied by a few commanders, choosing not the eastern gate that had been opened but the south. The soldiers guarding the ramparts had laid down their arms after a surprise attack by Chandra's men, who had been hiding in the city in wait of this moment. They called his name softly in the night, then opened the gate for Chandra to enter. At Chandra's quick gestures, his men formed silent lines, then fanned out quickly and decisively. Even the horses were quiet as the city rose around them.

He knew the silence could be deceptive. A quick glance around confirmed Pataliputra was the most well-planned city he had ever come across. The gate led to an army encampment and beyond this were the smaller houses of those who served the army – the weapon makers and the cooks. Further across another small moat were the brick houses and mansions of the merchants and the nobility, fenced in by walls and high gates.

As he continued, figures emerged from hidden corners and lanes. These were the city's poor who now came forth, with folded hands, a gesture that bespoke surrender and was also a plea for their lives. They had nowhere to go. But outside the bigger houses, as his soldiers burst through the gates, they were challenged. Enemy soldiers now sprang from their hiding places. Soon, amidst the shouts of soldiers rushing at each other in murderous fury, the clash of swords, and the hollow clunking of raised shields , there was also the sound of frantic running and screaming as the common people fled in panic. But his soldiers remembered his commands well. The innocent citizens were not to be harmed – a city needed them as much as it did its soldiers.

Such skirmishes continued through the night. As Chandra's army raced through the city taking control of it, his men always encountered a few disparate groups who put up fierce opposition. There were always some Nanda soldiers who remembered the pledge taken when they had joined the army and now could not bring themselves to desert the city.

As he reached the city's northern gate, a fetid smell made itself evident, making the soldiers mask their faces. The poison had worked, its effect seen in the quarters where the peacock-tamers had supplied their meat. It was the part of the city housing the inns and resting places for the traders and merchants that was caught in decay. Despite the stench of a deliberate unearthly death, thieves were openly looting everything in the area, their faces masked as they upended boxes and ripped apart sacks. As Chandra spurred his horse onward, they drifted away into the darkness.

When morning broke, the signs of war were clearly visible. Stray fights still broke out – spears flew in the air, swords flashed high and dust rose in heavy clouds everywhere, such sounds always followed by the shouts and victory cries in his name: *Victory is ours now. All hail Chandragupta of the Mauryas!* It was the most triumphant sound he had ever heard, and it stamped itself into every quarter, every section, every brick in the city.

Soon they found themselves in a cordoned section of the city. The temple dedicated to the Devi, the city's patron goddess, had its doors shut, its earthen lamps snuffed out – an eerily symbolic sign that the city had met its end. Even its priests had run for safety and soldiers lay dead on the streets. It was here that the empire's biggest city seemed a dark decaying shadow of its old magnificent self. But it was soon filled with the cries of victory – sounding down the streets, knocking against the walls.

The palace gates had only a few guards remaining, who stood with their spears upended and swords facing down in a gesture of surrender. A palace could not be abandoned, for this signalled complete surrender. The defeated soldiers bowed low and acknowledged the shouts of Chandra's soldiers with their own, confirming the truth – that Magadha and its chief city, Pataliputra, had a new ruler. The ride up to the forecourt was long and Chandra paused often. This was where the Nandas had lived their gilded, secluded lives. Chandra stopped, reined in his horse and took a deep breath as he saw the stables, the meeting halls, the assembly places and the palace court where the king and his nobles met daily. This was the heart of the kingdom but it was here the city seemed most empty, trapped in a slumber for centuries.

The reason for that deep silence was apparent. The royal stables, he noticed, were empty, and the main palace doors wide open. Dhana Nanda had indeed fled, taking everything with him. An escape that had been pre-planned, judging by its thoroughness, for there was no sign of the royal family and the doors of the royal treasury were left gaping open. Dhana Nanda had chosen to escape the moment the news about the first battle had reached him. Chandra smiled in contempt; his life was his, but the city's riches belonged to the city. A tyrant, now deposed, had no claim to it. As Magadha's new king, Chandra would see to it.

20

CITY OF DREAMS

Chandra rode his horse around the periphery of the palace, taking in its magnificence all over again. Through its open gate, he saw a city now open and defenceless, yet eager to welcome a new day. Its new defenders, Chandra promised himself, would be of a different mettle.

He lifted his head and saw once again, some distance away, the city's immense, imposing walls. As a young boy he had always seen them from afar and admired their power. He rode into the inner courtyard, from where he had a glimpse of the central assembly that Chanakya had often told him about. A massive statue of an elephant gazed down at him from far above. Abruptly, he brought his horse to a halt. The gate at the other hand, from where Dhana Nanda had fled, creaked in the early morning silence, and the torn flag of the Nandas slid down almost of its own volition. The solemnity of the moment seeped into him.

He got off the horse and bent to touch the ground. He gathered some earth and let it stream down onto his head, feeling its graininess against his closed eyes, his dry cheeks. 'From this moment on, the earth here is sacred,' he whispered. 'I will protect and defend it till my last breath.'

Chandra heard horses behind him. He turned to see Chanakya with soldiers following in orderly lines behind him. He dismounted and handed his reins over to one of the soldiers. Chandra looked at the man who for so long had been his teacher, his adviser, who had made this journey possible. He bowed before him. 'I seek your blessings for my journey ahead,' said the younger man.

Chanakya raised him by the shoulders. 'The honour was always mine, O king,' he whispered, before he bowed in turn. Then, turning around to the sea of faces behind them, he raised his voice and Chandra heard the joy and exultation in his every word, 'Raise your spears and swords to welcome your new emperor. Today, a new dawn rises on Magadha and Pataliputra.'

The raised shields and swords turned silver and gold on catching the sun. There was a rousing, triumphant call, the sound rising and travelling far. Chandragupta breathed it all in and knew that it was both a journey's end and a new beginning. He jumped onto his horse, a smile on his lips, and drawing his sword up high, led his men once more through the city that was now his. The ride was joyous, the men calling his name repeatedly, interspersed with mirth and triumphant laughs.

The Chedi soldiers and others from the Vanga kingdom of the south had joined them now, just as their kings had promised Chanakya. Some had begun looting the granaries and the distilleries of the city. Some soldiers were drinking themselves senseless. Vats had been overturned and alcohol flowed freely. Even horses swooned and lay bloated in the city's streets. Chandra rode out into their midst, unmindful of his soldiers struggling to keep up with him. His hair had escaped from its rough band and now sat heavy like a black cloud upon his shoulders. He had scratches and bruises sustained from the battle of Pataliputra, but they did not matter. The war was over. As the news of his final victory reached the cities and villages, ordinary people rejoiced, knowing that order and peace would return to their lives.

'Clear the bodies of the dead,' he ordered. 'As for the granaries, they belong to the people and are not for you to loot.'

'Can you see how much the Nandas were hated?' said Chanakya. 'No one really cared, no tear was shed for them. A city has its own life without its rulers, yet a ruler has no place without a city.'

Chandra nodded. He would ride through the city, down every street, pause at every corner and will the frightened people to come out of hiding. It was only later that he would give chase to the Nandas, trail them to where they had escaped. But from now on, he was the king of his people and they no longer had anything to fear. 'My lord,' he heard some soldiers call after him but he rode on ahead. The drunken soldiers tottered to their feet, embarrassed now. Some picked up their swords and remembered where their true duty lay. He heard windows opening, feet creeping up in excitement, the jingle of bangles and anklets giving them away. As he turned a corner, he heard conch shells erupt in a rousing welcome. He knew then that while the formal coronation needed an auspicious time to take place, the people of Pataliputra had understood that he was their new ruler and were making their acceptance of him known. It was a joyful and willing welcome. It was then that he paused, for the briefest moment, to raise his sword to his lips and then skyward in a gesture of victory.

That night, he retired to the palace, once the Nandas', and now his. But he could barely sleep; every now and then he rose to look out of the window at the city that was now his. Soldiers kept watch, passing each other along the ramparts. And on the streets, horsemen rode by at frequent intervals. From now on, this was their city to guard.

As he looked across the city's walls, he was suddenly beset with a new impatience. His conquest was over only in part. Restless, he made his way down to the stables, where he was stopped by two of his soldiers. The first soldier bowed low, insisting he would have a horse ready for the emperor and the other, waiting his turn, said he had important news.

It was news Chandra had been waiting for. Dhana Nanda, his wife and his daughter had been spotted in their chariot headed westwards towards the plateau, where hidden monasteries could provide a safe haven. He stopped still, then flung himself on his horse in one swift movement and shook his head firmly to his soldiers' offer to accompany him.

He headed for the road that led westwards. Every gate, every road now lay open to him, and it was a new feeling of freedom that he experienced as he rode away from Pataliputra. He breathed it in, and though he caught a whiff of danger too, it only added to his exultation. He felt blessed as he felt the new sun on his bare shoulders, the breeze as it played with his hair, the dust as it rose and fell around him, as he urged his horse to go faster.

He knew Dhana Nanda could not have gone far. He rode past the city gates, down the starkly empty roads, the silent trees and the stray carts scattered around. Abandoned horses glanced at him as he passed, vultures cawed harshly and circled overhead. These were remnants of the recent battle, evidence of soldiers who had fled in the course of battle and carts left behind by the fleeing royal family. The dust struck him on the face, then moments later, the forests rose and filled up his vision, even dimming the sky in places. What lay ahead was a battle he had to fight alone, where he had to claim his own destiny. The stones on the hard rocky path hit him painfully, but he did not care.

After riding for several hours, he saw his own soldiers ahead, waiting for him. Though they had hidden themselves among the trees, Chandra's eyes picked them out. He raised his sword, wary and conscious that he must never let down his guard. His men emerged, and Chandra saw that their swords were not drawn and that they approached him slowly.

He caught up with them, and spotted the monastery they pointed towards in the far distance. He knew then that he had finally caught up with Dhana Nanda. His men were certain of what they had seen – the two well-shod horses tethered to a tree and the chariot, now empty, that was hidden nearby. The Nandas, they surmised, had perhaps stopped here for some hours and intended to move on.

Chandra raced on, leaving his men many paces behind. The road gave way to a thorny path that was soon lost in a dense undergrowth. As his horse made its way ahead, he saw a taper that flickered to life from an upstairs window before its light was snuffed out hastily. The horse whinnied nervously as he rode up to the monastery.

The monastery was run down, a stairway with chipped stone steps leading up to its door. A light, not visible before, now flickered from an upper floor. Chandra tethered his horse nearby and walked silently towards the main door and entered the monastery. His sword moved against him and he gripped it hard, drawing strength from it. There could be a fight and he was always prepared for one. The Nandas had been responsible for his mother's suffering; she and the man he would always call his father had spent an entire lifetime on the run. And now Dhana Nanda had run away without even putting up a fight. The loneliest man, he thought, was a king who has lost his power.

'Are you looking for my father?'

He smelt her before he saw her, a fragrance made of flowers and perfumed oils. Gazing up, he saw her looking down at him from the top of the stairs. The light drifted on her gleaming black hair, which fell loosely on her shoulders. Her dark eyes held his as he walked up the stairs, breathing her in, watching her. There was no fear in her eyes, only an assurance that befitted a princess. Was this Dhana Nanda's daughter? he wondered. He remembered that one of his many spies had informed him about the princess, who was rumoured to be the loveliest of all but very arrogant, and had not yet found someone of her match.

'He is sick,' she said imperiously, almost as if she were addressing a minion, but softened her tone to a quiet plea when she spoke next. 'The monks think he cannot live.'

Chandra let his brows rise in contempt. 'He has sought shelter in a monastery – that is unbecoming of a king.'

'A king? He is more than one,' she said, her chin lifting, her face aglow despite the shadows within the monastery, her tone even and undisturbed.

'His own people did not want him.' She flinched now and he went on deliberately, 'And if they did not want him, how can he be more than a king?'

She did not answer. He felt his own anger abate and said, 'I need to see him.'

She glanced at his sword, prompting him to say, 'My sword has never been raised against an unarmed man, even a coward. And from your words I understand he is sick too.' He let his lips curl into a sneer.

He heard groans of pain coming from one of the rooms as he walked the last steps up to her. She stood blocking his way, determined not to let him pass. She was tall, and yet he forced her to look up at him as he neared, noting the smudged kohl near her eyes, the tendrils of hair that had escaped from her braid and sat loose on her cheek, and the pulse that beat erratically against her neck. Very deliberately, he placed the blade of his sword on her hip.

'Very well, then,' he said, bending to her, and drawing in a sharp breath as he felt a sudden unexpected desire to make this woman his. He pressed his hand around her delicate arm and forced himself to look down at her, 'Lead me to him then, O princess.'

He made her turn around slowly, a thin smile of intent on his lips, indicating that he would walk behind her as she led him to her father. As he followed, he found himself having to turn his gaze away from her long loose braid, her graceful steps, her tinkling anklets. He quickened his pace, irritated at himself for such momentary distractions. As they turned a corner, the sounds of someone calling in pain grew louder, and she stopped abruptly, falling against him. When his arm gripped her waist, he felt the dagger she had hidden close to her skin. He raised his sword and pulled her against him, so her back rested against his chest. 'If you had used that dagger against me, it would have been the last thing you would have done.'

She turned her head slightly to look into his eyes and then took the dagger out from her upper robes, defeated. He could have drowned in her gaze. She lifted her other arm and placed it against his neck, moving it along his shoulders to his back. He knew what she was looking for. Her eyes widened, and her touch on his skin, moving over the mark that always gave him away, made him tense. Her lips formed into a taunting smile.

'So it *is* you. The man my father called the enemy. And now, your enemy lies at your mercy.'

He knew she spoke of herself first, and that she did not know the whole story. He was the long-lost prince of the Nandas; he belonged to the family, but not truly so. He would bury this story once and for all. Decades, years, centuries later, history would tell his tale in the way it was meant to be told. For now, he would not do what Ajatashatru had done – kill a man who could be, had to be, related to him. The mark told its own story. A new story of Pataliputra could begin without history repeating itself.

His expression gave nothing away, but his eyes never left the princess. It was as if he could not stop looking at her. The princess watched him too, but her look of hostility had vanished, just as his wariness had. Her words came in a whisper and he felt them like a soothing balm, 'A king has an aura. You have it, as if you were always meant to be a ruler.'

He smiled – he could not help it – and touched her hair, feeling its silkiness. 'And when a king is defeated, you know what happens to his women, don't you?'

'They become slaves.' She threw the dagger at his feet and said, 'I am prepared for that fate. I do not want your pity.'

'That is not the temperament a slave should have.' He touched her hair again; it was a tempting mass of black silk in his hands. Its fragrance drowned him and he longed to bury his face in it. To forget his past and give himself up to the present. To surrender to his tiredness and seek refuge in the silky darkness of her hair.

But his words were lost in the shadow that loomed against the doorway, as the burning taper shifted menacingly, its flame moving in an arc.

'You dare talk to the enemy, daughter?' a new voice broke in, trembling in pain and a savage anger.

'Father, I am trying...'

Chandra saw the helplessness in her eyes, how she was torn between admitting that she was trying to save their lives, yet not giving up her regal pride even for a moment. The royal women of Pataliputra, he had heard, never flinched from or concealed their desires. They were used to being obeyed, having their secret, innermost desires satisfied. The man who had spoken was half in the shadows, his silken robes gleaming purple even in that dim light, the knuckles of his unusually white hand gripping the low wall. Dhana Nanda, it was known, hated the light, and had turned pale in his efforts to keep it away from him.

'It would have been better if you had killed yourself.'

'Father, your wishes shall be fulfilled once…'

She never finished her sentence, for her father had flung his dagger at her. Chandra saw the arc of silver like a bird swooping down. It grazed her neck, inflicting a sharp cut, as he pulled her back into his arms. Her cry echoed in the hall, drowning out the sound of the dagger as it fell with a sharp clank on the floor. For a moment, Chandra stared at the man who was his sworn enemy. And in that moment, he felt the bitterness leave him, leaving only a dangerous calm.

Dhana Nanda's lips quivered, his heavy jowls hanging loosely. His eyes glittered like a snake's and, despite his illness, he held himself straight. 'So you are the upstart who dares challenge me? It is only a matter of time before you meet a worse fate.'

Chandra felt the dampness of the woman's blood seep into his clothes and did not hesitate. Between killing the king he had deposed, and saving his daughter, he opted to rescue the woman.

Chandra thought of Chanakya. 'Forget your humaneness for once,' he would have said, 'and your need for compassion. You are now a king – think like one.'

'I am taking your daughter away,' he said quietly. 'Stop me if you can.'

'May your dynasty be as poisoned as mine is,' said the other man, not understanding that he had just surrendered in words to the younger man. He was a deposed king who knew his own soldiers would send him to his death if he was sighted. His life lay in a new king's hands. Chandra saw the realization contort the other man's face. Dhana Nanda raised an arm to shield his face. He fell back against the wall, in a gesture of defeat.

Chandra held the princess close, hoping his warmth could offer her some comfort. 'I am taking the princess away,' he repeated.

'Magadha will see for itself how abjectly you have surrendered then.' Chandra then ran down the steps, the princess in his arms. He took off his cloak, and her eyes widened with the fear she no longer tried to hide. Tearing off bits of his robe, he tried to stem the blood flow, for the dagger had cut a long gash in her neck, though the wound was not deep. There were flecks of blood on her shoulders, her torso and upper arms, and she tried in vain to dab them away. He hoisted her up on the horse and climbed up behind her. Then he began the ride towards Pataliputra, battling the sudden rainstorm that had begun some time ago. It gave him an excuse to not look into her eyes, to refuse to acknowledge, for now, his own raging emotions. She moaned softly in pain and anguish. She had perhaps guessed that she was returning to the palace she had left only a short while ago.

It seemed as if he had not slept for days now and that he would never sleep again. Time and again the city swam before his tired eyes and the reins slipped away from his hands. He looked at the woman's head against his chest and felt a longing sweep over him.

He saw Chanakya long before the open gates of the city came into view. He saw, too, the fluttering white cloth the men behind him held up. The city was finally at peace. Chandra stopped, letting Chanakya and the horsemen ride up to him.

It took Chanakya only a moment to understand what had happened. His harshness changed to a sharp gaze of concern as he saw the woman.

'What have you done?'

'What do you think?' Chandra said, his lips twisting in a smile. The next moment he was held firmly by Chanakya.

'O king,' he said in a voice loud enough for everyone to hear, 'you risked your life by going out to face that tyrant. And now your body is burning up with fever.' He turned to the horsemen, 'Summon the royal physician – and quickly.'

'I'll ride to the palace with her,' he said, tossing his hair back. 'This woman needs help.'

'She is your enemy's daughter, O king. You must show her no mercy.'

'A soldier does not kill women, especially unarmed, defenceless women.' Then with some sarcasm, he added, 'And not too long ago, you might have advised me to use her well.'

'She could be poison for you, you know,' said Chanakya, expressionlessly. 'The Nandas would not mind using their women as weapons.' It was clear his hatred of the Nandas was unabated, and would never die.

They rode in slowly and dismounted at the stables. Chandra smiled and turned away before he unexpectedly fell forward, still holding her to him. Then he felt Chanakya's cold fingers on his shoulder. He looked into the older man's flint-eyed gaze, and heard him whisper, 'It's not very far to the palace now, O king. Everything will be there as you'd have wanted. It is yours to live in and to rule from. Take every step, all the way to the inner chambers on your own. Never let anyone see you in a weak moment.'

Chanakya's hands moved to his forehead and lingered there. 'You having a raging fever that can choke the life out of you. Fight it like you have fought all your battles so far.'

Chanakya's face swam before him. He tried to nod but felt he was being singed by a fire that he couldn't get away from. Then he shivered as if doused by cold water. It made him delirious, causing Chanakya's expression to turn from concern to anger.

'The royal physician will be here soon,' Chanakya whispered after what seemed to Chandra a long time. The ride to the palace had been much longer than he expected and he was reassured by

Chanakya's steady presence by him. The sight of the palace, its stones a gentle gold in the sun, gladdened his heart. He saw the palace guards and behind them, the female attendants who bowed in unison, unhesitatingly. He saw the welcome curiosity in their eyes, a shyness in the women, three of whom now came up, hands outstretched to take the princess from his arms.

'Nothing must happen to her,' he said. As she slipped from his arms, he suddenly felt bereft and only then acknowledged the throbbing pain in his head.

A long time later, he woke to hear Chanakya say sharply, 'Why have you stopped fanning the king?' Then he heard the tinkle of an attendant's bangles before the cool breeze fanned his forehead again.

'This, before you, is the new king of Magadha.' He heard the note of pride and certainty in Chanakya's voice.

The footsteps hesitated. He saw the hovering shadow from the corner of his eye. 'This is the king.' This time Chanakya repeated it for the man who had just entered.

Chandra raised his head and opened his eyes with some effort. The darkness fell away, and the soft light felt welcoming.

The man whose eyes met his was short and wiry. Chandra could detect his hesitation at once. 'You have seen what you have to,' said Chanakya, 'now do your duty.'

'My duty?'

'This is the royal chamber where secrets stay and never leave – or have you forgotten?'

The man touched Chandra's forehead to detect a fever. His skin was cold and slimy like a snake's and Chandra flinched.

'I can tell a traitor by his very touch,' Chandra said, his teeth clenched in pain.

The man dropped his hand as if he had been struck. Chandra closed his eyes, not able to tolerate the fear in the other man's eyes. Fear in another man had always made him shudder; he found it distasteful. Fear was what drove human beings to sin. It was Chanakya's sardonic laughter that broke through his thoughts. 'No king he has served has ever spoken to him like that.'

'If the city is not cleared of rogue soldiers and the detritus of what...' Chandra couldn't bring himself to say the name, '...that coward king left behind, the situation could be worse.'

'The new city council is looking into it, O king. It is as you wish. The royal household is up and running and our men watch over the old staff. The soldiers will ensure that the situation is under control. The treasury has been sealed with immediate effect,' Chanakya said.

They exchanged glances and Chandra's own faltered as fatigue caught up with him again. His relief surprised him. Did Pataliputra matter so much to him then? It was the city that for long held his mother's secrets, the city who's name had made his father's face darken, the city that held within it magnificent secrets and terrors, the city at the heart of one of the world's biggest kingdoms.

'Not king but emperor,' Chandra felt Chanakya's firm hands on his forehead for a moment and heard his softly uttered words, before Chanakya moved away, and his familiar, raspy voice rang louder in that quiet room.

'Tomorrow he will be formally crowned emperor of Magadha. Chandragupta of the Maurya dynasty. There will be no doubt about his rule. The truth will spread from here and strike dread in all his enemies. And he will be a king like none other.' Chanakya's voice seemed to echo in the entire palace, and several bangles jangled as if in applause.

A long time later, he heard footsteps again. From the stillness around, Chandra knew it was very late. He heard Chanakya turn his head – the bones of his neck often creaked, and the silence made the moment audible. When he spoke, his voice low, Chandra surmised that he was speaking to the royal physician who had entered.

'You did take your time, didn't you?'

'Yes,' replied the physician. His laughter sounded nervous. 'This is a special medicine for the…king.'

Chandra was sure Chanakya, too, had noticed the physician's hesitation to call him king. This told him he must not stir or give any sign that he was now fully awake.

'I had sent my man out to get some special herbs. They grow deep in the forest and he was nervous about going alone. The entire city is. So we got the mendicants in the forest to help.'

'The medicine is ready?'

'Yes.'

Chandra heard the soft rattle of a wooden spoon on something metallic. The physician's quivering fingers made the bowl shake, his pestle as unsteady as he was.

Chanakya bent and sniffed. The sound of his breath reached Chandra, and he forced himself to stay still for the long moments that stretched as Chanakya's head remained bent over the bowl.

'It does indeed look special. I have never seen any medicine of this colour before.'

The physician laughed a high-pitched cackle as if he could not help himself.

'The king will recover in no time. You will see. He will spring from his bed and ride away like a tiger.'

'I see – you seem very certain of this medicine's properties.'

The man nodded. Chandra knew if he opened his eyes he would see the feverish excitement in the man's eyes, the murderous thoughts of death coursing in his veins. How many men waited for the news outside? What would happen to Chanakya later? What would they do with him? What about the men and soldiers who had come with him from distant Taxila, from the mountains and beyond? The tribesmen who were now camped outside the city, ill at ease in the plains, away from their homes in the hills? There would be far more bloodshed just from the loss of one life – his.

'Drink the medicine first,' ordered Chanakya. 'Before anything touches the emperor's lips, I have to be certain. Drink.'

'Sire,' the physician sounded flustered. 'You mean that my lips should touch the dish meant for the…emperor?'

'That is just what I meant. You pounded the herbs and made the medicine. You know the right portions. You must taste it then.'

'I already did.'

'Never mind, do it again.'

Chandra could hear the pestle shaking, probably because of the physician's fear. He heard the liquid swirl in the vessel, a man's frightened choking, his strangled gasp.

He heard the click as Chanakya gestured with his fingers. The fans dropped from the hands of the women who sat beside him. They rose, their bangles shaking erratically as they held the man by his arms.

'Drink. Make him drink it.'

He heard the sharp intake of breath. The bangles now jangled more chaotically, the noise drowning the sound of a man moaning. Then there was utter stillness, all except the hollow gulping sound of a man drinking. Then came the crash of the vessel followed by the sound of a body crumbling – the physician was dead.

'Let this be a lesson to all traitors.' Chandra did not know who Chanakya was speaking to. Someone put a wet cloth on his forehead; the coolness soothed him, and he sank into the darkness once again. Then he heard Chanakya's voice, low and reassuring in his ears, 'We must be very careful. This isn't the last time someone will try and take your life. Everything meant for you, O king, has to be tasted first. We must find someone willing to do it for you. A slave, even someone slavishly devoted to you.'

A vision of the princess of Magadha rose before his eyes, dishevelled and yet magnificent, proud even in disgrace.

The heat woke him up. The attendant dropped her fan, and he heard her voice call out gently yet clearly.

'The king…he has opened his eyes.'

Her words set off a buzz – there was a flurry of activity around him. He could hear voices echoing in the corridors and the sound of running footsteps.

After some time, his hair was washed and brushed back. Someone wiped his face with a fragrant cloth, so soft that he felt reborn. Then his feet were washed and as he felt the touch of soft hands on his skin, every trace of dust, of gritty earth, of long journeys across mountains, plains and harsh land disappeared. He did not see the face of the woman who bathed his feet. He felt other women pulling gently at his hair, untangling the knots, rubbing in sweet swelling oils, and he closed his eyes to give himself up to their gentle ministrations.

'O king, it is our privilege to serve you,' said the woman at his feet. The women behind her echoed her words, and he felt the shower of fragrant jasmine on his skin. 'On the day of your coronation, we and every citizen of this city, devote ourselves to your care and protection, sire.'

Their ministrations over, Chandra walked to the assembly hall, clad in new robes, feeling refreshed after his long sleep. The palace wore a freshly washed look. Elephants stood outside, and horses too, in an orderly arrangement. As he entered the assembly hall he heard every step he took in the hush around him. It was a momentous occasion; a city had fallen silent to mark it.

He bent his head briefly on recognizing Chanakya. The older man bowed before he walked up to Chandra, anointing his forehead with sandal paste. Then Chandragupta turned and walked up the few steps to his throne. He brushed aside the silk curtains, acknowledging the smiles of the attendants around him before he seated himself. There were silk cushions placed around him and a footstool for his now leather-shod feet. It was the throne where tyrants had once sat, but he would grace it, bring honour to it as all rightful kings must. He did not feel even a remote strangeness but was completely at ease on the throne. Perhaps kingship was a state of mind more than anything else.

He saw the assembly of faces before him. There was Chanakya, and behind him were faces that looked familiar and yet shadowed by the past. He had seen some of these men when he had ridden out across the city as its proud conqueror. Now that he was ruler, he had to look at them differently. They had been Mahapadma and Dhana Nanda's closest advisers, men who had remained because they knew no other state than Magadha. Would he be the king they deserved?

Chanakya gestured, before he intoned solemnly, 'Magadha has a new emperor now and Chandragupta is his name. Chandragupta of the Mauryas.'

They bowed before him. The women cheered and the priests raised conch shells in the air and blew into them. The elephants trumpeted outside as if on cue and he smelt the fragrance of jasmine and sandal once more. He folded his hands in acceptance and then raised them. A silence fell over the assembly and then they shuffled to their seats on the floor. One by one, they would pay their respects to the new king in order to leave no one in doubt about their loyalties.

One of the nobles, with the blackest of eyes and the shaggiest of hair, stepped forward, neatly side-stepping Chanakya.

'I am Rakshasa, the prime minister.'

'You were the prime minister. No one takes my adviser's place,' Chandragupta said. Suddenly he felt excitement pulse in him. He saw the breeze waft in through the windows. 'Ministers and advisers are appointed at my will.'

'I understand, my lord. I am here to offer my services,' he said as his dark eyes held Chandragupta's for a moment longer than necessary. Chanakya stared straight ahead and said nothing. Rakshasa was the man who had seen to his downfall before. But the wheel of time had turned, and Rakshasa was now well and truly at the mercy of the new king.

'Where is your offer of loyalty?' Chandra asked.

'That is unconditional,' Rakshasa said.

The others behind him repeated this declaration loudly, their words echoed in the corridors outside.

'My life and service are all for Magadha,' said Rakshasa. 'There is nowhere else I can go. My learning and my loyalty do not stretch beyond Magadha.'

'But what price will your loyalty in turn demand?' asked Chandra shrewdly.

Rakshasa was surprised but apart from the sudden flickering of his eyes, he betrayed nothing. 'I have nothing to offer but loyalty. But Magadha already has that.'

'In that case, Magadha needs you,' Chandra said in the insistent way he had, when he knew he would get his own way. 'Serve Magadha like you have always done. Make it as strong as it once was. As your king, I would expect this of you.'

There was nothing deceptive about his acquiescence as Rakshasa bowed one last time. 'I will serve Magadha with my life.'

'As will we.' The other ministers spoke, almost in unison, bowing low in obeisance and respect, and the genuineness of their gesture was all too clear.

After all the ministers had made their loyalty known and the official coronation was over, Chandra heard the sounds of drums thumping outside the palace, followed by the clanging of shields and the sound of a trumpet.

Only Chanakya discerned the frown on his face. He spoke quickly.

'O king, you need to appear at the window. The people of Pataliputra have gathered to see you. They want to greet their new king and celebrate the end of tyranny.'

21

A NEW KING-EMPEROR

The palace window overlooked the main square of the city. Chandragupta stood at the window and faced an ocean of people below.

'Raise your hands, my lord. This land and this sky, everywhere the sun falls now, is yours to rule over.'

'Strange soldiers are in our midst,' said the man called Rakshasa.

'They are soldiers who have saved lives. Else there could have been mayhem and bloodshed; many lives could have been lost,' said Chandragupta firmly. 'Their very presence was enough to drive the tyrants away.'

Chandra raised his arms above his head and was greeted by a roar from the crowd. He saw the rows of people moving back, bringing to his mind the image of the receding sand dunes of the desert. When he looked down again, he saw the frightened face of a child held up for him to see.

'We call him Moriya, my lord.'

The man who spoke up was immediately surrounded. Soldiers stepped in and clamped him so hard by the shoulders that the child almost fell from his arms. The child's mother pulled the child from the soldiers and held him close to her breast. Her cry, raw and trembling with emotion, reached Chandra. 'We meant no harm, my lord. Are we welcoming another tyrant in place of the old one?'

The soldiers had circled the man, the woman and the child who was now wailing piteously. He saw the crowd fading at the corners, a resentful section looking at him with hostility. He looked back to see Chanakya's disapproving gaze and for a moment, just before it vanished, the malicious gleam that appeared in Rakshasa's eyes.

'Leave them be,' Chandragupta said, raising his hand. His voice rang out in the silence and he was glad to hear it sound commanding. He saw the faces below and he said it again, 'I respect your wishes for your child. May he live in more peaceful times than ours.'

There was a rousing roar. The soldiers fell away and the child held in the arms of his relieved parents bawled even louder.

'Throw down your shawl, my lord.' It was Chanakya whispering to him. 'The royal robe, throw it down to your new subjects.'

He took off the silken yellow garment and watched it float down, catching the light of the sun. He stood there, bare and vulnerable, before the people who would be his subjects. There was silence among the crowd; he gazed down, his eyes as anxious as those that were looking up at him. The robe had fluttered down, a floating golden cloud safe in the outstretched hands of his people. A moment later, a thunderous applause sounded in the air.

'This is your new emperor, Chandragupta,' intoned Chanakya. Chandra observed how the faces of the people lit up with hope. Chanakya went on, saying the words like a ritual incantation, 'The new king-emperor of Magadha. Your saviour. The tyrants are gone forever.'

Some people were weeping openly. He saw women glancing up from behind their veils. His eyes flickered over them, still watchful.

He saw the men next to him, all wary, but their faces now held no malice or antipathy. Then his eyes fell on one, and Chandra noticed how he gripped the stone railing hard, and the frown that knit his eyebrows. It was all gone in a flash before Rakshasa was smiling too, but Chandra knew Rakshasa would not be easy to convince. Chandra needed every able man to lend a hand in establishing his empire. And able men, he had learnt, could make for redoubtable enemies.

It was only that evening when they were riding out into the city at his insistence that Chanakya explained his unease. It was about Rakshasa. 'Everything will soon fall in place. A kingdom has its own life, it just has to be better structured for it to be prosperous. But Rakshasa…' Chanakya shrugged before he continued. 'He has always been loyal to Magadha, and the Nandas, in that order. He will serve you once he is convinced you are a worthy ruler. After all, he has nowhere else to go. The Nandas abandoned him the moment all was lost for them.'

'And the princess?' asked Chandra.

Chanakya gave him a swift look. 'She chose to go back to the monastery once her wound was treated,' he said. 'This is not the time to get distracted, O king.'

It was a quiet street they rode on, the palace walls looming close. Where the street turned, the shadow of a peepal tree stretched and moved mysteriously. In moments, the gentle swaying of the branches turned to a violent rustling – then without warning, two horsemen rushed at him, swords extended.

He heard the throbbing of horse hooves almost at the same instant that a piercing whistle rose shrill into the darkening sky. In another moment, he had drawn his own sword out.

The waiting men, his own guards, slid down from the palace ramparts and rushed towards their king. He saw two other horsemen now emerge from a side-street, their swords drawn, intent on attacking him. Fighting as one, Chandra and his guards beat off the advancing assassins, stopping them at once. Chandra killed one with a swift stroke of his sword, the blood splattering him and those around, falling like dark blotches on the king's horse.

'Finished them, my lord,' said one of his soldiers. Two men lay dead. Another lay injured on his horse, which had now bolted with the assassin on its back.

When one of the men raised his spear as they chased after it, Chandra heard his own voice, firm and resolute.

'No, don't throw that. It could kill someone.'

'They will tear the man apart,' said Chanakya grimly, 'whenever they catch up with the horse.'

'It will be a pity about the horse.'

'You are learning fast,' said Chanakya. And after a moment, he bowed. 'Forgive me, I had no right to say that, my king.'

'You only said that because there were people following us,' Chandra tossed the words over his shoulder before riding on ahead.

22

A KING'S DEATH

'King Puru is dead.'
Chandra had learnt by now not to show shock, but the news filled him with sadness. Chanakya did not need to tell him how it had happened.

Malayketu had invited his father to talk about peace. The murder happened when the king's guard was down, when he was at his most vulnerable.

Chandragupta remembered the heaviness in the old king's eyes, his measured moves, his words unwillingly spoken – he realized Puru had been a man who might have welcomed what happened to him.

'He walked to his death,' said Chandra

Chanakya nodded. 'Yes, into a trap. His bodyguards were killed too. They died defending him to the last.'

They were on the palace ramparts from where they had a panoramic view of Pataliputra. Just down below, the palace gardens stretched to the gate. Looking out at his city, Chandragupta felt pride surge into him. In spite of the destruction it had seen recently, its walls broken, its buildings crumbled, he felt his heart swelling up with an emotion he could not name.

Chanakya said, 'It is your capital now, O king, yours to rule and defend and raise to all its glory.'

'Till my dying breath,' he responded.

He looked beyond at the forests, at where the river simmered blue in the sun and at the mountains in the distance.

'One day I will go there again.'

'Sooner than you think, my lord,' said Chanakya. 'The tribes and herders need to be controlled, their lives regulated. They need to make their loyalty clear once and for all. The days of the small republics are over.'

'But will they listen to us?'

'It is in their interest. A new system of governance is in place. The arbitrariness of the old will no longer prevail. The forests have elephants that the empire needs. And they are part of our empire. Elephant paths and tracks will be chalked out by elephant-herders who will provide for the empire. And in this way, everyone who is part of, or has anything to do with the forests, will lead lives as decided by the state, and the king who rules over it.'

'Are our soldiers still on guard?' At Chanakya's nod, he said, 'It is still early days, but this peace should hold.'

'Many of the Nandas' ministers have sworn loyalty to you. Others have left.'

Chandragupta knew what that meant, too. Perhaps they had killed themselves honourably – in defeat that was the only way out. 'The ministers will soon begin their work,' he said, 'and there will be rules and regulations chalked out so people can once again go about their lives and forget that there was once a tyrant who ruled over this land.'

Chanakya raised his head to the skies as he replied, 'That they already have, O king. Can't you sense it from the peace you see in your city?'

In the distance towards the western skies, Chandragupta turned to see a low cloud of dust. Chanakya noticed it some moments later and frowned. It seemed to gather in volume, a tiny storm of red and brown dust not too far away. They watched it, till the dust cloud continued on its way, farther into the forests.

'Dhana Nanda will not give up. His men, fewer and weaker than ever before, are still fighting for him.'

'They have no choice.'

'Yes, indeed,' replied Chandragupta with a brooding look in his eyes, 'you would give anything for loyal men like that.'

Chandragupta rode on ahead, charging at such a pace that he set off a furious storm behind him. His soldiers were anxious to keep up. He was rushing on heedless, as he realized much later, to the place where he had found himself only a few nights before – the Dandaka forests that skirted Magadha to the west, where the elephants roamed free. He rode down ravines, past trees whose branches crouched low over him, fording over canals, where the sun was warm and low on the water. Only when he heard nothing behind him did he slacken his pace.

The monastery lay on the ledge, overlooking the now dry river. It looked deceptively empty and uninhabited, but he soon recognized the movement for what it was. A shadow flitted over the rocks, but Chandra's arrow was already flying high, then sinking low. A man's dying scream resounded through the valley and beyond, dislodging small stones that fell in a certain rhythm to the ground.

He let his horse pick up pace then, knowing this was a trap he had chosen to walk into, feeling the arrows fly above him, some missing him narrowly. Peacocks flew out from their hiding places, deer leapt out of bushes, the sky seemed to darken for an instant.

He turned a corner, unsheathing his sword, his face hidden in his horse's neck, so that he could not be seen by any lurking assailant. Right in front of him was the most unexpected sight. An old monk sat on the ground, cradling the injured soldier in his arms. Chandragupta recognized him right away – it was Bhadrabahu, the old monk of the hermitage at Viratnagara. The monk raised his calm brown eyes, the lines on his face as deep as the land Chandra had just galloped through.

'There will be no bloodshed here,' Bhadrabahu said.

'The blood they wanted to spill was mine,' Chandragupta replied, but he lowered his sword. The monk's gaze was compelling.

'Revenge has its own cycle of violence. O king, what have you gained then in winning a kingdom?'

He heard slow footsteps and turned swiftly sideways. A younger monk stood with an apologetic smile on his face. He held a bowl and a cloth.

'You see, O king, even the smallest, most innocent of reactions startles you. You have lost your sense of peace.'

He had a low, mesmerizing voice. Chandragupta smiled ruefully as the import of that statement sank in.

'I have to; I have to stay a step ahead, or the violence will only continue.'

'You have to only begin to rule wisely and well. If you shed blood, your subjects will simply think you are like the kings of the past. Win your people's trust – the way to do that is not by shedding blood.'

Bhadrabahu saw the question in Chandragupta's eyes and smiled. 'That is for you to find out. Your advisers and ministers will help you rule but it is you who have to win people's hearts. You are their king and yet you have to be one of them. Greater than every part and among every part too.'

He learnt in the next few days that it was Bhadrabahu who had granted the Nandas shelter in his monastery the night they fled Pataliputra. He learnt it from the spy who came to give his daily report, and Chanakya added, 'Bhadrabahu was the one who roamed the streets of Pataliputra when the first disturbances had broken out, and the poison in the birds and in the granaries took the first lives.'

'In fact,' went on Chanakya, 'the monk you met will soon be here. I am told Dhana Nanda wants to make peace. Bhadrabahu will come as his envoy, at the Nandas' request.'

'Then the great monk shall be made welcome as a special guest,' Chandragupta said simply.

That morning, he stood at the immense wooden gates of Pataliputra, with Chanakya beside him, guards and attendants flanking them on every side. They waited a long time till the sun rose high but the monks did not come.

'They cannot take you for granted, O king,' said one of his ministers. 'They cannot make you wait.'

As Chandragupta walked back into his chambers, his feet soothed by the cool, darkened interiors of the palace, the sound of someone riding up alerted him. He waited as the rider, a lone monk on horseback, came into view. Chandragupta gestured from the window for the monk to be led up.

'I have a message for you, O king.' Perhaps he was too dazed from his long ride for the emissary did not bow as he approached the king. His orange robe was pulled over his face and he appeared short of breath. As Chandragupta gestured for the monk to speak, he noted to his surprise that the hands pulling at the robe were delicate and slender.

'Speak up,' he said again, not knowing why he was so distracted. The voice he then heard was faint and husky, a voice he felt he had known not so long ago. But he listened, his eyes on the bent figure before him. Bhadrabahu had been told that King Chandragupta had reneged on his promise and had sent his men to kill Dhana Nanda. The monk on that count had delayed his journey. But Dhana Nanda, angered by this news, understanding it held no hope for him, had set off himself, only to be killed in the most treacherous of circumstances.

The monk was looking up at him now, and Chandra gazed back into eyes that were deep blackened pools holding despair and anger. 'My father was saved time and again by the monk. This time, the monk himself was cheated, given the wrong information so my father could be killed by your men.'

His surprise changed to shock, for he knew who the voice belonged to. It was the princess Durdhara, whom he had saved from her father's anger, who had insisted on returning to the monastery for she would never be a kept woman, especially as a royal prisoner and a daughter of the hated Nandas. He felt her words sink in, unable to look away. He knew he had missed this voice and everything else too. It was a voice that had once stirred his senses in a way quite unlike anything else had before. She removed the orange robes to reveal that she was no monk; and he saw her simmering translucent robes and her hair hanging loosely.

'My father did not deserve to be king any more. There were too many people against him, even his own. The monk advised him to give it up, to seek peace among them. But there were those who advised him that he had to kill you. They gave him the wrong information and duped him.'

She went on, 'He was stabbed through the back, pushed down the cliff. If you look out near the cliff, you will see the people roaming there already. They are looking for him to desecrate his body. They hated him, and if they know I am here, I will meet the same fate.'

He rose to the windows and the guards at the gates saw him. The king's orders were passed on from one tower to another. 'Stop the people, make them return.'

Then Chandragupta's proclamation was read out on the streets. 'There is only one king now and Chandragupta is his name. The Nandas are Magadha's past, a past well-forgotten. The present will be better – more secure, more promising – just like the future. I, Chandragupta, promise you this, and I request you for your loyalty.'

When he met Chanakya, it was again a battle of wills.

Chandragupta said, 'I know it was you. You spread the story about my men wanting to take his life.'

Chanakya didn't utter a word. His silence was acquiescence enough; his need to avenge himself against the Nandas had driven his deception.

'It will not help to incite people,' said Chandragupta brusquely. 'The monk is right. We cannot perpetuate this cycle of violence.'

His eyes held Chanakya's before he said quietly, with determination, 'To end all this, to put the past behind, it is important that Durdhara be my queen. Our alliance will ensure that no more violence can take place and that the feud between the past rulers and the current is over. It will seal my rule over Magadha and bring peace among the people.'

Chanakya's eyes blazed. He had disapproved of her from the very beginning. He would rather the Nandas, every one of them, were exterminated from the face of the earth. But Chandragupta would not allow it. A new cycle had to begin.

Chandra turned away. The other reason for his desire to marry he wished to keep secret from Chanakya, though nothing escaped his canny advisor – he had fallen in love, with not just a voice or even her beauty, but with the most wilful woman he would ever know, one who was his equal in every way.

However the path he had chosen was not an easy one. Durdhara resented Chanakya's presence. Chandragupta knew enmity would soon grow between the two people he was closest to – one, his teacher whom he had known since his youth, and the other, an elusive, haunting woman whose secrets he would never know.

Her flashing gaze held his the day they were married. It did not falter or wilt when smoke from the sacred fire rose high, nor when he held her hand in a solemn promise to himself. The past would never come between them. He wanted her to love him for who he was and he knew he loved her too, a love mixed with undeniable lust. Now he smiled sardonically as she bent to wash his feet with milk and then wipe them with her hair. 'Are you my slave then?' he asked quietly so only she heard him.

'It is as custom demands,' she said, casting her eyes over the watching assembly, 'a queen does as the people want.'

'You are not my queen here, are you?' he asked her later when they were alone in their decorated, scented chamber. It was strewn with flowers and redolent with the aroma of incense sticks. The silken curtains were soft around them but nothing compared to the softness of her skin against his. He ran his lips over every bare part of her and then some more. He wanted to tell her that he loved her as much in her regal finery as he had when she had been in her torn garments at the monastery, but he couldn't. Her hands were in his hair, on his face, and on his skin, marking him as well.

'I give you every freedom you desire, my queen,' he whispered, as he leant over her, tired and spent, 'I only ask that you return to me always.'

She never answered him, and in the days to come, she would do what she wanted and he let her. It made him happy to see her for those moments when she was his, and he knew that she was never truly anyone else's.

When she left for the monastery, as she did occasionally, there were always other women to provide comfort to the king. But there was one evening Durdhara did not return. He knew from Chanakya's dark looks that something was wrong. The truth was revealed most reluctantly.

'Our horsemen had her in their sights but she gave them the slip. She did not go to the monastery like she usually does. We have sent out our soldiers and must wait till our riders return. You must not go, my lord. If she has not returned, if there is no sign of her, we could be right in thinking her life is in danger.'

Before they could do anything further, they both heard the horseman riding towards the palace who Chandra immediately summoned to his chambers. 'Come in,' he said, impatient when he saw the shadowed feet under the curtains. The man who entered lifted his robe and showed the tattoo of the sun on his upper arm – the secret symbol of a spy. 'Is there any news?'

'The soldiers are looking for the queen, O king.'

'Still?' Chandragupta stepped forward. 'It is night already, and she has been gone since the afternoon!'

'Sire,' the spy went on, 'we noticed Malayketu not too far from Kushinagara. Our spies say he is meeting other chiefs in secret, to form an alliance against you. He was dressed like a trader, but we recognized him.'

'O king,' said the monk in charge of the monastery when Chandragupta strode in. 'She was here, but left early. She did not want any escort, she said.' He hesitated before he went on, 'She said your guards were following her.'

'If I do not find the queen, your monks and your monastery will be in the gravest danger. You failed to protect a woman – a queen.'

The monk bowed low, a look of misery on his face. 'We accept our responsibility. We pray she is safe.'

He did not respond; in his mind he knew that if Malayketu was responsible for her disappearance, this new, most undeserving king of Gandhara would never be safe again. He would not have any refuge, no place to call home. But it was his queen he had to find first. He left the monastery in search of her.

He rode fast, past the rocks on the hills, pushing aside the branches that came in his way, but found no sign of her. He knew she could not be dead. His hair lashed his face as he rode on, bent low over his horse, and unknown even to himself, he was whispering her name. He was riding north through the Dandaka and Naimisha forests on the road that led towards Kushinagara. After hours of riding, he saw a figure lying under an old banyan tree, by the side of the road. His horse stood still as he dismounted. He gazed into the darkness and moved cautiously, noticing that it was an almost lifeless form. It was Durdhara. She looked up at him the same moment he came close, leading his horse towards her, the beating of his horse's hooves echoing the heaviness in his heart.

He lifted her the way he had done once before and held her close against him. He was bringing her back to the palace once more, as if destiny drew her back to the palace time and again. She whispered his name over and over again, and he knew she was glad he had found her. It was a long time later when she uttered the name that stilled his heart the moment he heard it – *Malayketu*. His hands tightened on her shoulder, before he relaxed his grip, knowing he must comfort her. Revenge could come later. For now, he could not believe he had found her and for those moments that he held her, he did not even think of the man responsible for this. When she tried to speak again, he urged her gently to be silent. There would always be time for conversation later. They did not exchange a single word; there was no need. Durdhara's breathing was ragged and broken, and her hands feverish and shaking. Her hair was dishevelled, her blouse in disarray. He smoothened her hair and clothes, whispered words of comfort as they rode back towards the palace.

All through that long journey, thoughts raced furiously in his mind. She had been abducted on her way back from the monastery, just where the road was most deserted. Malayketu and his men had been waiting for her. Only a king as vile and devious as him, who cared not a whit for the rhythms and rituals of proper conduct, would stoop to such a level. Perhaps he had deceived her in disguise. Chandra's resolve to hunt down Malayketu grew with every step he took.

He brought her back to the palace, quiet as he held her against him. She was moaning and ever so often he stopped to comfort her, holding her close, soothing her. He did not mention what she must have already told herself, the warnings she had not heeded. 'Leave the past,' he told her, brushing her muddy, tear-stained face. 'Leave it behind like this night that will soon leave us.'

In the palace, attendants stepped forward to help their queen. He passed Chanakya as he walked down the dimly lit corridor, but he ignored him and stayed with her while she rested, till he heard the rooster's call and saw dawn breaking.

When her eyes flew open once and she looked up at him, he bent to kiss her brow, reassuring her she was safe. She had nothing to fear any more. But she silenced him, and the anger returned to her eyes.

'They meant to humiliate you, my lord. But Magadha's queen is made of sterner stuff. They could ravage me, but did not dare attack the kingdom, even the palace.' He nodded and pulled her close, murmuring in her ears, 'I will avenge this, my queen, even if I have to pursue him to the ends of the earth.'

Then he laid her down gently, insisting she must rest. To Chanakya, who waited outside with barely concealed impatience, Chandra said nothing. There was no reply to every veiled statement that Chanakya threw the king's way. 'There are some rumours going around the place' he said. 'People are suspecting the queen of betraying you.'

'No, she did not. She never would.'

'Where was she then?'

'That does not matter,' he said. 'She is back with me now.'

'My lord, you do not understand. Her marriage to you was a matter of convenience. Dhana Nanda's sons would not dare harm you anymore. Most of his subjects have easily accepted you. But you still have enemies and they could use her against you.'

'Her marrying me means she is my wife – I have to defend her no matter what happens.'

Some nights later, an attendant was caught trying to put something in the king's morning milk.

Then one day, his robe was found smeared with a strange liquid that his new physician said was a poison that seeped into the skin, making the victim die a slow, painful death.

After these incidents, he had to give in to Chanakya's advice. 'You must not sleep in the same room ever, O king. Stay one step ahead of your enemies.' It was that very need which made Chanakya show him the letter he intended to fool Malayketu with. 'My king,' he said, 'Revenge is yours alone. The bigger battles, waged with your armies, deserve worthy opponents. I, with Rakshasa's agreement, am just trying to be of some assistance.' He waited till the emperor nodded in a gesture of permission and then continued, in a tone of extreme satisfaction, as he unfurled a small scroll.

'Do you see this? It's a letter from Rakshasa intended for Malayketu. It says, that he, Rakshasa, has changed his mind.' Chanakya's eyes scanned the scroll as he read it aloud quickly.

Contrary to my earlier agreement with you, I intend to reveal to my lord, the emperor Chandragupta, the plans you have in mind. I cannot betray Magadha. Your plans will come to no good. Your allies from the mountains will soon join Magadha's cause. As a man of honour, I am writing to tell you this.

Chanakya had the same conspiratorial grin as always as he looked up at Chandra. 'It will have Rakshasa's seal as well. It will drive Malayketu to mad anger. His allies are marked men. Now all his plans will fall apart.'

'We will wait for the letter to do its work,' agreed Chandragupta. War had to be fought by means that were devious, even if unjust. There would always be innocent victims too, but sometimes it was all part of destiny's game. And then, there were some plans he was determined to execute on his own.

23

THE ACCURSED KING OF GANDHARA

Chandragupta rode all night to reach Kushinagara – he had put off dealing with Malayketu for too long. The spy who had followed Chanakya's express instructions to deliver the letter to Malayketu hadn't reached very far. The king, in the robes of an ordinary messenger, intercepted the spy, showing him his royal seal, the new one especially designed by the bronze-workers of the city. It showed him riding a lion with the moon in his crown.

'Give me the letter Chanakya has given you. I will deliver it myself.'

The spy was unwilling to relinquish his task. 'But will you be safe, O king?'

'Don't ask that of me, my man,' Chandragupta said. 'If I cannot protect myself, I dare not rule over my people and decide on their safety.'

He did not mention the anger that surged beneath – a white blinding rage against Malayketu that he had to keep in check for now. These were the men who had dared touch his queen, his wife. It was an unforgivable insult. This time he would make sure that Malayketu would be brought to justice. The king of Gandhara would be condemned to a life in search of penitence, though Chandra doubted the king would ever find salvation. It would elude him even if he roamed every corner of the earth in his quest to be forgiven. Malayketu had committed the terrible act of parricide and now Chandragupta would make sure that he would be forever stained by it. He would not challenge Malayketu to battle. If things went according to plan, and Malayketu walked into the trap that had been carefully devised for him, he would seek revenge on his allies, believing them to be turncoats. His crimes, always underhanded, were committed in the most disgraceful of ways. This time, he would act against his own interests and there would be no one left from whom he could claim loyalty. Men, women, people all over would flee even from his shadow.

'The house, my lord, is well-protected,' said the spy with a desperate note of warning in his voice. 'He is never where you think he is. And he never sleeps in the same room twice. He is a very careful man, my lord.'

'Careful people make mistakes too. Now, it is time for you to go. Don't let me see you following me, or else...'

Chandra left his sentence unfinished. He knew the man, his faithful spy who had tried so desperately to warn him about the dangers ahead, would wait for his return at the gates of Patliputra. Farther away in the palace, Chanakya and his ministers would be waiting too. Chandra's lips were set in a stern line as he rode on. It was time things fell into place, just like he wanted them to.

Chandragupta rode late into the night, changing horses twice during that long journey. At every outpost, his men greeted him with awe in their eyes as he revealed his identity, then acquiesced willingly as he swore them to secrecy about his journey. They promised to wait, armed and ready, for his return. All was silent at Kushinagara when he rode up; the thought of the encounter that lay ahead keeping his fatigue at bay. Outside the house where Malayketu rested for the night – pointed out to Chandra by another one of his spies – he showed the message bearing Rakshasa's seal to a guard, demanding a meeting with Malayketu immediately.

'I have important information that I must pass on only to the king Malayketu. Any delay could cost him dearly.'

This got him past Malayketu's men without much suspicion. A little while later, he stood in the hallway of the mansion in Kushinagara that Malayketu had taken over. It belonged to the richest merchant in the city, a man who was a fervent devotee of the Buddha and known for his generosity. He had been forced to hand over his mansion as the base from where Malayketu plotted against Chandragupta.

Chandragupta hoped he would not be recognized. Dressed like an ordinary messenger, his face muddied and perspiring, his cloak of rough cloth bearing the ravages of a long horse ride, no one spared him even a glance. But at Sakala, during his days on the run, Malayketu had had a good look at him and was now thirsting for his blood. After all, Chandragupta had not carried out his wishes. To compound Malayketu's anger, Chandragupta was also the man his dead father Puru had willingly allied with.

'He would always send other men to fight his battles,' thought Chandragupta, 'So he could kill his old father in the most cowardly manner, and waylay an unarmed, defenceless woman...'

He shook off these thoughts and walked up the long curved staircase, showing the seal of Rakshasa again to the guards at Malayketu's door. He said imperiously, 'I have a message for the king of Gandhara; only him and none other. It cannot wait.' The guards did not notice the way he gritted his teeth over the words.

Suddenly a door was flung open and there stood the man himself, his quarry, showing his annoyance. He rubbed the sleep from his eyes, tossed his disheveled hair aside, while the women with him discreetly vanished into the shadows. He lurched forward, his eyes puffy after the night's debauchery.

'There is a message I thought you must see, sire,' Chandragupta said, bowing low so his hair covered his face. He was glad of the disguise it provided. 'A letter that could mean a lot.'

'It's about time then!' Rakshasa's seal glinted under the light of the tapers, and he saw how Malayketu's eyes widened at the sight.

'You must see this letter. I come from Pataliputra.'

Malayketu's head jerked up at the mention of Pataliputra. He snatched the letter and read it quickly, his hands shaking as he reached the end. Chanakya had laid out a clever trap – Rakshasa, unable to betray Magadha, the land he had served all his life, had instead persuaded the five kings of Kuninda, Malla, Darada, Nepa and Kekaa, all located in the terai, to throw in their lot with Chandragupta. They would no longer be allied to Malayketu. Malayketu's face contorted with rage, and his hands were trembling as he looked up at the disguised Chandragupta.

'Are you sure of this?'

'It bears the minister's seal, my lord.'

Chandra held up the seal again to show clearly who its owner was. The elephant and the quill in front belonged to Rakshasa, the loyal, committed minister of Magadha. He lowered his voice deliberately as he continued, 'After their meeting with the emperor's representatives, the kings will be resting in an inn not too far away, my lord. Only I know this. If you go there, you can present them with this evidence.'

Malayketu looked at him, his mind working furiously. His eyes gave nothing away. The anger blurred his senses, so even if, subconsciously, he had recognized Chandragupta for a moment, he did not dwell too long on it.

He disappeared into his chambers, returning only once to toss a gold coin in Chandra's face. It fell to the floor and Chandra saw Alexander's face on it. 'This coin won't work anymore, my lord.'

'Get it melted, that's what everyone is doing these days.'

Chandragupta kicked the coin roughly aside, hearing the clink of the coin as it rolled down the stairs. His eyes held Malayketu's gaze and he saw the clear look of disbelief in them.

'You dare insult...'

'It isn't your coin, my lord,' he said mildly. 'I wouldn't pick up a coin that had the face of the invader on it.'

Chandra's contempt for the man rose like bile, but he swallowed it. He couldn't help thinking this was the same man who had raged against the invader but had no compunction in using the invader's coins.

'I will have my own coins soon. My father allowed traders to bring in these other coins and thereby lost his right to rule.'

He draped his cloak around himself, and Chandra saw the glimpse of the dagger hidden in a sheath next to his chest.

'Trade is inevitable – you need to have a suitable exchange rate for it.'

Malayketu gave a short bark of laughter; his men sniggered too. 'When I am back, O wise man from the east, I will appoint you my adviser. I shall make you my Chanakya.'

As Malayketu walked off, driven by his blind rage and thirst for revenge, he did not know how close to the mark he had struck.

Moments later, Chandragupta walked out into the dimly lit streets, which seemed to be under a pall of grey – an undefined grey that signified the amoral zone between good and bad, wrong and right, where a murder could be justified for sundry reasons. Chanakya would approve of his actions. For Chandragupta, it was personal as well as political. His revenge was a necessity. He could even cite a moral reason for giving false evidence and information to Malayketu, to impel him to kill – with Chandra's enemies out of the way, his kingdom would be safe, his people unharmed. The greater good would always permit lesser evils.

The streets were silent as he rode away. Looking up, he saw the cloud formed by birds of death that had congregated over a once holy city, where the Buddha had drawn his last breath. He hoped scholars would write over this murder, erase it from books, so that it would be as though it had never happened. Five men would be killed in their sleep at a time when no warrior attacked another, even if guided by motives of revenge. Chandragupta had played a role in it and knew he would not be forgiven by posterity but that was only if posterity remembered he had been the instigator.

Halfway on his journey homeward, he stopped at the outpost of Bishnagar. His men had waited for him, just as he had commanded. They spread out, hiding themselves among the trees that lined the road. He knew for certain that the murderer and his men would be headed this way, as Malayketu was bound to, once the truth of the mass regicide was discovered. His plans to avenge himself on Rakshasa too would come to nothing, for the news of the minister being taken prisoner, in connivance with Chanakya, would soon reach him. A Magadhan spy would ensure this.

Smiling with grim satisfaction, Chandragupta bided his time, resting under a tree. He woke when he heard the soft, unmistakable sound of a snake. A long, green, dotted snake sinuously glided past him, its throat still swollen with its recent meal. For that reason, the snake would have no venom to spare and Chandra would escape its bite. He wondered if he should see that as another omen.

Then he heard the horse. From its pace, Chandra could tell that the creature had been driven to a frenzy by its crazed rider. Chandragupta stepped out onto that dusty wide road, broadened by years of travel by traders, monks and armies. He would be the only one out at this hour. He saw Malayaketu from a long way off, his hair flying wildly around his face, his clothes darkened with blood. The four horsemen behind him were trying hard to keep pace with their master.

Chandra flung himself atop his own horse and rode out into the road, signaling his men to keep up. Malayketu's horse reared up when it suddenly came upon Chandra, rising so high that Malayketu was thrown off. Chandra saw him fall in a perfect arc to the ground. Malayketu's tired horse then bolted, through the trees, running down the road, then coming back to its rider. It seemed that the horse knew there was nowhere else to go, and all the while its rider looked around wildly, too dazed, already in a mad unforgiving world of his own. Chandra heard the clash of swords as his men battled Malayketu's men and he knew the contest was one-sided. Malayketu's men were tired after a long ride; his men, on the other hand, had been waiting for this contest. It allowed Chandra to give his full attention to the man now at his feet.

'You have murder in your eyes and blood on your hands,' Chandragupta said, his voice showing a calmness he did not feel inside. 'So where do you think you are going?'

Words failed Malayketu, his face pale, his hands trembling, his hair still red as he tried time and again to wipe the blood away. 'Five men, killed in their sleep, by someone who calls himself a warrior. The most ignominious crime of all. You shame every warrior, and you call yourself king!' Chandragupta taunted him.

Suddenly, with a yell of terrible anguish that made even Chandragupta tremble, Malayketu lunged forward, a dagger drawn, but his own horse, which had been standing nervously by, now reared up and kicked him to the ground.

Chandragupta mocked him further, 'Even your animal no longer does your bidding. You cannot hold your head up high any more, you coward.'

A look of spiteful defiance came over Malayketu's face but he could not hold Chandragupta's gaze. By now, recognition had dawned on him. 'So it was you,' he said, gritting his teeth.

Chandragupta answered, 'Yes, it was me. You have killed your own allies and now you are alone, hated and despised by all your fellow kings. Just as you deserve for your sins. You killed your father by inviting him to talk about peace and you ravaged a woman just to spite me, the king of Magadha, and now you have committed the most cowardly and dastardly of acts. I should kill you but my sword has always been raised against brave warriors.'

Malayketu fell at his feet. No tears came but the howls ·that sprang forth from his mouth made Chandragupta shiver. It was the cry of a man who knew there would never be any hope of redemption.

Chandra ran the edge of his sword along Malayketu's arm. He did not intend to kill but to scar. 'When this wound heals, it will leave a scar. It will be a permanent stain that will mark you out from the rest. And the world will know you as a feckless warrior, a disloyal son, a traitor and a sinner in every way. The world will forever curse, spit and swear on you. You will be a symbol of ill omen, women will shudder from your gaze and children will run at your very sight.'

Malayketu took a few steps backwards, holding his injured arm, the tears and his dishevelled hair blurring his vision. Chandragupta did not look back even once as he mounted his horse, turned around and rode back furiously. It was morning by the time he reached Pataliputra.

As Chandragupta rode towards his palace, he held his sword and the seal embedded in his necklace up high so it would catch the sunlight and his guards would recognize him from afar. He wondered if he, too, had the look of a murderer in his eyes.

Chanakya and the queen were waiting for him. He sheathed his sword in its scabbard, and with some relief watched an attendant take it away. He felt light, as though a great burden had been lifted from his shoulders. He exchanged looks with both of them before indicating that he wished to go to his inner chamber, and saw his queen's eyes darken with a concern he had never seen before. He allowed himself to be led away, his hand in hers, while his adviser watched them leave, a bleakness in his eyes. One more enemy had fallen but there would always be others.

24

EMPEROR

The officials who had deserted Dhana Nanda's service on account of his miserliness now came back in even larger numbers, offering their services to the new king. There were others who came from afar. Students from the great universities at Taxila, Nalanda and Ujjain came to Pataliputra, while ships returned from the southern kingdoms, offering the finest silks and ivory ornaments.

That year the rains came on time and did not overstay. The crops were abundant and the granaries full. People saw this as a good sign for the new kingdom. When the monks returned to the monasteries and bandits stayed away from the roads that led to Pataliputra, it was a sign that normalcy had returned.

'There are good times but these do not last,' Chanakya told him. 'The need is to ensure that their effects stretch over into the bad times. These can come on us suddenly, with no warning. A state should be able to function with equanimity at such times in the same way it does when good fortune reigns.

'If it runs in certain order, a city, like the universe, will never go wrong. Nothing untoward will harm it. The city is like a wheel, always moving forward – its officials are the spokes. And as a city does, the kingdom follows too.'

It had taken Chandragupta only a few days to make his regulations effective. There were men regulating traders, other officials regulating measures and weights. Others oversaw the production of goods, for these had to be of a particular kind and quality. The entry of ships and carts into the city was monitored and every part of the kingdom carefully checked. Traders and foreign officials had to have a pass – a special seal – and could not enter certain parts of the empire. The city of Pataliputra was especially regulated. As part of its restructuring, pleasure houses were made, and these were inhabited by women offering every kind of comfort – women who also had ways of drawing out secrets and other information from every outsider: merchant, trader or even a visiting delegate.

The king's army was soon set to order as well. An elite group of warriors, with no ties to any other faction or group, ensured no lawlessness prevailed. The second rung of warriors had earlier worked under the Nandas, while a third group was made up of soldiers who came from distant lands or other kingdoms. A fourth group comprised farmers and artisans who could wield a sword if necessary and then there were the bandits whose bravery could be an asset. They were all kept in control by officials who supervised them, helped by a system of espionage that Chanakya had devised. In a special room in the palace, there were scrolls relating to every official, and every official transaction was recorded so that the government's functioning was clear, carefully balanced and well-regulated.

As the seasons changed, and a year moved into another, Chandragupta was to learn more lessons in kingship, but there were times when he was called away. There were always battles to fight, necessary ones, and Magadha always needed to be made more secure. Everything he did was in the interest of Magadha. The empire's borders now stretched beyond the land of the five rivers in the north and close to the Krishna river in the south. His armies had crossed the plateaus of the west to reach the port cities that lay beyond. It brought in more revenue, and the empire was stronger than ever before. But it all came with new responsibilities.

Four monsoons had come and gone when Chandra had to set off for the northwest again. A messenger had come with the news that Philippus, the satrap appointed by Alexander, couldn't control his fellow officers. There was open rebellion against him and with it came every reason to fear that such dissent could spill over into Magadha. Gandhara was under Mauryan sovereignty but friction like this wasn't always contained by borders. Soldiers were a fickle lot.

The night he reached Taxila, a city that was but a night's journey on horseback away from Philippus's realm, Chandragupta heard the news that the conspiracy against Philippus was too entrenched and widespread. Nothing could stave off the inevitable. To destroy the might of a petty satrap, Chandragupta knew, an entire army was not necessary. He would do it with a few loyal soldiers. The intention was also not to arouse suspicion in the enemy's mind. He only had to wait for the right moment – and it came not too long after.

One night, Philippus had a fierce argument with his fellow officers. It all began with a boast, a spear throwing contest and then a few drinks too many. Soon it degenerated into insults. No one would ever know who said what, though details of all that was said, the insults hurled, every snide exchange and every brutal threat made, were carried as gossip far and wide. It was a night of accusations and curses that could never be taken back or forgiven. The argument was that the Macedonian women were promiscuous, their children born of fathers they never knew. That the Greek men were peasants, uncouth and rough men, who did not know how to fight or make their women happy. They could be led by the nose like the very goats they domesticated.

The argument soon managed to escalate into a mighty brawl. One tent collapsed around the wrestling men so it looked as if a sea raged turbulently beneath the cloth as it heaved over the mass of drunken men fighting each other.

This was the precise moment Chandragupta had been waiting for. He, with a small band of men, had come over in separate groups. They hid close to Philupus's encampment, keeping watch over their activities. Chandra knew Philippus was in the tent next to the collapsed one. He felt the blood throb in his veins as he prepared to attack. The potion he had imbibed, prepared especially on Chanakya's instructions, made him light-footed and agile. He could jump through air if he wanted to. His sword could fly too, mowing down enemies at will.

His hair blew in front of his face as he crept towards Philippus's tent. He wished he could tie it up, but he had left it loose in the manner of a Greek soldier. He cut a neat slit through the cloth and stepped in. No one noticed his entry, for the men were still fighting. He nearly slipped as he advanced slowly, ordering his men to stay behind. They would intervene only if he took too long. The ground under his feet was squelchy, for liquor and blood had flowed too fast and freely.

Perhaps Philippus had seen him. His eyes bore the look of a man who knew he faced an inexorable threat. He had moved away from the brawling soldiers and stood alone, near the tent's entrance. As Chandragupta neared him, his eyes widened and he stepped back, losing his balance and falling. Chandragupta's dagger caught him neatly and blood spurted out. There was no cry of startled surprise as the viscous liquid gushed in a thick stream.

It was only when Chandragupta had slunk out again – after wiping his dagger on the tall grass – that he heard the shouts. No one was following him, but the shouts made him run to his horse and spur it on to make a speedy escape. The enemy soldiers behind him were inchoate, shrill and maniacal – sounds that belonged to hell, he imagined. These were men who had no control, men who were left at the mercy of sinister forces. Yet he was the man who had murdered in cold blood. He rode on faster, pushing these thoughts away. This death was necessary. He kept telling himself this, and shut out every other thought creeping into his mind.

He did not return immediately to Pataliputra, though he knew it was dangerous to stay where he was. But one death created more enemies, and he had to overcome them all. He had to make the northwest frontier of his empire secure before he could return home. His head ached, and his heart too. It would never be over, for he knew that the best of Alexander's generals, Seleucus Nikator, ruled further to the west, a man blessed as the son of Apollo himself and undefeated in most of his campaigns. One day, sooner or later, Chandra knew he would have to face Seleucus in a decisive contest.

Two days later, as he camped at Mehrgarh, an ancient fort town south of Taxila, the news came. It was early morning when the horseman rode into the yard with the message.

'He has indeed gone, the last of Alexander's satraps who remained on our land.' Chandragupta unrolled the scroll that the spy had written. It was as he said. Eudemus, the satrap, had ridden away with his troops. The time for the annual festival of the sun was due, and he had left. Chandragupta looked westward. Seleucus was all that remained to be overcome, the border between them invisible but clearly etched in his mind.

He turned to his cheering band of men, the faithful few who had accompanied him to the northwest regions of his empire. 'The general from the west may have abandoned his position but he still claims this land. Do not let your guard down, ever.'

'Your empire,' Chanakya was saying, 'now stretches to a journey of ten nights on horseback. And our horses are the fastest on earth.' In his mind, Chandragupta saw his kingdom spread out, from the Himavat mountains in the north to the Krishna river and beyond in the south. There was the sea and the dry desert of his youth that made up the western provinces of his empire and in the east, his kingdom bordered the Brahmaputra, a river to match the spirit and majesty of the Ganga and the Indus.

'Where the mountains look over us, and the rivers begin and end,' Chandragupta mused, 'that entire stretch of land is ours. There shall be no other foreign invader ruling over us. King Puru fought but he gave in and the Nandas were worse. A king who becomes too complacent doesn't deserve to be king. He was greedy for all the wrong reasons.'

Part of the ill-gotten treasure of the Nandas went to pay Chandragupta's officials and soldiers, who were then deputed to different regions of the kingdom. There were always men to watch over these officials and soldiers; always someone watching over someone else. 'An administration should work on a perfect system of checks and balances,' said Chanakya, 'that's what makes an empire truly functional.'

In the west were the fabled rich kingdoms of the Sahyas and Saurashtra, and Chandragupta's armies rode there, faster than the enemy spies could carry information. And no army was quite as big as the Mauryan army now; it was almost like a small kingdom on the move. Wherever his army stopped, it became an encampment not very different from Alexander's. There were the elephant camps and makeshift horse stables, the immense communal kitchens and smithies, and then his own tent, always guarded zealously by men he trusted and women soldiers too. Over it all, the lion flag of the Mauryas fluttered high, a sign of reassurance to those under his reign and a threat to those who opposed him. However, the area beyond the Indus in the northwest, even farther ahead of where Alexander had once set up camp, was still threatened by Seleucus' presence.

With every mile he advanced, his empire grew bigger. Territories were ceded in some instances and in others, they were conquered altogether. There were other smaller kingdoms in the west such as the Bhojas and Mulakas who accepted Chandragupta's sovereignty. An annual tribute was levied and ambassadors were exchanged. A defeated king or one who chose to surrender was treated with honour. Humiliation, Chandra realized, only created more enemies. Power gently exercised lasted longer than an evil tyranny. The future of his dynasty depended on that.

There were the old routes set up by monks and traders but his soldiers made new ones, roads that made Pataliputra the centre of his empire and at the intersection of all major trade routes.

At Kalinga in the east, the king's messenger rode out towards his forces, holding high the white flag of surrender. Chandra had won over another ally, in line with Chanakya's formulation of his foreign policy. A powerful state would offer its protection to a weaker one, and come to its assistance when the latter was threatened. Diplomacy was another means by which a stronger state exerted its power, avoiding war in the process. But even in the avoidance of war, a strong army remained essential.

For it wasn't just a question of winning a kingdom and holding on to it, but to continue to maintain peace. Peace, he was learning, was impossible without first waging war. Peace needed the best army with the bravest soldiers and strict regulations to preserve it.

More than just securing his conquests, most of those first years of his rule were spent on matters of state; passing judgment on small issues such as how much mercy to accord a farmer whose crops had failed, and to frame rules for this, and on bigger matters like the number of presents to be sent to neighbouring rulers, and the guards to be stationed at border regions. All this required a mix of graciousness and watchfulness. He found he had to fight sleep in order to carry out his duties. He knew that he had to keep a balance between fighting battles and good governance to ensure peace and prosperity in his kingdom. Meanwhile, the larger battle with Seleucus loomed ahead.

25

MEETING A LOST FRIEND

It was as he set siege to the kingdom of Kangra in the far north, encamping by a village near the city of Arithapura, that a villager brought the news that someone had been captured. The captive had been offering a reward to anyone who would accompany him in his search for gold-digging ants.

'My lord, he had promised to give all his gold to those who lead him there. He really wants none of it for himself.'

This strange declaration intrigued Chandragupta. He wondered what drove men mad in search of gold, to accumulate it in hoards hidden deep in the earth as Dhana Nanda had. Now, here was a man who was hunting for gold, and making rash promises.

'All the gold is yours, my lord,' said Rakshasa. 'So if he has audacity enough to offer a reward, it is you he is challenging. It is a most serious offence, king.'

The prisoner was brought to him. He lay flat on the ground, and had been dragged with ropes that bound him all over. A fair-haired and lean man with a short beard, his hair was much longer than Chandragupta remembered but there was no doubt as to who he was. It was Megasthenes, the cheeky young man from Alexander's camp, the ineffectual fighter who had now been reduced to an even more pitiable state. Chandragupta dismounted from his horse and demanded the man be set free.

One of his captors spoke up, 'My lord, we captured the traitor. He was about to set off...'

'That was cowardice,' Chandragupta interrupted sharply. 'It took the whole lot of you to subdue this one man, who...' He took a quick glimpse at the man lying prostrate on the ground, his vacant eyes not directed at anyone. '...was really armed to the hilt, wasn't he?' he asked sarcastically.

Another soldier offered him a seal the man had carried, and he looked at it with interest. The seal showed a man who wore the moon on his crown – Chandragupta identified him at once as Seleucus, who claimed allegiance with the moon, just like him. His lips twisted at the thought. It intrigued him as well... He knew he could not put off a contest with Seleucus any longer, but first, he had to deal with Megasthenes.

His voice rang out in raw anger, 'If he's a challenger in any way, it is I, the king, who has to deal with him. None of you have this authority. In torturing him in your own way, you defy me.'

His men nodded, looking abashed. 'We beg forgiveness, my lord.'

But Chandra's thoughts were also far away. He remembered how much Megasthenes' bravado had annoyed Chanakya during their earlier encounter. 'I will deal with him soon. Keep him tied so he does not dare escape.'

The old city of Arithapura was not too far away and Chandragupta and his men reached it well in time after their departure from the village. He was ushered into the chief's house to rest when he reached. He woke up a while later, on hearing a sound that filled him with a sense of unease. When he heard the sound again, he rose quickly, pulling his cloak around himself in the chill of the morning, and walked out into the courtyard.

Megasthenes, their prisoner, was strung up on ropes, dangling upside down from a tree, his moans broken by the twisting and creaking of the ropes. His head swayed and was caught in a terrible angle, his hair brushed the ground, making that soft, sweeping noise time and again.

Chandragupta tightened his cummerbund, shrugged his hair out of his face and walked noiselessly past his guards. Two were still awake and their eyes widened on seeing him, but he silenced them with a wave of his hand. He took a sword from a sleeping guard's hand and covered the ground in a few moments, cutting off the ropes that held Megasthenes with quick sharp strokes. Then, hoisting Megasthenes over his shoulder, he took him closer to the fire.

The man shivered and curled into a foetal position. His golden hair, streaked in places with dirt and blood, picked up the light of the fire and glinted strangely. He shivered again, and moaned in pain. Chandragupta picked up his shawl from the threshold and draped it over the man.

Then all was quiet, the stillness broken only by the sound of restless animals in the faraway forest. Megasthenes was looking at him, the old mischief all gone. Instead in his eyes, caught in the waning fire, Chandra saw an alertness – a quiet, understanding wisdom.

'It was all by your orders, O king.'

Chandragupta did not look away. Instead his lips curled with disdain. He said, 'You threw a challenge – my men read the signs. You might not have survived to tell me this. They are loyal in every way and took action.'

'Death can come so suddenly, so very unreasonably,' the other man said suddenly, almost as if he were speaking to himself. He was lying on his back, looking up at the stars. 'Alexander, the great conqueror, succumbed to an illness and he never reached home.'

Chandra thought of the passing of time. News of Alexander's withdrawal had come to him earlier in the midst of his campaigns. Perhaps it was when he was at Shravasti or – he tried hard to remember – some days later, at Prayag? The news had sunk in slowly, and then, with his commanders, he had returned to the task at hand – preparing for a siege or a surprise attack. Since then, three monsoons had gone by and he was now conqueror and ruler of Magadha. He had devoted his time to getting things in order, setting up new administration and eliminating rivals. And then there was his queen. He had fallen in love among all these other things.

The sadness he felt at the news of Alexander's death was momentary. A conqueror had come and gone, yet nothing would remain of Alexander, in these parts especially. Chandra realized that the memories of those days and nights had all blurred in his mind.

Megasthenes was speaking again in his low, hypnotic voice. 'When you consider all that has gone before, the vast universe, you realize, O king, how small your place in this world is. It does not matter whether you live or die.'

'Are you telling me it does not matter that I live? That I should not bother with doing my duties as a king? Even in keeping my kingdom secure for my people?'

'No. All I know is that for however long we are here, we live according to honour. Not because of our own needs, but to sustain order and chaos in the world, for the sake of our fellow men and fellow beings.'

'You talk like a man of sense,' Chandragupta said. 'Yet you were greedy for gold!'

'Ah, but there's a difference.' Megasthenes raised his head on his elbow, wincing before flopping down again. 'I wasn't greedy. It was those ants I wanted to see. You see, my lord, I have travelled too far and too long. In many ways, I am now jaded with what I have seen. I read about these ants in a book on my long journey here.' He frowned, trying hard to remember. 'Or maybe it was one of those storytellers I met at some inn or roadside. Or.the wandering monks or perhaps the man who robbed me in the deserts of Persia, when I had wandered out, leaving the soldiers and revellers behind.'

'But aren't you Alexander's man and now Seleucus'?'

'I am his ambassador, for that is my pretext to travel. No one else was willing to be ambassador. I was never made to be a soldier, not even to serve in Alexander's army. Soldiers followed him, and as long as he was there, we thought the world was secure. But it wasn't to be. He couldn't persuade his soldiers to stay with him. Like any of us, he couldn't even save the one he loved.'

His voice dropped. The skies were lightening now. The soldiers had woken and noticed that they were beside the fire, their footsteps automatically falling silent as they neared Chandragupta.

He knew what the man was referring to – the death of Alexander's best friend. In spite of all his watching over, his penance, his withdrawal, no heavenly power had listened as the life slowly drained from Hephaestion. Even the conqueror had been left helpless. Everyone said that his friend's death had hastened the emperor's own illness.

'You are lost in thought, O king. Don't take my words to heart. There was a time when Alexander stopped listening. He should have turned back once he lost his friend. But he had lost too much of himself with that death so he no longer recognized reality for what it was. Hindsight of course grants us all this wisdom…'

Chandragupta remembered the man he had seen. Someone with so much power – the conqueror of every place he had trod upon – had trembled on his feet, as if he wasn't really sure of his place on earth. Megasthenes said the next words so softly that Chandra felt he had heard them in his head.

'I travelled far and away. But even I knew his death was inevitable. Thus ended the life of one of the world's greatest conquerors.'

The crackling of the kindling diverted Chandragupta's thoughts to the past. It seemed so timeless. It was the sound that had accompanied all his night journeys, from his boyhood to the present. There were other timeless truths too. But he would not let himself dwell on another emperor's weaknesses or even his sad decline – he had his own empire to make secure. He looked at Megasthenes, a taunting smile on his face. 'It is to Seleucus, your master, that I offer my challenge. There can't be two emperors in the shadows of the Himavat.'

26

SELEUCUS

Several days and nights passed as he made the long journey once more, riding with his army from east to west, leaving Pataliputra to head towards Taxila. The seasons had changed and only when Chandragupta reached Taxila did he realize he had come a long way once more. Gazing out at a moonlit night, he thought of Durdhara, and hoped she was looking at the same moon too. It had already been a long time since he had left the palace. He found himself restless, as he did on some nights. The wind seemed to urge him on; the river sang as it lapped the banks time and again. He saw the moonlight fall across the river, spreading over it like several moons glittering on the water.

He had been told by a messenger that the queen was with child. She had appeared on the royal ramparts and the city had broken out into joyous celebrations. That night there had been much revelry in the encampment, but he had only half-heartedly joined in. He wished he had been with her in that moment.

Lost in his thoughts, he felt a sudden movement behind and turned around swiftly, his hand on his sword. The moonlight glimmened on his sword – and on an alarmed Megasthenes as he stood there, one leg over the rampart.

'Do you always react like that?' Megasthenes asked plaintively.

'I don't like people who creep up behind me,' he said, without sheathing his sword – which Megasthenes noticed. Megasthenes regarded his friendship with the Magadhan king as something precious and fragile, for a king could never really trust anyone. He always found the Magadhan emperor eager to hear news of people and customs from distant lands, but Megasthenes also understood that Chandragupta never let his guard down, however friendly he might seem in conversation.

Megasthenes came forward and Chandragupta noted how soiled and muddied his robe was. He smelt of horses now.

'I did not hear you come riding by.'

'I wouldn't be such a fool as to let myself be heard or seen. Your men kill first and ask questions later.'

'It's what they are trained and supposed to do. My life is always in danger. The empire, especially in these parts, is still unsettled in some ways.'

Megasthenes nodded. 'I am not really an enemy so perhaps someone did let me through.'

He laughed at the nonplussed expression on Chandragupta's face. 'It's all right, there is nothing to fault your men for. From some tribes in the north, I learnt the art of levitation and the skill of jumping through air, across roofs. You would know these skills that roving warriors of the area have made into a fine art.'

Chandragupta sat on the ramparts, watching the soldiers talk amongst themselves, change positions, walk along the camp, tend to the fires, every once in a while looking up, knowing the emperor was there, watching them. It was also a way of reassuring themselves that all was well. In a world of constant uncertainty, he had to provide them with some stability and meaning.

'From the manner of your entry, you evidently have some momentous news to give me?' he asked sarcastically.

The other man bowed, and admitted, 'Over there, in the lands beyond the Indus, the threat grows again, this time from men of my own land, belonging to a ruler I represent. A ruler who grows stronger and more ambitious by the day. Someone who knows your plans and is making his own.'

Megasthenes said these words slowly and deliberately and Chandra realized that he was a man torn. A man bound by loyalties of state, Megasthenes was now caught in the dilemma of his own loyalties, those formed by the heart. And these, Chandra thought, as his wife Durdhara came to mind, were always unwillingly formed and harder to let go.

Chandragupta held his breath. This was the moment he had been waiting for. The war with the Nandas had been won quickly and decisively. Destiny had been so heavily stacked against his enemy that his victory now seemed like a foregone conclusion. There were other smaller kings who had unquestioningly accepted his authority because Magadha was always more powerful than them.

But the challenge posed by Seleucus Nikator, the satrap of Alexander who was now master of the eastern part of the Greek empire and who had declared himself king, was something else altogether. The promised battle with him that Chandra longed for, would decide once and for all if he deserved to be king; if he could indeed claim to be Alexander's worthy successor as a great conqueror. He felt his heart beat faster, the blood drum in his veins, as he heard all that Megasthenes said.

Seleucus' armies, according to Megasthenes, had reached west of the Indus. 'Seleucus is not much different from you, my lord.' He stopped as he saw a flash of apprehension across Chandra's face. 'Why am I telling you this, you wonder?' Megasthenes continued softly. 'War is inevitable. This piece of land, fertile and strategic, cannot hold two emperors. It will be a fight to the finish, and a resolute one. If you play your cards right, it can be bloodless and come to a quick conclusion.'

In that faint light, as the sound of the encampment faded and rose around them, he saw Megasthenes' expression change. His eyes no longer had their look of dancing mischievousness. They held a sad, serious light, and his mouth was set in firm, determined lines.

Chandragupta sneered. 'I can't believe what I am hearing. You sound like a man of peace.'

'It would be hard not to be one, O king, if you have travelled as far as I have. The truths of the wandering monks stretch farther and deeper than the truths of a soldier.'

Megasthenes dug inside his robes, the jangle of coins breaking the silence of the night. Chandragupta saw the coins dance in the moonlight, turning silver as they fell on stone.

'Here is what he looks like.'

Chandragupta held one up realizing he was staring at another king. He shifted, and still the shadowy face was clearly visible – the piercing eyes now silver and all-seeing, the thick neck and the thin, cruel lips that the metal had moulded to perfection.

'They say he is invincible, the son of the god Apollo, himself.'

They exchanged the briefest of smiles then, two young men in mutual complicity. 'Apollo did sire a lot of sons. That mustn't have left him a lot of time for other things.'

'Yes, a story to claim superiority over others. They say Apollo himself marked him as his own.'

Megasthenes rolled down his sleeves. A cold wind had begun to blow and the river had turned grey. He pointed to his shoulder. 'He has a birthmark like an anchor, something you cannot miss.

They say when he was born, the mighty Apollo pressed his face on his shoulder to leave his mark.'

Chandragupta nodded, for the story did make for an enduring legend.

'The great king...' Megasthenes often referred to Alexander this way, and his tone never lost that half-mocking sneer. '...he once wanted to see which of his generals was the most loyal, and would be willing to risk his life for him. Not to see the man's bravery, but just to make an utter fool of him.

'It was on the banks of the river Tigris, deep in the deserts beyond Persia, and everyone was drunk. The river was in turmoil, and it was utterly and totally dark, the way it can get in the desert, when the blowing sand makes you forget the light forever. You could not only hear the river close by, you could hear jackals howl and wild asses bray with abandon. You would not be mistaken if you thought they were drunken soldiers. The torches rose higher, and for some time that kept the animals away. In that quiet, as the generals professed their loyalty one after another and as the laughter died away, the great conqueror flung his diadem into that cold, raging river.

'We saw it move like a crescent, a bright necklace of light sweeping in that darkness. It continued like a comet that had come very close to the earth – an omen. No one realized it then. The splash of water it created as it fell was like a small tidal wave itself.' Megasthenes stopped when he saw the disbelieving smile on Chandragupta's lips. 'I am not exaggerating; you think all I do is tell you stories, but I see omens everywhere. Even in that arrogant gesture, which would be the last gesture that the greatest of all emperors made, or the silence that followed. I wondered what it meant when Seleucus dived in. He wasn't the strongest, or the most favoured, but he seized this once chance that fate had placed in his hands.'

Chandragupta nodded. 'I have heard of his bravery. He was one of the elite guards, one of the most skilled swordsmen in the world. I learnt my skills just watching them in the camp. See...'

He hurled his sword up into the air, towards the sky. It flashed like a thin rod of lightning, slicing the night sky neatly, and then returned as swiftly as it had gone up. Amazed, Megasthenes held his breath as Chandragupta cartwheeled and caught it by the hilt.

Megasthenes regained his composure and continued with his story.

'None of us actually knew who jumped to recover the diadem. They all just heard a second, louder splash and that was when the laughter died away. One of them had jumped, in accordance with the command that came from the lips of the greatest of all conquerors. Then everyone began speaking up, hoping to identify one another by voice.

'Alexander was too drunk to care, but then came the sound of someone furiously thrashing in that river. Everyone strained to see – one of the soldiers found a lit torch and held it up but we could only see the bulrushes turn golden and white as they moved in the wind, softly, unconcerned. The thrashing died away, but you could tell someone was there. I knew who it was, and that this time he would prove himself.'

'And he did?'

Megasthenes smiled an old man's smile.

'Out of all of them, all those jackals, he was the bravest. A man who was a warrior, a man his leader could trust absolutely. The diadem shone even through the water and you could see Seleucus rising with it. In that darkness, someone threw a spear at him, startling everyone, and Seleucus veered erratically to avoid it. I knew then that he would always be cautious.'

Chandragupta raised his hand. 'Yes, I know what you mean. That he had been the most daring, but he did not want to be foolhardy. Tell me, what would you have done if you had been threatened by all that envy? What would the greatest of all emperors, when he was younger, have done?'

'He would have fought. Seleucus was an elite swordsman after all, not only because of his courage but because his caution and his own ambition made him so. He dived underwater and waited as the other men stared into the river. When he eventually emerged out of the water, they were still in the stupor of drunkenness. The diadem was on his head as he swam. The strangest thing was, the emperor was awake then, and I could see how he squinted his eyes against that blinding light. For a moment, we couldn't believe it – that Seleucus had put the emperor's diadem on his head, not accidentally or carelessly but very deliberately. Both the emperor and I saw the reckless look on his face as he looked at us through the weeds.

'Seleucus placed the diadem at the emperor's feet, but Alexander turned away. Even in that state, he could speak decisively like an emperor – "Go away, before I decide to teach you a lesson."

'Seleucus vanished after that incident, but like all stories, it became a legend. Stories abounded about the man who had taken up the emperor's challenge and had then dared to openly mock him, the man who swam away in that cold dark river till his strokes were faint and the ripples died away. And a long time later, when emperors had turned to dust and generals were at each other's throats, Seleucus surfaced out of nowhere. For he was a man who could bide his time and wait. But the wait has been a bit too prolonged this time. He is now a king but almost no more a warrior. He hasn't fought battles in some time now. He has had no worthy challenger, or so he thinks.'

27

THE WARNING

It was dawn when they set out towards the region beyond Gandhara across the mountains, their direction secure as long as the sun lay behind them. They were headed for the borderlands, the still unclaimed land flanking the eastern end of the Zagreb mountain ranges, on which both Seleucus and the Magadhan Empire had their eye.

As the world grew dustier and rockier around him, Chandragupta knew he was moving farther west than he ever had before. Megasthenes rode ahead, his back straight, his hands strong on the reins. Unlike Chandra, who now belonged to a land he had claim over, Megasthenes was a 'nowhere' man, an emissary, a man forced to live away from his home, or someone who really had no home. Their positions could change if relations between their kingdoms suffered. What made men like Megasthenes give their lives to the cause of diplomacy, making themselves vulnerable to being homesick all their lives?

Megasthenes stiffened when he felt the sharp edge of the sword on his back. 'I really don't know if you are leading me into a trap,' said Chandragupta.

Megasthenes did not turn around as Chandragupta pressed the tip in deeper. Instead, he stopped his horse and sat ramrod straight. His breath came in quick gasps, but his stance was still unwavering.

'That was your intention, wasn't it, you traitor?'

'That is the name even Seleucus might call me. I have no way of proving otherwise, O king. But we were not going far – if you can trust me for a few miles more, you will see for yourself this strangest and most unpredictable of Alexander's generals.'

'But how do I know I can trust you?'

Megasthenes stretched his hand out with a smile, but Chandragupta pressed his sword in even deeper. Blood ran down his back and tears sprang in his eyes.

'I have no way of assuring you, O king. Only my own trust and faith in my abilities to see the future are my defence. The future tells me that you do not see war and violence as an end in itself. I will lead you to another tribe, men who live with the falcons and the hawks, training them for the pleasure of kings. They dwell high up in the mountains and can tell you more.'

He pointed far up. Chandra, his sword still firmly placed against Megasthenes, looked up at the looming mountains, pockmarked in places by stunted trees. He saw hunched black figures and realized a moment later that they were birds, proud falcons and eagles that were emperors of their own universe.

'Men climb up those heights to capture the young birds. They are a king's passion, their sport, a symbol of all that they stand for. These men can tell you more about Seleucus and where he is. Perhaps then you will plan your move well.' He turned his head and looked at Chandragupta, who nodded curtly and withdrew his sword.

They rode a short distance after which they tethered their horses to a tree and looked around. High up in one of the trees, where the leaves moved a trifle faster, a branch creaked. As Chandragupta strained his eyes for a sharper view, a man made a spectacular leap forward, jumping from tree to rock before tossing a rope up to an overhanging ledge and climbing quickly up the higher rocks, pulling the rope up behind him before vanishing.

'We can wait here. It won't be long,' said Megasthenes.

Chandragupta rested with his head against the tree. It was the furious call of the eagles that caught his attention. The man they had seen before was now shinning down the rope along the rocks, his eyes alight with triumph. Chandragupta saw two eagles circling overhead in agitation. The two birds formed a thin black ring in the sky that narrowed and widened as the birds kept pace with each other. A smaller bird, evidently a fledgling, struggled in the man's arms. He had secured it from the birds' nest and was now smiling at his prized catch. He clamped thick iron bands onto the young fledgling's beak. The two onlooking men could hear the small bird's harsh breathing and the terrible fluttering of its wings. High above them, perched now on the highest branch of the tree, spent with their circling, its parents shrieked in frustration. Chandragupta saw their flaming yellow eyes flare up in anger.

'We need to go – their wrath can burn these old mountains up,' Chandragupta said.

He knew these birds from his boyhood days and now lifted his bow and aimed arrows straight into the sky. The pair of birds shrieked and flew high into the air, becoming two black specks in the wide blue sky. The two men dashed for their horses and went up to the bird-catcher.

'He pays a good price, doesn't he?' asked Megasthenes.

'Ah, he does,' said the bird-catcher. 'He wants the finest birds to train, those who will follow him around, circling over his head.'

Chandragupta realized they were talking of none other than Seleucus. He held out his hand. 'That bird's mine, I saw it with you first. Hand it over.'

Megasthenes grinned as he saw how startled the bird-catcher was. 'Do as he says, Upasika. You don't know how skilled a fighter he is, or how determined a king.'

'A king!' exclaimed the man, scanning Chandragupta's face. At once his own face turned pale and red in succession. 'My lord, I had no idea.'

In reply, Chandragupta gestured to the surrounding land, demanding the man's acquiescence. 'This is my land, and all its birds, too, belong to me.'

'But...'

He drew his sword and the man's fear was clearly evident. The bird in his hands had stopped fluttering. It was exhausted from its struggles, looking helplessly from one man to the other.

'You will tell Seleucus that the great emperor Chandragupta demanded it. From now on, all lands west of the Indus, right up to the deserts where King Darius once ruled, are his. The land this bird and his forebears flew over is King Chandragupta's now, and all its inhabitants are Chandragupta's subjects.'

'But...' stuttered the man.

'I am sparing your life,' he said, showing him his sword. Reflected on the shining blade was the bird. Chandragupta knew he had to possess it to send a message to Seleucus. 'I am letting you go this time because your master needs to get this message, but...'

This time, as the frightened man's hands shook, the bird slipped off and took a quick hop and jump across before it settled itself on Chandragupta's arm. He spoke to it in the way he remembered, urging it to be comfortable and pointing to his shoulder.

'You can show Seleucus how serious I am, too.' With a swish of his sword – so quick that Megasthenes gasped in astonishment – he ran his blade down the man's forearm. 'You can present this dark, gaping wound to Seleucus should he disbelieve you, or think you deliberately dishonoured his request.'

The man screamed in pain. 'My lord, my lord, how can I dare go against your wish...' Tears of pain coursed down his cheeks, but Chandragupta did not relent. 'In our times, upstarts can become kings too, and tell themselves stories of success.'

Chandragupta's lips twisted as he thought of his own story, not too different from Seleucus'. His heart beat faster as he realized that the battle he had been waiting for was finally at hand.

The man rode away, whimpering in pain, his blood falling in short, quick drops, leaving a trail behind him. Chandragupta now enquired of Megasthenes, 'What do you think? Do you think Seleucus will come surrounded by his army, leading his men on his fine horse, with all those divine birds around him?'

Megasthenes did not answer, too shocked by what had just happened. He looked around at the rough scrubland stretching all around him. His eyes lifted to take in the mountains and the thorn bushes growing at a height, all now silent and watchful around them. 'This land will always see battles, even though the years have seen monks and saints travel through it with their messages of peace.'

'I did think of sending Seleucus your head on a platter,' said Chandragupta with a smirk. 'But then I would not have had a fascinating storyteller for a companion.'

That night at Taxila, he left Megasthenes behind and rode on westwards. 'Don't let this man out of your sight,' he said to his soldiers, pointing to Megasthenes, not looking at him. It was always a two-edged game with him. But Megasthenes' life was in danger, not just from his men but from Seleucus' too. 'He fights no battles because he isn't one of us. And because of that, we must protect him too. Not a hair on his head is to be harmed.'

Horsemen had ridden all night to deliver him the message that his armies were marching in from Pataliputra and Ujjain, that tribes and hillmen had joined in as well.

'My lord, look...'

They saw the bird flying towards them and heard the determined tinkling of its bells as it neared. It swooped down low from the sky; the golden afternoon lit up its wings, which glinted, making them shade their eyes. Then they saw a group of bird-catchers descending from the hill. They came up to Chandragupta and bowed.

'Seleucus knows,' was all that the chief said.

They beat their drums and signalled with their cymbals. The falcon stopped, peering down as it took one slow, complete circle in the sky. Chandragupta kept looking up, never turning his gaze away till he saw the bird drop the scroll it carried so carefully in its beak. Then the bird rose magnificently in the afternoon sky – and in moments it was gone. Its grace had left them all spellbound.

28

THE STAND-OFF

Their armies faced each other, just as Alexander's armies had faced King Puru's, on either side of the Jhelum. The river was at its broadest here, and fields of ripening yellow wheat stretched on both the banks. The Mauryan army on the eastern bank could not see Seleucus' tent amidst the sea of tents that had sprung up overnight. In the manner of all enemy armies facing each other, the two sides tried to goad each other, each wishing their opponent would commit a mistake.

Chandragupta knew such a situation could not last for long. All day long, small battles raged, arrows flew fast and furious across the river, as did insults. Sometimes flaming torches were catapulted across too. Drums were beaten, shields clashed, and trumpets were blown at all hours simply to terrorize the other and make them lose sleep. But these had other effects too. The elephants, kept in a state of half-hunger, were chafing. They would soon lose control. The thought that their agonized trumpets perhaps sounded more fearful to those in the enemy camp brought little comfort. Sometimes small groups of Mauryan horsemen would participate in small skirmishes across the river and come away victorious. Sometime, they lost. The tally continued to mount by the day, but each side refused to give up.

Chandragupta was impatient. The sounds of battle – swords clashing, shields striking against each other with rhythmic force, the hooves of horses stomping on the ground – were fearful and undying. There was the smell of expectation everywhere, of confused animals and the fires that never seemed to die down. That was the Greek way of befuddling the enemy; the other side would never know where soldiers lay in wait, where the next battle could happen.

Surprise the enemy with their own methods, he remembered Chanakya's message, written to him in secret ink. *Send a spy and sow dissension,* his wily adviser had said.

But it hadn't worked, he thought to himself and shuddered. A spy's head had only recently been sent back in a horse bucket. Even the bravest of his soldiers had turned pale when the lid had been removed. The severed head had been placed in a bed of horse dung, and the blood had mingled with the hay. The smell soon pervaded the entire tent. They had burnt sandalwood incense for the entire day to purify the air and remove that stench, which disturbed the animals more.

Sleep evaded him. The need to be on guard, a constant change in his sleeping quarters, especially as he was surrounded by people, had stolen his sleep. He missed his days in the forest, when he did not have to be on the look out all the time. He was secretly afraid of Megasthenes betraying him as well. Had he trusted Megasthenes unthinkingly or had he treated him with the same contempt everyone did?

He remembered the conversation he had with Megasthenes just before he left camp. 'Seleucus' beloved birds will be alarmed by this constant noise. They will be jittery and upset. You can press him for peace because he'll be open to it at this point.'

Chandragupta did not believe him and Megasthenes evidently expected this.

'Look wisely and carefully. His tent will be the one where the birds will perch,' said Megasthenes. 'Be it hot or cold, if they are active or tired, they will know where Seleucus' tent is. They say it was his wife Apama, princess of the dry desert land of Persia, who was first fascinated with birds. My lord, you mustn't doubt me this time. Too much time will be lost if I am to prove this to you. But look for the tent I described. Peace will prevail then and victory will be yours sooner than you expect.'

The waters of the Indus were cold, and the first gentle splash hardened Chandra's veins, turning his blood to ice. But the cold allowed him to see things more clearly – the blue waters, the cold night sky and, behind him, the four soldiers who were his closest guards, more loyal to him than clansmen could ever be.

They were decoys, all dressed as him, hair tied up and knotted the same way as his. Every precaution had been taken to guard against the possibility of his assassination. It was again a strategy of Chanakya's, devised in consultation with Rakshasa, for under Mahapadma, the Nandas had been experts in using threat and subterfuge against their enemies. 'Never underestimate the enemy, my lord,' Chanakya had said. 'Even he has weapons and strategies that you can learn from. And most importantly, you must learn from his mistakes.'

What was Seleucus' mistake? That he loved his Persian wife so much that he had acceded to her love for birds and this fondness was proving to be his weakness?

The falcons moved from one tent to another. They looked agitated, their sleep patterns irrevocably changed because of the raging fires, the shouts of the soldiers and the elephants' piteous, heartbreaking calls. The nights continued to grow longer, and the sounds endless. The two sides had faced each other for days now.

At an opportune moment, Chandragupta and his men advanced, crossing the river at its wildest and most unguarded point. They looked like Seleucus' soldiers, many of whom were from the mountains farther north, and from Persia. The soldiers right by the riverbank, on guard in Seleucus' camp, were huddled together, trying their best not to fall asleep. They were hiding their faces in their long cloaks, their spears and long swords firm in their hands. The restless and disoriented birds continued to swoop overhead in that kingdom of tents.

Suddenly, one of Chandragupta's soldiers tripped over a peg. He tossed away his cloak as it caught in the rough edge, prompting a few of the Persian soldiers in Seleucus' army to look in his direction. Chandragupta took off his helmet, hoping to divert their attention. His long hair fell loose from its tight knot and tumbled in abundance over his face and shoulders. He pointed at the birds, speaking up now in Old Persian. 'Things have changed. When birds do not sleep at night and elephants and horses rage all day long, you can tell...'

He ducked as the spear flew above him and the enemy soldiers broke into raucous laughter. 'I can tell the world is indeed becoming strange,' one soldier said, laughing with his companions, 'when a soldier is given to philosophizing.'

They dared not sigh in relief. The theatrics had worked. In the darkness, the soldiers had not seen Chandragupta's face. He tied his hair quickly, for its fragrance could give them away. They lay against the rocks again, waiting for the sounds of laughter to die away.

Careful now. He mouthed his warning emphatically and his soldiers nodded.

The birds continued to fly higher in circles, sometimes crashing into each other. In the end, as if unable to help themselves, they shrieked, giving in to their pent-up despair. A spear pierced the air between them to silence them, but it resulted in hundreds more flying up from everywhere, from the tent roofs and ropes that stretched to the ground. Someone lit a fire and raised the torch high, but the birds panicked only more, and their shrill cries now filled the sky. Chandragupta and his soldiers inched forward softly, their faces hidden in the long cloaks they wore in the manner of Seleucus' soldiers.

Other soldiers, farther away, now aware something had disturbed the birds, realized something was amiss. They rushed outside the tents, their swords catching the light of the fires, their confusion manifesting in cries of alarm in multiple languages – Koine Greek, Bactrian and Old Persian. It suddenly felt as if morning had set in too quickly.

The five of them surged ahead with Chandragupta in the lead, knowing they had to take advantage of the melee and barge into Seleucus' tent. Its yellow top, now dotted in places with distressed birds, flapping their wings ineffectually, was visible from some way off, and as king and commander of his armies, Seleucus' tent was the biggest one around. As they neared, Chandragupta signalled to his companions that he would go in alone. His soldiers taking their cue, began shouting up at the whirling birds, drawing attention away from Chandragupta. Those who stood guard at the tent's entrance were momentarily distracted. One of them was tackled quickly by Chandragupta who dragged his body into the tent's folds. He knew the other guard would meet the same fate at his soldiers' hands. It was imperative that this work be done quickly and with quiet ruthlessness.

He saw Seleucus the moment he burst into the tent. The general looked up, his attention drawn by the sound of a body being dragged in. His hands, as he donned his armour, stilled and Chandra noticed how the metallic glint of his armour shone even in the greyness inside his tent. Chandragupta let his eyes take in everything in one swift glance. It was a tent far bigger than any he had ever seen, and he could see the famed diadem shining in the darkness. He was also aware of Seleucus' steely-eyed, unwavering gaze fixed on him. The other king had been caught by surprise but like a true king, he was not giving anything away.

For a long moment they stared at each other. Seleucus was a lean man, but shorter than Chandragupta. This height made his appearance deceptive, and his fellow generals in Alexander's army had mocked him for it. Perhaps that was why he surrounded himself with all the paraphernalia of royalty, as if to make up for his lack of height.

'They said you were brave, and indeed you are,' he said, speaking slowly in Old Persian, and choosing his words carefully. He knew it was another king he spoke to, regardless of the unconventional circumstances of their first meeting. 'A trifle foolhardy though, if I may add, O king.'

'I had to meet you face to face. I was told you don't really want a war,' retorted Chandragupta. 'My men are more battle-ready than yours. Isn't that obvious?'

The mockery was not lost on Seleucus. He knew Chandragupta had walked into his tent almost unnoticed. Seleucus had no idea how many of Chandragupta's men waited outside. He took a step to the side and Chandragupta stopped him, pulling out a dagger and placing it very deliberately on the low divan between them.

They stared at each other, not saying a word, while the birds above them refused to settle down. He heard their fluttering over the hard cloth, the mad scrambling as they looked for a foothold and then flew away again. The chanting of the soldiers only grew louder.

'I will hear out your proposal, O king,' said Seleucus at last, his face flushed with humiliation, 'but first you must let me assure my soldiers. And I promise...'

Chandragupta raised his hand, and Seleucus had no need to finish. True kings acted in honourable measure towards one another.

Seleucus gripped his sword and walked with determined strides to the curtains.

'It's all right, calm down and go back to your positions. Stand guard. Do your duties and the birds will do theirs,' Seleucus roughly barked out orders. Chandragupta listened to him, a knowing smile on his lips. He felt a grudging admiration for Seleucus, a king who would never let anything tarnish his honour; he would never reveal that he had been surprised in his own tent. Chandragupta remembered what Megasthenes had told him not too long ago – Seleucus was more king than warrior.

The next moment, a movement inside the tent and the sound of rustling, drew his attention. He picked up his dagger and whirled around in one fluid motion. Responding instinctively had become second nature to him. Then Chandragupta drew in his breath at the unexpected sight of a young woman.

She lay in an alcove inside, her face framed by the thick silk that covered her head, turning softly now in sleep. His spies had told him Seleucus' daughter, called Helen, was a sprightly young maiden, who often, disregarding her mother's advice, accompanied her father on his long campaigns. She loved riding out into the cold desert and also loved the mountain air. Chandragupta, remembering all this, realized his spies' descriptions hadn't quite measured up to what he saw. They had missed telling him something else as well – that she was chained to the bed, almost as if Seleucus feared she would run away any moment.

Helen was the loveliest woman Chandragupta had ever seen. As she awoke, pulling the thick blankets away from her, he saw the puzzled look on her face. The calling of the birds was now greatly diminished and as her eyes focused on him, she pushed the golden tresses of her hair away from her face. Chandragupta knew he had to quickly effect a change in plan. He lifted the dagger and raised a finger to his lips in warning. The presence of an intruder king in his own tent was an embarrassment to Seleucus, but if his daughter sounded the alarm, soldiers would burst in readily. He looked around quickly, assessing the situation for himself.

His eyes strayed to the entrance of the tent, where the tent folds moved, revealing Seleucus' presence. Chandra also saw the swift shadows moving against the tent cloth, and knew the soldiers were returning to their positions. They would soon pick up any suspicious sign, such as the presence of a different guard outside their king's tent. In one swift move Chandragupta picked up the diadem that had once been Alexander's and was now treasured by Seleucus. Then he heard her voice – clear, low and musical. He saw her parted red lips, the blue of her eyes, and the golden tendrils of hair that had escaped from the headscarf she had hurriedly put on, and then he heard her say, 'You can't...you can't.'

He looked back, and this time her blue eyes flickered with nervousness as his eyes, grey and intense, rested on her. 'Father always has a way of getting it back.'

Chandragupta smiled thinly, ignoring her warnings. She shrank as he moved towards her, intending to find his way out through the entrance on the other side. There would be guards there too. He placed the diadem inside his thick cummerbund and held his dagger more securely. Then his glance strayed towards her one last time – she was now sitting up, her elbow on a cushion, her blue eyes wide in disbelief. The contest with Seleucus would have to move to another day. He had the diadem after all and Seleucus, proud of his position as king, would hate to be mocked. The thought of a rival king and his guards entering Seleucus' closely guarded tent and stealing the latter's most prized diadem was an embarrassment.

Aware of this thought, Chandra bowed mockingly towards Helen and then brushed past where she lay as he made for the other exit. The curtains parted softly around him. He thought she had smiled and that he must have smiled back too. One surprised guard looked back but Chandra had dashed out, weaving through the small gaps between different tents. The guard would not dare barge into his king's tent to inquire. The momentary confusion would help Chandra get some distance between him and his pursuers.

He made his way back through the milling group of enemy soldiers and towards his own camp. His soldiers, waiting for him by the river, gasped when he prised open his cloak, and held up the magnificent stone-encrusted diadem. Its glow seemed to spread and fill the night.

The skirmishes began to acquire a new intensity, and it seemed as if the war would not be resolved between the two equal foes. Several nights later, the first of the emissaries made their way to the other camp. Blood had flown freely by then. The exchange of arrows and insults continued, but the armies fell silent when white flags moved between the camps indicating the passage of royal messengers.

It was Chandragupta who wrote to Seleucus first. The cycle of vengeance had to be stopped, and the need to blame innocent men for letting intruders into Seleucus' tent had to be snuffed out. Chandra's spies had reported how some among Seleucus' most loyal guards had already paid the price for their negligence.

Chandragupta knew Seleucus was still smarting from the intrusion. It was obvious from the kind of silence that persisted in the opposite camp, broken only by the shouts that would erupt every once in a while. Chandra had the diadem placed on a velvet cushion outside his tent.

'Innocent men who made no mistake but guarded you with their lives should not pay the price for our intrusion. This is the blood sport of cowards and tyrants. The diadem is mine now,' he wrote to Seleucus.

This time the reply was not delayed. 'My guards forgot their duty and should pay the price. You took the diadem from my tent and disappeared. You should have stayed and fought.'

Chandragupta's lips curled. Later, the emissary would tell Seleucus that he had mocked the Hellenic king, who had once been one of Alexander's most trusted generals. But only Seleucus knew what had transpired between them. The revelation that an enemy king had breached his tent would make him an object of open ridicule. No king could survive that loss of face, or even dare make war.

Indeed, the story of how Chandragupta had sneaked into Seleucus' tent was soon all over the two camps, rumours giving the story more colour and drama. No matter how much the accounts diverged, none of these placed Seleucus in a good light.

'There is no point in fighting an unnecessary war,' Chandragupta wrote, 'one which we both do not want. It is a wise king who does not choose war over other options.'

In this atmosphere, battles dwindled in intensity. As messengers began moving from one side to another, other rumours too floated freely – of how one king wanted to return home because his wife, in an advanced state of pregnancy, was asking for him; of how another had quietly accepted defeat, besides the fact that his daughter had been seen riding up to the riverbank, close enough to the enemy, looking for the enemy king she was now totally besotted with.

'This war is over; you could not vanquish Magadha in your short battles. This land you and I choose to possess by force will never know peace if we go on. But a permanent peace is possible.' Chandragupta wrote in a note sent across to the other side. Later, two special emissaries followed. They had Seleucus' diadem with them and one last message from the Mauryan emperor.

All lands west of the Indus belong to Magadha, and whatever lies even farther westwards, beyond the Malayvat, is yours. And you shall also have five hundred of my best-trained elephants, and keepers too, to look after them.

Seleucus had glanced at his daughter and then nodded – that was what Chandragupta's emissaries soon told him. The soldiers repeated the story to every town, village and outpost they passed, that, Alexander's chosen successor, had indeed said, or whispered, 'I accept your conditions.' Seleucus had not, at that moment, told Chandragupta's men of the condition his own daughter had placed on him. She, who rode fearlessly and for miles in the desert, who rode for so long at times that her father, fearing she would be kidnapped by his enemies, often had her chained, had now made an impossible request. She had always longed to see more of the world, a world beyond the mountains and the desert. She would even join the handsome enemy king's armies if this gave her a chance to do so.

Seleucus' last message reached Chandragupta as he led his army out, at the beginning of their long journey back to Pataliputra.

The message was delivered by a warrior bound by oath not to reveal the contents of the message to anyone but Chandragupta.

It was wrapped in a sealed bag under his tongue, hidden just as Seleucus wanted. It simply read – 'I would be honoured if you accept my daughter as your wife. It would cement our agreement once and for all.'

Chandragupta stared at the scroll, the thought of the beautiful princess flashing through his mind. He had heard more stories of her, urging his spies for such reports, acknowledging his guilt in not thinking as much of Durdhara as he once had. His eyes lingered on the elegant inked notes. He wished he had a way of reading the princess's mind. Was this what she wanted, had she readily acquiesced to her father's wishes? Perhaps she too had heard stories of him too and Chandragupta knew, stories were often just that, and quite far from the truth. They had only seen each other by the light of a taper. The two kings now had an uneasy friendship which could very easily be ruined by a woman, even a daughter.

Would Seleucus really want Helen to marry him – an alien ruler, his empire centred in the plains, and would she, a princess used to the cold and arid desert, accept it? It seemed inconceivable. How would a princess of the dry desert region live in the dull heat of Pataliputra? How would she bear the frenzied rain that poured down on the city? And most importantly, how would Durdhara – his queen – accept her?

Lamps lit up in every village that Chandragupta passed by or rested in for the night. Myriad colourful patterns decorated every wall and every mud floor. The closer he came to Pataliputra, the more he felt Durdhara's presence, sensing her impatient wait, her sadness at his absence. He could not tell her about Helen yet, or even about Seleucus' offer. There was a chance she already knew, especially about what had transpired inside Seleucus' tent, but for now his heart had to keep its own secrets and heed its own counsel.

He was glad Chanakya joined him once they reached the plains; his trusted adviser could tell when he had to choose between his own interests and that of the state. As a king, the two were entwined in his self and he found it hard to be objective.

'You must indeed consider the proposal. It will secure the western frontier forever,' said Chanakya with little hesitation.

'But as a son-in-law, he would see me as a threat as well.'

Chanakya laughed, the harshness of the sound bouncing across the old stone walls and floors. 'I doubt it. His own position is never as secure as he would like it to be. So if he's sure of you in any way, that is some relief.'

Chandragupta nodded, yet he hesitated. As if Chanakya understood, he said, 'The monsoons will arrive in the plains any time now. It is time for you to return. Say yes… A marriage can be solemnized whenever the time is right.'

PART III

DHARMA

29

OF POISON AND OTHER MATTERS

Chandragupta paced the terrace at night, deep in thought. His armies had reached Kushinagara on their march back to Pataliputra and Chandragupta had decided the Kushinagara fort was a good place for his men to rest for the night. His soldiers would later say that their king never slept, and it was he who saw the horseman first in the dawning light. He realized – from the direction the messenger came from – that he had to be a bearer of his queen's message.

The messenger stopped below the terrace and bowed before him. He looked up and said, 'The queen has been asking for you, my lord.'

'Is she unwell?' Alarmed, he ran down the winding staircase of the fort and out into the open courtyard where the horses were being washed.

'She has been counting days, my lord,' the messenger said. 'The whole empire is awaiting the birth of the heir. May he have the sun god's protection.'

Chandragupta quickly mounted his horse and was soon on his way. It was with relief that he sighted the stone walls of his fort at Pataliputra. He realized he could now conjure up Durdhara's lovely face more clearly. It was this thought that filled him with gladness, and made him jump off and dash through the flowers showered at him as he entered the palace. And then through the open door, he saw his queen.

She was reclining on a silken couch, looking pale, yet beautiful. For a while, she warded him off, holding him at arm's length. 'I am told you have changed – yes, you do look preoccupied.'

He averted his eyes for a moment. She turned his face back towards her and smiled, but he recognized the sadness in her eyes.

'You never sent a messenger for me, my lord.'

'There was a war to be fought.'

He felt her stomach, and felt a movement against his hand. 'I see he is already a warrior.'

He felt soothed in the cool comfort of her chamber. His hands, which were caressing her feverishly and passionately, stilled – for she held his face in her hands. He could not turn his eyes away as she spoke.

'I heard about her, my lord, and what she wants of you. I was told of your sleepless nights, the way you restlessly prowled the riverbank looking across at the other side, the horizons your eyes scanned...and I knew you weren't looking for me – I had not even strayed into your thoughts.'

Her voice was low and sad. He thought of another woman's laughing eyes and turned away.

'There is nothing I can hold on to, my lord.'

'You are afraid of losing what you have,' he said. 'Wasn't that why you agreed to become my queen?'

He stumbled over the possessive word. He saw her turn pale, but something made him continue. 'You did not want to let go of what you knew well, of what you were already used to.'

As he said this, he saw every emotion flit across her face – anger, pain and a terrible betrayal. He understood then how she felt. How could he have thought of another woman when she had fallen in love with him and he had given himself up to all her fiery passion?

Hating the look in her eyes, he said gruffly, 'You need to rest now.' She lay there, unable to move. As he touched her, he realized that for all the impression she gave of strength, her fragile, bird-like bones gave her away. When he spoke to her next, his voice sounded distant, and he chose his words carefully, 'Sometimes I find, as king, there are things one must do for the sake of the state.' He thought of her father, of the Nandas and the many kings before, and how they had forgotten this distinction. The king was the state, but the state mattered more. He did not say this to her; instead, he kissed her once again, and wished there was indeed something he could say to reassure her.

'My lord.' But he had only imagined her whisper it. She stood up from the couch, her face turned away from him and stumbled. He sprang to her rescue and steadied her. All her new heaviness was strange, he thought, as he held her close, his face buried in her neck. He realized she smelt different, more of the unborn child than anything else. Some of her love for him had faded as well, just like he had changed in irrevocable, unknown ways.

Then, placing her down on the low couch, he held her close, stroking her hair, caressing her, willing her sad memories away. She placed her hands on his stomach instead and they sank in the deep cave that formed. 'Love has made you starve.'

He laughed and found his old love for her returning. For some days he basked in her love, knowing for some time, he could keep thoughts of battle away. He could even keep Seleucus and his proposal waiting, though thoughts of his lovely daughter flooded his mind at unbidden moments. He returned to the present, knowing he was a warrior who thrived on battle but such moments of peace and love had been hard fought over too.

Just another day, he always told himself, unable to tear himself away from Durdhara and the peace he felt in Pataliputra. But it was not to last.

That afternoon was a particularly joyous occasion. The ceremony to celebrate the impending birth of the heir to the throne had brought a glow to the queen's face. She refused to rest, turning down Chandragupta's pleas that she do so. 'I will have all the time to rest, my lord, when you are away.' And only he heard the sadness in her tone this time.

Soon, the attendants streamed in with an array of food. They led the two of them ceremoniously to a low mat, but he waited for the queen to be seated first. She walked heavily and he helped her, feeling her rest against him, revelling in the way her veil slipped off her shoulders and revealed her swollen breasts. They were fuller, more rounded, and she smiled as she caught his eyes on them. Every woman was a temptress, he thought, smiling back.

'You look older,' she said, noticing his frown lines, the wrinkles at the corners of his eyes and his hard, weary hands.

'Older before my time,' he said.

Her smile was sad. She stopped him as he leaned across to sample the food. 'My lord, you are forgetting.'

Her hand stopped his wrist and he heard the sound of her bangles sliding back. He smiled at her reassuringly, to tell her he was well aware of the precautions enforced on him since his early days of kingship. The food served to him was always tasted first, on Chanakya's advice, and it was always one of his trusted guards and attendants who volunteered. Ever since their days of wandering, Chanakya had worked with poisons and herbs believing that the ill-effects of most poisons could be countered if the body was made accustomed to small doses of it, taken in gradually and over time. The body then became inured and even indifferent to the poison.

'Only someone who has your trust has to offer to do this first. We cannot take a risk,' Chanakya had said, that first night at Pataliputra as he, lay sick. He remembered that and so, as he saw Durdhara playfully lean over his own plate, he did not hesitate, wanting to indulge her. He was certain there was no danger.

He watched as she bent forward and took a morsel of the fragrant rice. Her eyes were on him all the time, a look almost teasing at how concerned he appeared. He would remember it all later. How he saw himself reflected in her large, blue-black, kohl-lined eyes, and how her eyes suddenly narrowed in awareness, then widened in surprise, before she fell back.

He was on his feet in a flash, knowing what he must do and yet somehow he felt his movements were slow. He prised the fragrant rice out of her hands, his hands reaching for her mouth that was clamped shut in pain. He felt the dampness on her hands and her forehead, her low, pained moan. His hands trembled and the drumming sound he was unable to recognize at first was his own heart. He leant over her, his lips on hers, desperate with fear. All he wanted now was to suck out the poison she had so willingly taken. Guards and attendants were running towards them, he could hear their footsteps as they rushed forward. Then he felt a hand on his shoulder and he was jerked back roughly.

'O king, you must move away,' someone said.

He could only stare as the attendants burned incense before Durdhara, making his eyes tear up. She stared at him with the same beautiful eyes he had come upon that distant night in the monastery, and slowly they closed of their own accord. He wanted her to know that he had loved her all along, even through all his betrayal and his days spent away from her. Would she ever know that? That fiery mocking gaze had dulled, misted over and he saw the froth bubble up and run from her lips. He wiped the froth away as she moaned.

She looked at him one last time, and as he took his fill of hers, he saw they were wide open in fear and alarm. He felt the baby's sharp kick once again. She whispered, 'Save my child, O king.'

He looked up uncomprehendingly and saw Chanakya standing before him, the man who until recently had supplied him with most answers. His teacher looked on expressionless; he only hoped this time the king would agree with what he said.

'Move away, O king, move away. The physicians and midwives are here.'

They carried her away and he saw the curtains fall, a soft sound that seemed to snuff out the warmth and comfort he had known only a few minutes ago. He heard her scream, again and again, and he turned to Chanakya in anguish, 'The poison in my food – I should have stopped her.'

As always, the harsh eyes did not look away, nor did they give anything away.

'It wasn't that potent, O king, but in her state it proved lethal… The last few days, with your return…perhaps it excited her too much and weakened her…'

Chanakya was unable to go on, the hesitation making him swallow his words.

'Save her!' Chandragupta insisted. 'Save her, with all that you have.'

He flung open the curtains but the sounds were different now. He leaned against a column, looking at his queen, her eyes closed, no longer in pain. The midwife pressed a soft bundle into his hands. He found himself looking at the shining black eyes of the smallest child he had ever seen.

'Your son, but he has been born too early,' said the midwife, her voice quavering. Her smoky-grey eyes were clouded over and she sobbed piteously. 'I have been the royal midwife for a long time, ever since the time I came to the palace, dragged here by the evil Mahapadma. Perhaps I held you too. '

Chanakya pushed forward. 'Do not waste the king's time at this moment, woman.'

But Chandragupta silenced him with an imperious nod. He slipped off his bangle and gave it to her, saying, 'Tell me more.'

'I have delivered the babies of the women of the Nandas, a hundred and more times; it seems a hundred, how can I who never looked up at the stars count what passed through my hands? There were many babies I killed – their cries smothered as I held them to my breast. I remember the women I was forced to kill too.'

She cried, falling at his feet. 'But not the queen, not this one. The poison had already taken her – all I could do was save your son.'

He shivered at the sight of a woman older than his mother bending down at his feet.

She gazed at him. 'Your mother…I remember her too. She was the most spirited woman I ever knew. She had your questioning eyes and your restlessness. They could never hold her in this palace.'

Her last words were in such a faint whisper that only he could hear. 'I fear, I am afraid, this kingdom may not be enough to hold you in. It is your mother's spirit that you have in you. Your land worships the sun, O king, but age has granted me this ability to see beyond. Your rule will be remembered for the gentleness it bestowed on its subjects – a gentleness like the light of the full moon.'

He sat with his queen, holding her hand, now cold and of the earth. He remained with her till the last candles died out and dawn stole in like a quiet thief. He kissed her, caressing her forehead and murmuring in sorrow. Her fiery eyes were closed forever. The hands that had pointed a dagger at him, ridden a horse expertly, clasped him fiercely with passion, now lay by his side, open and cold.

'At least she died a queen. Destiny could have willed it differently,' Chanakya said, having come to the room to check on Chandragupta.

Chandragupta understood what Chanakya meant – here was a woman born into royalty, and even if the fates had conspired against her, she was determined to die as a queen. 'Are you saying she was as manipulative as you want me to be? In that case, she would have made a better student.'

Surprisingly, the older man smiled. 'She loved you, O king. Like your subjects do, like a queen should. But more as a woman… but I have no answers for that. None at all.'

His voice softened in that quiet dawn, each man understanding the other's loneliness.

The smell of the fire that turned his queen to ashes lingered long after the embers burnt out. As he entered his chamber, he heard his son's muffled cries. His steps quickened as he made his way to where the sounds came from. One of the attendants stopped him gently at the entrance of the room.

'O king, the prince is very sick.'

He brushed him aside and pushed his way past the other attendants. They looked at him alarmed and watchful, knowing he was angry at the way destiny was contriving to cheat him of love. His wife was gone and now his newborn son was struggling for his life. The curtains swished angrily and the baby's cries dimmed. There he was in his cradle – and to Chandragupta's astonishment, the cradle was moving though there was no breeze or wind to rock it. His son's tiny fingers were firmly gripping the bars, like he would never let go. Tears glistened on the infant's cheeks, and the creaking cradle was the only sound Chandragupta heard. In spite of himself, he smiled. His son was already making his presence felt.

'My lord.'

The old midwife reached out a trembling hand and then withdrew. She said softly, 'He will live, and live long, my lord. My old eyes that cannot see your face too clearly, can see this. Long after you and I are gone, his reign will be the most peaceful any king of Magadha will have known.'

Chandragupta placed his hand on his son's head, the damp curls knotting around his finger as he bent down to speak the words he hoped no one would hear. 'May you know no war, little son of mine. May you know the peace that eluded your mother and which will never be my lot.'

As the taper nearby cast its soft glow, his son's eyes searched for his. He knew that infants heard their parents' voices deep in the womb and he thought of his own mother – he had at least known her, while his son had already lost his.

'Bindusara, that's what the queen wanted to call him. That he would be pure as a pearl and as truthful,' said the old midwife, her eyes fixed on him, twinkling as if she knew secrets untold.

'I would like the queen's wishes to be respected,' he answered, his voice choked with tears.

30

THE PRINCESS WHO WOULD NOT BE QUEEN

At the border that demarcated his empire from Seleucus' realms, Chandragupta saw the princess approaching on a noble Arabian horse, the finest of its kind. Through her thin veil, he could see the same derisive smile on her face as before, and knew she had noted his admiring glance at the horse she was riding. The Greek soldiers rode on the most splendid Arabian horses and he had made them a part of his deal with Seleucus. Behind him were the five hundred elephants with their mahouts that he had promised Seleucus in exchange.

Then he saw Seleucus and his soldiers riding up to him and they both bowed to each other.

'Your elephants, sire,' he said to Seleucus, 'each one the best and well trained.'

'Your horses,' said the other king. Chandragupta noticed the king's two young sons standing at their father's side. He did not miss the antagonism in their grey eyes. He had heard reports that they were not happy with their father reaching an agreement with that upstart new ruler of the east. Chandragupta tossed a disdainful glance at the horses, as Seleucus added, 'They are the best, and your soldiers will have no trouble with them.'

'Our soldiers know how to train even the roughest and most recalcitrant of horses.'

As the two came closer, ambassadors of both sides unfurled their scrolls and cleared their throats, waiting for the other to finish a complete sentence before starting their own. This declaration of peace would be perfectly synchronized.

'At this gathering, before our armies, in the presence of our gods, who speak the same truth with different names, we solemnly promise to be each other's allies in times of war.

May an occasion for war never arise, in your time and all those glorious kings who rule after you. May war never threaten the peace that now reigns and may this ever be the case forever.

That at this august gathering in the presence of our gods, with our people assembled around us, we exchange these gifts in the hope of long-lasting peace.'

The trumpets sounded, the horses stamped their feet, and on cue, the elephants raised their trunks and trumpeted.

The princess surged forward on her horse, led by her father. He placed the reins of her horse in Chandragupta's hand. 'And as a token of my trust, I give you my most precious possession.'

Chandragupta said nothing. He saw from the flush suffusing her face that she had not expected his silence. He ran his fingers, soft with sandalwood paste, over her face, her cheeks smooth under his fingers; he felt the throbbing vein on her forehead and stopped.

'I am no one's property,' she said, her eyes bluer than before. Then, snatching the reins from his hands, she flicked her whip before riding away.

His commanders drew their swords and waited for his command.

'Bring her back – safely, unharmed, using no force,' he said expressionlessly.

The four of them turned and galloped away after her.

'O king,' he said to Seleucus. 'I have one more condition. From now on you shall treat the tribes of the bird-tamers and falconers well and fairly because they are subjects of this land. Your daughter is safe, she will be my queen and will be treated honourably.'

Seleucus nodded his agreement. And the falcons, the birds Chandragupta had seen over Seleucus' tent before, were now subdued. A falcon each sat on both his shoulders and a few hovered overhead, watching everything with bleak, hooded expressions.

His commanders had caught up with the princess in no time and, keeping their distance, they bowed to her respectfully.

It had been a difficult exchange. He felt vulnerable the moment his officers left. If anything went wrong and the armies were given the order to clash, he needed them to command and arrange their platoons.

But it was a son of Seleucus whose hand rushed to his sword first, a look of total hatred on his face. He was a boy, barely out of his teens, and his wild mane of hair rolled about his shoulders. He snarled in aggression, despite a warning glance from his father. His ineffectual, untamed anger amused Chandragupta who, nodding to Seleucus, asked the younger man – if he was so keen for a battle, would he agree to a duel, even with an upstart emperor like himself?

The prince surged forward with a war cry. Chandragupta raised a warning hand to his own soldiers, who understood their emperor's intentions. Rash princes had no idea of statecraft or the high price that peace demanded and this impetuous one would soon learn a quick lesson. Chandragupta raised his sword high; it flashed like a beam of fire as he pointed it towards the prince, who came at him swinging his weapon with unrestrained excitement. Chandragupta twirled around, his sword never stopping, his shield thwarting the prince's every move, till the latter, frustrated, lunged at him. His move promptly caused the prince to lose his sword and fall to the ground, where he was pinned down by Chandragupta.

The duel was over in a few moments. The prince's breath was loud and harsh and Chandragupta's soldiers laughed long and heartily. Seleucus put his sword down to ask heavily, 'What would you demand now, my daughter's life or my son's? Or both?'

Chandragupta did not answer. Looking up, a bleak expression on his face, he knew the princess had not gone far. 'I spare their lives,' he said, 'but this victory is one battle that you, O king, must not turn into an undying war between both our dynasties. It was a lesson meant for your upstart, vain son.'

It was her horse that let Helen down, recognizing its kin in the other horses. The proud Arab stallion she was seated on had trotted forward, in spite of her best efforts to turn him around, and nuzzled against one of the other horses.

'O princess,' The chief commander had held out his sword in surrender, assuring her of his intentions. 'I will escort you back and it shall be my honour.'

'I chose to come back. Your commanders were tiring of chasing me,' she said mockingly, much later when they were in his tent.

Chandragupta shook his head and sighed. He had not had time to mourn the queen he had lost and would continue to grieve for her secretly. Perhaps Durdhara had wanted this. He looked at the scratches and bruises she had left on his arms and hands, remembered how she had held him as she lay writhing in pain, as if in the moment of her passing she had somehow flowed into him.

'And the peace between our dynasties would soon be over. Where would it all end then?' He looked at her, then asked, 'Are you indeed your father's possession?'

His question enraged her, just as he had intended. She turned to face him then, her hands beating his chest and pulling at his hair. In turn, he caught a handful of her hair in his fist and leaned into her, smelling the flowers in her hair, the scent of her neck, and smiled. The wedding had been a simple affair, and he had wanted to get it over with. No grand ceremony like there had been with Durdhara. The women attendants had given her a ritual bath before sending her to his tent. For all her insistence that she was different, she was a pawn – just like soldiers were, just like any other exchange between two enemies.

'Being a queen is different, O princess,' he said with deliberate, savage contempt. She was even more beautiful than Durdhara, but lacked her mystery and her queenly allure. It struck him that he had thought more about Durdhara since her death than in the days before, when she had longed for his return. Now he looked down at Helen's blue eyes and knew they were both trapped in some measure. He, in his kingship and in memories of his wife; she, who was now queen of an empire in the plains. 'You have nowhere to go now, you know,' he said quietly, and she did not comprehend his sudden pity. 'When will you understand this?'

He pressed his lips down on hers. She stiffened for a moment but in the next instant kissed him back, biting his lower lip. He picked her up while she was still struggling and scratching, blowing out the candles as he took her to the low bed. Holding her hair in his hand, her face imprisoned in his grasp, he heard the wind slap against the tent and dance below the gaps where it was tethered to the earth. A fire raged deep in his heart – the fire of yearning and unfulfilled desires. Later, he gazed at her as she slept and realized she would never be tamed. She was wild and thrashed about restlessly in bed even in her sleep.

Her restlessness became even more apparent on their journey back to Pataliputra. All the way they had raced each other on their horses. There was a time when she gave him the slip and it took all his knowledge of the ways of bird and beast to find her. There could have been wild elephants where she had run to, he warned her later, but she shrugged, unafraid.

In the palace, the attendants and courtiers were spellbound by her fine looks. The infinite braids of her hair had to be undone carefully. Open and unfurled, her hair was a golden-brown cloud that changed colour in the light. He longed to see it unbraided at night, but she refused – sometimes teasing him, at other times simply unwilling to do his bidding.

One night as they were lying down, she veiled his face with her cloud of hair and then pointed his dagger at him. 'Do you believe I could kill you? Do the job for my father?' He pushed her away easily, tossing her aside before he walked away. He heard her voice, teasing and insouciant behind him, 'I did let you go this time.'

'I wouldn't want you to think that I could be killed so easily, O queen. Your father's men would have no chance. No one can defeat us. Didn't Alexander try?'

Her laughter filled the palace then and afterwards, making Chanakya frown in disapproval.

'A wife must not behave like that, a queen definitely not,' said Chanakya.

He did not tell his teacher of how her father had tried to tame her spirit. He would chain her to her bed every night with thick anklets and tie her braid to the bedpost, lest she slip away. She wanted freedom from her father, and he understood why she ran away often. It was simply a way to escape bondage.

31

THE MESSENGER'S NEWS

Chandragupta waited for the queen for a long time. His horsemen were growing irate and their horses were restless, but she had left at dawn and not returned. He grew anxious, scanning the skies for any ominous signs, but there were no birds circling around hungrily. There were only low, thick monsoon clouds. He knew he could not delay his southern march any more.

The north was under his control now. The regions along the upper Ganga, once the kingdoms of Kuru and Panchala, and further beyond along the Himalayas, Kambhoj and Gandhara, were all part of the Magadhan empire. In the west, his domain had moved beyond the Aravallis and included the kingdom of Saurashtra by the sea. In the south, Vidarbha formed the border with the kingdom of the Andhras and he was now headed to conquer the lands beyond. He had men in place for this next stage – governors responsible for the provinces and commanders in charge of different armies. There were two different sets of authorities to balance each other, to keep an eye on each other's activities, with judges and the authorities of appeal making up a third rung. Among all these layers of government were the spies; men and women who moved around effortlessly, listening to secrets that emerged in the darkness and that would seal a foe's fate forever.

When the queen did not return, Chandragupta decided not to wait any longer. The bugles sounded and he leapt on his horse, riding until he was at the head of the columns of horsemen so that he could lead his men away at dusk. The priests who had returned to the temple of the sun, and Chanakya himself standing at the very ramparts of the fort, looked on disapprovingly.

It was not the auspicious time for armies to march, Chandragupta knew. At twilight, his soldiers would have to ride faster to set up camp for the night. Later, those who saw his army on the move would say they had seen nothing but swift movement – swirling dust clouds that danced like dervishes along the earth, falling from a sky drained of every colour.

They stopped by the Krishna river late one night, not too far from a cluster of villages. A storehouse, set up as part of Chanakya's principles of statecraft, ensured that his army was well supplied. The moon was full; and they had not met any of the wild elephant herds that roamed the forests in these parts. He had seen the lamp lights flickering in the caves of Amaravati and knew this was a resting place for monks and travellers. Many times on his way, he had looked back, straining his eyes for any sign of his queen. And he realized she had got under his skin, just the way Durdhara had. The thought made him angry.

As his men set up camp by the river, he climbed onto the highest rocks, watching the lamps dance, ebb away and rise again below him. The Jain monks were at their evening prayers, looking like upright rocks themselves. They looked serene and untroubled, oblivious to the presence of the army among them. He had seen them often over the years – from his days as a tribesman and later during his time on the run – and now their serenity struck him with an astonishing clarity. Warriors rode roughly and arrogantly claiming the land, and these monks became one with the land they walked on, touching everything and every being on it, with their gentleness and compassion. He wandered among the monks now, and noticed how his soldiers, alert as ever, followed his every move.

'Go to sleep, rest,' he said, in a gently reproving tone. 'There's nothing that can harm us here.'

They smiled, but he knew they would still keep an eye on him. They knew their king was given to dark moods and a tendency to wander off alone. But standing there on the high rocks, seeing the detachment of the monks, he sensed a restlessness in himself, as if something significant was about to happen. Not an attack, for the forests were still, but perhaps it was too still. Then, standing on the highest rock, casting his eyes as far as he could, he saw movement – it could only be a lone horseman coming towards their camp.

Chandragupta waited, his calmness changing into a sense of impending doom. He breathed in the night, hoping his queen was safe.

As the rider approached, the soldiers in the camp rose to attention. He saw the difference in response between his soldiers and the monks, who continued praying with no sign of being disturbed. He envied the difference and recognized his own agitation.

When the rider drew closer, they saw that he was a royal messenger. The tapers caught his trident raised high, the sun on the flag he held. The soldiers let him pass. Wary and curious now, Chandragupta strode down the rocks. He tried to hide his eagerness and anxiety.

It had to be news about his queen. Chanakya would never have dispatched a rider post-haste otherwise. He knew she couldn't have been trampled by elephants or met a gory end. Chanakya was not likely to keep such news to himself till his campaign was over. It was something else, far more sinister. She wasn't in danger, he could tell, but the empire was.

'What I have to say is only for your ears, O king,' said the messenger. He wasn't afraid but looked very embarrassed. His voice quivered – he couldn't look Chandragupta in the eye when he greeted him.

'Tell me. I have nothing to fear.'

The messenger looked most distressed, then he gulped and went on. 'What I have to say could not even be written down. I need to tell you in secret.'

'A king's life is open – he has no secrets and nothing to hide from his people. The moment he does that, there will always be a chasm between him and his people.'

The messenger remained silent, and looked even more miserable. Chandragupta suddenly heard the tinkling of bells; monks approached, holding silver plates arranged with small lamps and the evening's offerings. 'It is to nature and the end of another day that we offer our thanks. It is amidst nature we live and offer our lives, going wherever we are needed,' said Bhadrabahu the head monk. The monk was smiling. Chandragupta felt that time had not moved since he had last seen him. 'Everything continues in its own cycle, the universe is boundless and we are thankful for our place in it. This is an offering of gratitude for this harmonious balance and prayers for it to prevail under your rule, O king.'

Chandragupta bowed, accepted their blessings, and turned back to the messenger.

'The wheel of life moves on. Didn't you hear the holy monk just say that? Whatever makes you afraid, or feel shame, cast it aside and tell me.'

'O king, our spies who went in search of the queen spotted her with Megasthenes, in the chambers of the diplomat.'

The soldiers who heard this gasped and turned red.

'The attendants revealed this. It was clear that it was your queen in the chambers – even in the darkness, her golden braids…'

Chandragupta raised a hand to stop him. He had heard enough.

He turned to see Bhadrabahu still standing there, with a wise, sad look in his eyes. 'O king, do not ever act in haste...and regret it later. You wedded her and you owe her a chance to explain herself.'

'But...does she not not have duties to honour?' he burst out.

'A woman has needs too, perhaps not easily expressed. Being in a new land, among strangers, she may not be used to new ways. She is a princess of royal birth used to living by her own rules.'

Chandragupta turned to the messenger and said, in calm, clear tones, so that his words reached everyone, 'Return to Pataliputra at once. The queen must be escorted to her chambers without being harmed. And she must not be allowed to step out till I return. Otherwise, I will kill all her guards and attendants myself.'

He cut his thumb with his sword's edge, smeared it on the messenger's scroll and handed it back. 'This is a sign that you met the king, and these are his orders.'

'But...'

'And if the queen tries to escape...' He stopped and forced himself to continue, 'The guards must prevent her at all costs. She will be safe in the palace.'

Suddenly the thought struck him that he had become just like Seleucus; his order insisting the queen remain in her palace mirrored her father's ways of chaining her to the tent stake. A woman wasn't a piece of land to be conquered. In his long journey to be king-emperor, other relationships, he understood, came second.

It had already been a long, arduous campaign moving beyond Vidarbha, and to its southwest, skirting the kingdom of the Andhras that he intended to deal with soon. Now a part of him did not want to return. His empire was vast and he needed to move often, to ensure it was administered well and efficiently. This time, as before, some of his ministers accompanied him. Conquest of a region had to be followed by ensuring that proper systems of governance, administration and reportage were in place.

The kings of Asmaka and Kuntala met him at the gates of their forts and made him welcome. It was a campaign intended to cow everyone down into submission without bloodshed.

Reaching beyond Kuntala, in the kingdom of Dakshinapatha, he ruthlessly and deliberately cut short a war. The enemy soldiers were no match for the Mauryan army and he waited once the gates to the fort had been breached. A massacre could be averted, and a victorious emperor could assert himself in other ways. In an agreement with the king, who surrendered and agreed to become a vassal of Magadha, it was laid down that the Raichur region between the sources of the Godavari and the Krishna would form the demarcating point between the two kingdoms, and traders would be safely escorted to the borders of the Magadhan empire. If Dakshinapatha was ever threatened by the rulers further south, Magadha would intervene and its armies would have rights of passage through the region.

'O king,' said Rakshasa, the minister, 'as long as King Trivikram reigns over Dakshinapatha, our rule will hold. But he is old, has a young son and some impatient stepbrothers who can barely wait to grab the throne.'

'We will fight those battles if it comes to that. For now, we cannot depose an old king and place one of our own on the throne. That would antagonise the people. And it is peace with the people of Dakshinapatha that we want,' Chandragupta replied.

32

THE DHARMA OF FRIENDSHIP

The Krishna river was dangerously close to breaching its banks and his men were out helping the boatmen when the news reached Chandragupta. It was Rakshasa who broke it to him. Megasthenes had left Pataliputra, giving everyone the slip. 'We have our orders not to kill him since he is Seleucus' ambassador but we do not know his whereabouts. The message is that he could be headed here, O king.'

'He shall not be harmed.'

'But, my king, he...'

Chandragupta thought of the cheeky grin and the floppy brown curls of the man he almost considered his best friend. By now, he had either lost all his friends, or they had turned against him.

He emphasized, 'He is a citizen of another land. His protection is our duty. He shall not be harmed.'

Rakshasa spoke in a quiet voice, 'But he is also your friend, besides being a diplomat, my king. As a friend, his trustworthiness has come under question. Are the rules meant for a diplomat applicable in this instance?'

'Yes,' Chandragupta replied harshly, looking at the man whose eyes were lowered. He realized he was simply asking the question that was on everyone's mind. 'As a king, I will not make any rules favouring friends. But it is the welfare of my state that matters. If the news of Megasthenes' escape or even the rumours of him being in danger reach the western frontier, there will be war. And all our armies are presently in the south.'

The camp was settling down fast as evening came upon them. It was raining intermittently and the mist that had gathered brought in cold air. He draped a warm shawl around himself. 'Go to sleep,' he told his men. 'We will take turns to guard.'

He went about on his horse, his shawl flying around him. It began to rain harder, and the men retreated into their tents, which they had placed on higher ground so as to avoid any rain water seeping in from below. The rain drummed on the rocks, echoing in the low mountains, as if a thousand ghost horses rode all night long.

It was when he felt his legs would not hold any longer that he turned towards his tent. As he was about to enter, he sensed the presence of someone close by. The tent, too, seemed to hold its breath till he saw its ends move. Chandragupta was sure the unknown intruder was waiting for him. And he knew who it was.

'You could not have got in on your own,' he said, entering the tent and wiping himself with a soft towel. He did not even look at the man in the corner.

Megasthenes looked up. He had been resting on his haunches and there was exhaustion written all over his face. But his eyes lit up on meeting him. The king felt a momentary lightness sweep into him on meeting his old friend but he quelled his feelings.

'No,' Megasthenes grinned, looking his younger self again despite the visible fatigue. 'But I can't give away the monks or even the people you have promised not to wage war against.'

'I can always change my mind. Just like I can strike you dead, and no one will question me.'

The rain picked up pace, lashing against the tent harder. Megasthenes said, 'Yes, you would be well within your rights. I am ready to take any punishment.'

He knelt before Chandragupta and spread his hands before him, showing him that they were empty, that he was unarmed. Chandragupta saw the tired lines that now marked his friend's face. He looked like a man who had constantly waged a battle with his body and the higher demands of his soul.

'Why did you give in to the queen? You knew what you were doing,' demanded Chandragupta, his bewilderment and raw anger evident in his tone.

Megasthenes bowed his head before answering, not looking into Chandragupta's eyes.

'I asked her why she had escaped from her chambers and sought refuge with me. There was no answer. I knew what she would say, or perhaps I understood her silence. She is a kinswoman after all. I suggested that the reason was that she was simply bored, that she could not have enough of the freedom you gave her. "No," she said, "I may have been restless, but I do not feel I fit in with the way I am expected to live as the queen." I then asked her, "Wasn't that what you wanted? To be Chandragupta's queen?" She replied, "All I knew was what I didn't want."'

Chandragupta stayed silent and turned away, wondering why her words hurt him. He had thought that she had desperately wanted to marry him, that he was the centre of her universe. But this wasn't true.

'She knows what she doesn't want. But what she doesn't know, she doesn't want,' Megasthenes continued, almost to himself. 'These are not the wilds of Persia, O king. Pataliputra is the most organized city in the world. Aside from Athens, there has been no city like this. Everything has to be ordered, everything in its place like the universe itself, because it is Pataliputra.'

'I wish you would stop speaking in metaphors all the time, Megasthenes. Tell me, does it matter what a king should be like?'

'What do you mean?' Megasthenes asked, looking at the small fire that had been lit just outside. Chandragupta went to sit by him, the tent flaps swinging open in front.

'There are tyrants who call themselves kings,' answered Chandragupta. 'Then there are those who surround themselves with all kinds of paraphernalia, like Seleucus, the king you serve, and there are others who are greedy for more conquests, but then perish.' His voice faded as he watched the kindling catch fire. 'If everyone were allowed to be king for one season, as was prevalent in the tribe I grew up in, envy, greed, selfishness – these would disappear. People would live for each other and one man would give his life for another. But then there will always be someone greedier and hungrier for power. As if all the riches and power they accumulate in this world could be taken away with them when they die.'

A sudden grin appeared on Megasthenes' face. Still suspicious and cautious, Chandragupta quickly drew out his dagger. But Megasthenes restrained him. 'No, I am not mocking you, O king. I only wanted to tell you of the time we broke into the tombs of the great pharaohs. The kings of the Nile were buried with all their treasures and their queens and their attendants. The tombs were guarded but I managed to break in. It was a sight I will never forget. Jewels and gemstones were scattered everywhere in the depths of that cold chamber, with creatures of the night swooping past me – rats as big as dogs and bats as large as eagles. So what does this tell you?'

He waited, breaking the silence to say, 'When we leave this world, we depart alone. With nothing. Even the pharaoh's flesh had rotted, as will mine one day, and his bones had turned to dust. That is what we all become – dust.'

'Back to the earth,' echoed Chandragupta. 'Whatever we are attached to, whatever we call our possessions, everything is all left behind. But what about the soul?'

'I haven't understood that yet. I followed the monks for a while, I saw their privations, their strictly regulated lives. I tried to emulate them and sometimes became so devoid of thoughts and even of food that I felt I was light enough to float into the sky – I imagined the soul was something like that. But it was only momentary, leaving me feeling tired and exhausted, and...' he looked around, rubbing his stomach, '...very hungry.'

Chandragupta laughed. Then he told the Greek, 'You cannot go back now, you realize that.'

'I came to see you and tell you my part of the story. My truth. Yes,' he rolled his eyes, 'your adviser already had rules for foreigners of every kind in the kingdom. The regulations in place and the category of spies who should shadow them.'

Chandragupta realized he was tired. He looked up at Megasthenes from the tough camel hide he had stretched out only a few minutes ago and saw that his friend's face had turned grey. The fire, not too far away, cast a glow on his neck.

'So tell me, Megasthenes, what should my dharma be?'

'Your dharma is to do your duty as king. As a parent to all your subjects, you have to be the protector of all the land that makes up your kingdom.'

'You speak in riddles worse than Chanakya.'

'O king, you trouble yourself unduly. Sometimes the truth has a way of revealing itself.'

Outside, light began to break, and Chandragupta heard the chafing of horses, the smell of dung carried up by the wind and the monks picking up their chanting as the dawn of a new day drew upon them.

'Tell me, Megasthenes, what should your dharma have been?'

Megasthenes replied slowly, his words halting, 'I have my own dharma, as I decide it for myself. It all makes me suspect in others' eyes. I could belong somewhere, but in truth I belong nowhere. I recognize no borders and no boundaries...'

He stopped and looked at Chandragupta, who simply said, 'What would have been your duty as a friend?'

'Not to hurt my friend,' he said simply.

'And if I were a friend to you, should I forgive you?'

'No,' said Megasthenes. 'Instead, save me from my weaknesses.'

'In that case, I do not want to see you ever again. You're a weak man who cannot control his craving of the flesh.'

Megasthenes stood up. 'I came here willing to die at your hands, O king.'

'You knew I would never have killed you.'

'Yes, you see O king, you understand without being told what your dharma is. I came here to confess, to throw myself at your mercy and I knew you would listen because you were my friend. And listen impartially, for that is where a friend's dharma also lies. Forgiveness by itself is of no use.'

He bowed before Chandragupta and disappeared, as if he had never been there at all.

33

A KING'S DILEMMA

The siege of the Andhra kingdom had already lasted several days, worsened by the relentless rains and the presence of looming dark clouds that blotted the sun. The coconut and mango trees around them stood drenched and grey, rendered colourless in the rain.

A soldier came up to Chandragupta, who looked on from a rock above the banks of the Krishna. An attendant held an umbrella over him to protect him from the rain. 'The rains do not seem to ease, my lord.'

The other soldiers agreed. 'We cannot cross the river.'

'But what about the other side?' Chandragupta asked.

'The land immediately below is on lower ground,' said Uddipana, one of his advisers who had accompanied him on the long march south. 'The dykes holding back the waters have been pulled down to stall our invasion but it is the farmers who have suffered. Their rice fields are damaged. Kaunteyadeva, the king of the Andhras, does not deserve to rule for failing to protect his people.'

'It is a gamble Kaunteyadeva had to take,' said the king instead. 'To safeguard the rest of his kingdom, he had to sacrifice the farmers and their produce.'

In the afternoon, Chandragupta heard a man shouting. It was in a language he did not understand. For the briefest of moments, the rain had stopped, but the clouds continued to hang low and sullen as he rushed out. There were mud-brown pools of water everywhere and flies had begun to swarm over them. He knew he could not wait in that outpost any longer. It would soon bring disease and ill health.

Then he saw the man who had been shouting. He was barely able to stand up, but held close to his heart a child, swaddled in cloth.

'O king, they say you are just. That you will ensure justice. Tell me, has my child suffered for any reason at all?'

Chandragupta saw the child's face, which had been ravaged by illness, splattered with pus-filled sores.

The farmer spoke in a strange language so a soldier translated his words. 'He says that if this one dies, it will be the fifth child he has lost.'

The man spoke up again, blubbering through his tears, while the soldiers tried to restrain him. 'He says he heard about your miracles, how you were able to drive away lions and tame wild elephants, so he begs you to save his child.'

Chandragupta shook his head helplessly.

'O king, all I beg of you is to save my son.'

Chandragupta did not need a translator to understand what the man was saying. He moved forward but his soldiers formed a protective ring around him. 'O king, we do not know who this person is and what his actual intentions are.'

Someone whispered, 'It could be a spell, an enchantment cast on you. My king, there is no way of ascertaining the truth.'

Chandragupta pushed them all away and cradled the child, calling for his own physicians to take a look at him. He saw the grudging look on his men's faces, as if they felt that this was a step he should not have taken. He knew the unasked questions they had in their mind. What if more such people arrived? Would that not provide a reason for an invasion by the Mauryan army, given that the other king seemed oblivious or helpless towards his people's needs?

Perhaps, if he had not come with his armies, the mudbanks would not have been pulled down, the farmers would not have suffered, and this man's child would have survived. But would that still be enough to satiate his kingly ambitions?

'Even miracles do not come on their own,' he wanted to tell the man. 'There is always a price. I lost my wife, and my son was born. The lions were not too hungry when they sniffed me, so it wasn't a miracle but a question of their needs. The elephants were tired. Sooner or later they would give themselves up to be tamed and I, for my part, did not give in to my own fears.'

The monks were still in their midst. He could see them in their caves, following their daily routines despite the rains. They would move on once the rains relented. That evening, he went to visit the monks at the caves. Bhadrabahu was at his prayers and the king waited, soaking in the serenity of the place and felt momentarily soothed, till the questions came to him again. Would the great monk have an answer? How could a king alleviate his people's suffering, especially if suffering was ingrained, and if it always involved a choice? The other king, his enemy, had to make a choice, the suffering of many against that of a few. How could he take advantage of the moral dilemma his rival king evidently faced?

The monk opened his eyes and smiled as he saw the king. 'Did the long wait yield any answers?'

He shook his head, and the monk smiled again, 'Sometimes all you have to do is ask questions. But they may not always lead you to answers; they might lead you to more questions instead.'

'Is there ever an end to it then?'

Bhadrabahu noted the king's sadness. 'O king, you are in many ways above it all and yet the choices before you are far more than anything a simple monk can comprehend. You are responsible for your people but only to the extent your dharma allows you to be. How to balance things – between ambition and the concerns of your people, between providing for them and for your kingdom's future, how much peace to ensure, for your time and for the future – are all choices that you alone have to make. Sometimes the answers to these questions may present difficulties for you. Sometimes as king, you have to listen to the man within you, the soul of a man, not the king.'

'Do we have to be alone to find our answers?'

'That is the strangest reality. We have attachments and bonds to our earthly possessions. All of us have our cravings, and yet in the end we are all alone with our doubts and questions. Sometimes admitting we have these can be an answer in itself. At least we are on our way.'

The monks left soon after for lands south of the Krishna, in lands he did not hold; lands which lay ravaged by the sudden rains. He wondered if he should march onwards, but the long encampment had taken its toll on him as well as the army. He knew his men were restless and anxious. They yearned to go home.

When Chandragupta reached Pataliputra with his army, he was welcomed with a wonderful homecoming. Every house was lit up and painted afresh. The streets looked newly washed, the smell of jasmine and marigold hung everywhere. War, misery and the suffering he had witnessed seemed a long way off – it was as if such things had never been.

In the palace grounds, guarded by high walls and manned by able men and women alike, he rode up before all his soldiers. He had missed this city – his city. As he neared the walls, he saw Chanakya, and smiled. Then his smile faltered, for he noticed that Chanakya looked older – there were lines on his face although the glittering harshness he remembered still remained. He suspected he saw a tear in the cold, hard eyes of his adviser.

Chanakya had already known when the king-emperor and his army would reach Pataliputra. The falcons' cries overhead had informed him so and the horsemen who appeared at regular intervals had passed the message on, confirming his suspicions.

'It has been a long journey for you, O king,' he said, his eyes flickering over Chandragupta. Perhaps the older man saw that the king looked old too, beyond his years and infinitely more wearied.

'Yes, it has,' Chandragupta replied, accepting his old teacher's welcome, 'I thought I would be glad to come home but…'

He let his sentence trail away. His adviser knew him well, knew the emptiness that now tormented him. His soldiers were well into their revelry – some had to be picked off the streets as the potent spirits got to them, while some lurched into the nearest pleasure houses. Chandragupta met his ministers and senior officials. He was shown into the impressive records room where every document and record pertaining to events and officials was kept. 'No one is allowed to enter this room,' said Chanakya, 'except for the two of us. There are also some records that no one dared to write down.'

He looked puzzled and Chanakya explained, 'A written record could fall into the wrong hands – of someone working against us. Suppose one of your ministers is plotting against you. Or if an ambassador is spying on you. The spy system will work separate from other departments. The lower level officials will report to the senior ones and all of them will be paid from the central treasury. This will ensure they do not develop loyalty to governors or heads of provinces. They will pretend to be employed in ordinary jobs and will never reveal their true identities. All reports will reach you directly. A spy, if he has anything to reveal, will have immediate access to you though he will come to you in disguise. Interference will invite punishment, and a spy's death will be treated as extremely suspicious. And of course, there will be women spies too, especially in our pleasure houses. This will help us keep an eye on foreign merchants and...' for the first time Chanakya faltered, then he cleared his throat as he completed his sentence, '...diplomats.'

Though Chandragupta's expression didn't change, his amazement only increased as Chanakya led him into a dark, quiet room that adjoined the records room. With the light coming in from overhead windows, he could see men writing silently. The only sound was the dipping of their quills in ink and the scratching of their nibs on palm leaves as they wrote. They looked up once when he passed by and bowed before resuming their work. Something about their devotion to work reminded him of the meditating monks.

In the royal chambers, the queen was waiting for him. He had to bite his lips to hide his shock when he saw her. She looked wraith like, with her pale shimmering skin, and her almost dead eyes. He felt as if he were seeing her for the first time, and was confused at his own reaction. If he looked hard, a shadow of the elusive young princess she had once been shone in her eyes, which also bore a new cunning and anger. She beat her hands against the bedpost; the heavy gold bangles were thick and loud against her skin.

'This isn't the wild, lawless land you came from, where rules do not exist. You are the queen of Magadha now.'

'Do you have any idea what being a queen means? It means being closeted, locked up.' He saw the emptiness in her eyes as she spoke. 'Even my horse has more freedom than me.'

'But there are rules here. A dharma to be followed. You are my queen.'

'Did you buy me as you would a slave? I did not see money being exchanged between you and my father.'

'It is the price I paid for peace.'

'No,' she said, in anguish. 'My father got five hundred elephants as the bride price. The trained and skilled elephants you and your men are so proud of. I was a bad deal in return.'

'But you wanted to get away from there.'

'Not to this kind of a life.'

'You have your attendants here and nothing to want for. While I only have my duty.' He wished she would understand, though he could not understand her.

'Suppose I choose not to accept my duty?' The last of her defiance asserted itself.

'Your duty came to you once you became queen and you are bound to honour it.'

He walked away, questions and doubts once again hammering in his head. That evening he rode out on a horse that had not been broken, and moments later, saw his son riding up. He knew instantly who it was, it could be no one else but Bindusara. He had come riding out from the Dandaka forests that surrounded Magadha. It was feared for the presence of wild elephant herds but his son had emerged unscathed – calm and fearless. As his son approached, Chandragupta saw clearly the diadem on his head and the peacock tattoo on his arm.

'I am glad the forests are your playing ground now,' he said in half-amusement, noting also the sword that rested gently on Bindusara's lap.

The boy looked pleased at his father's remark. The men with him turned their horses away, letting father and son ride together.

'Has the guru been teaching you? You should be prepared to become king at any time.'

The sense of his own mortality confronted him as he looked at the boy. It had been a long time since he had last seen him. So many seasons had passed, making him feel old at the very thought. All of a sudden his son appeared rather grown-up – a young man. All Chandragupta remembered of his birth were his mother's dying moments and the taste of the poison on her lips.

Bindusara replied, 'He says I have a lot to learn. I wish I could learn more from you.' As the sunlight caught his son's hair and their horses picked up pace, Chandragupta remembered the boy he had once been. Free to ride wherever he wanted, chasing the rare green peacock. He had never found it again. Perhaps he never would.

'Did your teacher say anything about the peacock? I thought he might give you a lecture that since you will be a king you cannot have the sign of a tribe on your arm.'

His hand ran gently down his son's arm to the tattoo of the peacock that the boy sported. But his son, not noticing, went on, 'The guru said that when he first saw you, you told him you were going to be a king like Alexander.'

Chandragupta could see glimpses of that day in his mind. He remembered watching the man from far away, the man who had walked long miles in search of revenge – in search of him. He remembered little of that first conversation now.

'I wish you would tell me your stories yourself and I didn't have to hear them from the master. The one about the peacock you were looking for and the lions that you talked to...'

'He knows my stories better than I do myself, son,' he smiled.
'I don't even remember the peacock one – all I know is I am still
looking for it.'

He did not tell him what he remembered of the lions. He could
not tell him the story of the old lion he had saved, the thorn in its
foot and the old creature limping away in agony. Now he was no
longer sure if he had seen tears on its tawny cheeks.

Bindusara reached out as they rode side by side and touched
his father's sword.

'This is the sword that you used against your enemies.'

'Yes, and I hope you never have to use it. The reason I have
used it is because this land – this empire – needs peace. For too
long, there has been war.'

His words were broken by the long soulful cries of the cuckoo.
'One day, my son, there will be time to look at birds and trees
and wild animals, and there will be no worry about war, or about
people's sufferings.'

'There is little you can do about war or suffering. It is inevitable
– if there is peace all the time, we would have to invent war.'

Chandragupta turned to look at his son. 'Has the guru been
telling you that?'

'No. But he said if there were a cycle, just like our own cycle of
birth, death and rebirth, peace eventually has to give way some time
to war, for without war we would forget the value of peace.'

His son's wisdom weighed him down. He was unsure of what
to think and he urged his horse forward. Bindusara caught up with
him, and Chandragupta saw that he had his mother's narrow face,
but his eyes were gentler and his hair fell straight on either side
of his face. He felt a sudden urge to keep his son away from the
dangers of kingship. He knew he had willed his son into a trap
not of his own making. It was his destiny.

He took out his sword and held it up high in the air, conscious of his entire being in that moment. The horse beneath him seemed to still its movements – every flick of its tail, even its harsh breathing – as it waited. Chandragupta flexed his arm and then hurled the sword away – as emotions welled up in him and memories of a time of peace raced through his mind. He hoped it would fall in the river, for that was where he had aimed it, and that the river would claim the sword for itself and carry it swiftly away. He did not want his son to live as he had. He wanted to bequeath him everlasting peace, if that were possible.

He heard another horse breathing softly and realized Bindusara was by his side. There was hurt and the puzzlement in his eyes. 'That sword would have come to me, father. Did you think I was undeserving of it? Why did you throw it away?'

He had not thought of his son's hurt, but only of his own fears. Looking at him now, he saw his own mortality in Bindusara's eyes. Would he see his son grow up? If he was no longer king, would his son look at him with the same respect in his eyes? He caught his thoughts, wondering what it was about being a king that made him so suspicious even of his own son.

'No, it was my way of conveying that I wish you a time of peace; that you may never have to use a sword.'

'But I am a warrior, I've been born one. And as your son, I will be like you in every way. My teacher said that when I hold your sword one day, it will pass on the same power you have to me.'

'A sword depends on the skill of the soldier, my son. You must learn things on your own. The path I have followed may not necessarily be the one you will take.'

He saw the pain and sadness in his son's eyes and understood that he was not explaining himself well.

'You will be king one day, my son, and every king rules in a different way.'

Chandragupta did not tell him what he really wanted to – he didn't wish his son to be burdened by kingship – so he said instead, 'I only want you to rule over a land that knows peace. That you do not have to fight wars. That you are never threatened, nor are your people.'

'Whoever finds that sword will fight hard to win peace,' Chandragupta said after a long silence.

He did not know why he said that. He was filled with a sense of foreboding. In spite of what he had achieved – the rules he had laid down, the impressive administrative and military framework he had devised with Chanakya, all the records and scrolls that held the secrets of how an empire could be made to work – eventually all of it would be of little use in protecting his loved ones. There would never be a time of absolute peace. His own family would see bloodshed and feud. It was an eternal cycle that guided most circumstances and he, even as the most powerful king Magadha had ever seen, was powerless to stop it.

They moved back to the palace and he saw the lamps on in the queen's chamber. Oddly, his spirits lifted. The warmth of those oil lamps reached him as the evening turned cold and the wind began whistling in the trees. He turned to his son, 'See, I returned with you protecting me. Do you need any other proof of what you are capable of?'

'Soldiers followed us too, father,' said his worldly-wise son, smiling in return. Maybe his son would, after all, be a far more wise and practical king than he had been.

34

A PALACE FOR A QUEEN

The relief on his soldiers' faces as they entered the palace compound made him laugh. Where was the despondency he had felt a moment ago? It was all gone, dispelled by the warmth of their welcome, until one of the women attendants came to him with a worried look on her face.

'Sire, the queen has refused to eat for the last two days.'

He turned and met the harsh gaze of Chanakya, and knew he had something to say to him. Chanakya said, 'It isn't the way of queens, or even wives, to behave as your queen does, O king. What will your subjects think? They know she defied you and that she was not punished for it, and that she continues to defy you.'

'Punishment is not always a remedy, is it?'

'Your queen, O king, is our queen and it is important that she conducts herself suitably. A man is perfectly justified in banishing his wife if he doubts her loyalty, for the woman is expected to retain purity and bear children in his name. A man would like his son to be his own. Remember the time of the Nandas, when there was utter chaos and lawlessness – the world itself had turned upside down. Those things must no longer happen. Order must prevail and it is the queen who must set an example.'

'Why only the queen? Why is it the lot of women to suffer for us?'

'They cannot truly be warriors, my lord. Along with destiny, duty is an intrinsic part of a man or woman's life. There are rules that lay this down; even rules that define who can punish or who deserves punishment. For those with the power to punish must be seen to be just, too. A wife is answerable to her husband first and he is answerable to the community – every community is sustained by its households, of which the king is master. Ministers are answerable to the king, so are diplomats representing their kings – it is the king who is supreme. He is the symbol of dharma, the righteous way of living, and if he acts in such a way then he need not be answerable to anyone. This is what the Buddha said and what all our great religions espouse as well. There is really no difference between statecraft and religion.'

There was something in his voice that made Chandragupta catch on to that one word. *Diplomats.* Chanakya had spoken evenly but there was no mistaking whom he had alluded to. Megasthenes, as a diplomat, had a duty to follow King Seleucus.

He had seen the shadow that had fallen from above. The queen had overheard everything. Did he have a duty towards her as well?

'Our duty as men, O king, is to set things in order and preserve the universe, and women have the duty of maintaining it in the home. That way the different aspects of the universe are perfectly balanced and complement each other.'

'The queen is my wife, so I must consider the situation as one that is strictly between man and wife.'

'This is where you may be wrong. Rules and justice do matter. Even a woman wronged by her husband can expect justice. There are punishments for every crime and sin, and these should be justly awarded.'

The image of his queen stuck in a magnificent palace, lost in a lonely life, came sharply to him. He knew then, though Chanakya had been subtle, that he had been unfair to her. In his effort to be a good, righteous emperor, he had forgotten his self – the part of him that existed as a father, as a husband. He remembered his son's sadness on losing his father's sword. He had thought like an emperor and disregarded his son's feelings.

Leaving Chanakya behind, Chandragupta drew the curtain to his queen's chambers, waved the attendants aside and walked up to her. He said tenderly, 'The world knows you married me of your own will. So why are you unhappy?'

He saw a strange look in her eyes, or perhaps her eyes only mirrored what they saw in his.

'You left me alone, and there is always...' she said, her words trailing off.

'Always...?' he waited for her answer, his eyes narrowed.

He saw her blue eyes gleaming in the light of the tapers overhead, and understood what she was trying to say. Durdhara's presence was always there – something he had not missed either. It was his dead queen who had lived in the palace, who had been born there, and who had come back as queen. She had almost willed her return to this palace as his queen and wife, and even after her death, lived in this palace as a memory.

'All the attendants do is tell me her stories. What she liked to do, hear, see, speak about...and how she was your most devoted subject and yet had a commanding presence that no one has been able to forget. I feel that same presence seeping in through these walls, strangling me, eating me alive.'

He listened to her patiently. Then, seeing that he had her full attention, he asked her the question foremost in his mind. 'Did Megasthenes offer to take you away?' He held her face in his hands. She winced at his touch and he felt an anger sweep through him.

'I am giving you a chance to answer, to atone. Do you think a man likes being cuckolded? Or that a king likes being betrayed, and to a foreigner, at that? Yes, a foreigner. Because it seems you have forgotten you are no longer a half-Greek and half-Persian princess, but the queen of Magadha.'

'But why did I have to change myself too?' she asked. 'I had no idea that marrying you would mean I had to become a different person. Someone condemned to always live in your shadow, or even in the other queen's shadow.'

As the night passed, he found himself telling her what he knew, the little wisdom he had gathered. He also understood her need to be free. A few hours later, in the light of the early morning sun, he showed her the spot where a new palace was to be built. 'It's a place not really far away from Pataliputra, but secluded enough,' he told her, 'to allow you the freedom you crave.'

'A palace more magnificent than this one?' she asked.

He held his smile, telling himself not to be disappointed in her avarice. It was just the kind of inclination the Nandas had been hated for – their palaces and love of luxuries, much greater than the love for the people they ruled over. A king should never make himself so utterly remote, he thought.

Surprisingly, Chanakya did not disapprove as he thought he would; he said a new palace was the best thing the king could have thought of to keep the queen occupied. 'Besides his conquests, a king should make sure that his presence is larger than life. His magnificence should eclipse that of every other king. It should stamp his presence on his people's minds and hearts and even on time itself. What you build, O king, will live longer than you, or even your kingdom. It will reflect your glory in every way,' said the wise Chanakya.

In the span of one season, the new palace acquired substantial proportions. It was spread in every direction, always visible from the walls of the old palace. Even Chandragupta himself was surprised at the speed with which it was being built.

The architect met him just once. He was so obsequious that he had refused to look up and bowed with every question put to him. 'Apollodorus has been building stupas for the Lord Buddha,' said Rakshasa, by way of introduction, 'and monasteries too, but he is up to the challenge of building the most splendid palace of all. It will be the crowning glory of all his achievements.'

The architect had moved to Pataliputra from Egypt and spoke a mishmash of languages. Perhaps that was the reason why he hid his face, because he had stopped trying to make himself understood. He devoted himself to his work and he made sure the workmen obeyed his instructions, standing with his whip and his rod, making an assistant repeat his instructions until they were well understood.

The imposing three-arched gate would stand on pillars driven deep into the earth. The columns of the new palace were evenly spaced. All of them were slender and finely proportioned, each one holding aloft an exquisitely carved animal. Chandragupta loved the lions, as lifelike as the lions he had encountered. When he felt the stone teeth with his fingers, he experienced the same burning sensation as when he had warded off the lion so many years ago.

The arches at the entrance had the same ornate carvings that decorated the entire palace. There would be mirrors in the main hallway, even on the floors, so that they would appear like limpid pools. In turn, the pools at the intersections of every hall would look like mirrors. The rooms inside were spacious, with lofty ceilings, and the corridors were lined on either side by arched windows. Chandragupta could ride his horse easily in the wide corridors, if he wanted to.

But the more he looked for his queen, the more elusive she was. She would smile if he chanced on her in the corridors of the unfinished palace, but when confined to a single space in the vast rooms, a haunted, lost look appeared in her eyes.

Every time he returned, he saw these two sides in her. He began to hear other stories too, of how she was driving Apollodorus mad. A tyrant to all his workmen, he had been reduced to a teary, desperate man before her. She did not like the way the palace was being built, and pestered him to redo his work time and again.

What happened next was inevitable. Apollodorus disappeared one night, leaving the construction incomplete. The news that he had abandoned his duties without warning reached Chandragupta when he was campaigning in the west, where the Sahyas had risen in rebellion and had to be subdued. He had crossed the fast-flowing rivers of the Punjab, past the bandit lairs that now lay abandoned. His army, large and swift, would ensure that the rebels were brutally suppressed. It would seve as an example to all frontier people, so they never felt emboldened enough to throw off the Mauryan yoke because of their distance from Pataliputra.

The messenger from the palace reached him at night. He was no soldier and had taken his time.

'It is Apollodorus, O king. He has run away – he could not take the constant interference in his work.'

Chandragupta's lips set in a stern line and he clamped his jaw hard, unwilling to give in to the weariness that always seemed to close in.

'And the queen?'

The man hesitated. He breathed in again and his chest heaved painfully. He was unable to utter a sound for long moments, his gasps getting deeper by the second. He tried to speak but could not. Then he collapsed at the emperor's feet. The long journey under a relentless sun had evidently left him exhausted and drained.

Chandragupta was stone-faced. He said flatly, 'Take him away, and make sure he recovers. As for my reply, it can wait for a while.'

He looked at his advisers' faces as he walked away. They would expect him to announce the most stringent of punishments for Apollodorus but he wondered if, in his zeal to be the perfect ruler and the just emperor, he was making a fetish out of dharma. The great sages, the Buddha and Mahavira, and all the tirthankaras had believed in this – that every being had a dharma, a duty assigned to him or her since birth – but these sages had not insisted on force. But the belief that every man and woman had a dharma to follow, even if other circumstances or destiny prevented them from doing their duty made him feel that he was a tyrant in some way. Had he become a slave to dharma's demands, and would any relenting on his part signify weakness?

35

UNANSWERED QUESTIONS

The architect was not found for days and Chandragupta found himself fretting about his palace. How different did that make him, after all, from the Nandas?

He was in the northwest of his realm – a place familiar to him in many ways – where the land was rockier, greyer and harder. His feet hurt through the soft leather of his shoes and his hair felt dry and frizzy. Touching his hair with his fingers, he remembered with fondness the comforts of his palace. Every evening in Pataliputra, the attendants had tended to his hair, and he always drifted off under their gentle ministrations. One day they did think he had drifted off to a faraway land of sleep, for he heard their voices gently float over him. But they spoke in faint, melodious tones, and he was sure he was dreaming for when he awoke he was alone. He remembered all too clearly what he had heard.

'He has too much hair, don't you think?' they giggled.

'Shh...'

His hair was matted, but their hands were gentle on him. 'It would tickle, having all that hair run on my body.'

'In a nice way too, you naughty girl. But it is true what they say about him. That he is the best of kings and the handsomest of all men.'

He had to be dreaming...his hair fell in fragrant, luscious waves around him as he drifted off again, hearing their voices carried to him by the wind.

'None of the Nandas had hair like this. Except for the old man, the monstrous father, whose hair was white and silver. Our hands trembled to touch it. But all his sons lost their hair. Remember how we could see clumps of hair on the floor every time they left the bath? The tyrant himself would never fall asleep, unlike this one. He would never relax, and we could never drop our guard either. He believed all his strength and longevity lay in his hair.'

The older woman's voice sounded sadder and further away. 'And that Nanda ruler was a barber's son. You would think a barber's son would not have so much strength, or so much love for his hair. But stranger things have happened.'

'And are circumstances different now?'

'The fear isn't there but it is all the same. After some time, the men lose their interest in you, especially if you aren't setting up a household with them. But if you are content to live your life in the shadows, it's fine.'

'But one doesn't want to turn into a shadow.'

He was lulled into sleep by their voices so if the older woman had comforted the younger one, he had missed her words. Perhaps she had been captured in war or in a raid. When he woke again, he heard someone else speak, for the voice sounded different now.

'You know, his mother was brought to the palace, but she came most unwillingly – her heart was never in it.'

His heart stilled and he felt a soft hand over his.

'But that's not true, is it?'

'She was a woman from one of the forest tribes, those who had the forest trails carved into the lines of their palms. She had come riding out to fight the elephant-keepers and that's when one of the princes, either Kaivarta or Mahendra, caught her and kept her here in the palace.'

'But she escaped?'

'Yes, that is what I heard. Or he let her go. Familiarity can lead to love, after all. And love is strange. For all our secret potions and arts, we still don't know why it happens, what causes it, why it lasts and why it dies.'

There was silence, except for the gentle brush of the comb on his hair and the woman went on. 'It was because the other princes were fighting over the woman that this Nanda prince let her go. He didn't want her to fall into his brothers' hands.'

There was silence once more. Perhaps this was the silence not of confusion but of acceptance. 'And then he died too.'

'Yes, he was the weakling – at least they called him that.'

'What happened to her?'

'I have no idea. I only remember how she used to be when she was here in the palace chambers. She was lonely and kept to herself. Later on, after she left, I heard from one of the palace maids that she was given refuge by the Moriya tribe, the peacock-tamers. She was extremely sad because she had to leave her son behind, I was told.'

'But he got away too? Why could he come back as emperor?'

This time, the voice was harsher. 'Girl, you are making me talk too much. He may seem to be sleeping but you never know. Do you think the story of the lions is entirely false?'

'This one is blessed. Can you smell him? Don't go too near, he may awaken. He smells of sandalwood and wild flowers, as if he were of the forests themselves. Why do you think he was able to conquer so many hearts in so short a while?'

'Girl, his fragrance is part of what we do, it is part of our routine of looking after the king. But he is a man of wisdom and learning. He has an understanding most men do not have. And it will all come to use for the kingdom. Finally Magadha will see some peace with him as a ruler. Do you know what living in peace means, girl?'

Perhaps the other girl shook her head, for the older one continued, 'It means that even if there is uncertainty, as there is always bound to be, this king will think of his subjects first. Our sufferings are his now. We will not be reduced to a state of humiliation as we had when the Nandas ruled. There is a thing called justice that exists in Magadha now.'

'But justice is strange. When confronted with contradictory claims, like those of power, or even attachment, it is justice that always gives way.'

'Ah we shall see, we shall see. A restless queen lives in the palace – we shall soon see what happens to her.'

The monks led by Bhadrabahu, he was told, had moved farther away. The rebellion of the Sahyas had been crushed – as an emperor, he realized he was capable of infinitely greater cruelties simply to keep his hard-won empire in control. Yet his eyes and heart sought the monks everywhere, as if they would have the answers that still eluded him. A kingdom could never be totally at peace, he had now learnt. Did that mean the king had failed his duties? And if he persisted in pursuing peace for the kingdom, did that indicate he was too attached to his worldly being, when all the great sages said attachment was what caused misery?

The monks, his spies reported, were deep in the jungles of the west, an area he was familiar with. It was partly in those regions that he had been on the run with Chanakya – a land he felt safe in, with its deserts on one side, and the dry forests on the other, the branches of the trees low enough to scratch one's face. He remembered the sounds of its animals that carried in the quiet sifting sand, the settlements that one came upon quite by surprise, where the camel-herders lived and traders stopped by.

It was not an area the monks usually preferred. But he heard they planned to travel as far as the low Vindhya mountains of the west. These mountains were, in many ways, harsher than the cold mountains of the north because in summer the rivers ran dry there, and the heat was so strong that feet cracked and bled on the rocks. Beyond the Vindhyas, there was Saurashtra, and then the sea from where traders and other foreigners came. A vast blue sea upon which the biggest ships and boats sailed, much larger than the river boats they were used to. The world, he realized, would always be larger than a king could ever dream to hold as his own territory.

Sometimes, as he rode past with his armies, past hamlets and settlements, he felt he had left the palace, the missing architect, the restless queen, far behind. All this land, the soldiers said, belonged to him. And he smiled at their pride.

All this land is mine for as long as it keeps peace. The presence of his army meant peace was maintained at all times. The show of force was necessary to strike fear not just among his enemy but in his people too.

To keep a land at peace, its armies only grew larger, more monstrous. Angry men composed each army – restless men whose duty it was to kill. Yet, he always had to tell his soldiers to kill with a purpose. Bandits, herdsmen, villages – all vanished at their approach because the army was too big for them to maintain. He had fought wars to bring about peace and now he wanted some of it for himself.

Peace can never come on its own. Time and again, the old monk's words came back to him. Why did the monks go about, talking about peace, then? Perhaps, he thought answering his own question, because we would forget about the healing power of peace.

Far away, as the night faded, he would see the monks' lamps flickering in welcome in the darkness. He knew that was why he had ridden out at night, in the hope of seeing them again.

A messenger brought him the news that Apollodorus had been found, cowering in the house of a courtesan. The messenger who reached Chandragupta had picked up the message about the architect's whereabouts from two others, who had set off from Pataliputra several days ago. Chandragupta was then faced with a dilemma only he could resolve.

The courtesan had hidden Apollodorus had been initially charmed by him, but then sedated him and called the soldiers when fear had got to her, knowing that if he was caught with her, she too would bear the brunt of the inevitable punishment. And the man himself, now afraid of retribution, said he had been tired – the palace was eating him up, there had been too much interference – but he had not dared to take the queen's name. As Chandragupta thought about it, he wondered who deserved punishment and who deserved forgiveness.

'It took me two whole days to get here, O king,' said the messenger breathlessly. 'And the men who rode before me took seven days, using ten horses. They spoke of the way it had rained where they came from. The earthen walls of the fort fell down on sleeping people and you would never believe me, when I say that the rains were indeed terrible because here it is so harsh and dry.'

Chandragupta made his decision. He told the messenger to return, and his army was ordered to begin preparations for the long march home. He saw the relief on their faces, and understood that adding land to an empire that was already the greatest they had ever known made no sense. A lone horseman that wandered into a village, a town or a small kingdom was no longer opposed, and later, a headman, a chief or even a small-time king would turn up to pay tribute. The idea of returning filled him with longing and restlessness. Pataliputra was home, yet it always seemed a different place every time he went back.

Whenever he returned from a campaign, he found the welcome grander than before. With every mile that they covered towards Pataliputra, he saw – though it was summer and the heat was settling on the plains – a growing lightheartedness on his men's faces. Their laughter could be heard more often, their complaints about the hot conditions in which they marched were now all in jest. From afar, he saw the glow in the eastern skies and knew the lamps had already been lit in Pataliputra. A fire would burn for several days in the palace courtyard, and freshly washed and painted elephants would stand at every street corner. He could already hear them trumpeting. If he placed his ear to the ground, he could hear the sound of elephants moving in herds, and the breathing of the earth itself.

It was his son who waited, on his impatient horse, at Pataliputra's northern gate. He was flanked by his ministers and advisers. For a moment, Chandragupta was alarmed. Wasn't this how Bimbisara was killed too? As his son Ajatashatru waited to welcome him from a heroic campaign? Wasn't this why Mahapadma Nanda always ensured his sons were witness to every victory spectacle, and why his victories were always bloody, murderous affairs? But his son rode forward, excited. He saw that Bindusara was bigger, but had not lost his childlike, innocent smile.

'This is the last time you go campaigning on your own, father,' he said.

His son asked later, a prince's question to the king, 'What shall we do with the architect, my lord? The queen...' he trailed off, and his father did not miss the contemptuous tone in his voice when he referred to the queen.

Bindusara hesitated at his father's silence, then said softly, 'The master said I am the prince, the future king, and must not recognize such ties openly. Except the one I have with you, because everything I am, and will be, comes from you.'

Chandragupta did not answer. He thought about his past and where he came from. The deviousness that had made him plot a murder, even kill on so many occasions – where had he got that from? Or the restlessness that made him chase a green peacock for miles and miles just to see it, but never to capture it? He had made his own dharma and wondered who would punish him for any lapses.

At the head of the steps stood Chanakya, smiling thinly as he looked at the young prince. 'My king, even the prince says exemplary punishment has to be meted out to the architect.'

The debate among his advisers, one that his son actively participated in, raged long into the night.

'But there must be reasons why a man would be driven to the dereliction of his duty, abandoning the work he has done all his life?' asked Bindusara, a lock of hair falling over his forehead as he leaned forward.

'If a man desists from doing his dharma, he should be punished to set an example,' answered Uddipana.

'When does a king then show mercy?' Chandra broke in. 'Is mercy a sign of weakness? Look at the palace. It is a fine work of art, unfinished as it may be. All the arches and columns, and the stone gates with their figurines, are glorious. The man's work is immortal and it is a pity that nothing of him will be known. It will all be in the king's name.'

'In the glory of the king lies the happiness of the subject,' said Chanakya.

'A man runs for fear of his life, even if he is the greatest architect of all. People must think I am quite a demon to make that happen. How does that make me different from the great Nanda?'

'There is a difference, my lord. The artistes of the Nandas' dominions worked like slaves, as if they were the king's bonded labourers,' said Rakshasa, 'but artistes are not ordinary men of labour – they are men of their word.'

They were interrupted by the tinkling of bells and the clash of cymbals. The gong at the main gate sounded some moments later, and as the echo faded, the chanting of the monks reverberated through the air as their prayers acknowledged the day's end.

Every other sound died away, and to Chandragupta, it seemed every dark thought died too. He heard someone playing the flute in the distance, accompanied by the increasingly loud calls of owls and frogs as the night darkened.

He remembered the night when he had suddenly found himself the ruler of Magadha. He had ridden into the city, and found it in utter darkness. People had cowered in fear, or had lost themselves in a thankful sleep, while the former rulers had already fled. Burning with the heat of victory, he had given chase. Chandragupta had no idea why he had done so, except that his overwhelming impulse had been to capture the enemy. The rules and rites of the victor were the same at each point of history and written down in reams of cruelty. Alexander's men would return with each defeated man in chains, his head half-shaven, or sometimes even a severed head on a plate. Perhaps, it was the loss of his friend that had made Alexander so unexpectedly generous towards Porus, or it could just have been his arbitrariness. The Nanda king could reward a hunter for killing a peacock but could cut his head off or mete out a cruel punishment if he had killed a tiger, for only the king had the right to kill one. And yet, even the Nanda king's tiger hunt had been a mere façade, as everyone knew too well. Records were being erased and rewritten to show that. A different account was being recorded by the scribes in their chambers – inked on palm leaves, the story of the Nandas was being told anew. Mahapadma had never had the courage to kill a tiger. Hunters followed him into the jungle, and aimed their arrows the moment the king lifted his own bow. It was said the hunter had to succeed for he was doomed to death or exile if he missed. Success was rewarded only at the king's whim.

'Why should a tired, unmotivated man be killed just for the sake of my ego?'

It was the question he wanted to put to the monk, Bhadrabahu. The messenger told the king and his advisers about Bhadrabahu's arrival, and about how he was unwell and had gone to stay at the palace of the rich merchant Democretus. 'He begs you not to consider it an insult that he chose to stay somewhere else. He will meet with you when you have no pressing duties to attend to.'

He saw Chanakya's eyes glittering in the darkness. Chandragupta knew his old teacher, who once had all the answers, could not help him at this juncture. He had helped a young man make his own destiny and become emperor, but now the emperor wanted to find himself again. He said to the messenger in careful, measured tones, 'Tell the great master that when he has rested, I will come to meet him.'

36

Ill Fares the Land

Bhadrabahu looked tired, but his smile was radiant when Chandragupta walked into his chamber. He had once again returned to Magadha with his fellow monks. This was where they would be every monsoon before branching out to other areas in other seasons. Their lives were dedicated to the service of others – they tended to the ailing and the needy; at other times they would find an isolated place to meditate and absorb themselves in prayer.

'This time,' Bhadrabahu said, surprising the king by standing up, 'you should have had your crown on.'

Chandragupta bowed. 'Before you, I am no king. I'd rather be Moriya.'

There was no mistaking the compassion in the holy man's gaze. He said gently, 'There are some things even a king cannot avoid and it is your destiny to be in that position – to be the greatest emperor this land has ever known.'

Chandragupta could say nothing. This was what he had wanted ever since his boyhood. The challenge to seize the hawk-eagle's nest, to prove to his friends that he could do it, just as he believed one day he would be the greatest king in this land. But he had not accounted for the isolation, the loneliness and the constant dilemmas kingship imposed on him.

Once again as if he had read his mind, the monk went on, 'Having doubts and confusion is but an acknowledgment that you understand what it is to be human. Lesser beings than you have doubts too, but they have rules to live by, while you have to enforce them. Sometimes you need the acceptance that all this is inevitable to pass through this transient phase called life.'

'If this is transient,' Chandragupta asked, 'why must we be concerned about dharma, instead of pleasing ourselves?'

'Because we do not live for ourselves alone. And seeking happiness for oneself doesn't really make us happy,' the monk said. 'Did the palace make your queen happy? Or the fact that she became your queen? Or is it that some people are fated to be unhappy?'

'She is happy sometimes, I am told.'

The mystics and physicians had ways of keeping her calm, and this had unexpected effects. Her tears and smiles appeared at the strangest moments. He felt she was no longer a creature of the earth.

'Sometimes,' went on the monk as if he had not heard, 'dharma could simply be a question of offering one's understanding. And being strong enough to accept it, even if one is accused of weakness.'

Chandragupta couldn't help smiling. He had never before been conscious of who he was – Bhadrabahu in his gentle way was reminding him of it. 'A king must never be seen as weak. You know why I am here. The fate of a man rests in my hands once again. I cannot ignore the fact that he dared leave his work incomplete.'

'Perhaps it is not the palace he should be building, O king.'

'But this kingdom and empire stands on the shoulders of everyone doing their duty, their dharma, as best as they can. If governors do not rule in the king's stead, if ministers do not administer their functions wisely and fairly, if the spies lose their sense of alertness, warriors their daring, farmers their conscientiousness, the kingdom would weaken. But it all begins with the king and his sense of duty.'

'That rests on fairness and the ability to be merciful when it is called for.'

The firmness in Bhadrabahu's tone surprised Chandragupta. The monk lowered his gaze, as if he realized his harshness and regretted it.

'There are already things you do not see, O king. But that is not your fault. Most of your empire is at peace, but peace does not last. All we can hope is that it will last through our children's lifetime too.'

Bhadrabahu told him more as Chandragupta led him to the divan. With his own hands, he washed the monk's bloodied and calloused feet, which told him how far the old man had travelled.

'In the border regions, they are pulling down the forests, setting up army outposts to make your empire secure. The elephants are being driven out of their natural homes. In those border regions in the north, where we monks are coming from, the rivers are in spate from the sudden rains. Boats have capsized in the floods and crops have been destroyed. Once again, people are rushing to the cities, and there is not enough food there. Now that you've secured these regions, it is here that your generosity and compassion will leave their mark.'

Bhadrabahu paused, for he had the king's full attention. Then he said, in his gentle, self-effacing way, 'The architect gave in to his weakness. His abondoning of the palace was not an insult to you, but to himself, to his skills. My king, give this man a chance to atone for himself.'

'So it shall be.'

The king-emperor made his decision quickly. The granaries and storehouses, as Chanakya had written down in his *Arthashastra*, built across the provinces of his empire and standing near the main highways, well within reach of most of the cities and villages too, had to have more grain.

'The granaries shall be well supplied,' the emperor declared. 'And those who need it, will have it. My soldiers will fan out, spreading the message, offering help where it is needed. Soldiers do not just make war, they keep the peace too. The rains will come where they have failed,' he said, leaving the chambers. 'They must…' he added as an afterthought, knowing some things were beyond him.

In the days and weeks after his talk with Bhadrabahu, he rode out to the villages around Pataliputra and those by the foothills, assessing the conditions for himself. He heard his advisers out carefully and every night took stock of the situation as his officials reported to him on the other provinces, in the border regions and even in the neighbouring states, for any distress in the latter regions could affect the Magadhan empire too.

Every day, from every province of his empire, soldiers would ride out to guard the crops, keep the elephants in check and in some instances, the tribesmen too. The rains had failed in the dry regions of the west and in the upper reaches of the mountains. Here, the herdsmen and pastoralists were in need of grain and more grass for their cattle, as the grasslands had turned dry and yellow in the unending heat. Bindusara, whom he had appointed the governor of Taxila, would leave every morning to monitor the granaries. Chandragupta was reassured by the confidence he saw in Bindusara's eyes, the easy majesty with which he sat on his horse and rode away, satisfied with the way his son was taking on his responsibilities. Then there was always Chanakya, making his plans, writing them down, so they would be used for posterity.

'In times of famine, the kingdom should never find itself ill-prepared. In the granaries, grain shall be stocked and it shall be doled out, in accordance with each person's need. Farmers must compulsorily pay their share of produce as revenue and it shall be judged by officials of the agriculture and revenue departments. Young children and the elderly and shall receive more. And soldiers too, for in their welfare lies the peace of the land. The palace will have its own granary,' Chanakya wrote.

As the king looked openly doubtful about these rules, Chanakya sought to reassure him.

'This is necessary, O king. You represent the state, and if there are shortages here, in the heart of the empire, think of the message that will send. That the king does not have enough, and so what of his people?'

'The king's granaries should rightly be thrown open to the people.'

'The king,' disagreed Chanakya, 'does not have to do that. It is the duty of the people to ensure the king has enough stores in his granary. And the king's duty is to make sure the people have enough of their own too; not to open his own granaries to them. The palace is the heart of everything. You symbolize power, O king. How will you decide who is really more needy? Leave it to the state and its officials, to figure this out.'

It was an argument Chandragupta had no answer for.

Yet the granaries came up in places he willed them to, and Apollodorus, the architect, gladly joined in the task. The granaries the architect built would be safe storehouses, where the grain would suffer no damage or rot. These measures offered immense reassurance as the heat blazed down the plains from the north to the east and showed no signs of abating.

One night, the meeting with his officials went on for long. When it was over, Chandragupta leaned back on the couch, his ears picking up the faint bird calls of a new morning. Then he heard the scraping sound behind. His instincts would never let him down, though he did not whirl around this time. He smiled, it wasn't just that he was much older but that the changed circumstances had made him different. He no longer felt threatened.

It was his spy. 'The great monk, sire, may be planning his departure soon,' he reported.

'But why?'

The messenger bowed low. 'His holiness never stays in one place for too long. It is against the principles of attachment; principles that demand serving the needy, and already, the absent rains have changed the country. It would be their duty to visit areas where there is suffering and the great monk feels he has wasted too much time here. He should have left a long time ago, he says.'

'He is leaving to share in the people's suffering? Because he has nothing else to offer?'

Sensing the king's confusion, the spy bowed, and the king granted him permission to speak on.

'No one can leave the city without your permission, my lord. The roads are not safe to travel on.'

From a place far away, he heard himself say, 'No monk needs my permission to go wherever he wants. And if he has to leave the city, I will escort him myself.'

Bindusara and Chanakya, who had entered the room shortly after the spy, had heard their conversation. As if they realized that the king had made a momentous decision, they nodded, and said not a word.

37

IN THE FOOTSTEPS OF THE MONKS

One evening, a few days later, in a solemn ceremony presided over by priests, Chandragupta crowned his son the king.

'He will be the ruler of Magadha,' Chandragupta declared.

'In your absence?' an official asked.

The suddenness of his decision had made his officials forget protocol, for a king's decision about his own throne was never to be questioned.

But Chandragupta only smiled. He had no answer to the official's question. He had lived the wandering life before, and had borne pain and suffering. But this time it was different. He was the king-emperor who had conquered everything – but not his own self.

He waited for the queen to bid him the ceremonial farewell, but there was no sign of her. He waited till the auspicious time had passed, but she still did not appear. The women of the palace gathered and in the streaking light of dawn, he saw the courtyard fill up with their silent presence, the low gleaming lamps glowing brighter as the wind died away.

He felt the shame of not being acknowledged by his queen, seeing it reflected on the faces of the women and the courtiers who waited to send him off. Realizing that the atmosphere was one of hostility towards the queen, he said to his son, 'See that you don't punish her too harshly.'

That would be the last command he would give Bindusara, knowing even then that she would be exiled and left to her fate. The queen who wanted to be free would finally be left alone. He wouldn't think of her any more. His heart cracked, but he forced himself to be strong. The sound of the wailing women and the quiet shuffling of people filled the air as more and more gathered in the streets to watch him go.

He descended the palace steps as he watched the monks appear. All of them walked in a single file, behind Bhadrabahu. Barefoot, they chanted simple hymns in a low tone. He was reassured by their hymns as he turned and folded his hands before his people, but he could not trust himself to say anything. He hoped he had served them well. Behind his son stood Chanakya. Bindusara prostrated himself before him, and he accepted the gesture quietly, his mind already far away.

Do not leave us, O king.

He did not know where the plea had first come from but it was picked up in a chorus. The wailing grew louder – it appeared to come from the earth itself. It was so beyond his understanding that he did little but fold his hands once more as he made his departure. If so many people could bid a king farewell in this fashion, the kingdom that was once his and now his son's would be safe.

Taking off his fine leather slippers, he handed them to his son, who was waiting at the foot of the staircase. He then ordered Bindusara not to follow him.

'It is far better I leave this way, for there is never a right moment to renounce everything and leave.'

He did not say more – he did not voice his fear of becoming just like the Nanda king and all the other kings who had clung to their thrones, ages past their glory days.

And still the people – his people – followed him. He could hear his horse following him too, its hooves gentle over the earth. He did not lead the monks but followed them at a distance, already noticing the dampness and the grime on the road. The wind blew in from the river, leaving its mark on the soil. He felt his heart fill up as he bent and touched the soil that lay under his feet and that coated the cracks of his soles. He had done this before he entered Pataliputra and he did this on leaving. Pataliputra had forever left its mark on him.

He caught up with the monks and Bhadrabahu said, 'O king, with every step you take, you leave all your old attachments behind. It is necessary. As monks, we do not belong to any aspect of the world or let it take hold of us. Life is ephemeral, and true happiness is in realizing you are part of the whole, never separate.'

'I have always felt that I had to be in control of my destiny.'

'That is an illusion. There are many circumstances we cannot explain, but you will see, you leave your empire in safe hands.'

At the banks of the river, he bid his horse farewell, his last faithful companion – for it had followed him from the palace till the banks – and folded his hands before the assembled people.

He saw his old teacher too, who had followed him all this way to the river. Chanakya stood tall, still unbent, though the wrinkles had set in deep and the darkness in his eyes was unfathomable. Chanakya, who had all the answers, had finally no answer to his own confusion, his agonizing dilemma, his need to find meaning beyond being a great king. He thought of the blood he had on his hands, the men he had driven to their death, his two queens and whether he had been just with them – one whom he had abandoned in her loneliness, and the other whose loneliness he could never conquer – these were secrets he was taking away and he had no reason to justify those actions. He had done all that he had because he wanted to be emperor and bring justice to Magadha, but that answer could not soothe his soul.

He walked towards Chanakya, wishing to bow before him in respect. But Chanakya still remembered the protocol.

He said, 'You are still the man whose adviser I once was, my king.'

Chandragupta looked at him. 'You made me what I am.'

This time Chanakya smiled, and his eyes misted over. 'You became what you were meant to be. I helped you, and perhaps, in serving your cause, I served mine too.'

He fell silent and stood looking down at Chanakya. The first time he had met the boy, they had been at eye-level, and even then he had never lowered his gaze before the older man. Nor had Chanakya ever expected it.

Chanakya went on quietly, 'This time you are seeking answers that do not lie in the practical plane. You are seeking the truth that can only be yours, and I know I cannot stop you.'

'But you will be there for Magadha?'

'I don't know anything else. This is what I have lived for, and will continue to live for.'

Chanakya bowed before the king-emperor one last time. The wailing of his people rose again. Every step was like a stab in his heart, adding to the heaviness he felt. With every step he took, the words shaped themselves in his mind.

This is my kingdom that I leave behind. But it is not mine any more.

A stone turned over as he stepped on it, and a lizard escaped, jumping back towards his city.

Did he have the freedom to change his mind? But wouldn't that freedom mean giving in to attachment all over again? A little creature lived by the simple attachments it had formed; did it behove a human being to do the same?

This is my city, and yet, no longer my city. I leave behind this, too.

Drops of rain fell, and under his feet, the cracks of a starving earth appeared to be smiling now. A last howl erupted from the crowd behind him. It sounded far away, like a rushing river he had long left behind.

O king, even the gods weep for you.

He did not raise his face to meet the gentle rain. He saw the monks walking steadfastly ahead; the rain slowly drenching their robes. The brown earth turned a muddy red, the rain formed a heavy curtain and he looked straight ahead as the monks hesitated. Some moved towards the nearest tree. This was when he led them, finding his way unerringly through the heavy streaming curtain of water, towards the river.

When he looked back one last time, he saw nothing but the tall towers of the fort and its high walls. If there were guards still standing there, he didn't see them. If they had turned away, and were once again watching over the walls, their absence was a relief for they were doing their duty. And the thought that they would not be watching him did not cause him grief, only a detached satisfaction that his kingdom was safe.

Let my city, my kingdom, my people be at peace. May there be no bloodshed or war in my son's lifetime.

That was all he could wish for. A lasting peace was just as impossible as an endless war. Soon everyone tired of it. *We were not meant to be happy.* Chandragupta bent to wipe away the mud on Bhadrabahu's feet when he noticed the old man trying to do the same. Some of it still stuck to the soles of his cracked feet which had been stained in places by his blood.

His feet reflected the earth the monk had walked on and Chandragupta suddenly felt humbled. Bhadrabahu was a man with no attachments, yet the earth attached itself to him.

A boat arrived miraculously in that pouring rain. The boatman's hands faltered as his eyes met the king-emperor's and recognized him. He folded his hands and trembled as he stood before him.

'My king,' he whispered in awe. Although it was raining, Chandragupta could see the tears course down his cheeks.

'I am not king any more. I am a man waiting to cross the river. You are the boatman and I am in your hands.'

When the boatman reached out with his hand, Chandragupta shook his head, gentle in his reprimand. 'Help those more in need, that is your duty. The monks have travelled farther than I have.'

He heard the soft thump as the monks stepped on to the boat, seating themselves on the wooden seats under the thin cloth awning, surrounding Bhadrabahu who sat in the centre.

He remembered the last time he had seen Pataliputra from a boat – it was when he had just returned from a campaign and had gone out on a royal barge to watch the evening lamps lit up all over the city to celebrate his victory. Now he looked at the brown walls of the fort and the sky beyond it. The rain had lifted. Rays of sunshine burst out from behind dark clouds like gilded columns, and the monks smiled as they saw a rainbow.

He smiled too, for he heard the bells ring in the city that had once been his capital. Life moved on – cruelly, inexorably, inevitably and necessarily.

They descended from the boat and walked into the forests to the east, the forests he had known since he was a young boy. Through the foliage of the trees, he saw the capital city, and remembered his nameless longings in the past. Longings that had turned to reality and then vanished just as soon. Such was the truth about attachments.

He led the way, and the monks followed him, picking him as the natural leader, just as it had been in the world he had left behind. They crossed forests, rivers, high plateaus, places he had traversed before on horseback. He let the hot dry earth burn his feet, just like the sun that scorched his face. His hair, once fragrant, frequently massaged and washed, now lay in thick matted coils around his head.

When the heat began to singe, when there wasn't enough food, he felt light. The night sky looked gentler, the stars nearer, and the heat seemed to slide over him.

He must have walked a long distance and for a long time, too. The monks with him were soon replaced by new ones, every face looked familiar, yet not the same. He saw people in towns and villages, who offered them food or a place to sleep for the night. As the earth seeped into him when he lay down to sleep, he thought of this land which he had once ruled over. It was only now that he truly felt he was a part of the land. A king never claimed land, it was the earth that claimed everything in the end.

He knew there was a shortage of food. It was visible in the unnatural harshness of the heat, the trees that looked old and bent before their time, the abandoned houses, the old and the young who had been left behind. He saw skeletal cattle and heard at night the ominous sounds of wild animals coming nearer and nearer. He heard the sounds of tigers and saw the fires that rose higher and higher, while those who remained tried to keep the wild animals away.

Once again, he found himself on guard, sitting awake over those who slept, with a spear he had fashioned himself. Was there any hope in running away from himself – escaping who he had been?

Those he watched over were profuse in their gratitude. He forced himself to harden his heart, not to think too much of the abandoned people in villages that stood alone, helpless in the heat, languishing in the absence of rains. Villages that had been destroyed by elephants or caught in skirmishes – all these were sacrificed in the upkeep of a big empire. He had learnt that this was the rule of the universe – the small gave way to the big, the weak to the mighty, but was there justice in that? What if the small and the helpless followed the righteous path – where did that leave them?

As the days went by, he felt the burning red soil more and more under his feet. At night he looked up at the black, towering mountains. He had learnt enough about the forest to sleep in peace as snakes brushed past him, as elephant herds thundered past and leopards slithered down the mountain slopes. Once animals had been at his mercy and he had understood them – now he found himself among them, hoping they would understand what his presence among them meant. He was mostly left alone, and in that quiet solitude, he learnt once again of the wisdom of animals.

He heard voices, saw things that made him believe he was imagining it all. Sometimes he lay on a rock, lulled by the quiet, when bears came and sniffed at him but let him be.

The wind blew his clothes away, and once someone wrapped him in a shawl. His hair was bathed, leaving it fragrant as it had been in the palace. He never saw who it was, though there was a lot of gentle laughing like before and he felt soothing hands on his hair and face.

Wherever he went, the world would generally be a kind place. But he had no desire to return to where he had come from. The moment you step away from something, it becomes the past.

Chandra walked alone amid the craggy red rocks that lay beyond the vast grey plateau. He heard a sound he recognized. The harsh, sorrowful cry of the green peacock. He remembered the way he had chased it as a young boy. How running after it had taken him far away from everything familiar, far from all that he knew.

He saw the bird now, perched high on a rock, looking down at him. Teasing, very much present, beautiful as nothing he had ever seen. He looked till his eyes closed in the bright light of the sun. He wondered if the peacock would still be there when he opened his eyes, whether it would always be there.

But the rock stood stark and bare when his eyes rested on it again. He climbed the small hill effortlessly, his steps buoyant; it almost felt like he was flying. And then he saw the bird again, strutting about not too far away. As he drew closer, the bird stretched its neck and looked around, as though it had been waiting for him. He stopped and watched the bird as it watched him, and then when he took a step forward the bird took off, its magnificent tail trailing behind. He quickened his pace, jumping from rock to rock, feeling light and free, as though he had finally broken away from the past and its attachments. He felt he could walk the darkest of valleys, pass flower-filled gardens, ford the deepest rivers, and the peacock would always be somewhere ahead, sometimes on the wet soil, sometimes flapping its wings in the sky, but somehow always near enough.